Broken Moon

Anna Kelly

POOLBEG

Published 2011
by Poolbeg Press Ltd.
123 Grange Hill, Baldoyle,
Dublin 13, Ireland
Email: poolbeg@poolbeg.com

1

A catalogue record for this book is available from the British Library.

ISBN 978-1-84223-352-8

Typeset by Patricia Hope in Sabon 11/14.5
Cover design by Poolbeg Press Ltd.

Printed by
CPI Cox & Wyman, UK

www.poolbeg.com

Note on the Author

Anna Kelly was born in Dublin, where she continues to live. She often wondered where her writing had come from, and discovered that it is in the family history: a grand-uncle was a writer, and three of her cousins have preceded her into publication in various fields of literature.

As a mature student she returned to education, studied Irish Culture and Heritage, and set to writing in earnest. A love of her country and its social history provide inspiration for the settings in her books.

Following *Daniel's Daughter* (Poolbeg 2008), this is her second book. She is currently working on her next novel.

Also by Anna Kelly

Daniel's Daughter

Acknowledgements

Writing is a solitary thing, as they say, but there the solitude ends. For without the experience and input of others no book would ever be published. And without the encouragement and support of family and friends it would be a difficult solitary thing.

My thanks to my sons, my family, and friends, and anyone who posed the question: *"When is your next book out?"* It was music to my ears and your support is invaluable.

My thanks to all the terrific team at Poolbeg Publishing, especially Gaye Shortland my editor, for her excellent advice and guidance.

But difficult or solitary, for me writing remains hugely absorbing and enjoyable and I sincerely hope you enjoy this book.

Anna

For Mary and Margaret,

Love always

Chapter 1

"Grandy, Mummy says is your bag ready?"

Three-and-a-half-year-old Isabella Harcourt skipped out onto the terrace, her untamed light-brown curls bobbing carelessly about her pretty face. She climbed onto her grandfather's lap.

Myles Nugent put his drink on the balustrade beside him and settled her in a more comfortable position. She had a habit of reaching up and twiddling his thick grey hair around her fingers.

"I'm ready, pet."

"Mummy says I can bring Daddy in *my* bag," she told him, her blue eyes dancing with importance, and her mouth set in such a way that her dimples deepened, while she watched closely for his reaction.

"I'm sure he would be very pleased, Izzy."

He knew Sophie hated him calling her that, it annoyed her, but then there seemed to be no pleasing his younger daughter since she moved back home. This past year had

1

been a tough one for them, Sophie especially, and he had serious worries about her. Perhaps when the next couple of days were over she might get back to being more like her old self again.

He affectionately pushed some curls back from the child's forehead, only to watch them tumble forward again. Pleased with his approval, she smiled widely and stretched her arms high above her head before hopping down.

"I'll tell Mummy you're ready," she called as she ran back into the house, all hop and skip, her head lashed by thousands of wildly bouncing curls. Myles so enjoyed her antics; she was a joy to watch.

He picked up his glass, listening to her excited voice floating down to him from the open bedroom window above his head, while he watched the ferries on the sea below make their way effortlessly across a benign Dublin Bay.

It was a glorious early summer evening: one of those rare times when the blood-red of the sun in the west swamps the sky with a warm reddish-purple glow and spills through the wispy cinnamon clouds, making promises it does not always keep.

His home on the south-facing side of the Hill of Howth afforded a stunning view across the bay to Dun Laoghaire and its busy harbour, with Killiney Hill behind it and little Dalkey Island sitting in the sea just off shore. The Sugar Loaf Mountains and Bray Head rose beyond them like distant shadows on canvas in palest grey and faded away into the background.

Maeve had been passionate about this view.

Ferries criss-crossed the water and the nearest had

made its way around the Baily Lighthouse and now crossed Dublin Bay towards its berth above the mouth of the River Liffey. The furthest one was leaving Dun Laoghaire for the open sea.

One of Maeve's favourite things was parties on the terrace on evenings such as this. She was passionate about a lot of things, a lot of people. If any of it had been directed at him, Myles Nugent's life might have been somewhat more fulfilling. Retirement, even as early as was his, had a way of not working out as one thought. Maeve died during the first six months. Ironic that, just when he thought he had all the time he needed to woo her back.

Now here were Sophie and Isabella living with him this last year. It suited Sophie to be back in her father's house. He believed when she moved back home that it was a temporary measure and that she would move back to her own life again, but while she and Izzy were here he was glad of the company. Sometimes he wondered how long Sophie would stay. Sometimes it even *worried* him how long that might be. She had her own apartment, but it seemed to him that his younger daughter had grown more problematic in the last year, and sometimes he felt she was more or less taking refuge from life by being in his house. And that was something which he was sure wouldn't be good for her long term, and he didn't know how to handle it. Besides, while he adored Isabella and was glad of their company, their presence only served to magnify the fact that his own life lacked a certain something.

Taking his glass with him, he turned his back on the ferries and the glistening water and made his way indoors and up to the bedroom he had shared for over thirty years with Maeve. It was as she had left it the day she died, frilly and feminine. Delicate muslin curtains hung on the tall sash windows. All of the elegant furniture was painted white. At the time, his eldest daughter, also called Maeve, declared that a sacrilege. She appreciated the natural qualities of the wood, with her artist's eye, and bemoaned her mother's determination to have an all-white bedroom which necessitated painting the furniture also.

- Sophie was always urging Myles to change the décor. He would reply by saying that he would call in decorators and have it done. Eventually Sophie gave up. Now his bag sat beside the bed, ready for the trip tomorrow. One small bag: they were not staying long, it would be a brief trip, and the quicker the better, he thought.

He placed his glass on the bedside table. A good measure of the golden liquid still remained but he left it there; it didn't solve anything. He walked over to the window. The curtains fluttered lazily on a light breeze. The nearest ferry was almost at her berth. There's another journey over, he thought, and another about to begin.

There was a light tap on his door. A waft of Sophie's perfume swirled ahead of her on the created draft. With a slight fleeting frown she noted the half-empty glass. Myles no longer tried to explain his habit of often having a drink to hand. It would most likely be the same one for hours on end which he would take about the house with him. He wasn't at all sure he could explain properly, even to himself, his habit of holding onto the glass. He sometimes thought it was because it gave him the feeling that he was doing something. But Sophie preferred her own assumption. He ignored the frown.

"Did you tell Bradley that we will be away?" she asked.

"Yes, I spoke to him this morning. He'll call over and

keep an eye. I phoned Maeve too, just to let her know where we'll be."

Since Maeve's move to live in Kerry to pursue her artistic career, the sisters didn't see much of each other and that didn't look as if it was a problem for either of them. It always struck an odd chord with Sophie though, how much Myles mentioned his elder daughter, how much he seemed to keep her in mind despite the fact that she was blissfully getting on with her own life and, to Sophie's way of thinking, without much thought for any of them. But it appeared that out of sight did not mean out of mind, certainly not in this case, not where Maeve was concerned.

"You all packed?" Her father's voice brought her back to the present.

"Just about. I'm giving Isabella her bath in a few minutes. Would you take the bags down to the hall for the morning, please?"

Tomorrow was an important day for Sophie, and it was making her anxious and a bit strung out. Myles wondered how she would feel when she got there, if she would feel relief or sadness, or both.

"Isabella is delighted she's to have the urn in her bag," he remarked.

Sophie flapped a hand in front of her face and quickly turned to leave.

"Wrong again," he sighed as the door closed.

It was difficult to read his younger daughter. Any mention at all of the urn or indeed anything remotely related to it was likely to go down the wrong way. He took his bag down to the hall and went back for the others. Three bags! What on earth did they need three bags for?

They would be home again in a couple of days. He struggled along the landing with two of them, hearing the splashing and laughter of Isabella in the bath, and the admonishing of her mother, complaining that she might as well be in the bath also, she was getting so wet.

Lighten up, Sophie, Myles mentally urged, as he lifted the handle at one end of a large hold-all and dragged it along behind him on its two small wheels. She's still only a baby!

At twenty-seven Sophie seemed filled with anxiety. Had she grown up like that, or when exactly was the fun knocked out of her? How come he hadn't noticed the confidence slide out of her and the angst and the insecurity creeping in? Was she like that during her brief marriage? He didn't think so. Had he been *so* absorbed in his own loss that everyone else seemed fine, he wondered.

After Isabella's bath, her mother wrapped her in a big bath towel. Grandy would dry her off and see to it that her pyjamas didn't go on inside out or back to front. It was the usual after-bath ritual, and Isabella wouldn't have it otherwise.

"Grandy will," was a regular declaration by the child, as she ran into her bedroom with the bath towel trailing. Sophie listened to their laughter, and the familiar frown flashed across her beautiful face. Why was it she didn't share times like that?

Later, when Myles went to say goodnight to Isabella, she was at the window clutching Ted under her arm. Sophie said Ted needed to go in the washing machine, but Isabella wouldn't allow that to happen to him. He was *Ted*, she insisted, she didn't want him different. She kept him safe with her. She was safe with *him*.

"Not asleep yet, Isabella? We have a long journey ahead of us tomorrow, pet – you should be in bed."

It was a clear night. From north to south the bay was illuminated by an almost full moon. A narrow strip of cloud drifted across its face, dividing it in two.

"Look, Grandy!" Isabella cried, pointing out the window. "Look at the broken moon! Do you think Daddy can see it too?"

She surprised him sometimes. He wondered if she had any real memory of her father, or indeed of her grandmother who had died eight months before him, but that was less likely. Nonetheless he assured her that Daddy *could* see it too. Happily, she allowed him to lift her into bed and tuck her in. And Ted had to get as much tucking in as she. Grandy was best at tucking in, he never skimped. By the time her mother came to say goodnight Isabella was fast asleep.

In her own room Sophie took a pair of soft chocolate-brown leather trousers from her wardrobe and considered whether or not she should wear them for travelling. She held them up to her waist and looked in the mirror. Then she tossed back her long blonde hair and cringed at her reflection with annoyance and disgust.

"You're fat!" she told the perfect image. "Look at you. Fat! What would Peter say if he could see you now?"

She flinched visibly at the unguarded mention of Peter, who had dark curls and the eyes of a photographer that managed to look into her very soul. Peter, who told her when they first met on that unforgettable shoot that *she* would be 'his' woman. Peter, who had promised to take care of her till death did them part, and now she was taking him back to where they met, to leave him for all time at the wild rocky cliffs of Dun Aengus. A tremor shot through her as that thought came uninvited into her head. It shouldn't have been like this . . .

She flung the trousers onto the bed, and rummaged through her wardrobe but among her extensive range of designer clothes she found no alternative to wear tomorrow that would satisfy her. She turned in frustration to her chest of drawers and pulled out the middle one. Reaching in behind the carefully folded lingerie, she took out a bottle. It was all she had, and it would have to do.

Chapter 2

Betty Morris couldn't remember the last time she had taken a bath in the morning. She hated holidays, and she had four days due. Four days! What was she going to do with herself for four days? In the shop she'd argued to be allowed to work them but "Rules is rules" Trish had said, she had to take them by the 28th, and that was that.

"Where do you go on your own for four days?" she'd asked.

Trish had an answer for that. "Give me four days to spend on myself and I wouldn't have a problem. You don't know how lucky you are, Betty Morris."

Betty didn't exactly agree with that. She had too much time to herself now that her son and daughter had moved into their own homes, Olive being the second to leave and that was only three weeks ago. Buddy had moved out two months ago, and the stuff he didn't take with him was still in his old room. He had his own mortgage now. His job with an estate agent enabled him to find a property he could afford, but his old Gillette razor was still sitting in the same spot in her bathroom cabinet.

"What about all those half-empty bottles of aftershave?" Betty asked him.

She could still hear his laughing reply. "I'll get them later, Mam – won't be able to afford so much wastage from now on!"

She gave them each as much as she could by way of a cash house-warming present. It was money she'd been saving for times such as this, but things had become so much more expensive in the last few years that what she had planned to give wouldn't go as far as she'd have liked. So she added to it, and now her savings were very much depleted. She knew in order to splash out on herself, as Trish had urged, you need sufficient to be able to make a splash with in the first place.

She grabbed the sponge and squeezed the lavender-scented water over her body, thinking how nice it would be to spend these four days at a spa being oiled and massaged and pummelled and pampered and having her meals handed to her. Breakfast in bed and lunch and dinner served up in the most relaxing atmosphere. The luxury of it would be sheer bliss!

But, she figured, she could have some of that if not all. A break with lashings of aromatherapy and the like might be a bit pricey but surely she could manage a B&B and some entertainment? Then at last feeling a tingle of excitement at her imminent freedom, albeit forced, she dressed and put some clothes into a bag – no need to take much, it would be only a few days at best.

By midday the Number 90 bus had inched its way laboriously through the traffic on the south quays, and eventually deposited Betty and her bag at Heuston Station. The sheer volume of the travelling public at the station was a bit of a shock. People hugging people. People waving goodbye. People reading the electronic noticeboard. Queues that snaked their way around seats and kiosks, with people inching their luggage forward with their feet. Queues for takeaway teas. Queues for newspapers or magazines. The queue for the ticket office was no different.

"Where is the next train out going to, please?" Betty asked when she finally got to the window.

The young man behind the reinforced glass threw her a peculiar look, and then checked his computer screen.

"Galway," he said. "Four minutes."

She asked for a return ticket. He slid it under the glass.

"Platform two."

The packed train was already moving away from the platform when she settled into her seat. Galway, she thought, what am I going to do in Galway? What if I can't get a B&B?

Thoughts sped through her head as if keeping in time with the racing train, and she had trouble holding onto them long enough to think one through. She ought to have a good think as to what she was going to do with her future, now that she had the time. But the spurt of optimism she had when getting out of her bath this morning was waning fast and she was having serious doubts about having come on this trip in the first place.

She had been in Galway once before, as a child, and

11

her memory of it was very vague. Anyway, it was a bit late now for 'what ifs': the train was already moving through open countryside. A mobile phone rang in the seat behind her and she immediately thought of Olive, and decided to phone her later. There was a fair sprinkling of foreign accents around her in the carriage. Her life had moved into another sphere, and was taking her into the unknown. Being with other travellers had a buzz about it. A feeling of expectation moved around the carriage and infected her with the realisation that she had options, and she was free to explore them.

The skies became cloudier as they sped westward. Hawthorn bushes, magnificent in full bloom, stretched across the countryside, bordering fields as well as the railway line. Yellow gorse covered the ground in places, making a striking splash of colour among the green. She knew it smelled like coconut. Her neighbours at home used to grow it as a hedge, and when he was young Buddy was forever being pricked by its sharp thorns.

When they arrived at the mighty River Shannon and rolled into Athlone station she ate her lunch – two chicken salad sandwiches she had bought in Heuston before boarding the train. West of Balinasloe she noticed the land was much more rocky and uneven. The coconut-smelling yellow gorse grew here in abundance. Then the train travelled through peat bog, which stretched to the horizon, and dry-stone walls began to make an appearance. The clouds were thick and grey but the rain did not fall. Athenry Station, all red-brick and green paint and covered platform reminded her of the song about 'The Fields of Athenry' that Olive sang religiously at one time. A strong smell of silage seeped into the carriage. Country smells. To the south-west the hills of Clare could be seen in the distance, and before long the high limestone hills of the Burren came into view. Dry-stone walls now bordered every field, and the many inlets of Galway Bay told her the journey was almost over.

Two and three-quarter hours after leaving Heuston the train rumbled into Galway's crowded Ceannt Station. Large groups of vociferous backpackers all babbling away in foreign languages added to the mêlée on the platform. She followed the crowd down into Eyre Square.

It was a very busy place, and a pleasant sight to behold despite the dull day. The replica russet sails of the Galway Hooker rose sharp and stark from its plinth at one end of the square and the grassy open ground was decorated with trees and furnished with seating. The Great Southern Hotel dominated one side of the square but Betty passed on, looking for somewhere she could afford. The streets were jammed with people and there was a great buzz about the place. What was it the posters on the station wall had said? *Fly to the edge of the world in less than ten minutes*' and *'Sail to Aran'*.

The Aran Islands, tranquil, peaceful, a short hop away. She enquired about the boat and the flight and opted for the 'less than ten minute' short hop. Extravagant? Yes, but she decided on the quick flight rather than risk the longer, possibly sea-sicky ferry crossing. She was feeling a bit excited about the little adventure till she arrived at the airport. Sitting out on the tarmac the nine-seater fixed-wheel craft looked more like an overgrown toy, and didn't look much stronger than the Airfix models that used to hang from Buddy's bedroom ceiling. Her trepidation was not helped when her bag was weighed, and then they asked her to stand on the scales herself.

"You're joking," she laughed in disbelief.

It was all about balance in the plane, they told her patiently. Heaviest people were placed in the centre, halfway between nose and tail. Her seat was in the front, beside the pilot. She stepped from the tarmac into the front seat as if she was getting into a car and pulled the door closed, sitting on her own side of the bench seat.

If she moved her arm she brushed against the pilot, the interior was so narrow. If she reached out her hand she could touch the controls. The throttle was beside her left knee. Two more levers were beside that, one with a blue grip and one with red. In front was a control panel with countless switches and dials, a vertical speed dial, an altimeter, a dial with an orange outline of a plane, a dial that resembled the wings of a plane on the horizon. The control panel in front of her was a replica of what was in front of the pilot.

The propellers swung into action and her attention was immediately diverted. The noise was deafening. The plane began to race down the little runway and in seconds was lifting sharply into the skies. Betty held her breath and would have gripped onto something for reassurance as they soared but she was afraid to touch anything, so she settled for making the Sign of the Cross upon herself and then clamped her hands over her eyes. Curiosity got the better of her and she took a look down as they flew out over Galway Bay. The sight was fascinating. The clouds had blown eastwards and ahead in brilliant sunshine she saw the three Aran Islands strung out before her, sitting like jewels in a glittering blue sea. A couple of minutes later the plane banked and aligned itself with a tiny runway that looked no bigger than an

Elastoplast-strip stuck on a patch of green at the eastern end of the largest of the islands, Inis Mór. Then they were landing.

When the plane rolled to a halt, Betty collected her bag and climbed into the minivan that would take her to her accommodation, which she had already booked in Galway.

Well, here I am, she thought. Now to make the most of it.

Chapter 3

The sleek white Aran Islands Ferry passed the lifeboat at anchor, slid into the little harbour and docked at the end of Kilronan Pier. The crossing of Galway Bay had been as smooth as glass. Looking west out over the Atlantic Ocean the sky was clear blue to the horizon. Passengers poured down the gangway to where some minibuses stood lined up waiting to offer Island Tours to curious day-trippers.

Further along the pier bicycles were on offer for hire. Passengers started the walk down the pier, among them an excited Isabella who ran all the time in front of her mother.

Myles took care of the two larger bags. Sophie carried the smaller one. Her face was set in a frown. She remembered the last time she had set foot on this island. She was happy and carefree then. She was at the height of her modelling career and expected a certain deference from all on the shoot, but the tall dark-haired photographer was well used to prima donnas in front of his lens and he soon made it very clear how it was going to be. His way . . . or they all went home.

She remembered the wind, the strong wild wind that swept in off the Atlantic Ocean across the limestone landscape, bared the rock and bent the few sparse trees. She had complained about the wind, the cold wind that continually obscured her face by blowing her long hair across it just at the wrong moment. Peter Harcourt used it to his advantage, and insisted on taking those shots, saying it accentuated the warmth of the garments she was modelling, the protection they afforded from the elements. Sophie was furious. What was the point of having *her* model at all if her face could not be seen, she demanded. Any other model would have done if that was what he wanted. Two inflated egos clashed. Later in silence she licked her wounds, wondering how she was going to handle this self-opinionated human magnet.

In the next few days they became inseparable. When shooting was impossible because of the rain, he took her to the ancient fort of Dun Aengus, deserted by tourists and everyone else in the rotten weather, to show her the fierce magnificence of the island in the grip of something akin to fury. It crossed her mind briefly that he was mad to visit this place in these conditions, but she pushed the thought aside almost as it formed and followed him. The path to the ancient fort was rocky all the way up and slippery in the rain, but with Peter guiding her and holding her elbow to steady her she was as sure-footed as a mountain goat. They moved through the concentric dry-stone semi-circles of the fort to the innermost area and the edge of the sheer cliff. Huge swells lashed its base, and sent white spray soaring into the sky. He watched it with a reckless gleam in his eyes. She could feel his intense passion for the place.

"Look at that!" he enthused above the wind. "Didn't I tell you it was magnificent? When I die I will have my ashes scattered here," he told her, "over these limestone cliffs. Where else on the planet would be better?"

"You're mad!" she told him, shouting over the wind, turning her back to the rain and feeling secretly alarmed at the appalling idea of such an attractive body ever being reduced to ashes.

"I want *you* to do it, Sophie, if I go first!"

She stared at him in disbelief as the implication of his words drove home, wind and rain drenching them both. His arms went round her, holding her firmly against him, his body shielding her from the worst of the weather.

"Promise me Sophie! Promise!"

She promised.

That was how it was. Never in her wildest dreams did she ever think she would have to keep that promise.

They made for the relative shelter on the leeward side of the massively thick high stone wall. There on the grass, sheltered by the ancient fort, they made love with the thundering sounds of the Atlantic Ocean vibrating through their bodies, as it crashed against the base of the cliff hundreds of metres beneath them. She remembered how he seemed more alive the more the weather worsened.

"Are you okay, Sophie? Sophie?"

Myles was looking at her with obvious concern.

With a start she forced herself back to the present.

"We're here," he announced, stopping and placing the bags on the ground. They had completed the short walk from the pier to their accommodation without her noticing. Inis Mór was having an effect on her that she did not expect and she was not at all comfortable with it.

She and Peter had been here for only a few days, and it was exactly as she remembered it. The beach so close to the pier, the roadway behind it, the tourist office, the sweater shops, all within a few hundred metres of the ferries. She remembered every detail of those first few days with him, but she was not prepared for the strong awareness of his presence that accompanied her return to the island. Somewhere in the depths of her mind it occurred to her that Peter might well have preceded her here. He was so much at one with the wildness of the place, perhaps his spirit returned as soon as it was released from his body.

She shivered involuntarily.

The sounds of her daughter's shrieking in excitement made her jolt her attention to the present. Isabella ran across the garden to the low wall opposite and was jumping up and down in delight as she called to two donkeys grazing in the field next to the B&B garden.

"Would you look at her?" Sophie exclaimed in annoyance. "Next you know she will be over the wall! Isabella, come here – we can see the horses later!"

"Donkeys," Myles muttered.

"Whatever."

In their accommodation Isabella and her mother shared a twin-bedded room. The cases were dropped on the beds and Isabella dashed immediately to see Grandy's room.

"Oh, Grandy! You can see the sea! Just like at

home!" She thought for a moment, her head cocked to one side. "Is that *our* sea?"

Myles picked her up and plonked a loud kiss on her forehead and put her straight down again. No, it wasn't *our* sea, that was the great Atlantic Ocean out there and it went all the way to America, he told her.

She was so impressed. She decided that information was important enough to pass on and off she went across the landing again. "I'll tell Mummy."

Sophie was removing the urn from Isabella's bag and the child suddenly stopped short, horrified.

"Mummy! We're not leaving Daddy *here*? This is not *our* sea!"

Sophie was stuck for an answer for a moment or two. She didn't really expect Isabella to make any sense of what the trip was all about. She struggled with her feelings before finding her voice.

"This is where he wanted, Isabella, you know that. He said this is what we should do for him if he died."

This reminder changed things for Isabella. Daddy wanted here so that was alright. But it was not so simple for Sophie as she continued the unpacking.

Myles knocked at the door.

"It's a beautiful evening. I'll take Isabella for a walk while you unpack, if you like?"

He was careful not to aggravate her with 'Izzy'.

Sophie put down the bundle of clothes she had in her hands.

"No, I'd like to come too. I could do with it right now. I can finish unpacking when Isabella is in bed."

She smiled at him, wanting him to see that she needed the company. It was a peculiar feeling that troubled her since their arrival, and she did not want to be left alone with the urn. For a year now she had lived with it every day, waiting for a time she felt would be best to carry out her husband's final wishes. She thought she'd grown used to its presence in her life. But now that she was back on Inis Mór she was not so sure about anything, not so sure that anything could put an end to her nightmare.

And the urn bothered her so much. She was keen to be done with this business and go home, and she was also acutely aware that it was not going to be easy, that it was not even guaranteed to make things any better. What she expected to feel afterwards she had no idea. She knew her father hoped it would be a kind of catharsis, a metamorphosis, but surely you had to be free to move on in order to experience a healing or a change of any kind? Sophie's turmoil was exactly that, turmoil, and only she knew the cause. Was it too much to hope that it could be sorted by the simple act of scattering ashes? The sound of her daughter's voice carried on the still evening air, and in a serious effort to dispel the unwelcome feelings that persisted she threw a cream cashmere sweater about her shoulders and followed her father and Isabella downstairs.

Chapter 4

Betty's accommodation was on the eastern side of the harbour, just along the road beyond the Dun Aengus restaurant. From her window she could look out and see the lifeboat anchored in the bay and the island ferry berthed at the end of Kilronan Pier. The tide was way out now, exposing the rocks on the foreshore, and a huge expanse of hard-packed sand. There was hardly a ripple in the water, either in the deep harbour or at the water line. The skies were clear and the sun was still warm. It was so peaceful and idyllic that she was very glad she hadn't stayed in Galway itself.

She made short work of her unpacking, what there was of it. Never had she given so little thought to what she would take when going away. Not that she was ever away much. But this place tempted her to get out there and feel the peace, the tranquil way of it. She left her B&B and crossed the road to the sea wall, and walked along till she came to a gap where she could step through.

She wandered along till she found a suitable spot among the rocks and sat down. Seagulls wheeled silently overhead. They glided and dipped gracefully, then soared again, taking on a golden tinge to their plumage in the late evening sunlight. The faint sound of an engine reached her ears. A sail-boat slid slowly around the tip of the pier, its sail already down. Betty watched fascinated as it cut its engine while passing the ferry and its momentum carried it silently towards the pier wall. Ropes were thrown and quayside workers tied it up. Further out on the water a Galway Hooker danced through the rays of the evening sun and an entranced Betty sat on, allowing time to drift like the boat, and her head to empty of all its troubles. It would be sacrilege to allow her predicament to impinge on this tranquillity. Tomorrow would be time enough to deal with reality.

The sound of a child's voice floated towards her, followed by a female voice calling. At first Betty could see no one. Then from her left a little girl came running along the hard-packed sand, holding something under her arm. Fascinated, Betty watched her. Dressed in a pair of pink trousers and a cream T-shirt, the child's hair was what caught her attention. Masses of short bouncy light-brown curls sprang up and down as the child ran towards a couple of seagulls picking in the sand ahead of her. The gulls immediately soared into the air at her approach, and the child's attention went with them. She tripped over a rock which was partially embedded in the damp sand, and crashed down with a thud. A short stunned silence followed, then a shrill wail shattered the evening peace. Betty was already up and running to help the little girl back on her feet. Tears ran down the child's face as she held her hands out, palms upwards. They smarted and were caked with sand. There was sand stuck to her chin and in her mouth.

"There there, pet," Betty soothed her, "you're alright, you're alright."

She took a packet of tissues from her jacket pocket and began to wipe away the tears and the offending sand as much as she could.

"Grandy!" the child wailed, looking around.

Two people came running up, and fussed over the child. Betty took the young woman to be the mother. The man could have been the father, he had such a fresh clean-cut look about him, but she knew he was the grandfather by the way the little one addressed him.

"Grandy, I fell!" She held out her arms, tears streaming afresh down her face. He picked her up and held her to him, soothing her with hugs and kisses.

"Teddy fell too," she wailed, the tears ceasing quickly as she remembered her bear.

"Really, Isabella! You should watch where you're going," the mother exclaimed, trying to brush sand from the pink trousers in a rather agitated fashion.

Betty picked up the teddy bear from the sand. She brushed him off and held him out to the child. She felt it was time for her to bow out of this family scene. The grandfather took the toy and acknowledged her for the first time. The smiling eyes reflected his sincerity.

"Thank you very much," he said warmly. "We appreciate the lady's help, don't we, Isabella?"

With the teddy bear's nose he brushed some grains of sand from Isabella's cheek as he spoke. The child clutched her teddy, looked at Betty and nodded solemnly.

The mother spoke to no one in particular. "It's getting late. I think perhaps we should go back." She turned to Betty. "Thank you for your concern." Her perfectly made-up lips formed a little smile. It hovered about for a moment or two but never reached her eyes.

"You're welcome," Betty replied as the well-dressed trio moved away back along the beach.

The mother, tall and slim in a pair of soft brown-leather trousers to die for, settled her sweater around her shoulders. The man carried the little girl for some of the way. The child gripped her teddy by his arm, allowing him to dangle down her grandfather's back.

Betty returned to her rock and sat for a while, but the feeling of solitude was gone. Food, she needed food. The last time she had eaten was on the train in Athenry. She headed back to the roadway and walked the short distance to the village. She passed the American Bar where a man with a guitar led a singsong of sorts in the open air.

He sang country and western. Appropriate for the American bar, not exactly what you'd expect to hear on Inis Mór, Betty found herself thinking ruefully. She passed the huge stone cross in the centre of Kilronan and then the delicious mouth-watering aroma coming from the Waterfront Restaurant decided for her where she would have dinner.

Dining alone is a fairly speedy affair, she discovered, with no interruptions to your eating for talk, or to sip your wine slowly while you listen, and in no time at all she was back at the cross, her hunger taken care of, and much too much awake to consider going to bed. She went for a short after-dinner walk and then up the steep slope which led from the seafront up to Joe Mac's bar, drawn by the sound of traditional music. This was as good a place as any to kill a little time before early bed. Outside, people strolled about at their ease, enjoying the wonderful evening. Younger tourists were beginning to appear, all dressed up for a night out. Dressed was hardly the proper word, she thought. Necklines plunged way down, almost meeting hemlines on the way up. Many dedicated followers of current fashion trends opted to leave their midriffs bare also. Fake tans and genuine sunburn vied with each other for attention, and judging by the vast amount of bare skin, they both got attention in equal measure.

Music was in full swing and the small bar was packed to the door. She squeezed her way in and was lucky enough to nab a seat near the end of the counter just as its current occupier vacated it; it was still warm. She ordered a coffee and sat back to enjoy the atmosphere.

Very cosmopolitan, she observed; every race and creed was represented in the little bar by the looks of it. Spanish, Germans, Chinese, French . . . languages from every corner of the world. When a voice beside her said, "Hello again" she was almost surprised at hearing words she could understand.

The man from the beach held out his hand and introduced himself. "Myles Nugent."

She smiled and shook his hand. "Betty Morris."

He was wearing an immaculate white cotton shirt, open at the neck with the sleeves rolled back to the elbows, and grey trousers. Betty wished she had brought something nice to wear, something that would have been more suitable for evenings. But, when she left home this morning, going out at night was the last thing on her mind.

"How is the little one?" she asked, surprised that he appeared to be on his own.

"Isabella is fine, thank you – she's sleeping soundly." Then, gesturing to the barman, he asked her, "Mind if I join you?"

That was the end of her plans for an early night.

Later, lying in her bed, it crossed her mind that she had just spent a good number of hours without thinking once about her problems and nothing drastic had befallen her. In fact, she'd had quite an interesting evening. She couldn't remember having the opportunity of talking for so long with such an interesting stranger before. What on earth did they find to talk about? It didn't seem in any way strange when he ordered drinks. Or when he walked her back to her accommodation. He said he was probably going back on tomorrow afternoon's ferry. His daughter Sophie, he explained, planned to scatter her husband's ashes in the morning. He expected she would want to leave on the afternoon ferry, and catch the five past six train back to Heuston.

After he left Betty, Myles sank his hands into his trouser pockets, and rambled slowly back towards his own accommodation. The night was still calm and warm. Along the way people still sat at outside tables finishing their drinks. Music was ended for the night and some were doing as he was, sauntering along, in no hurry to bring an end to a very pleasant evening. He was glad he'd decided to take a walk after dinner, glad he had bumped into Betty Morris.

He glanced up at the sky. Some light clouds had rolled in. He smiled to himself and rambled on. If Isabella was awake now and looking out her window she would see that Aran had a 'broken moon' too.

Sophie sat in the armchair in her bedroom. The light from the en suite was enough. In the bed across from her, Isabella slept soundly. Sophie heard her father's key turn in his lock across the landing, and was glad he had not come to say goodnight before turning in. Earlier she'd sat in the guest sitting room reading for a while after putting Isabella to bed, but she was in no fit state to be seen right now. The glass in her hand had been refilled already a number of times.

She was restless. Peter would have had a better solution, but he wasn't here now. She fell into an uneasy sleep, where Peter hovered around in some indefinable place, but she couldn't figure out what it was that appeared to be bothering him. She couldn't see him clearly, but there was no doubt that it was he. She was greatly troubled that she couldn't know what he wanted. She heard herself being called over and over, and the distress became unbearable.

"Mummy, Mummy!" Isabella shook her arm.

With a start Sophie woke. The empty glass was on the floor.

"What!" she snapped, only half-awake.

The child wanted to go to the toilet.

"Then go, Isabella! And get back into bed."

Sophie lifted her tired body from the chair, placed the cap back on the bottle, and put the bottle into the bottom of her case. She told herself tomorrow would see an end to the limbo she inhabited, but even as she thought it she had her doubts. She had spent so much time hoping that when she scattered Peter's ashes it would also be a new beginning. But she knew it was futile because she was sceptical of new beginnings, for she couldn't see how new beginnings with old baggage could possibly work.

Chapter 5

The morning brought a big change in the weather. A wind had whipped up masses of cloud overnight, the skies were dark and threatening, and Sophie's feeling of foreboding strengthened. The water in the harbour lashed against its walls, and the lifeboat no longer sat motionless at anchor. Rain threatened.

At the breakfast table Myles threw an eye in Sophie's direction. Her expertly applied make-up did not conceal all, as she no doubt hoped it would. She looked tired and red-eyed, and she didn't bother to check Isabella about her table manners. He worried. Perhaps she shouldn't go alone to Dun Aengus this morning as planned.

"Everything okay?"

"Fine."

"Would you like me to . . . ?"

"No, thank you, I really must do this myself."

They continued the breakfast in silence. The weather was the topic among the other guests. But they were walkers, hikers, and had come well prepared for whatever the elements might throw at them.

The minibus Sophie ordered arrived late. By the time she finally set off with the urn Myles was very concerned about her.

The ancient fort was further across the island at the top of a steep climb which was a rocky pathway between two dry-stone walls for a good part of the way. The minibus could only take her to the car park at the base of the climb. She set out, remembering it all as if it were only yesterday that she had climbed this rocky path with Peter at her elbow, steadying her every step. How they laughed at the wind which whipped her hair, whistled in their ears, deafened their words, threw them off balance, holding each other to steady up, and then battling on again through the rain.

She kept her head down now, watching carefully where she placed her feet. With no Peter to ensure her safety she became rather nervous.

No trees grew on this bare expanse of limestone rock and there was no shelter from the wind. The fort ahead seemed benign enough, but as she drew nearer the weather worsened and rain began to fall. Sophie's mind flew back to that day when they made love in the shelter of the ancient walls. Peter's voice filled her head, his face spun before her. She felt as if he was guiding her onwards, drawing her closer, beckoning. When she passed beneath the single stone entrance in the innermost wall, its depth provided a little shelter and in the brief respite she sat down heavily, her legs suddenly unsteady. Looking out from her shelter towards the edge of the sheer drop she saw she had only a short distance to go. But the fort had completely lost its benign appearance. The high stone walls were now broody and dark. The Atlantic thundered away at the foot of the cliffs. She could sense its might vibrate through the earth beneath her. Its power frightened her. But she must do this for Peter. It was the least she could do; and she had promised – promised faithfully. They were alone when first here, and it was fitting that it should be so when they finally parted.

The desolation of the place was overpowering. Peter's face hovered before her, leading her out towards the edge. But she was not prepared for the trembling that gripped her as she moved slowly forward. Her hands holding the urn began to shake and the trembling spread through her whole body. The strength of the wind increased considerably. Finally, dejectedly, unable to force herself the rest of the way, she sank to the wet grass, her eyes staring out to the horizon while the rain beat down.

Then she staggered to her feet and stumbled back out through the entrance and down the rocky path, still clutching the urn, which seemed to burn itself into the crook of her arm. Rain hammered down from the south-west. Once or twice her ankle went from under her, but she was so upset that it didn't register.

Somewhere on the path she met the minibus driver. Worry had sent him up to the fort after her, despite her instructions that he should wait. It was no place to be alone in this weather, he said. It was no place to be alone in any weather. It was said that people were 'persuaded' to do strange things up there, and it was generally accepted that when things happened it was because of the compelling influence of the 'ancients'. In weather like this one never knew, one could never be sure.

Hearing this didn't do anything to help Sophie.

The driver helped her into the minibus, then watched her through his rear-view mirror as he reversed the van.

She sat motionless, staring unseeingly ahead.

"You alright, miss?"

There was no answer.

Myles' first reaction when he saw her was that she should get out of her wet clothes immediately.

"I failed him. I couldn't do it . . ." she whispered, clearly distressed.

"The driver tells me it's just as well you didn't! The winds at those cliffs can be very dangerous. Sweep a body off their feet, he says."

He took the urn from her arms and prevailed upon her to go and have a hot shower.

"We'll do it together when this wind dies down, don't worry. This weather is not set to continue so we'll be fine, you'll see. Peter will still have his wish."

Chapter 6

One thing about not having loads of clothes, Betty told herself, is that one garment goes everywhere with you. That one garment, on this occasion, was her anorak. She looked out at the rough water in the harbour and decided it was an anorak day. Browsing over the information leaflets she'd picked up in the airport while waiting for the plane, she decided to take a walk to the Black Fort. She saw the sign for it yesterday on the way from the airport, and it didn't seem to be too far. Just about far enough for all the thinking she needed to do. She hadn't phoned Olive or Buddy, because she discovered that in her hurry to be gone she had left her mobile phone on the kitchen table. She could see it in her mind's eye. And their mobile-phone numbers were in *its* memory, not hers.

She left her accommodation after breakfast and turned right along the coast road she came in on yesterday. Already she seemed to be here longer than that. It was hard to credit that it was only yesterday morning that she had left her own house. Perhaps she could assimilate herself into island life quite easily? She smiled to herself, thinking she must be the umpteenth visitor to think the same thing. The wind was strong this morning. She zipped up her jacket and lengthened her stride. The Black Fort was on the eastern end of the island and she walked with the wind comfortably at her back.

She allowed her mind to ramble back over last night for a while. But for some inexplicable reason it was Martin who commandeered her thoughts. That was quite a shock; she had not given much thought to her husband in God knows how many years. His desertion caused major life changes and left her with the daily problems of providing for their young children alone.

That was when she emerged from the shock and became angry. So angry that it empowered her to carry on. She consoled her children, got a job, and tried to make her meagre salary cover everything. The anger had died a long time ago. There just wasn't enough energy to sustain the lot. It was years before she realised there was life apart from her children and home and work. And by then it had left her behind. Olive and Buddy grew up and she began to feel old. She had been much too busy to keep up with the world, and she found with a jolt on her fortieth birthday that, just like Time, the world waits for no one.

"You need a new hairstyle, Mam," Olive told her plainly then. "Your hair has been like that since I was born, for God's sake! And it needs a colour, too."

Betty remembered looking at her reflection. "It's not too bad . . . maybe a decent cut, or something," she mused.

"*Something* is needed for sure! I'm going to get you a

new look for your birthday." Betty's hands went up. "Oh no, you're not! God knows what I'll end up looking like. I'll get a bit of a trim, that'll do."

But Olive had her way, and Betty kept the new look.

The road to the Black Fort curved around by the shore. The walk was deceptive. Because of the flat landscape it looked much shorter in distance, but she kept going. Lost in memories she walked as if on automatic pilot.

The day her 'life' ended began like any other: playschool for Buddy, a nap for Olive, shopping, cooking. She was looking forward to the party. A neighbour's daughter's twenty-first birthday. The girl was home from London for the celebration. She had spent the last four years working over there, and she had certainly grown up in the process. Betty found it hard to equate this confident young woman with the 'child' who left Dublin before doing her Leaving Certificate.

'The child' never went back. She and Martin took one look at each other and Betty was history. The neighbours, unable to look her in the face any more, eventually moved house.

She reached the signpost for the Black Fort, turned towards the path that curved around by the electricity station, and continued. People passed her on their way back, giving her a cheery greeting. Walkers. You could depend on them to be already heading back while you are only heading out, she thought. They shared a comment about the weather and kept going.

The ground was extremely rocky. Careful where you put your feet, she told herself, you don't want a sprained ankle all the way out here by yourself, or worse. When she broke the crest of the slope, the wind, strong and suddenly in her face, was a surprise. The black clouds over the sea were rolling in fast, and she realised only then how far she had walked. Staying to spend time at the fort was not really an option now. There was no shelter. The soft spongy grassy hollows were ideal for sitting and meditating in fine weather, but hardly sufficient to offer protection from the rain. She pulled her anorak zip up the rest of the way and started the long walk back.

By the time she got back to the house she was fairly wet, and the rain looked like it was down for the day.

She took her book and sat in the glass porch at the front of the house, in one of the two sturdy wicker chairs. A glass-topped wicker coffee table held information leaflets on the island. She turned her chair towards the water and sat looking out over Kilronan Harbour, across Galway Bay to the dark and heavy mountains of Connemara in the distance, the book lying on her lap, her hand resting on the open page. Rain rivulets trickled down the outside of the glass obscuring her view.

Her eyes were looking into the distance, un-obscured by the rain because it was the distance of the past, and her picture was as clear as the day it happened. Her husband's jacket hanging on the end of the banisters, when she expected he should be in work, the gut instinct that put her breathing on hold as she climbed the stairs. She knew well that faint familiar squeak of the bedsprings. The silent way she approached the half-open door. The girl, naked and on her knees astride Martin, her back to the door, his hands gripping her hips, keeping them moving in unison.

She didn't remember making a sound, but they

became aware of her. Her recollection of events after that was nothing but a jumbled mess, an unbelievably horrible mess. A scramble to get into clothes, her not wanting to look, but unable to look away, inaudible babble, the feeling of falling from a great height, and the awful awareness that her husband was not attempting to catch her.

Martin apologised, but he was leaving. The girl said nothing . . . there was just an infuriating toss of her long hair as she went with him.

Her family said nothing. Some weeks later a 'For Sale' sign went up on the neighbours' house.

The book fell from Betty's lap. As she picked it up her landlady came out with a mug of tea and some delicious home-made brown bread with jam.

"I thought you might be hungry after your walk," she smiled, placing the small tray on the wicker table. "This weather has lasted longer than was forecast. At least it's clearing up now."

Betty realised she had been sitting in the porch for quite some time. Yellow shafts of sunlight streaked through broken cloud and she watched the afternoon ferry as it moved away from the pier, taking its quota of visitors and day-trippers back to the mainland. Isabella and her mother and grandfather would be on it.

The winds that blew the rain-clouds away still disturbed the sea quite a bit. By tomorrow morning she hoped the weather would be a lot better for her departure. Either way she was glad that she had chosen the quickest way of crossing.

She went upstairs and took a nice long hot shower, and rubbed vigorously at her hair to dry it. The long dyed-blonde tresses of her neighbour's daughter flashed through her mind. That was more than twenty-four years ago. They probably had a fair sprinkling of grey by now, she thought ruefully. Time took care of everything. Time was the great leveller. She knew Martin had other children. Now and again over the years snippets of information came to her. Usually she didn't dwell on them. She had things to be getting on with and no energy to waste on something she could do nothing about. But the news of their first child was the worst bit. She bitterly begrudged that child its father, when her own never saw theirs. She brushed hard at her hair and gave out to her reflection in the mirror.

"What the hell has come over you, Betty Morris?" she demanded. "Can you not think of what you are going to do from here on? After all, that's what you came here for, isn't it? Yes, it is. Now get on with it, and come up with a plan, and no more of this misery backtracking, d'you hear? Smile! I don't want to see that miserable look next time I look in this mirror!"

As she spoke she waved the hairbrush at her reflection.

I'm going mad, she thought.

She dined in the Waterfront Restaurant again and felt quite at home this time round, taking as long as she pleased over her meal, but she still had time on her hands after dinner and decided on a walk. The scene was different from last night. People wore jackets and coats against the westerly wind, and only the very hardy sat outside.

Joe Mac's was as packed as last night when she went in for her taste of holiday atmosphere, and there was no chance of a seat at all. There were times when she wished she was taller, and this was one of them. Trying to get the barman's attention while obscured by taller Germans, or Americans, or practically anyone at all, wasn't easy.

"Is this okay?" A drink was placed in her hand. "Same as you had last night."

She looked up into Myles Nugent's face. It almost seemed like he had been waiting for her. She instantly checked herself. Don't be so stupid, she thought.

"I thought you said you'd be gone?"

"I have a seat." He took her by the elbow and guided her through the crowd to where his jacket was placed on a stool. He lifted it and she sat up to the bar. They clinked glasses.

"To what?" she asked.

"To bad weather," he grinned.

Smiling, he told Betty of how his departure was delayed. He didn't seem at all put out about it. He was quite happy to sit and talk, and talk they did.

Last night was a fluke, she had figured. To sit dug into conversation the way they had, was not an experience that would ever get the chance to repeat itself.

But his plans had gone awry and here they were again.

Chapter 7

For the second night in a row Sophie sat, glass in hand, bottle by her side, her eyes now fixed on the sleeping Isabella, even though it was not her daughter who filled her thoughts. Her cowardice had prevented her from fulfilling her promise, and that was the least she could have done for Peter.

She felt Peter's presence, and believed it to be an ominous one, but she thought that was no more than she deserved.

She had chosen not to join her father for a drink after Isabella was put to bed. It might help to cheer her a bit and take her mind off things, he suggested. He had tried to reassure her that tomorrow things would be righted, but to her that could not be.

Not ever.

She was well aware that she could not face the Fort alone again; therefore the scattering of the ashes could not happen the way it was supposed to. The way Peter would have wanted. The only means of consolation was in her hand. She poured again, wanting to rid herself of the morose feelings that persisted. But she wasn't so heavy-handed this time. She'd seen the look her father sneaked at her that morning, and she wasn't so sure that he believed her 'didn't sleep very well' comment.

The following morning was bright and dry. Banks of white cloud obscured the sun from time to time, and the wind was still fairly strong, but at least it dried the ground and the steep climb up to Dun Aengus was relatively safe.

They all went and Sophie made no objection. Isabella held Grandy's hand all the way to the top. Sometimes he lifted her when the steps up the rocks were too high for her legs, while she insisted she was getting bigger and she could do it herself.

When they reached the top the wind from the southwest swept up the cliff face and tore at their hair and clothes. Sophie halted after she went under the stone entrance to the inner area, and Myles took her gently by the arm, while keeping a good hold on Isabella's hand. Slowly they moved forward towards the cliff but Myles knew it would be impossible to scatter the ashes over the edge in such a wind.

Sophie realised it too, and stopped dead.

"There is only one thing to do," her father said gently. "You hold Isabella's hand, Sophie, and I'll take the urn."

"It's not the way he wanted it," she stressed.

She knew instinctively what he meant to do and she wasn't happy, but Myles waited till she passed the urn to him.

"Do you want to say a prayer, or anything?"

"I'm done with that," she answered, her expression a void.

He turned towards the sea and went as near to the edge as was necessary. The sun, already moving into the south, was shining into their eyes and they saw his dark silhouette make one clean movement as he threw the urn clear out over the edge. It was gone. No one heard the gasp that escaped Sophie. In her head she heard the sharp crack as it broke apart which brought to mind another breaking, this time of human bones. She was rooted to the spot as she watched a mental vision of the urn smashing into a million pieces at the base of the cliffs, and saw the fine grey ash swallowed by the Atlantic swell.

"Mummy, you're hurting my hand!" Isabella pulled her hand free.

"I'm sorry," Sophie whispered. "I'm sorry."

The words were not directed at her daughter. The child looked up and something about her mother frightened her now. Grandy was back beside them and she placed her hand in his.

"Can we go now, Grandy? I don't like it here."

Chapter 8

The long road of houses where Betty lived felt quite claustrophobic after all the open space and sea views on Inis Mór. The terraced two-storey houses were built in blocks of six or eight, with red-brick running uninterrupted from one gable end of a block to the other.

On the northern side of the narrow road, which was never built to accommodate all the family cars now parked along it, some houses had three steps up inside the gate, and their gardens were higher. Betty's garden path to her front door was flat, and the façades on her side were half red-brick and half pebbledash. The best thing about her house, Betty used to think when Olive and Buddy were small, was its proximity to the green open grassland of Fairview Park.

She closed her door and dropped her bag in the hall, intending to take it upstairs and unpack later. The first thing she needed was a refreshing cuppa. As she filled the cordless kettle she noticed the note by the bread bin.

Olive had called and used her key.

My God, Betty lamented, the first time she calls in ages, and I'm not here!

The note was written in capitals, and finished with an exclamation mark. A little smile flitted over Betty's features. There was something of the 'shoe on the other foot' about the tone of the note, but she decided to have her tea first before picking up her mobile. A subtle change had occurred in her relationship with her daughter and she was just becoming aware of it.

She sat, cupping the mug in her hands, with her feet on the opposite chair.

It was good to be home.

Grand and all as the few days were, and they were, she wouldn't have kicked off her shoes and put her feet up in the B&B.

She wouldn't have met Myles Nugent either. She'd never see him again of course. People you meet by chance like that, you never meet them again. You never ran into them before, and you never do again. Even though you both live in the same city, and even though Dublin is noted for being 'a small town'.

Ah well, it helped to make the time pass better, and did her a world of good.

There was the sound of the key in the lock, and Olive's voice rang out.

"Mam? You here? Mam?"

Betty's eyebrows went up. Two visits in as many days! "In the kitchen!"

They greeted each other with a warm tight hug. Betty

kept herself in check. She didn't want to gush over Olive and let her see how upset she had been at the lengthy lack of communication.

"God, Mam! You could have let us know where you were. I was worried. I couldn't get you on your mobile either."

"But I was only gone barely three days, and there's the mobile on the table. I forgot to take it."

She took another cup down and poured two teas, pushing one across to Olive.

"If that had been me you'd have been giving out yards!" Olive sugared her tea, and caught her mother's little smile.

"Ah yes, but you're living your own life now. I'm sure you wouldn't appreciate having to check in still."

Olive stirred her tea for a long time. Her thoughts seemed to have sailed off somewhere else.

"You know, Mam, I should've called around ages ago . . ."

Oh oh. A crisis already? A reason other than switching to a new life and all the time that manages to absorb?

"But I couldn't . . ." Another pause.

Betty waited, trying not to let her anxiety show. She didn't know what to expect. Before, when Olive had a problem they always talked about it. Work or boyfriend or whatever, they talked. Often they sat up, well into the night, talking about life, loves, relationships, and just about everything in between, till exhaustion sent them to their beds, the world all set to rights again.

"We were having problems settling in."

"How do you mean?"

"You know the way you want something so much you think it can only go right?"

"Yeah."

"Well, it wasn't quite as simple as that. We argued over such stupid things! I just couldn't bring myself to come around here because I was afraid I'd made an awful mistake, and I felt so stupid at having been in such a hurry to go."

"And . . . did you? Make a mistake, I mean?"

"No, I didn't." Olive's reply was definite. "I remembered the way you and I used to talk when I was at home, so we sat ourselves down one night and decided we weren't going to bed till we got it sorted."

"And . . . did you? Get it sorted?"

Her daughter's smile said it all.

Betty put her arms around her and held her, and her heart was glad. Glad that Olive had taken something valuable away from home with her. Glad it wasn't that *she* had been dispensed with, as she had thought. Glad that she had not given way to her despairing thoughts on the matter.

But all she said was: "I'm glad."

"So how did your little break go? You could have let us know you were off!"

Betty just smiled. Olive was just as astute as she, and Betty had not decided how she was going to explain her "little break". Certainly she had to come up with a reason as to why she just took off like that. She stuck to a limited version of the truth.

"Holidays due, and they wouldn't let me work them, so there you are."

She said she had gone away on the spur of the

moment. At least that much was true. She had no intention of saying how she needed time to think what she was going to do with herself now that she was living alone. She couldn't and wouldn't put that on her daughter.

Her relief at having her daughter 'back' again was huge. She felt the weight physically lift and laughed when she told of the tiny plane, and sitting beside the pilot, almost rubbing knees, and getting weighed in front of everyone.

Her kitchen knew the sound of laughter again. Like old times, she thought, the two of them laughing and chatting away.

Like old friends.

Chapter 9

When Maeve was alive they'd had Sally. Sally used to sing away to herself in the house, especially in the kitchen where the acoustics were better, but she was always out of tune, and she always had the words mixed up, but that never deterred her. Myles used to wonder sometimes if her hearing was okay. In her last few years with them her singing was not heard so often. Her breathing was a problem, and she became "quite puffed on the stairs" as she said. When she retired her family took her to live with them in Australia.

Eileen Hyland arrived after Maeve died. Eileen was supposed to be temporary and part-time, but she was still there. Eileen didn't sing; she didn't talk much either. She had a grown family of her own and a habit of rolling her eyes to heaven when a request was made of her. Her biggest concern was not being delayed from leaving when her hours were up.

The Nugents' home was an old house. It had two storeys to the front, but because of the steep slope it was built on, three storeys to the back. The front didn't have what could be called a garden. It was more of a short gravel turn-in that curved from the narrow road to a parking area in front of the hall door, but they were more than compensated for this to the rear of the house.

Beyond the terrace the garden was on two lower levels, separated by three wide granite steps. A wrought-iron fire escape wound its solid way down to the side of the terrace from the tall sash window of the landing. Myles often thought of removing the fire escape completely, but it was a unique element of the house, and he was reluctant to reduce its character. When Maeve used to have her terrace parties, the last few steps of the fire escape were a favourite seating spot for the guests. The view from there or anywhere in the garden was magnificent, unobstructed, and totally private.

Now Isabella was quite absorbed in arranging her dolls on the steps leading from the terrace to the lawn. She was being extremely precise about it, fixing the folds of a dress, placing a doll's long plaits first in front of, then behind the doll's shoulders, moving the arms just so, and all the time she talked, telling them the story of the trip to Aran.

Ted sat wedged in the forked trunk of the nearby palm tree, and from there he cast a glassy eye over the proceedings. Isabella knew, simply by glancing at him, whether or not her arrangements met with his approval. Apparently they did, and she continued her story as she arranged the dolls exactly right. The reason for such precision was not remotely evident to Myles, who watched her quietly from his seat on the terrace, but clearly it was of the utmost importance to her.

There appeared to be some pecking order in existence

among the dolls, and Isabella placed the oldest one, which had been her grandmother's, in pride of place on the top step.

"It wasn't *our* sea," she emphasised, and with a flick of her hand she indicated the sweep of Dublin Bay behind her, "but it was *very* big, and Grandy says it goes all the way to 'Merica."

She glanced at Ted, who'd shared the experience with her, and who apparently signalled his agreement by his silence, and so she proceeded to tell them all about how she chased the big white birds, and how the nice lady on the rocks helped her and Ted when they fell. Myles smiled at the child's logic. He figured Betty wouldn't mind being referred to as the "lady on the rocks". She had a great sense of humour, he reflected, and he couldn't remember when he was last able to relax and laugh and enjoy "the *craic*" as she called it, the way they had.

But she was gone back to her own life, and he to his.

Sophie was in the boutique, the first week in ages that her staff saw her there for any substantial amount of time, and she was in fine form. 'On a high,' they might have said if they had been asked. Much of her stock was 'exclusives', and many customers expected her personal attention. The sale was coming up, and the new season's stock was arriving daily.

The apartment above the shop was the home she had shared with Peter and Isabella. It was attractive, the large balcony off the sitting room to the front looking out over the Bull Island in Clontarf, but she spent precious little time in it after Peter died. Eventually she had packed the urn, and some things for herself and her daughter and moved back in with her father, temporarily of course, telling herself that he needed the company as much as she.

He made no fuss about her being back. He too assumed it to be temporary, perhaps till Sophie dispersed her husband's ashes, and so he set out to enjoy his granddaughter's company while he had it.

Somewhere along the line he became unsure of the correctness of his assumption. Sophie lived in his house as if it was her only home. Myles would have preferred to see her move on with her life, for her own sake, and he squashed uneasy thoughts that sneaked about in the back of his mind.

But if Sophie moved out, Myles knew that to be without Isabella now would be worse than losing a limb. Her light footfall, even when she ran through the house, which she often did since she could hardly contain herself, she just *had* to run, and her natural exuberance would leave a silence too awful to contemplate.

He watched her as she told her story, watched how she checked with Ted from time to time. He wondered what wisdom she figured Ted was imbued with behind his black glassy eyes.

Andy Fox finished in the lower garden where he was deadheading flowers and doing a bit of weeding.

"Constant vigilance," he always said of the battle against the weeds, "is the only thing."

Carrying his hoe and bucket, he moved to the upper level and began working along the flower border at the back of the oval-shaped lawn. He tended the garden a few afternoons a week for the Nugents, and often on evenings such as this, with the sun warm on his back, he would be in no hurry to leave.

A quiet man, Andy, not as young as he used to be.

Unless Myles came to chat or there was something to be discussed about the garden, Andy just got on with it. He had been "getting on with it" as he would say, for the past twenty-five years.

The small site had never been what could be called a garden before the Nugents moved in shortly after Sophie was born and she had been two years old when Andy began the enormous task of transforming the rocky, gorse-overgrown plot into what it was today. Maeve wanted the work done in order to maximise enjoyment of the stunning view from the back of the house. The ground had to be cleared, and to combat the slope Andy suggested the two different levels of lawn, with three granite steps leading from the terrace to the smaller upper lawn, and three more steps going down to the lower one. A balustrade of the same granite surrounded the terrace area. To Maeve he was a genius, because he had created her favourite place. It was his design, his masterpiece, and laborious backbreaking work, yet she never had much to say to him, and he always seemed ill at ease if she happened to wander about the garden while he was there.

Isabella caught sight of him and suddenly left her dolls high and dry. Ted was pulled from the fork of the palm tree and carried over to where Andy was quietly hoeing.

"You finding wigglies, Andy?" she asked as she reached him.

Ted was laid on the grass while Isabella watched closely as the hoe sliced through the soft earth and Andy used it expertly to aerate the soil. Myles couldn't hear what response Andy made in his deep, slow voice, but he knew that he would try to unearth at least one or two worms. Isabella was bent almost double, her hands clasped between her knees, as she scrutinised the soil for a "wigglie".

"There!" she squealed, pointing and backing off a little. She watched it for a while then Andy carefully laid some soil back over it.

"Don't want them birds to get him – them worms do good work in the ground," he said.

"We *like* them, don't we?" Isabella piped up, keen to be in agreement with him. Andy's weathered face broke into a gentle smile, and he nodded slowly, and continued along the bed.

There was the sound of a footfall behind Myles and Bradley joined him on the terrace.

Eileen had answered his knock.

"Sophie about?"

He sat in the chair opposite and crossed one long leg over the other.

"She's in the shop," his father told him, at the same time offering him a glass of iced juice from the table. "Did you want her for anything in particular?"

Bradley waved away the offer of juice. "I was just wondering what she's going to do about the apartment. If she's not going to go back to it maybe she might think of selling it. It would be an excellent buy, don't you think?"

Myles stared at him with something of a shock. "Have you said that to her?"

No, Bradley hadn't, but he was thinking of it. His eyes roamed around the garden, and he called hello to

Isabella, who, on seeing him, ran up to him to tell him that she was watching "wigglies" in the ground. After giving him a quick hug she turned back to her dolls.

Bradley recrossed his legs. He was taller than his father, and would have loved to have inherited his father's hair at least, for at thirty he was already showing quite a noticeable bald spot. Plain though he was, his personality was what showed first, and his clear blue eyes held his father's twinkle, behind which lay a similar logical practical brain. He had been his mother's favourite.

His father's expression made him curious.

"Something wrong?" he asked.

"I'm not sure." There was a slight hesitation in Myles' voice. He was hoping Sophie would be able to move on with her life now. He didn't think suggesting she sell her apartment would be any help at all at the moment. Reducing her options was hardly what he thought she should be doing.

For some reason he was reminded of the other morning when he walked into the kitchen. Talk between Sophie and Eileen stopped abruptly. Talk between Sophie and Eileen was not a regular occurrence as far as he could tell, and therefore struck him as odd.

A sliver of worry about his sister detached itself from his father and planted itself in Bradley's head. He opened his mouth to reply, but closed it again.

"Business must be good if you're thinking of buying," his father remarked, changing the subject.

Bradley changed his mind about the juice, reached for the jug, and poured himself a glass.

"It's not bad at all. I've just landed a couple of very

lucrative contracts which should keep us flying high for the foreseeable future at least."

His choice of words these days reflected his position as marketing manager of Flying High, a helicopter-hire company. His was the satisfaction of having been head-hunted, but even so Myles smiled ruefully. He remembered when well-established firms could practically depend on the future long-term. In the cut-throat business world today only a very few could look into the distance with confidence. Newspapers were full of shock reports of apparently solid companies going under.

Ruthlessness was the name of the game. Security did not come as standard.

"I thought if she *was* selling, you know . . ." Bradley mused, going back to the subject of Sophie's apartment. "Renting is just dead money. There's no point either in leaving it in the banks these days. With all due respect to the banks," he added, suddenly mindful of his father's thirty years of working for them.

"I've no doubt you're right. I think I got out just in time," Myles reflected, not for the first time. "At the rate things are going I'd say future retirement deals will be severely reduced at the very least."

They sat in silence a while, then Myles went on, "I don't think it would be a good idea for her to sell the apartment, not at the moment – she needs her own place. But if she mentions anything . . ."

Bradley nodded.

They watched Isabella as she played with her dolls, once again lost in her own world where the dolls were the players and she and Ted called the shots. Behind her they observed Andy Fox as he hoed systematically along the edges of the lawn. He worked in such an unhurried fashion that he never seemed to be moving very much, always giving the impression that he might not finish working where he was for quite a while. But the entire garden was his silent testament. Father and son sat back and enjoyed the fascination of watching a master perfect his masterpiece. Andy always wore a tweed hound's-tooth cap, the pattern obliterated on the peak by the constant handling with his soil-encrusted fingers. As they watched he lifted it with his usual sideways sweep, for no apparent reason other than to re-position it at an even more precarious angle over his right ear. Then he jerked his neck upward from his collarless shirt, jutted his chin out left and right a couple of times, and delved a well-weathered hand into his jacket pocket for a piece of tobacco. With the tobacco popped in between his yellow teeth, he continued with the hoeing and proceeded with such fluidity of movement he appeared as if he had never interrupted himself at all.

"You think Sophie has a problem, Dad."

It wasn't a question.

Myles looked far out over the bay, where boats moved silently in an east-west direction. The statement seemed to put flesh on the bones of his worry. One look at his father's face told Bradley they were thinking the same thing.

"I'd hoped when we got back from Aran things would be better, but no. And I'm sure drink isn't always her only remedy."

He glanced over to check that Isabella was well out of earshot.

Father and son sat in silence a while, each with his own worried thoughts, till Bradley changed the subject.

"Any word from Maeve lately?"

"Talked to her a couple of days ago," Myles answered, brightening, suddenly picturing his auburn-haired eldest daughter in her element, standing before her easel, looking out over the wilds of Kerry. "She was in the middle of her exhibition. Seems she's delighted with how it's going. Apparently she's had great interest expressed by a couple who have businesses in New York."

But Myles' darker thoughts hung about in the background despite the convivial conversation. It wasn't like Sophie to take an interest in household matters, Eileen usually just got on with it, and Eileen was never very sociable or chatty either, and he found himself disturbed again about the incident in the kitchen.

Chapter 10

The shop was in the thick of what Betty called "the fresh-out-of-the-oven rush". The first afternoon batch was out, and the mouth-watering smells of freshly baked bread and cakes brought passers-by in off Grafton Street in their dozens. Customers were three deep at the counter in the narrow shop.

No problem to Betty. She could have served them with her eyes closed.

"He was a bit of alright, your man," Trish Dunne teased as she leaned across for two fresh-cream doughnuts. Trish was the working manageress who preferred being one of the girls.

"He's not 'my man'," Betty protested under her breath, as she put a wheaten brown and three apple slices into bags.

"Could've fooled me."

Betty busied herself at the till, getting change of a twenty-euro note. She was late back from lunch, and the girls were unmerciful in making the most out of it.

This morning she had lifted her head to serve the next

customer, and looked right into the face of Myles Nugent. Surprise would have been too mild a word for it. Was it coincidence or had she told him where she worked? For the moment, she couldn't remember with shock.

"Hello again," he said.

Before she could answer he stooped and picked up Isabella. The child wrapped an arm around his neck and gave Betty a big smile.

"Teddy not with you today?" It was the first thing that came to mind.

"He has a cold."

"Oh." Stupid response.

"Izzy and I thought we might take you to lunch, in return for your kindness to her on the beach, if that's alright with you?"

Betty became very aware of the silence that had befallen her workmates.

"I–I'm not off for half an hour yet . . ."

"We'll meet you in the Westbury so – say about forty minutes, would that be okay?"

"Okay."

Myles put Isabella down and she waved goodbye to Betty as they left.

"The Westbury, well now!" Trish said, impressed.

Betty had a sinking feeling of dismay. "I can't go to the Westbury!" she wailed looking down at her flat shop shoes and the blue polo shirt and black trousers she was wearing under her white shop apron. "Just look at the state of me!"

"I could," Fran White insisted. "To lunch in the Westbury with *him,* I could convince myself I was wearing Vivienne Westwood!"

Their comments were no help at all, but there was

nothing she could do about it. At least her lipstick and make-up were in her handbag. She would just have to leave her jacket on.

She whisked off the apron and tided herself up as best she could and set off up Grafton Street.

No sooner had she joined Myles and Isabella than she forgot all about her attire. Imagine him remembering where she worked!

Isabella was a little dote with perfect manners for one so young, and so chatty. Betty wondered briefly where Isabella's mother was, but thought it rude to ask.

Then Myles provided the information when he volunteered, "Isabella and I sometimes come into town after playschool, while Sophie is working. We go to the Green and feed the ducks – we like that, don't we Izzy?"

"They come out of the water and walk on the grass!"

Isabella made a walking movement on the tablecloth with her fingers, wide-eyed with the telling of it.

Betty was fondly reminded of Olive at the same age. How fast they grew!

"How about we have dinner, you and I?" Myles asked, taking her totally off guard.

"I'm thinking end of the week," he suggested, "whenever suits you."

Betty agreed and could feel herself blush faintly.

Then she suddenly remembered the time and stood up to leave, all apologies at having to dash back.

Now she dragged her thoughts back to her work and her nimble hands began to assemble a cake box. She asked herself a million times during the afternoon if she was mad to agree to dinner. Dinner was different to lunch. Dinner, as Trish said, was a date.

God, a *date*!

Betty got really cold feet when she thought of it like that. She hadn't been on a date since she was going out with . . . with . . . no, don't go there.

Myles Nugent was out of her league. She thought of the clothes in her wardrobe. Christ, there was nothing in it she could wear – nothing! It occurred to her then how she'd forgotten all about her 'shop' gear while she was with him. And certainly he did not seem at all bothered by the fact that she wasn't decked out in expensive creations.

She carefully placed the customer's purchase into the cake box, tied it with string, and handed it across the glass counter-top.

Trish threw her a curious glance. "Not saying much, are you? Go on, tell us, did you say you'd see him again or what?"

Betty drew in a deep breath. "Yeah."

It was Trish's turn to draw a deep breath. "I knew it!" She turned to Fran. "Told you, didn't I? Pity you wouldn't put your money on it!"

"You and your gambling! I could hand you over my week's wages if I was to take all your bets," Fran retorted.

"Well, at least I don't read my stars to tell me what's going to happen in *my* life," Trish replied.

Years of working together made this kind of banter familiar and no one batted an eyelid. Family crises were sometimes aired in work, always voluntarily, no one nosed, and the support they received from each other was invaluable. For Betty it was the teasing banter that provided a lift when she was down, kept her on track when things were really tough. They were the safety-net that never gave way, no matter how far she fell. It was the way it was.

Fran and Trish had husbands. Trish sometimes voiced a strong wish that hers would run off with somebody, or else she was threatening to leave herself. Other times she just kept quiet and smiled. She was in one of her smiley phases at the moment. She had three daughters and the middle one was in an 'on again off again' relationship.

"What is it with the young ones today?" Trish would ask, shaking her head. "They don't seem to think in terms of commitment any more. They certainly don't take after their parents, do they? We can't seem to get rid of any of ours."

Fran usually looked to her stars, and not only when things got tough. She watched the papers daily and tried her best to tie happenings in her day in with what the stars had said. She knew the star signs of the others and watched theirs as well. She was permanently on the lookout for the financial security she kept reading about.

They kept up the banter while the shop was slack between rushes, but Betty was only half in on it. Her mind was wondering what on earth she was going to wear to this dinner. She had no idea where Myles might take her. There hadn't been time to say. He had simply said he would phone, before she rushed off.

My God, she thought, rushing off like that was very rude of me. Maybe he won't get in touch. Maybe he will change his mind, and I'll never see him again. Well, she told herself ruefully, that would sort out your 'what to wear' problem, wouldn't it?

Chapter 11

A silver Ford saloon car was parked unobtrusively among other vehicles outside the row of shops in the housing estate. From its vantage point it afforded a clear view up and down the road, particularly of the houses on the opposite side. Council houses, in blocks of four to six stretched along the avenue to the right and left of the shops. All around was the movement of people starting their day, and children going to the local school down the road on foot, being driven in cars, older ones on bicycles. Two men sat in the parked car. The man behind the steering wheel stretched his arms above his head and yawned. It was just before nine o'clock and they had been there a couple of hours already.

"Christ, I hate this," he said, keeping his eye on a dark blue Mercedes parked outside an end house further up on the opposite side.

The other man got out and went into the small supermarket, glad of the chance to stretch his legs. He came back with two take-away coffees and a couple of blueberry muffins.

"Breakfast."

They were received with an air of resigned acceptance, born out of years of having irregular unorthodox meals.

"Anything?"

The driver answered through a mouthful of muffin and coffee. "Nope."

A bus stopped on their side, picking up passengers outside the shops, obscuring the men's view for a minute or two. When it moved on a woman had come into view on the far side of the road. The watchers perked up, suddenly totally alert, breakfast put on hold.

"That one of them?"

"That's the mother. She's a bit early today."

They watched as the woman walked to the bus stop on the far side and waited. She wore a lightweight jacket over jeans and carried a large canvas shoulder bag. While she waited she rummaged in her bag, took out her purse and got her fare ready for the bus. Then she spoke on her mobile phone. Suddenly she dropped the purse and the coins rolled all over the footpath. Her efforts to hold onto the bag while retrieving the coins were watched with amusement by the men in the car. She picked up the last of the coins just as her bus cruised down the road to her stop.

"Damn! The bloody Merc is gone!"

"Aw fuck it! We shoulda known."

The driver immediately shoved the car into gear and it shot out onto the road, causing other drivers to jam on. But it was already too late. Two hundred yards further up a narrow four-way junction had given the Merc three other options, and it was nowhere to be seen. The silver car was brought to a stop. No point in chasing around aimlessly; they knew from experience it was well gone by now. The driver thumped the steering wheel in frustration, uttering a string of oaths, and mopped at the spilled coffee which had made a large wet stain on the leg of his trousers. The other man cursed furiously as he picked crushed blueberries off the front of his shirt.

"You thinking what I'm thinking?"

"Could be. And I'm thinking maybe it wouldn't be any harm if we forget the mother altogether and just concentrate on the Merc."

Chapter 12

Sophie tidied up the bathroom and put fresh towels on the rail. She could have left it for Eileen in the morning, but she preferred the Jacuzzi facility in this bathroom to her own en suite, and she wanted to have a bath later. Had her father been there, he would have replaced the towels after she'd bathed Isabella but he was out. This was the third time in two weeks that she and Isabella had dinner without him, and she had to perform the usual after-bath rituals for Isabella in his place.

Sophie had to admit that, for the most part, it was very handy indeed living in her father's house. Either he or Eileen would collect Isabella from playschool. It meant Sophie had no childminding problems. She'd become quite accustomed to the freedom it afforded her. Her apartment was something which kept popping into her head of late. It was not exactly that she was actively thinking of moving back in, but it was there in the back of her mind needing to be addressed, and her father's absences brought to mind the problems she would have if she were to move back to her own home.

Isabella was in her bed waiting for her to come and say goodnight. By the time Sophie appeared, Isabella was just nodding off. Being covered with the quilt disturbed her.

"Is Grandy home?" she asked sleepily.

"Of course not, it's much too early."

He hadn't said where he was going. Now that she thought of it, he'd given her a rather vague reply, and Sophie just made her own assumption.

"He's probably gone down to the club again, so he won't be back till later," she said as she tucked in the covers.

"No, he's out with Betty," the child muttered sleepily, pulling Ted closer as her eyes closed.

"What? Isabella, what did you say?"

Sophie strained her ears. There was no answer.

"Isabella!" She shook her daughter more firmly than she intended. "Isabella, what did you say? Who is Betty?"

"The lady on the rocks," was the drowsy answer, "when I fell."

Sophie sat motionless on the edge of the bed. For a second she couldn't think what her daughter meant. Then she had a flashback to the beach scene.

Vaguely she remembered a woman helping Isabella up from the sand. She tried hard to recall her but it was practically impossible since she had not given her anything more than a cursory glance. The only thing she could remember was the deplorable track suit with the white stripe down the outside of the leg.

But that was *weeks* ago. Was the child right? Sophie had just assumed the woman lived on the island. Apparently not. Had she been visiting there also? And had they met again? Had her father been seeing her ever since? Why on earth didn't he *say*? She figured she already knew the answer to that. What was he *thinking* of? She got to her feet and left the room, the sleeping Isabella having been instantly thrust to the back of her mind.

On the landing she stopped. Her father's door was ajar. She pushed it open, strode purposefully in and looked around. It was tidy, as ever. On the bed lay a jacket, as if he had changed his mind at the last minute and had chosen another. The smell of the aftershave he used hung in the air. The wardrobe door was ajar. All signs of very careful dressing.

But there was nothing out of the ordinary. What did she expect to see? Her mother's framed picture still stood on the dressing table where it always was. Beside it was a smaller one of Isabella. There was no sense of anything different, except within herself. An anxious and unidentified feeling had settled itself in the pit of her stomach. It didn't help when she thought of the familiarity with which that woman's name tripped off Isabella's tongue. She picked up her mother's photograph. The calm smile was undisturbed, the beautiful eyes looked out at her in everlasting assurance that all was well.

But it *wasn't*, was it?

How could it be that her father was seeing someone and had not thought to mention it? He could at least have done her the courtesy of saying. And her daughter knew, but not *her*. It was just unbearable if he was seeing that woman from the beach in Aran. Surely he could find someone more . . . more . . . suitable! But that said something about *her*, and Sophie never chose to listen to anything about herself. She turned and went downstairs.

She wanted a drink. She needed something to deal with the implications of this.

She decided on a course of action, or inaction really. Wait, she told herself, he will probably say it tomorrow. You can ask how his evening went and then he will say. Who knows, with any luck it might even be over. Brief, but over. Well, of course it would be over, soon if not straight away. How could he possibly want to spend time with . . . a track suit?

Either way she was afraid of what she might hear. Her father's wish for company was disconcerting in itself. She didn't like to feel the unease that was holding her gut in a tight grip. She wanted to quash the rising alarm that was rushing in. A good measure of anger was mixed in with the rest.

How was she supposed to cope all on her own? God! Why did Peter have to go and crash his car? Why couldn't he have been more careful? It was just so *selfish* of him. What about *her now*? Who was there now for her?

She poured a good measure into a glass and curled up on the sofa in a foetal-like position. The house was very quiet. The silence became oppressive. Picking up the remote control she flicked on the television and turned up the volume, knowing the sound would interfere with her thinking, and she did not want to hear her thoughts.

If Eileen was here . . . well, she wasn't. It was going to be a long night.

The following morning was warm and sunny. The doors to the terrace were wide open, letting the fine day into the room, and her father was already at the breakfast table when she came down. He buttered toast and bade her good morning. He was dressed and ready for the day. He looked exactly the opposite of how she felt.

It irritated her. She had the urge to make a snappy reply but bit it back. She sat down gingerly and poured coffee.

Myles saw the dark circles under her eyes, the lacklustre pallor, and noted the absence of a reply.

"Isabella has had her breakfast. I'll drop her into play-school if you like," he offered, noting the dressing gown.

"You're up and about early this morning," she responded, a little too quickly. The words were laced with a touch of sarcasm, but they were out before she could stop them. Her father's quick glance across the table went unnoticed as she supped the strong coffee, her eyes half-closed.

"It's a lovely morning. You going into the shop?" he asked pleasantly, pointedly ignoring her mood.

"Isabella said you had a date."

It sounded accusing and he looked a bit taken aback. She groaned inwardly. This was not how she meant it to sound, but it was just bursting out of her. She met his eyes.

"You could have told me."

It was so petty. He put his knife down.

"Sophie, is there a problem?"

It was too much. She couldn't bear it. Was there a problem? Of *course* there was a problem!

"Isabella said you were seeing that woman from Aran." Her voice was rising. She checked it, but couldn't keep it normal. "Don't you think *that* is a problem?"

Her father was at a loss for words. He looked totally perplexed.

"No, I don't, why should it be? If I want to see someone –"

"*Someone*? Why *that* someone? Surely you could find someone more . . . more . . ."

Myles glared across the table. He was not given easily to anger, but he felt it rising fast. His placid nature cautioned him to be careful. He had no wish to aggravate her, but she was way out of line.

His glare was ignored.

". . . more *suitable*!"

There, it was out, but the grip on her gut tightened rather than eased. Her head was splitting, her voice was not her own, and her father's face was set hard.

Into the razor-sharp atmosphere Isabella bounced, her playschool bag hanging from one shoulder.

"I nearly got my other hand in, Grandy, see?" she said breathlessly. She struggled to show him how close she came to managing the tricky manoeuvre on her own. "Mummy, look, I can nearly do it!"

Sophie gave an imperceptible nod. She was miserable. It had gone wrong. Her father was livid. He rarely if ever expressed anger, but she felt it now, it was palpable. He stood up from the table.

"I'll pretend I never heard that."

He said it so quietly that she felt even worse.

"I'm taking Isabella to playschool now, but I won't be able to pick her up. I'll see you later."

Sophie sat at the table, more miserable than ever, her cup of coffee suspended in hands that trembled slightly. Her thoughts screamed at her, filling her head with turmoil and noise. She heard the car drive away and an ominous silence descended. It was broken by the sound of Eileen coming into the house by way of the side entrance. Sophie rose immediately.

"Eileen . . ."

Chapter 13

Quigley McGurk sat watching his long feet quietly tapping a rhythm on the stone floor. His head hung down and his face, partially hidden by his long dark hair, was the epitome of dejection. This was how Maeve found him when she arrived back at her cottage. She'd spent the past hour, or most of it, walking over the hills behind her home. From her elevated position she could see way out to the south and west, over the beautiful sweep of Dingle Bay, across to the mountains of the Ring of Kerry directly south of her, and out west into the vast Atlantic ocean. Behind her the mountains of the Dingle Peninsula rose in shades of purples and browns and greens and the Sky Road, leading northeast to the magnificent and dangerous Connor's Pass, could be seen straight as an arrow.

A storm was rolling in from the south-west. Although she was still in bright sunshine the weather change could be seen approaching from the horizon.

Out beyond the Blasket Islands, the sky was almost black at the centre of the storm, and the sea was already choppy and argumentative in the bay.

She had sat on a stone wall and watched, contemplating the power of nature, committing the contrasting scene to her creative memory, ready to be drawn upon when she put brush to canvas.

In the kitchen she hung her coat on the back of the door and picked up the kettle.

"Tea?

Quigley's hair rather than his head moved. His arms were folded and rested on his knees, leaving Maeve to navigate her way back and forth round him. She was well used to Quigley. It wasn't unusual to find him at the cottage when she arrived home. He was the type that she figured to be a bit of a creative genius and his moods were very subject to silence when the creative juices flatly refused to flow. He shared a house on the outskirts of the town and liked to walk miles, deep in thought. Quigley often took refuge in her small kitchen, particularly when his page was, as he would say, "bare as a branch in winter".

"How long this time?"

The hair shook slightly more than at first. Apparently he was "beyond words". And that was a dire situation for a poet to be in. Probably the best part of a week now, she read into the dejection. But Quigley had been beyond words before, many times.

The thought came to her head to suggest he take a look outside the cottage to the west, to the edge of the peninsula, past the bay and out into the Atlantic Ocean where the black sky was spreading eastwards, and allow

Mother Nature inspire him, but she was afraid he might think she was trivialising his agony. She was well aware that he had his own mechanisms for dealing with a creative block, and she strongly suspected she was one of them. That pleased her, for she was not beyond knowing what it was like to be stuck for inspiration. It was a torment that visited them all from time to time. It wasn't uncommon to go into McCaffrey's pub at any time and find someone among their arty group sitting dejectedly over a drink, staring into its depths in search of inspiration. She smiled as she busied herself with the tea, and warmed up some fresh apple pie, in the hope that the warm food and a cosy atmosphere would dissolve the log jam and his river of words would flow freely again, while she waited patiently in the sure knowledge that he would talk, hopefully sooner rather than later.

Quigley was aware that he was in her way. From behind the hair, his eyes followed her as she made her way round him. He noticed the soft padding of her suede boots as she moved about, and how the light from the window highlighted the chestnut in her hair. He could be quite partial to an older woman, this older woman in particular. That thought ran uninvited through his head, and not for the first time. Sometimes it even stampeded round and round. But he did not really think of Maeve as older – there were not as many as three or four years between them, he figured – it was just his way of putting it. Anyway he had no idea how she would feel on the matter of herself and himself. He could hardly ask. Quigley McGurk could hardly ask anything of almost any woman. He was not without experience, but his shy ways made sure that experience was limited, and in the past it was younger girls he succeeded with, and that made Maeve's maturity a bit daunting – unfamiliar but interesting territory.

His pen was his voice, his eloquence, his heartfelt communication. He could pen verse about the exquisite pain of love, or the dramatic floundering of a wounded heart, or the ecstatic joy of lovers, but he could not ask Maeve Nugent anything. So he came to her cottage and sat in her way often and for as long as he felt he dared. But he was not there under false pretences. He was indeed suffering a patch as bare as a branch in winter.

Maeve put the tea and warm apple pie on the table. "There's a storm coming in from the south-west. Looks like a biggie," she said.

Quigley lifted his head. "I'd better be off so."

Maeve smiled. "It's not coming *that* fast – have your tea."

She pushed the cup towards him. He ran long fingers through his hair, pushing it back from his face. It was a good-looking face, with clear definite features, if only he would allow it to be *seen*.

"I heard you got a big commission from America," he said seriously, without looking at her. "Pat said it's going to be the making of you."

She laughed modestly at that. "Pat exaggerates, I think."

"Not this time." He stood his ground, feeling awkward in the process. Pat Keegan was a ceramicist with a studio in the garden of his house, and Quigley had been sharing with him for a number of months now. By Pat's own reckoning he "did all right". Quigley ate his pie as he waited for Maeve to go on.

Pleased at the thought that success was prophesied, a

smile played about her mouth. He watched how she pursed her lips as thoughts ran through her head, and suddenly jerked his eyes back to his cup as she looked directly at him.

"A hotelier couple from New York want some works for their hotel renovations," she said. "Apparently the husband's great-grandmother was a Dingle woman, and they want something by an artist working from here."

"And you just happened to be exhibiting when they came? God! How lucky can you get?"

This spontaneous outburst was almost a speech for Quigley, and she could see he was genuinely pleased for her.

"Have you any idea what your subject will be?" he ventured.

"Not yet. I'm going to have to go there and take a look at where exactly they want to hang the finished works. A series of three, they say. Size and lighting and location play a big part when a work is commissioned – everything has to complement the rest. Then it should come to me what the best subject matter would be. I hope," she finished, and caught sight of his wistful face and nearly regretted being so exuberant about it. "Any sprouting at all going on?" she asked gently, referring to the "bare branch" syndrome he complained of.

He slumped visibly on his chair, his thoughts going back to his own current unproductive situation. One word. That was all he needed. Just one lousy word, the right word, would get him going again. There was that shake of his hair again.

While he was thinking what would be a clever thing to say to keep the conversation going, he glanced out the window. He saw a broad figure approaching the cottage.

"Here's the Lord of the Manor," he said glumly. He got up and carried his cup and plate over to the sink. "Dammit," he muttered under his breath, "that bloody puff is everywhere."

Maeve had the door open before The Puff had a chance to tap on it with the top of the blackthorn walking-stick he always carried. She smiled widely at Conor, a smile that made Quigley's dark brows almost meet in the middle of his forehead.

The Puff removed his tweed hat, showing a healthy head of curls. He was proud of his hair. A true light brown and still no grey.

"Maeve," he beamed, "you grow more beautiful each time I see you. Ah, Quigley, there you are, my man – am I disturbing something?" Cleverly, he had wrong-footed Quigley with his innuendo.

Quigley felt a retort rise, but his mortification strangled it in his throat, and he wasn't "his man" either.

Maeve made his embarrassment worse when she said, "Of course not, Conor," as if the notion was utterly ridiculous. "Come on in. We were just discussing work."

Conor de Lacy was twice the width of Quigley, and although Quigley had the advantage in height, somehow it became a serious flaw in the presence of The Puff.

Quigley edged towards the door.

"I've got work to do," he mumbled in Maeve's direction, and bent his head as he went under the lintel.

He walked briskly in the direction of Dingle town, annoyed at himself for his lightning retreat. But Maeve had not encouraged him to stay. That irked him more than anything. That bloody Puff was only out for what he could get. Surely she could see that? Quigley often saw him having a drink in the town, but he had yet to see him actually pay for anything. The way he swanned about the entire area, anyone would think his family still owned every acre of land about, and all on it.

Quigley felt the wind increase, and lengthened his stride. He hunched his shoulders and dug his hands deep into his pockets. He was almost home when it occurred to him that if the storm hit now then The Puff would have a great excuse for staying longer at Maeve's cottage. The crafty bugger probably timed it like that on purpose.

Back at the cottage, Conor sat himself down and spread his arms across the back of the two-seater sofa, the only soft seating available. He was quite comfortable, by the looks of it. His walking-stick was propped against the arm of the chair, his legs stretched out in front of him. With a satisfied smile he watched as Maeve set a cup of tea in front of him and served him up some apple pie.

"So, Maeve, you're all set for the big time, I hear. When do you head for the Big Apple?"

"It'll be a little while yet," she replied. "I have things to do here first. Soon."

Conor observed her quietly as she busied herself about the kitchen. She was a fine woman, educated and very presentable, easily the best he had come across in quite a while, *and* she was on the brink of becoming a big commercial success, by all accounts. He told himself smugly that she was well disposed towards him.

So then, what was that rake McGurk doing calling on her so often? His glance noted the gathering storm through the window opposite. Rain was imminent. Maeve too noticed the failing light and realised she would get no more painting done that day, but she still had plenty of things she ought to be going on with. There were ideas in her head she wanted to put down on paper and, in the studio she had fashioned in the building at the back of her cottage, there were paintings from the exhibition waiting to be dispatched to their buyers. She was itching to be getting on with that also.

Conor looked quite settled. *Too* settled.

"I have some work I must do in the studio," she announced at last with an encouraging smile. "You're welcome to come across if you like."

She knew well he wouldn't. He stood up, trying his best to hide his annoyance.

He gathered his hat and walking-stick and smiled stiffly.

"One must not hinder genius. Another time, I think."

Taking note of the darkened sky and the direction of the wind, Conor decided to head towards the town, putting his back to the approaching storm. It wasn't as daft an idea as it appeared, given the worsening weather. His family was still of excellent standing about the town and no one would ever pass a de Lacy on the roadway. Conor relied on this often rather than taking out his own car, regularly seeming to be out for a walk, and it didn't fail him now.

In no time at all he was pushing open the doors of McCaffrey's pub. Out of pure habit locals moved aside for him, as they would have moved for his father, and his grandfather before him who, in his day, would have been inclined to feel he was paying too much wages if they could afford to be buying drink. Unless of course it was *his* drink they were paying for. Old habits die hard and space was made for Conor. He caught the barman's eye and without a word his usual was placed before him on the counter. At the same time he caught sight of Quigley just moving away from the end of the bar, pint in hand. Conor's mouth tightened. That rake was everywhere. He bothered him. He couldn't quite figure out the relationship if any, between him and Maeve. Too often for his liking he saw the two of them together, mostly at her cottage, yet Maeve always seemed to make light of it. What struck him was the comfortable way The Rake and Maeve could be together apparently without the need for words. That really niggled him. Asking leading but hopefully subtle questions threw no light on the matter. He lifted his glass to his lips with the briefest of nods to the barman, and received the briefest of nods in return.

Quigley took his pint to a table where a couple of acquaintances were sitting, but not before he saw the nod. That drink would join all the others on Conor de Lacy's ever-lengthening slate.

Chapter 14

Taking advantage of the fact that a luncheon appointment was cancelled at the last minute, Bradley decided to call in on his father and hopefully have lunch with him.

But only Sophie's car was there when he pulled up at the house. He hadn't seen her for a while, and now he was appalled at her appearance. She was not pleased to see him. She wasn't dressed even though it was almost lunchtime and, as she tied the belt of her dressing gown tighter, he noticed she was avoiding his eyes. Her whole demeanour was one of some agitation. When he asked if she was ill, she snapped angrily at him and insisted of course she wasn't.

He knew his father was worried about her. Bradley had put some of that down to the natural concern of a father. But this state his sister was in appeared to warrant more than a normal level of concern. He doubted it was a hangover, or only a hangover. Her eyes sat in dark sockets, and her usually pale complexion had a transparent, dull look to it. She coughed hard and he offered to get a drink of water. She protested, saying she didn't *want* one, but he left the sitting room and moved towards the kitchen anyway. He just noticed Eileen slipping into the sitting room. He didn't like Eileen, and the feeling appeared to be mutual. Had she been listening? He couldn't be sure. He didn't know her routine about the house, only that she usually left once Isabella was home from playschool and there was someone there to mind her. Some days she was there longer than others, but she rarely remained there all day. When he returned with the water she was quickly coming away from Sophie, and gave him the barest nod.

She could move when she liked, that one, either that or she was making herself scarce. Sophie took the water without a word. She was quite preoccupied. He asked if she knew where his father was, and suddenly she was very together.

"I'm not his keeper, am I?" she snapped.

He was silent before responding, so surprised was he at the vehemence in her voice.

"I just thought he might be home."

"Why should he be? He'd rather be elsewhere, don't you think?"

Concern was beginning to merge with alarm and even a little anger. "Sophie, what are you on about? What's going on?"

A look of pure contempt crossed her face. "Don't play the innocent. You know very well. I would have thought you'd have said something to him, man to man. Somebody ought to, he won't listen to me! He persists in seeing that – that – that woman! She's totally unsuitable.

A leech!" Her face had become infused with colour; such was the temper she was in.

Bradley was quite taken aback. That his sister should be against his father seeing anyone did not surprise him. He knew his father was very glad of Sophie's company, and that of Isabella, but Bradley worried that Myles really ought to get out more. His life since his retirement had narrowed a lot, and after their mother died, followed not too long after by Peter's crash, Myles seemed to be taking care of everyone. Surely he needed more than that? Sophie was too dependent on him, and not only was she showing no signs of getting on with her own life, she was objecting strongly to her father making any moves to get on with his.

Up till now Sophie had her father totally to herself. He was there at her beck and call all the time. Bradley suspected there were many reasons for that. Not least the fact that they were both widowed and Myles knew well the pain of losing a spouse. But also Sophie was adrift. In her marriage she had depended so much on Peter. Not like their parents.

Bradley suspected for some time now that Myles was lonely, and as a result he was only too glad to have his time absorbed with Isabella, only too glad to have them in his house. Bradley thought Sophie was spoiled by that. But then, she always was spoiled.

"I'm sure he can see whoever –"

She whirled on him cutting him short. "Have you *met* her? *Have* you? Clearly you *haven't*!"

He hadn't, although his father had mentioned her once or twice. More in the way of lunching with an acquaintance, was the impression Bradley got. No big deal. One way or the other, what was there to get het up about? But now that Sophie had brought it so much to the fore, Bradley realised that whatever way Myles described his 'lady friend' he could see a difference in him. Myles may not have verbally attributed a whole lot to this new acquaintance, but Bradley now formed an opinion of his own. He trusted his father's judgement of character. Perhaps Myles was not yet aware of it but there was a new light in his eye, a general lift to his spirit. He was usually in good form, but recently he was more cheerful and animated. In short, Bradley felt he was happy.

Anyway, his father did not need anyone's okay, and therefore no one had the luxury of giving or refusing it. That was the way Bradley saw it. But Sophie was not concerned with anything but her own view.

She didn't *approve*.

"I *have* seen her," she went on, fuming, "and believe you me she saw him coming. I only had to see the track suit, the anorak – my God, she's absolutely so wrong for him!"

"Have you two *argued* about this?" He could barely believe she would dare.

She was silent. With an indifferent wave of her hand she turned her back on him.

"It's late. I have to get to the shop, and collect Isabella later."

He stood up. He wanted to try to persuade her to consider her father.

"Another few minutes won't make any difference at this hour," he said, "I'm quite sure they can spare you."

The inference that the boutique could manage quite well without her brought an objection to her lips, but she was more enraged by his next comment.

"And I don't think you can decide what a person is like by their clothes. If he is happy to see this lady –"

"Lady? Hah!" she exploded. "Mother will turn in her grave! How could he *do* this to her?"

Bradley had half-turned from her. He had heard enough, this discussion was becoming ridiculous. He remembered well being aware of arguments between his parents. Arguments that never rose to the pitch Sophie was using now, but they were intense arguments that strung out the atmosphere in the house without a voice being raised. His mother was a wilful woman, and attention was her drug. She was addicted to it. It made her careless with her husband's feelings.

He hated to admit it of his mother, but in the latter years of her life he became aware of more than he ever should have known. He mentioned it once to his father. The quiet defeatism he encountered made him ashamed of his own lack of integrity.

He turned now on Sophie who was still spitting anger and contempt. His bearing halted her words. His face was set so hard that she caught her breath, not daring to utter another syllable. The dark circles emphasised her eyes, and the apprehension in them.

He was almost menacing as he leaned towards her, his anger reaching forward even more than he.

"Don't you even think of messing up things on him, Sophie, I'm warning you! He deserves someone. Judging someone by their income or dress is no way to measure character!"

Sophie's apprehension disappeared and her anger flared again. "Mother's memory does not deserve this, after the wife she was to him –"

"What did you know of anything?" His manner was derisory. "You were always away on some shoot or other, looking after your own life. You were too absorbed in yourself to see what was under your nose. You still are."

She was appalled he should insinuate that all was not well with their parents. She quickly convinced herself that he was in cahoots with their father, condoning this behaviour, the men of the family sticking together.

"Our precious mother was rarely home in the latter years of her life unless it was for some function or some party she threw, or whatever," he went on. "Otherwise she did just as she liked, with whom she liked, whenever she liked, and what Father felt about that made not a jot of difference! So don't talk to me of how he could do that to *her*. He *loved* her to the end no matter what, and he deserved better than he got!"

If Sophie's face was pale before, it now looked deathly. Her agitation became more evident. She pulled at the belt of her dressing gown, twisting it round her fingers, looking about as if an answer was somewhere to be seen.

"Liar."

It was barely a whisper. The colour drained from her lips. Bradley thought she would fall. He was alert for the unsteadiness he was sure would result, but she remained solid on her feet, twisting the belt into a knot.

"Liar. And you were supposed to be her favourite! Some great son *you* turned out to be," she hissed scornfully and pushed past him towards the door.

"Where are you going?"

He reached for her arm as she passed but she shook his hand away with more strength than he would have thought she had.

He was shocked at his own outburst. He immediately regretted having said so much. Straight away he worried how Sophie would react to the disclosure. He believed she was in no fit state to cope with the awful things he'd said. Never having voiced a word of it before, he wondered if he had just vented pent-up anger towards his mother on his sister. That he still had so much buried within himself was a disturbing revelation. The feelings left him with a distinct sense of unease and emotional discomfort. How to deal with that? Once said there was no way to bury them again. And his father? He certainly would not be pleased that these things had been resurrected. Myles had remained silent the last time he had mentioned it – Bradley's heart sank further at the memory. He'd made things a million times worse with his anger. He became aware that the door of the room had slammed shut. He reached out and wrenched it open.

"Where are you going?" he repeated after the disappearing Sophie.

"I'm going to work. I have to get dressed."

He could not see her driving her car safely right then. Even if she could, he doubted she would venture outside looking as she did. Not the glamorous Sophie Nugent. But he was more concerned about her safety, and Isabella's.

"I'll pick up Isabella for you," he called from the bottom of the stairs.

"You will *not*!"

"Sophie –"

"No." Her voice was most emphatic. "You will not!"

He went back into the room and sat down.

His unease persisted, but he was no longer sure

whether it was because of his disclosure or his concern, or both. The fight was gone from him. The anger subsided, leaving him with the overriding feeling that all was no longer well with the world. He wanted to go. Leave the house. Get away to his work, become immersed in something that would dispel this weight that had burst out of him and taken up position on his shoulders.

He could not have said how long he sat in the armchair, but great was his surprise when he became aware of Sophie coming back down the stairs in a hurry. She was transformed.

Dressed to meet the world, the change was astonishing. Her hair was piled on top, caught in a large grip, showing her carefully made-up features. Gone were the dark circles, the jaded skin. In their place was the face the public knew, the large clear eyes, the porcelain complexion. Because his mind was concerned with the argument and any outcome, the question of how such a metamorphosis could occur in so short a time only partially formed in the back of his mind.

She said nothing as she crossed the hall, her heels clicking on the tiled floor, her car keys in her hand. The look she flung him made Bradley feel like a traitor. And why wouldn't it, he asked himself? In his heart he had betrayed his mother. He pulled the hall door hard behind him when he left, the sound echoing through the house.

Eileen came from the kitchen and looked at the closed door, making a mental note of the emptiness of the house, and the fact that no one would be back for at least a couple of hours.

Chapter 15

Betty examined her reflection in the bedroom mirror, and decided she should have taken out some savings and bought herself decent clothes ages ago. She hadn't looked this good in a long time. Actually, she had to admit she couldn't ever remember looking this good before.

Olive had gone on the shopping spree with her. It was definitely a first for Olive to be buying with her mother *for* her mother, and she threw herself into the task with total enthusiasm.

At first it was very difficult to get Betty to try anything on.

"Look at the price, for God's sake!" Betty was flabbergasted.

It took a fair bit of patience and coaxing on Olive's part, but that was no problem to her – she was a long-time dedicated shopper.

"If you want to look good, you don't look at the

price ticket, Mam – you look in the mirror!" was the little gem of advice she gave. "You only look at the ticket at the cash register, if at all, and then only briefly." There was a mischievous grin on her face. Betty threw her a disbelieving glance, but followed her from one stylish boutique to another. Olive knew exactly where they should shop, and Betty found herself in little boutiques she never knew existed. It seemed to her the smaller the shop the higher the prices.

"At this rate I'll only be able to afford tights," she complained, but in spite of her ingrained thriftiness the amount of shopping bags they carried home was impressive.

"Don't lose any receipts on me," Betty cautioned as Olive was emptying one bag after another of the day's purchases. Olive assured her the only reason anything would go back was if it proved faulty, which she was positive would be highly unlikely. She took all the receipts, saying she would keep them safe, knowing that if she didn't her mother might well cave in and take some of these lovely clothes back.

"You'll put the eye out of him in this," she mused, holding up a simple dress with a deep V neckline which they had bought in a little shop in the Powerscourt Town centre.

Betty's cheeks turned pink at the direct remark, and she busied herself with the teapot.

"You need a nice necklace for it," Olive went on. "We should have got something while we were at it. We slipped up there but not to worry. I have the very thing. I'll bring it over later."

She hung the dress on its hanger, scoffing at her

mother when she said: "What will the neighbours say when they see me all dressed up?"

"We didn't do all this shopping to impress the neighbours, now did we?" she teased.

Betty could not suppress a laugh. How did she ever think she could escape the forthright remarks of her intuitive daughter?

But what to say about Myles? How would she define for someone else something as yet undefined for herself? Being with him, and finding they were so easy in each other's company and in tune on so many things, was so great that she almost felt that she ought to pinch herself from time to time to see if she would wake up. And it felt so normal at the same time.

"They'll think I've lost the run of myself," she said, thinking of her well-established pattern of all work and almost no play.

But it was strange; the shoe was very definitely on the other foot. How many times had they sat at this very table over a cup of coffee and discussed men? Olive's men. Olive would be deliberating matters that arose from her current relationship. Between them, mother and daughter would toss matters about, Betty always being careful to remind herself that she should steer clear of actually telling Olive what she ought to do, and trusting her daughter's good sense to make the right decision herself. It wasn't exactly the same thing now, but still there was a funny sense of déjà vu about it.

They sat, surrounded by Betty's new wardrobe, and spent ages chatting like two teenagers having a deep and meaningful heart to heart. What came to light was a concern on Betty's part which Olive eventually made light of.

"So what if he is a retired banker? Why should that make any difference?"

"It doesn't. Not to him, apparently," Betty shrugged. "It's just me. I'm hardly used to the places he frequents, now am I? I mean, *my* social life thus far has been almost non-existent, hardly the talk of the social pages now, is it? And the people who *do* move in those circles are hardly watching every penny either. *They* could go to the boutiques we were in today and not bat an eye buying up new wardrobes, and then maybe wearing them once or twice and I'll be prepared to bet they don't bother to even look at the labels either."

Olive was watching her mother carefully. "And do you think like that while you are out with him, wherever?"

"That's the gas part of it, no, I don't. It's only later I think about it."

"Well, there's your answer so: don't think about it. You could be only making problems where there are none."

Olive was firmly of the view that 'society', to give it an identity, went largely on appearances. At least initially, first impressions and all that. Integrity or character or intelligence or any of the other intangible qualities a person might possess were no yardstick in the initial stages. And if they were, her mother would be up there with the best of them, and if this Myles could see beyond the outer wrappings, then where was the problem?

"Lighten up, Mam, and just enjoy! If anyone deserves the attention of a nice man who appreciates her, it's definitely you. Like I said, don't look for problems, just enjoy."

She took up one of the shopping bags and took out a

beautifully cut jacket with a button detail on the cuff. Size 10. Why did clothes always look so much better in smaller sizes? And didn't she only wish she were small enough to borrow it?

"I want to see you in that dress with this jacket." She held it out as she spoke and then she took out a pair of high-heeled strappy sandals. "And put these on too. Then you'll need some highlights in your hair."

Betty protested. "But I like it like this!"

"Nice subtle shades will give that nice thick hair more interest," was the insistent reply. "Always a good idea to make improvements, you know."

Betty gave up. There was no arguing with her. Of the pair of them Olive was the expert, and Betty knew well that she would never let her go out looking like mutton dressed as lamb.

Now, with Olive gone home, Betty viewed herself in the mirror wearing the outfit Olive had picked out. She was quite pleased with what she saw.

'Clothes maketh the man,' was that the way the saying went? Well, she decided as she turned to take in a side view, clothes maketh the woman as well!

Undressing again, she began to put her finery away in her wardrobe. All she needed now was the occasion to wear them. And with any luck, Myles would provide that, and just maybe she would "put the eye out of him" after all, she told herself with a smug devilish little grin.

Chapter 16

Myles hung a number of balloons on the front gate. Isabella selected the colours herself, deciding it wouldn't look right if there was more than one of each. So six different colours flapped gaily in a strong breeze, anchored tightly to the uppermost bar by a deep pink ribbon. Isabella tilted her head and eyed the balloons warily, as if she suspected them of doing their level best to break free the minute her back was turned.

"You tie good knots, don't you, Grandy?" She wanted to be sure.

Grandy assured her they would not blow away. He was the best at tying knots, he told her, and that was good enough for her.

Back inside the house Eileen was putting the finishing touches to the lavish spread on the large dining-room table. She should have been gone over an hour and a half ago, but Sophie wasn't there and in what he saw as an emergency Myles roped Eileen in to help. She wasn't often asked to stay late, probably because she wasn't the most obliging person in the world. There was no question of her not being paid for the extra time, she knew that; it was just that when her hours were done she preferred to be out the door before she could be sidetracked. It wasn't that she'd actually refuse. It was more the gruff manner and the air of begrudgery she managed to exude while not even looking one in the eye.

Maeve always wondered why Myles didn't bother to look for someone else instead, someone more like Sally. He would, he said, but for some reason he had not even tried to put his finger on, he hadn't done it yet. It was, like the all-white bedroom upstairs, on the long finger, and no satisfactory reason why. But Eileen did them proud today. She had done the shopping for the occasion and put her best into arranging the table. The goodie bags and a magician 'with lots of magic' were already organised.

Sophie said she would be home early, in plenty of time to greet Isabella's guests with her. The magician was due to arrive halfway through the proceedings, the strategy being to distract and entertain the children before they became totally unmanageable.

Sophie doubted that would happen; they were well-brought-up children, mannerly and never rowdy or difficult. She met their mothers frequently when she called to collect Isabella from playschool, and sometimes their fathers. Lovely people. She had no qualms about her daughter mixing with their children. They were ladies and gentlemen in the making, she said.

Isabella needed her hair ribbon arranged in her mop of curls. Myles was a dab hand at tying ribbons to gates, but when it came to putting one in his granddaughter's hair he was defeated before he started. Bradley too was there for the occasion, but there was no point in asking him either – he'd sooner sell a helicopter. Isabella took the ribbon to Eileen who arranged it in her hair as the last thing she did that afternoon, then Isabella skipped out onto the terrace where her Grandy and Uncle Bradley were having a quiet drink before the "invasion", as they called it.

"Almost time for your guests, Isabella," said Bradley.

He admired the bow in her hair and she twirled to show off her party frock, then stopped mid-twirl as the doorbell was heard.

"They're here!" she squealed in delight running through to the hall, followed by her grandfather and uncle.

Sophie wasn't home yet.

The door was opened to the first of the miniature ladies and gentlemen who came in shyly, quiet as mice, subdued by the fact that for most of them Isabella only existed in playschool. Isabella's guests all brought her a present, and one or two of them had trouble when it came to handing them over.

But it wasn't too long before the strangeness of their surroundings wore off and they began to feel very much at home. The table laden with goodies was like a magnet, and Ruairi, a sturdy child with red hair and freckles, immediately decided he was having the gingerbread teddy bear with the jelly sweets for eyes and a chocolate button for his nose. The teddy bear's flat rotund body and head filled the plate and Ruairi longed to reduce him to crumbs.

"I'm having *him*," he declared, pointing and testing the firmness of the jelly eyes with his index finger.

Isabella soon put paid to that idea. "He's *mine*! It's *my* birthday and *I* say!"

97

Her expression warned the poacher off as she pouted her lip at him. She felt happy she had sorted that one out. Ruairi quickly withdrew his finger, but the gingerbread bear looked better than ever.

When Sophie arrived it was to the sound of ten children feeling quite at home, apart from a thin boy with a fringe which nearly obscured his eyes who sat quietly, clearly out-manoeuvred by all the action around him.

They had been waiting for Sophie to arrive before Isabella blew out her candles and, after Myles lit all four, he placed the birthday cake in front of Isabella. But Ruairi was pulling faces at her from the far side of the table, and she refused to blow, holding up the proceedings until Myles raised his eyebrows across at Ruairi. Ruairi slid down in his chair, and the candles were finally blown out.

Sophie began cutting the cake and placed a slice on Isabella's plate. David, wearing glasses, decided he wanted someone else's party hat instead of his own because it had Spiderman on it, and he made a grab for it. One little miss beside him was reaching across the table, using her finger to secure herself a dollop of cream from the side of the birthday cake, but before she could plant it on her tongue his unexpected lunge knocked her sideways and she fell from her chair with a clatter. The cream flew into the air and landed on his glasses, obscuring one lens. Thinking, for a split second, that he had been hit in the face he wailed loudly, causing a slight lull in the noise, and capturing everyone's attention, except Ruairi's. This was Ruairi's chance. Quick as a flash he broke off the head of the gingerbread teddy bear and bit a big chunk out of the side.

An ear-piercing scream startled everyone. Isabella, furious that her gingerbread teddy was spoiled, shook her plastic fork furiously in Ruairi's direction. The cream on it landed in the hair of the child beside him as Myles was picking up the little girl who had fallen, who was now in tears. Some of the others broke into fits of laughter, and a tearful but enraged Isabella screamed across the table at them all.

Sophie intervened, thinking to put a stop to this chaos. Why on God's earth did she ever agree to the party in the first place? Her patience was running out fast.

"It's a cake, Isabella, it's there to be shared."

"No!" was the insistent answer. "He was *mine*! Betty made him for *me*!"

Sophie looked like she had been slapped in the face, but no one noticed. An elbow suddenly overturned a glass of lemonade and it spilled all down the front of her soft suede skirt.

"That's it!" she was heard to hiss. "This is the last straw!" Had Myles not interceded immediately, she would have ordered them all home there and then. The lad with the fringe sat quietly, his face pale and anxious, his hat all askew, his pants wet from his having peed on the chair. Sophie didn't know where to turn – the place was a disaster zone.

Bradley tried to console the lad who had peed, but there wasn't much he could do to ease his discomfort.

The magician never arrived.

Later that night when all the mess was cleared up and Isabella was bathed and in bed, Myles sat down to unwind and picked up the evening paper, thoroughly grateful for the tranquillity of the house again. Despite watching all the news broadcasts on television he enjoyed a good read of the daily papers, and often tackled the crossword puzzle. Bradley had gone home and Sophie was in her room.

She had been very quiet since the party and seemed pre-occupied, Myles thought, but that was Sophie for you, one never knew what way she was likely to be. The house was quiet, the television was off and Myles was enjoying the peace.

In her room Sophie was also sitting in silence. But there was anything but silence going on in her head. The one thing kept repeating itself over and over again: "Betty made him for *me*, Betty made him for *me*!"

She rummaged in her drawer for something to ease the whirl of her brain, to settle it down so she could think straight, and hopefully dull the fear that gripped the pit of her stomach. The feeling that she was outside her safety zone grew. She wanted to get back there, to dispel the heavy weight she felt, the weight that pressed her down, made her breath shallow, and dimmed her light.

Myles never heard her come into the room. He simply became aware of being watched. He turned suddenly in his chair.

"Sophie! Didn't hear you come down. Would you be thinking of making a cup of . . . "

His daughter was looking at him oddly. Myles put down the paper.

"What is it, Sophie?"

He watched her move across the room. Something struck him about her. She's been drinking, he thought at first, then wasn't so sure. Straight away he was worried. Now that he thought about it, he should have sensed something was wrong. He should have known something was brewing, given her quietness in the latter half of the party. Amidst all that party mayhem, quietness had to be an ominous sign.

That little Ruairi really stirred things up; so much for Sophie's assessment of the "little gentlemen". The "little ladies" could certainly do their bit too. But now, as he watched his daughter warily, his gut told him something was different. Her words, measured and spoken quietly, stunned him.

"I don't want you taking my daughter into that woman's company. I don't want her anywhere near Isabella."

She seemed calm, too calm, and he was instantly aware that she was like a volcano, quiet before erupting. But she was way out of line. He said so. He said it was none of her business whom he saw; he wanted no more comments or remarks of any kind on the matter.

She laughed, a little too loudly, and just a little out of control. "I will not have Isabella exposed to the likes of her. You should have more concern for your grandchild. You don't know what someone like her could do!"

The accusation and the superior tone brought Myles to his feet, his knuckles white, crunching the paper in his grip. His cold anger matched hers. Her insinuations and her slights on Betty were intolerable.

"How dare you suggest that I do not have proper concern for my own grandchild? Or suggest that Betty is somehow –"

Sophie's voice rose as she cut him short, suddenly feeling in control of everything. She was shouting, drowning out his words, enjoying watching the anger he controlled with supreme effort.

"Somehow what? All that woman sees is money, and clearly she thinks you have plenty of it! And she means to get her hands on it one way or another! There are women like her all over the place – get a man with money no matter how they do it!

"I will move out of here," she hissed, her voice dropping threateningly, "take my daughter and go back to my apartment, and leave you to your fate at the hands of that *leech*, if you persist."

She savoured the shock that registered on his face. That should put a stop to it, she thought, bring him to his senses. Neither of them heard a sound, so engrossed were they in their argument, but in the doorway the small distressed figure of Isabella stood, gripping Ted close to her body.

"No! I won't go! I want to stay with Grandy!"

Chapter 17

Myles picked up his jacket from the back of the chair.

"I feel like a bit of a walk," he said, opening the door of the cottage. The rain had passed on, moved east, and the dark clouds were casting their deep shadows over the green fields in the direction of the town. Maeve watched him walk away from the gate. She sighed heavily. She was in the weighty position of a child seeing a parent troubled by a heavy heart. With a sigh she turned back to her work. She still had a lot to do before she set off for New York, and time was getting short.

Myles walked along the narrow road, watching the sea on his right-hand side change colour from the dull grey it had been under the rain-clouds to the sparkling mid-blue it now was with the sun shining on it. Strange, he thought, seeing two vastly different weather situations side by side over Dingle Bay. Puddles of rainwater lodged by the sides of the road and the landscape looked freshly washed. It was not surprising that there were so many creative souls living in this beautiful part of the country.

A streak of lightning flashed out of the storm clouds to the east, illuminating the landscape, and a low rumble of thunder followed like the growl of an animal disturbed in its sleep. Myles shoved his hands deep into his pockets, his head bent in thought, unaware of the warmth of the sun on his back. His thoughts were dark as the storm clouds that moved in an easterly direction ahead of him. Many things troubled him, spun round and round in his head, not least of them Sophie.

She was like someone out of control of herself; she seemed to have no grip on her life any more. How she behaved in the shop was a mystery. Was it when she got home her personality changed for the worse? He had fervently hoped after Aran she would settle, start getting back to herself again, and get her life back to some sort of organised normality, but it seemed that he had become the focus of all she deemed wrong with her lot. He felt her wrath even when she was being fine with him. The rapid and radical changes that were happening to her led him to believe she was on something other than alcohol, but he had found nothing. As far as he could ascertain there were no such substances in the house.

He knew Bradley was thinking along the same lines. He had the feeling that Bradley had already fallen foul of her. There was a vibe difficult to define between them but, although he had touched on the matter most pointedly, Bradley had not taken the opportunity to talk.

Eileen, apparently, was the only one not involved in any dispute with her so far. And that in itself was on the strange side. Myles would have thought that Eileen was more likely to get on Sophie's wrong side than anyone.

And there was Isabella.

His heart broke sometimes for the little pet. How eager she would be to show her mother what she had been doing in school, or to tell her what had been said at "news time", and how dismissive Sophie could be. A quick glance, a mere nod, an inaudible reply and her mind was already elsewhere. Isabella often turned to him and finished her story. No wonder she talked so much to Ted. Sophie hated the toy and the fact that it went everywhere with Izzy. In fact, Sophie hated anything that took attention from her.

Which brought him to Betty.

He missed her. Her light laugh, her interesting conversation, her resilience, her enthusiasm for life, her company. For a brief while his world had sunshine in it again. When he phoned Maeve, she had been quick to say yes to his unexpected request to come down for a visit. He was running away, he knew that, running to where he hoped there would be no emptiness, but he saw now there wasn't such a place.

Even before he had to tell her, he was aware that Betty had sensed something was wrong. There was an intangible shift and she felt it. But he would never have told her what Sophie said.

That walk on the beach at Dollymount a few days ago would be etched into his mind forever. It was a glorious sunny day. The breeze coming in off the water was nippy, but bracing. Howth Head sat before them in brilliant sunshine on the northern point of the bay, and the Sugar Loaf Mountain was the sentinel to the south. The sight of Isabella and Betty running on ahead of him stuck in his mind – their laughter, the sound of their voices carried on the wind, words indecipherable. Betty dragging a long string of seaweed, Isabella trying to jump on it.

Then the stop.

That was when his world had flipped. Betty was motionless, looking back at him, unaware that the seaweed had dropped from her hand. He walked towards them, with a growing feeling of never wanting to reach them. The sound of the sea was gone. The gulls wheeling overhead were silent. Only Isabella moved, wanting the game to continue.

Why hadn't he told her, she asked, and he knew exactly what she was talking about. Surely it should have occurred to him that she would hear, knowing how Isabella chattered about everything? But it hadn't occurred to him.

But he would not repeat what Sophie said, nor would he have offended her by repeating Sophie's threat. And he said he wouldn't have mentioned it because it absolutely didn't matter. His life was not governed by Sophie's views, and anyway Sophie wouldn't *do* that. Even as he spoke he didn't feel convinced. He didn't *sound* convinced.

Isabella ran up to them, effectively cutting short the brief conversation. But it mattered to Betty. She *couldn't* be the cause of a rift in his family. She *wouldn't* be the reason he might lose Izzy. She knew only too well what the child meant to him. While his world fell apart Isabella, oblivious to the devastation she had unleashed, ran about with the slippery seaweed gripped in her hand, trailing it behind her, calling on Betty to jump on it.

The game was over. There was silence in the car as Myles drove Betty back to her house. What he wanted to say could not be said in front of Isabella. She had overheard too much already.

They could meet. He would phone later.

No.

Yes, he would.

The look in Betty's eyes was absolute. The merest shake of her head and she turned towards the house, while Isabella waved goodbye through the window.

"Betty forgot to say bye to me, Grandy."

Now as Myles walked on deep in thought he became aware that someone had fallen into step beside him.

"Hello, Mr Nugent, nice to see you again. Staying a while, are you?"

Myles glanced up and recognised the tall figure of Quigley McGurk but couldn't put a name to the face.

Quigley didn't mind. He was used to people not remembering his name.

"Quigley," he offered, "Quigley McGurk."

"Of course. Sorry, Quigley, my mind was elsewhere. Yes, down for a little stay. Just out for a walk. Got out of Maeve's way – she's very busy with this New York trip. How have you been?"

Myles and Quigley had met occasionally on previous visits. They were introduced in the pub in the town where the 'arty types' congregated to bolster up each other's morale or to seek inspiration. Dingle had a niche for all types. Everyone found a home there.

"Oh, fine, fine. I'm just heading in for a pint," Quigley said. "Need something to moisten the neo-cortex. Could do with some company."

Maeve would have been flabbergasted if she had heard the relaxed easy chat from Quigley McGurk, but then, Quigley was talking to Myles, and Myles wasn't a very desirable chestnut-haired female.

"Sounds like a good idea. Lead on, man."

They fell into step and easy conversation, following the recent rain-clouds which were kept moving ahead by the westerly wind. Quigley tempered his long stride to suit his companion. It was evening and the sun was moving into the west, pleasant and warm on their backs.

At the pub, people were all congratulations and talk about Maeve's commission. They took it as a personal compliment that an artist from their area was so favoured. They had, of course, said the same thing to Maeve herself, and toasted her assured success, but now that her father was among them it was cause to do it all over again.

Plenty of pints had been consumed by the time the "Lord of the Manor" arrived in.

Conor de Lacy expected attention to switch to him, as it usually did when he put in an appearance, but Quigley felt annoyed by the shift in the limelight.

He sidled up to Conor at the bar and ordered two more pints for Myles and himself, which he lifted to take back to the table, just as Conor lifted his pint and gave Tom the barman *that* nod.

"That slate must be getting very full," Quigley remarked slyly as he moved away, leaving a livid but silent Conor with his glass halfway to his lips.

"*What* did you say to your man at the bar?" Myles had to ask. "If looks could kill you just got a dagger in the back!"

"Oh, nothing really," Quigley shrugged. "You wouldn't want to mind your man," and clearly that was the end of the matter as far as he was concerned, and he settled himself down to his pint.

But Conor didn't turn back to his drink as quickly. The Rake was getting too cocky by far, he thought.

He would have relished the opportunity to inveigle himself into Maeve's father's favour, but he would wait. Perhaps tomorrow would be more effective. He could call to the cottage, when The Rake was back in his shell, dumbstruck and hung over.

For what seemed like the hundredth time Maeve looked out the window. It was dark and the moon, visible in a clear sky, glinted its silvery light on the wind-driven waters of Dingle Bay. In her worry it looked like a scene that could spell trouble. It was hours since her father went out walking, and he had not been his usual self all day. Her subtle attempts at enquiries must have been too subtle, because they didn't work. Anxiety had taken root ages ago. His dinner was cold, sitting in the microwave. Her own along with it. She waited and waited and then became so worried the hunger went off her altogether.

A taxi pulled up outside. Thank God! She ran to the door. Myles was insisting to the driver that he didn't need any help to get up the path. Quigley, scrunched up in the back seat, was leaning out the window of the car. He caught sight of her silhouette with the light from the room behind her and saluted demonstratively, and even in the dark she saw the biggest grin she had ever seen on his face.

"Maeve," he began as words burst out of him, one arm out the window and outstretched, "my beautiful dove, wings of –"

He broke off, suddenly mortified by his own spontaneous effusiveness, and vanished into the dark recesses of the car.

Maeve smiled. That was so typically Quigley, but clearly the branch was not bare at the moment.

Myles waved the car off and turned to greet her. He looked sheepish, expecting admonishment, and launched into praise of his drinking companion.

"He's a genius, that Quigley, and great company too," he enthused.

Her father probably needed some man-to-man talk, Maeve told herself, and said nothing, but smiled as she guided him into the house. Anything that served as a distraction to take his mind off whatever was bothering him was okay with her.

But *Quigley*? Quigley was *great* company? She always suspected that he had another side to him, a side that for some reason he kept hidden from her, for she doubted very much that he was permanently tongue-tied in company. In fact, she had seen him in McCaffrey's with his 'arty' friends as he liked to call them, and Pat Keegan, and he could be as animated as the next when they were all wound up over the current topic.

Yes, perhaps she should definitely take a closer look at Quigley McGurk in the future.

Chapter 18

Myles woke the following morning, momentarily wondering where he was. The pounding in his head defied description. He looked around the comfortable bedroom and the memories of last night came rushing back. The crowded pub, the music and the *craic*, the fact that others joined their company, and the drink that flowed.

As he sat on the edge of the bed, gingerly holding his head in his hands, he could only assume that Quigley must be feeling as bad. He realised he was still in his clothes, except for his shoes and jacket. His shirt was open at the neck and cuffs. Obviously Maeve had thrown the duvet over him and left him to sleep it off.

He noticed she had left fresh towels on the end of the bed, and he took them into the bathroom and stood for ages under the shower. Feeling a little more human, he had a quick shave and went into the kitchen. It was deserted. Maeve was in her studio, but there was fresh coffee in the pot. He poured himself a large black coffee and sat down at the table. Lost in his thoughts, which centred on Betty, he was taken by surprise when Maeve came in.

"Okay, so are you going to say what's up? It's not like you to go and get plastered, now is it?"

She was glad to see he could still smile.

"That obvious, is it?"

"Very."

She made more coffee, put rashers and sausages on the grill, and waited. The silence lengthened. She cracked some eggs on the pan and made some toast.

When she placed the breakfast in front of him, he was thinking he couldn't eat all that, he couldn't even *eat*, but automatically picked up his knife and fork, and ate almost mechanically.

With a slight movement of her head towards her studio, Maeve stood up after a few minutes. "I'll get back over there, still a lot to do."

He looked directly across at her with a resigned look.

"Got a few minutes?"

She sat down again, not knowing what was coming, deciding the best thing was to just hear what her father wanted to say. But her apprehension evaporated as he spoke. She was both surprised and pleased by the things she heard. The way her father spoke about this woman told Maeve a lot. It wasn't anything he said exactly, for he really didn't go into much detail, but the telling was in the tone of his voice, the way he looked past her into the distance while he recounted his story.

So where was the problem?

As she listened further she felt her anger rising. How

very typical! Sophie hadn't changed one jot, had she? Still all out for herself. Maeve had forgotten, up to a point, what life at home with Sophie had been like. Living here in the peace and harmony of Dingle the memory had diminished, faded over the distance, so that she began to feel more kindly towards her.

Their childhood was marked throughout by fractious incidents in which Sophie invariably got her own way. Their mother erred on the side of peace, not being willing to deal with the quarrelsome nature of her younger daughter. Maeve was "the elder" she was constantly told, and as such she should have more sense. To Maeve this read as 'give in to her'.

Bradley was wise enough to stay well out of the way. Myles did not figure in these family situations, by virtue of the fact that he was seldom there. Sophie was never expected to behave responsibly; she was the younger, and was cunning enough to relish her position and reap the advantages of being the youngest. Maeve learned to steer clear of trouble eventually. When she discovered that she could immerse herself in her drawing and painting without being disturbed by her sister's demands, she realised she had found a true refuge. Sophie was loath to encroach on such a messy pastime. But she quickly learned to take advantage of her sister's passion and made her own of her choice of Maeve's things. Maeve realised that she couldn't have it both ways. But she opted for the painting which Sophie never went near, and she discovered that her 'things' were of significantly less importance. But Sophie soon found that this capitulation was not the answer either. With Maeve extricated from the petty squabbles, with Bradley keeping out of the way, with

Myles engrossed in his work, and their mother involved in her own life, there was no one to give Sophie what she sought most: attention.

As Maeve sat and listened to her father, the old animosity came sliding out of the past. It crept up on her gradually, settling on her shoulders like a familiar but hated cloak, and caused her brows to draw together in a frown. In her heart she felt the tension regroup and the lightness of freedom begin to leave her, but there was nothing for it but to keep it well hidden, and to submerge it before it had a chance to re-establish itself. She reached across and poured more coffee, and made a huge effort to keep a benign expression on her face.

"So here I am," Myles picked up his knife and fork again, "running away to the country to hide from life. Wouldn't you think I would know better?" He smiled ruefully. "Wouldn't you think I should deal with it myself, and not burden my daughter with it, especially now when you're so busy?"

Maeve immediately brushed his apology aside with a quick wave of her hand and a firm retort. "Nonsense. What're daughters for anyway, if you can't call in a marker when needed?"

"You always were the sensible one, Maeve. I used to think you would take after your mother, being the eldest, but you are your own person. I'm glad for you."

Maeve stood up and began to clear the breakfast things, pleased with but unused to such vocal fatherly approval.

"Will you give over, Dad? I'm glad you're here, that's all, and I wish it was for a happier reason." She turned to face him. "But I don't think you should give up without a fight. This Betty sounds like a person of integrity, a really nice sort. You haven't asked my opinion, I know, and it's not for me to say, but I *am* saying," she grinned cheekily at him, "and I *don't* think you should give up easily."

She could well understand Betty's reluctance. And she admired her for it. It was an awkward situation. But they had to find a way. Sophie could not be allowed to rule the roost in this manner.

"I have an idea," she said suddenly. As it formed she liked it more.

Her father looked up expectantly.

"Come to New York with me. Yeah, why not? It will give you time to decide how best to handle this, and I would certainly love the company, and it would give Sophie time to see exactly how self-defeating her appalling attitude is, wouldn't you say?"

Chapter 19

Isabella's grip on Ted's arm tightened and she ran out into the garden. Andy Fox was busily working away, raking up grass cuttings and piling them in the compost container. There was a lot to be done in the garden at the moment and he was spending as much time there as daylight would allow. Isabella didn't see him immediately and stood on the terrace, momentarily at a loss as to whether to stay or go back inside. Her mother and Eileen were arguing in the kitchen, and the child instinctively made herself scarce. With an unconscious gasp of relief she saw Andy, as he came into view in the lower garden, and ran towards him.

"I like the smell when you cut the grass, Andy. Ted does too."

Andy nodded sagely. "Smart bear that," he observed.

Isabella followed him about the garden and chatted away to him, or maybe to herself or Ted, and sometimes bent down to examine whatever caught her attention, but she managed to stay quite close to him, he noticed.

The sounds of raised voices carried out to the garden, a situation so appalling that Andy actually felt embarrassed. Things were tense about the place since Myles had taken off quite unexpectedly for Kerry. Family matters were not usually made known to him, certainly not by Sophie or "the nearly daily" as he liked to think of Eileen. Sometimes Myles would ramble out to him and let him know of anything that was likely to concern him in any way. In any case the atmosphere about the house would spill out beyond the terrace and he could not help but be aware of the usual quiet harmony that was the way of life within the Nugent household.

But this past week there was the awful fact that a perceptible air of discord pervaded and, as well as that, or perhaps more likely because of it, after school Isabella sought his company more than usual. Andy never had much dealings with Eileen, there was no need – but, without knowing exactly why, he was convinced he was the better for it. Compared to the length of service he had with the Nugent family, Eileen wasn't a wet day in the place. Andy felt she didn't rightly know her place, either.

Now and again Myles would chat about what Andy was doing with the garden and he always found plenty to approve of and admire. Occasionally Andy would elaborate on his plans for next season, or what the weather was doing to his work. Sometimes the chat would wander from the garden on to whatever was in the news at the time, but it would never be personal chat. Andy liked it that way.

He wished Myles was back.

Although the words were not decipherable, the voices coming from the house continued. Usually, by this time of day, Eileen would be long gone. Andy put it out of his mind and moved to work in another part of the garden where the shrubs and trees deadened the sound, and Isabella followed, aware only of the fact that it was better here with Andy.

Her mother seemed to be cross all the time. Some days Isabella had to stay in Ruairi's house after playschool till her mother collected her after work. At first that was fun, but the novelty quickly wore off and Ruairi soon reverted to being himself, taking every chance to aggravate Isabella when his mother's back was turned, and Sophie would arrive to collect Isabella to find a cold look in Ruairi's mother's eye, even though she smilingly insisted Isabella was no trouble at all.

In the house things had gone quiet. Isabella and Andy stayed where they were till a change in the weather and spattering of light rain brought a halt to the day's gardening for the moment.

"I will help you put the things away, Andy," Isabella enthusiastically offered, picking up the heavy garden shears, but Andy immediately took it from her, gently persuading her to take the hoe instead. He hid a little smile as she struggled to drag the long-handled hoe across the grass and hang onto Ted at the same time.

Sophie appeared on the terrace.

"Isabella! For heaven's sake, come in this minute! Really, Andy, the child should not be out in the rain!"

It could hardly be called *rain*, but Andy hid his irritation at the inferred disregard for Isabella who stopped dead in her tracks in the face of her mother's annoyance. Andy allowed himself a small shake of his head, and remained quiet.

Isabella dropped the hoe.

"Bye, Andy."

He adjusted his cap. "Thanks for the help," he said, giving her a quick wink, but noticed her smile was gone.

He made no reply to Sophie. He wanted no argument with her for he knew she would see a reply as argumentative. All the more odd then was the lengthy argument with that ill-mannered daily.

He tidied up the garden, put away the implements, and went into the small greenhouse. He inspected all the young plants and seedlings, and busied himself deciding which were just about ready for hardening off before planting in the borders. This was his therapy, the place where the cares and the Sophies of this world were reduced to nothing compared to the abundance of new life getting ready to dazzle the world with its beauty for one brief season.

Sophie had no such therapy. She'd had bad news that day. Her father was going to New York with Maeve. New York for God's sake! How thoughtless of him! Leave it to Maeve, she thought. She might have known *she* would come into the equation somehow, she always did. Always managing to get her own way without even looking like she had tried. What about *her*? Why couldn't they just for once see that she was making bits of herself with the boutique and Isabella and everything? How was she supposed to manage in the meantime? And Eileen? She was getting above herself alright, arguing with her like that. But if she ditched her position with them, God, what then? She had hinted that she could easily get another position. Sophie worried that she might take a notion and not turn up for work in the morning, as she had threatened. Whatever else, Sophie couldn't cope with another problem.

And as for that Andy Fox! He behaved as if she was of no consequence whatsoever. He never had a word to say, just licked up to her father, and wheedled his way into her daughter's affections with his quiet ways and his praising of her teddy! It bothered her that he might well have heard the argument. She would never trust one so silent about the place. He could suddenly be working within earshot and managing to look totally absorbed in his work at the same time. No one questioned his constant presence in the garden; surely he did not need to be there so much. The garden always looked so immaculate and *done*. What did he need to keep at it for?

Isabella was in bed waiting to be tucked in, with Ted in the crook of her arm.

"When Grandy comes back we will ask him to take us to see Betty," she told him. "You would like that, Ted, wouldn't you? She must be missing us, I think, 'cos we miss her, don't we?"

Sophie stopped in her tracks at the door. Her daughter's words hit her like a hammer. She had put all thoughts of this Betty out of her mind. The matter was over with. Done. Or it should have been. Fleetingly she wondered how it was with her father. Was it equally over for him? She dismissed the very idea even as it occurred. Of course it was. He had said nothing since. And hadn't he gone down to Kerry for a short break to put it all behind him?

Hadn't he?

She crossed over to the bed and tucked in the covers briskly.

"Mummy, when is Grandy coming home?"

"I don't know, Isabella. He's going to America with your Auntie Maeve for a while."

The child looked alarmed. 'Merica was very far away. She knew that. Grandy told her so when they went with Daddy. And he showed her just how far it was on the globe in his study when they came home. It was very, very far.

Tears welled up. "I want him to come home. Me and Ted does."

"*Teddy and I,*" her mother corrected her. "Anyway, we're just going to have to wait. Maeve asked him to go, so that's that."

She bent and brushed her daughter's brow with her lips.

"Goodnight, Isabella," she said and left the room. She went downstairs with Eileen on her mind.

It was not that Isabella minded Grandy being with her Auntie Maeve. She liked Maeve. Maeve always sat and did painting and colouring with her when she came to their house, and Mummy never said anything about the mess when Maeve was there. Maeve was able to do great paintings, and Isabella watched fascinated while a few simple strokes made people and animals come alive on the paper. Or sometimes the picture was warm sunshine at her cottage, or the big sea that was down where she lived.

Maeve had not come to her party. Grandy said she had important paintings to do for some people in 'Merica and she was very busy, but on Isabella's birthday

Maeve promised on the phone that Isabella and Grandy could go down and stay for a while. But Grandy was already gone there, and he did not take her with him.

Some time later in the sitting room Sophie was startled by the unexpectedness of the voice at her elbow.

"Mummy, my bed is all tossed."

"Oh, for goodness sake, Isabella! Can you not just go to sleep? Come, I'll tuck you in, and this time go to sleep."

"Will you read me a story?"

Sophie let out an exasperated sigh, and marched her daughter back up the stairs.

Chapter 20

Eileen didn't miss much. There was the silver Ford again, and there was no doubt that it was the same one with the same two men in it as well. It cropped up from time to time, but she didn't bother too much about it any more. A minor inconvenience, that's all.

She crossed the road and went into the newsagent's rather than to the bus stop, and bought the morning paper, making no attempt to avoid being seen by the occupants of the car. Then she started walking back in the direction of her house. Whether she was late for work or not didn't matter. Sophie and cleaning her house wasn't ever Eileen's first priority.

The man behind the driver's wheel let out a string of expletives, spittle clinging to his greying moustache.

"We've been sussed."

The other man didn't see how he could know that. His thin pale face registered utter surprise.

"What? How do you know?"

"I just fuckin' *know*, don't I? That's why I *do* this fuckin' job, isn't it?"

He thumped the steering wheel with a clenched fist, then he took a couple of coins from his pocket. "Here, go in and get me a paper till we get the hell out of here." He turned the key in the ignition with a vengeance.

"I got the coffees."

"Get the bloody paper! Do something fuckin' useful!"

Paleface went, wiping splatters of spit from his forehead. There were times when it was better just to put up and shut up. This job was proving to be so frustrating. How anyone spent decades doing it he didn't know. But what they would do now he had no idea. Where or how they would go from here he didn't know either, and they had wasted all that time, because that's what it was, a complete waste of time and apparently for nothing. What had gone wrong?

In the house Eileen watched and waited and the argument with Sophie yesterday replayed in her mind and annoyed her. Getting into an argument like that was careless.

She didn't like Sophie, and she never had. She was a spoiled bitch, a very spoiled bitch. She figured Sophie didn't much like her either. She was surprised that she was still employed there. When she started she hadn't expected to be kept long – she wasn't exactly what they were looking for. But while Eileen wanted to do no more hours than was agreed, it turned out that this house actually suited her very well, for the moment.

What Mrs Nugent had been like when she lived Eileen didn't know, and it was odd that she was hardly ever mentioned. Eileen arrived some time after she died and quickly formed the impression that she had been a woman who liked her luxuries. One look at the house she had been mistress of and it wasn't hard to imagine that. Her picture still stood beside the bed, and if it was a good likeness she had been a very good-looking woman. Eileen never heard what she died of, but from what she did know of the woman she figured Sophie must be the spit of her, especially in her ways, pampered and over-indulged. Apparently the house was alive while the mother lived, with parties and dinners, entertainment and so forth, but there wasn't much sign of that about these days.

Sophie had changed drastically since her husband was killed. Alcohol was detected in his blood, and not only that, other substances were discovered too. No surprise to Eileen that. The accident had made it into the news bulletins: one more fatality to add to the carnage on the roads. The press were very interested because Peter was such a well-known photographer, and Sophie's face was very recognisable too. There was no other vehicle involved, no one else injured.

But Peter's crash went out of the news very quickly. No one was willing to talk to the press or anyone else, pleading privacy in their grief. The matter was routinely investigated by the authorities as far as Eileen could tell, and questions were asked, though no one questioned her.

Sophie was more difficult now, but Eileen didn't mind. In some ways it actually suited her better.

Still, it seems she could have been more concerned with her family. As a family they were like a ship without an anchor to Eileen's way of thinking, and she was not at all sure that they'd ever really had one. Things had certainly deteriorated after the son-in-law's accident.

That little child needed a full-time somebody. Often she trailed about outside after that oddball of a gardener, particularly if her mother was in bad form. Dividing Isabella between her mother and grandfather was an unsatisfactory stop-gap measure. She knew this because she overheard things, and she always made it her business to overhear as much as she could. How else was she supposed to be sure that the Nugent household would suit her? True, Eileen didn't miss much.

And, yes, there was a weird one, that gardener. Eileen was wary of the man. And she felt instinctively that *he* didn't miss much either. She knew the child chatted away as she followed him, a fact that sometimes worried her. '*Out of the mouth of babes*' and all that. She was glad his domain was the garden. Glad she had no dealings with him other than when he came in to the kitchen for something to eat, which wasn't often; it was mostly for a drink of water – gardening was thirsty work – and she busied herself with something or other till he was gone. Granted, he always nodded his thanks or tipped his cap wordlessly, and she would acknowledge it with a nod in return, but she was always relieved when he was gone back to his soil and his compost.

She begrudged him the edge she knew he enjoyed. The Nugents thought the world of him, and it made her all the more careful around him. Yesterday's argument worried her for that very reason. What had that manure-riddled scarecrow overheard?

Her thoughts jerked back to the present, and she stretched her neck to see down the road. As far as she could see the Ford was gone. She closed the hall door and hurried towards the bus stop again. It wasn't that she was all that full of conscientiousness or anything about her work, but it would be highly inconvenient if she was to lose this job, and she certainly could do without lateness causing a repetition of yesterday's argument.

Chapter 21

The mood in the shop was deflated and sombre, the atmosphere leaden with disappointment. The budding romance was over, taking with it the possibility of a lift out of the ordinary, a bit of excitement shared for the fun of it. Fran felt let down because she thought she should have seen it coming, the stars should have given some sort of warning. But no matter what either she or Trish said or did, it was proving difficult to lift Betty's spirits.

Isabella's words went over and over in Betty's head, confirming the apparent gulf between her and Myles: "Mummy said she would take me away and I don't want to go, I want to stay with Grandy."

Betty saw again the vision of Sophie on the beach on Inis Mór, the supercilious manner with which she barely acknowledged the fact that Betty had gone to help. The way she immediately turned to leave, the woman who had kindly rushed to help her daughter already dismissed from her mind.

There was no way to change a mindset like that, Betty was sure of it. The cards were stacked against her before any of them had even met, and she was convinced that Sophie would not be the type to change. Her manner, her demeanour, told Betty wordlessly but stridently that they undoubtedly inhabited different worlds and Sophie's was the superior one.

Betty had felt she had no option but to remove herself from a situation where her presence could only cause conflict. She did not listen to the little voice telling her that this wasn't the only conflict in Sophie's perceived superior world, or to the feeling that Sophie's issues could be deeper, or darker.

But the girls in the shop were great, they did their best to cheer her, and she only had herself to blame that their efforts didn't work. Trish bet there would be another romance just around the corner, now that Betty had finally made a move, and Fran told her she ought to go out anyway and make use of all those expensive clothes she had bought.

What a waste, Betty thought, what a stupid, conceited, expensive waste. She felt ridiculous now when she pictured herself in those pricey boutiques, eyeing herself this way and that in the mirror. What did she think she was doing? Just how long did she think it could last?

He'd said he would phone. What else could she have expected him to say? How could she have been so dim as to think she could be anything more than a passing fancy to him? Despite the vast gulf she felt between herself and his daughter, she half-hoped it would be different for him. He was never going to phone her now; she had been so adamant that he shouldn't. He was hardly going to stick his neck out and risk another rebuff.

How could she have done otherwise, she asked herself? What sense would there have been in continuing on when his own daughter was so dead set on splitting them up? It could make for nothing else but conflict and grief in his house, and Betty knew that was too big a hurdle for any one or any emotion to have to scale.

Perhaps if Sophie lived in her own apartment things could be different. Distance between her and Sophie was vital if she and Myles were to have any chance at all. Then maybe Sophie wouldn't mind so much, or be so opinionated on the matter.

Yet in spite of acknowledging all the problems she saw, some silly little feeling somewhere inside Betty was still daft enough to hope.

Nothing distracted her for long and at home the silence was more oppressive than ever.

And Trish was lamenting the loss of the comfortable lifestyle she foresaw for Betty who had only got a glimpse of what it would have been like not to have to work just to survive.

It would have been nice.

Later that night, in the bathroom of her terraced council house, Betty turned off the taps and swished her hand about to disperse the mountain of bath foam. It formed lots of smaller peaks floating about like drifting icebergs. They felt cold to the touch despite the rising steam. Then she lowered her tired body into the comfortably hot water, and lay back.

Idly she moved her foot around and watched the icebergs drift and collide, form other masses, like continents moving on the planet's surface. She slid down in the bath till the water crept up to her chin, and it lapped at the end of her short auburn hair at the nape of her neck. There was a certain element of comfort in the enveloping warm water. She lay very still for a long time while the icebergs melted.

She sighed deeply.

I can't do this, she thought dispiritedly, it's too hard, just too bloody hard.

The television was turned on in the sitting room and the door was left open, just so that there wouldn't be dead quiet in the house. In the house next door someone flushed the toilet. She listened to the familiar sound of the pipes jerking into action, gurgling, swallowing down water. Olive's old dressing gown still hung on the back of the bathroom door. She didn't want anything that didn't match her new apartment, and she considered it too frumpy to take with her when she moved in with her boyfriend.

"That is so *yesterday*, Mam," was what she said about anything she was leaving behind.

Betty felt so "yesterday".

At forty-eight Betty felt totally irrelevant. She hadn't known till now the difference that Myles Nugent had made to her life, and it made her wonder how she had gone through so many years without being really alive. Without her noticing, he had brought her world alive. She realized now that before Myles she had seen her days as stretching out monotonously before her, and he had planted an air of expectancy in her very bones, an enthusiasm that wasn't there before. It was gone now, she'd ended it; she had extinguished the one bright spark in her life.

Now it seemed it was all about the next generation. In magazines, on television, in the media, it was all about the school leavers, the first-time house buyers, young working parents. All about *them*. She used to be one of *them*. Once.

Her life had slipped by working to feed and clothe her children, keeping a roof over their heads, educating them. It had been her sole purpose, her entire focus. She'd have done it a million times over. Hard work was never a problem.

But now was a different kind of hard. A cruel merciless kind of hard.

The camaraderie with the others at work got Betty through her day. But the minute she got in the hall door the shutters slammed down again with a resounding silent bang, underlining her return to solitary life, and the silence drummed at her ears till she felt it would deafen her.

Day after day of pretending she was fine was taking its toll.

The heat of the bath made her drowsy. She noticed the calmness of the water, as it lapped gently against her chin. The icebergs were all gone. How calm it was beneath.

No problems there. There was no *room* for problems in the silent world beneath the surface. It occurred to her how just the merest slide downwards could sort it all out.

The idea took hold very easily. Here was the obvious solution, already enveloping her like a warm comfort-blanket. She imagined the feel of the water, warm and soothing as it crept up the insides of her nostrils, filled her ears, covered her head. Problems could not follow. She could keep her eyes closed while she welcomed blissful oblivion. She could do it.

And when she took a deep gulp, as she surely would, she wondered fleetingly if it would take long. A minute even? Quicker perhaps if she just went with it, mustn't have to do it twice. Focus only on the blessed nothingness it promised beyond.

Only on that.

She figured, with the water being nice and warm, she wouldn't turn cold too quickly. Betty didn't like cold. She would be gone and still be warm. Wouldn't that be something? She might not even be blue when they found her.

They?

Now there was a thought: who were *they* likely to be? Wait a minute, she had to think about this. If it were her daughter, would she understand? Questions began to flood into Betty's head, questions she needed answers to.

If Olive had children what would she tell them when they asked about their gran?

Grandchildren! In time it would be all about them too. Life had taught *her* that the hard way. She lay there and admitted to herself she would have *liked* to see what Olive's children would look like.

Well, she still could, couldn't she? Unreasonable though it was, she began to feel a bit selfish at the prospect of depriving them of their gran, and grandchildren might not be *that* far away, because with a little bit of luck Olive and her partner might learn that the best-laid plans sometimes had a way of not working out . . . so she just had to be a little patient.

A tiny feeling of anticipation seeded itself in her heart. Maybe now was not quite the right time for this. There were still possibilities in the future – she just had to remind herself of that. She hadn't realised she'd been feeling quite that low. A more optimistic feeling began to take hold and it slowly replaced the dangerous negatives. With that thought she sat up slowly, somewhat shocked at herself now for how she had almost allowed herself to slip so easily into oblivion. She got out of the bath, towelled herself dry, lifted Olive's dressing gown from the back of the door and wrapped it around her.

Chapter 22

The tail end of the storms that lashed the east coast of America just before Maeve and Myles' arrival there reached the east coast of Ireland a number of days later in the small hours of the morning. Gale force winds had been forecast, but the storm that howled across the eastern counties and Dublin Bay was much stronger than expected. Trees outside the Nugents' house swayed and moaned mournfully, bent threateningly towards Sophie's window by the force of the wind, and the waters of the bay were whipped into a wild and ferocious frenzy against the outcrop of land that stretched out behind the house and garden before dipping into the sea.

Every fibre of the Nugent family home seemed to rattle under the onslaught. Sophie was woken by the noise of torrential rain lashing against her window. It filled her head with pictures she didn't want in daylight, much less in the dark of night. Why was it that foul weather always brought Peter so vividly into her thoughts, always in a negative manner? Yet she knew that if he were here now she would probably not even have woken. But he wasn't, and she felt to blame.

She listened to the old house creak and groan and wished her father was home. He had phoned earlier on to see how they were. He didn't know how much longer they would be away. Maeve was not quite finished her business yet and the hotel owners who had commissioned her work seemed to have taken quite a liking to her. They delighted in introducing this "artist from Ireland" to their friends and some business acquaintances, and insisted on showing them excellent hospitality. They wanted Maeve to have as long as she needed to develop a good feel for their hotel and the location of her finished work. Maeve had no objection to that, nor indeed did Myles. They were shown some of the sights, were being well looked after and he was enjoying the break.

Sophie had strained her ears for any tell-tale signs in his voice that he had put that leech out of his mind. The impression she formed was ambiguous and unsatisfactory and the issue bothered her for the remainder of the day. She always sought refuge in alcohol and then sleep but tonight that bolthole was denied her by the wind and rain battering the house in explosions of energy.

Isabella too was disturbed by the gales and, leaping instinctively from her bed in the dark, she ran to the protection of Grandy's room. But there she stopped in her tracks. Grandy's curtains were not drawn and his bed was empty and she remembered with dismay that he was in 'Merica with Maeve. She turned and crept quietly into her mother's room.

"Mummy?"

Sophie groaned inwardly. "Go back to bed, Isabella, it's only the wind – it's the middle of the night."

But her daughter stood there silently and began to shiver. Sophie pushed back her covers: there was nothing else for it.

"I'll tuck you in," she said, trying to keep the annoyance from her voice while taking her daughter back to her bedroom. "You must go to sleep – you have playschool in the morning."

Silently under her covers Isabella drew Ted towards her and buried her face in his knotted fur. Sophie got back into her own bed, seeking the oblivion of sleep. It did not cross her mind that she expected four-year-old Isabella to deal with the storm in a manner that at twenty-seven she was unable to manage herself.

The following morning the storm had passed, leaving a strong wind and bright patchy sunshine in its wake. The garden and terrace were strewn with bits of branches and debris carried on the storm-force winds during the night. Andy had his work cut out for him when he arrived. His usual pristine garden looked ragged and neglected with fragments of small shrubs and bits of old branches and fronds from the palm trees by the garden steps lying all over the lawn and the flower-beds. But that was Mother Nature for you, would be Andy's way of looking at it; you did your best and hoped she did not take too much umbrage at your puny efforts to tame just a tiny bit of her terrain.

Sophie paid no attention to the state of the garden. That was Andy's department. She was only concerned with getting Isabella to school and herself to the boutique. A tired Isabella was being particularly difficult this morning and Sophie wished for the millionth time that Myles was home. How he always managed to get better out of her wilful daughter she would never know, but he did, and it took the effort away from her, and she was very glad of it, particularly at times like now when she almost had to force her daughter's rigid arms down the sleeves of her coat, with time running against them.

News of the devastation caused by last night's storm made the news headlines that day, and in the shop it was the talking point of the customers who remarked on the severity of it. Sophie added her own observations each time, and inwardly bemoaned the repetitive comments, but it was necessary to have a good rapport with her customers, if she was to make a sale.

She collected Isabella from playschool that afternoon because it was Eileen's day off (she had asked for the next day as well, as she was going to a wedding), and without her father home to look after the child Sophie had no choice but to take the rest of the day off herself.

It quickly deteriorated into chaos.

Izzy ran upstairs to tell Ted about her day, which she always did if Grandy wasn't around, but today Ted was not waiting to welcome her home as usual. He was busy lying on her bed, drowning. Isabella's wail brought her mother running up the stairs.

She found her daughter holding a soggy teddy bear who dripped wet onto the floor.

"Ted is all wet!" the child wailed.

Sophie's first reaction was annoyance at Isabella for messing with water, but she instinctively knew Isabella wouldn't allow the toy near water and her eye was drawn upwards. The sagging of the ceiling shocked her as she watched water seep through the plaster and land on the bed below. The plaster over a large area was a greyish colour, indicating the extent of how far the water had spread and Sophie, half expecting the bulge to collapse in on top of them, was immobilised.

"My bed is all wet too," Isabella was crying, looking in disbelief at her sopping wet bedclothes.

But her mother was paying no heed. All she could think was why wasn't her father here to deal with this crisis. What the *hell* was she supposed to do about it? Was it a burst water tank, or was it a result of the blasted storm she kept hearing about in the shop all morning? Ushering Isabella out of the room, she closed the door on the problem and then realised the whole house could well be flooded in no time at all.

She fished out her mobile and swore impatiently, waiting for it to be answered.

"Bradley! You have to come over now. The house is about to be flooded!"

Isabella burst into tears with fright at her mother's words.

"I want Grandy, I want Grandy, and Ted is all wet!" she cried, still carrying the dripping bear.

"Oh, do shut up Isabella, I can't hear Bradley! No, Bradley, I don't know where the water is coming from. No, I certainly am *not* going up into the attic. For goodness sake, the ceiling looks like it's about to cave in!"

Thanks to Bradley's prompt intervention roofers were soon at work, assessing the damage and making the roof temporarily weather-tight, which was the immediate need. A thorough assessment was carried out and it became obvious that there must have already been damaged tiles on the roof, letting in water each time it rained. Some of the roof trusses were rotting and needed replacing, and between that and the subsequent water damage it was going to take time and a lot of repair work to put right.

Sophie told Isabella she would have to sleep in Auntie Maeve's old room for the time being, but Isabella wanted to sleep in Grandy's bed. Sophie told the child that Maeve's was best "just in case Grandy arrives home" but in her heart of hearts she knew that was hardly the reason. There was no indication from him when they spoke that he would arrive unexpectedly, but the closeness between her father and daughter was something Sophie had a problem with, and although she could have guessed Isabella's choice, it still irked her to think that of the two rooms available Isabella chose her grandfather's room first.

"Ted would like Grandy's room too," the child insisted, which reminded Sophie, now that the disaster was being sorted, that the bear needed to be dried out as well. It was a great opportunity to put the toy in the washing machine. A clearly upset Isabella sat watching him spin round and round in the washer-drier, and then rejected him when he came out. She left him on the worktop by the washing machine. He didn't look like Ted, he just wasn't the same. But she quickly got over that when it came to bedtime.

Lying in Maeve's room was different. The shapes and shadows were nothing like the ones in her own room that she was used to, and the window was much smaller, making the room seem darker, and suddenly Ted's company was very necessary. Isabella got out of bed and went downstairs.

"Mummy, I want Ted."

It was some time before she settled and finally fell asleep.

Sophie too found she had difficulty getting to sleep. She was overtired and anxious and it had been a right calamity of a day, one she would not forget in a hurry. Without Bradley she didn't know what she would have done, but at least the roof had been made weather-tight and the repair work would begin tomorrow.

Something disturbed Isabella's sleep. She opened her eyes and for a minute felt a stab of panic till she remembered she was not in her own room because all the water had got in, and Mummy would have to get her a new bed when the room was ready again. She felt the soft familiarity of Ted's fur against her face, then suddenly leapt from the bed in the dark, a sudden streak in pink pyjamas, and ran into her mother's room.

"Mummy!" she whispered urgently. "Mummy!"

Regardless of triggering her mother's anger, she shook Sophie till she woke.

"For God's sake, Isabella, what on earth is it now?"

Isabella's voice held all the fright she felt. "Mummy . . . there's a man in my room!"

Sophie's patience was non-existent. What on God's earth would her daughter come out with next? But despite her annoyance and her tiredness, it crossed her mind that it wasn't too unlikely that after the day they'd had that Isabella would have nightmares.

"You've been dreaming, Isabella, it was only a dream."

But the child just stood there resolutely. Sophie tried for once to hide her impatience and she got out of bed.

"Isabella, you were dreaming. Come on. I'll tuck you in, then you can go back to sleep."

Reluctantly Isabella followed her mother back across the landing.

"I saw him. I did," and after a second she whispered in a very small voice, "Ted saw him too."

Chapter 23

Maeve and Myles' plane touched down at Shannon in the midst of pouring rain. Maeve was keen to get home to her cottage. Her head was chock-full of ideas for her commission and she was keen to get started. Knowing this, Myles said goodbye to her at the airport. He felt he had been away from home long enough and if he were to accept her invitation to go back to Kerry with her now, well, perhaps he would only be in her way. The main things in his mind were the storm damage, and Betty, though not necessarily in that order all the time. The storm damage had been the most urgent but fortunately Bradley had stepped in and looked after things. He had kept him apprised of the repair situation, and he was aware that Bradley knew what he was talking about and would deal with the situation every bit as well as he would have himself.

And then there was Betty. She had not left his mind

since she had left his life. They had unfinished business, regardless of what she said, that much he was sure of.

Maeve didn't feel that her father would be in the way if he stayed in Kerry. Having him with her this past week and a half was something she would have liked to continue. Since her mother died, she felt he was very much at a loose end, and she was sure he would have liked living in Kerry. She had noticed how he fitted seamlessly into her way of life while he was at her cottage. How easily he made friends – such as the unlikely Quigley McGurk and the imposing Conor de Lacy who seemed to think her father's friendship was worth cultivating.

But Sophie had commandeered him completely during the past year and Maeve knew he worried about her. What exactly that worry stemmed from was something he didn't explain but, knowing Sophie of old, Maeve was sure his worry wasn't without foundation. And then there was Isabella.

In any case, she sensed he was keen to be home, particularly after what he told her about the storm damage. Maeve had the sneaky feeling her sister might have exaggerated it just to get her father home. That would be Sophie.

When he arrived at his house Myles was surprised to see it looking pretty much as he left it. Apart from the newer tiles on the roof there wasn't much else to be seen on the exterior of the house.

When he entered the hall and called out he was home, a loud shriek greeted him from the back of the house and a wildly ecstatic Isabella ran into the hall and launched herself into his arms. With her arms wrapped around him as if for dear life, she gushed on all about the storm and the rain and her soggy bed. Words tumbled over each other in her attempt to tell him everything all at once.

Sophie's greeting was in complete contrast to her daughter's.

"I thought you would have let us know that you were arriving today." She managed to make it sound like he had slipped up somehow.

Sophie was concerned as to whether he had got over that woman while he was away but there was no way she could tell and she certainly couldn't ask.

Myles said he wanted to surprise Izzy, and that he undoubtedly did. She was still right beside him as if he would vanish if she took her eyes off him for a second.

Over dinner Sophie filled him in on the happenings since the storm. Isabella's ceiling had been re-plastered and she could go back into it when it was painted, and a new bed had been ordered. Otherwise the repair work was practically done.

Conversation was going smoothly when Isabella innocently asked, "Grandy, will we be going to see Betty now?"

His hesitation was just long enough to cause severe alarm in Sophie. The atmosphere changed instantly and the tightening of her expression spoke volumes.

"We'll see, pet, we'll see," he answered soothingly, and his tone was telling Sophie clearly that there was nothing she could have to say on the matter.

But Sophie wasn't having it.

"Mark my words," she warned, her voice low and thick with threat, "that will be the biggest mistake ever –"

The look he shot across the table silenced her. She found it was becoming harder to read her father. There was a steeliness in him she had not noticed before. This was obviously that woman's influence and it was not the reaction she had expected to get. But then she had never challenged him openly before. Her methods had always been quite subtle – understated but successful – and she was suddenly feeling on very shaky ground.

The atmosphere did not improve that evening and, after tucking Isabella into Maeve's bed, Myles went to his bedroom and read by the window for a while. Sophie's sullen company was not at all inviting, and the long flight home, the time difference and the train journey had totally exhausted him.

He was glad to be in his bed early and he would have slept late the following morning if it had not been for Sophie's alarmed voice waking him. Still halfway between sleep and wakefulness, he wondered why on earth she was shouting for Isabella like that. Something immediately felt very wrong and he had just about lifted his head off the pillow when she burst into his room.

"Isabella's gone!" Sophie's face registered panic and incomprehension, her hands fluttered wildly before her face. "She's not in her bed! And the door is wide open!" Her frantic voice broke off.

He did not wait to hear any more, the tone of his daughter's voice was enough to send him running to the child's room, while logic was telling him that Sophie had to be making a mistake, of course Isabella was somewhere in the house. But she wasn't.

Sophie was following him agitatedly as if he could somehow conjure up her daughter. But he couldn't. The child was not in her bed, not in the house, and though it was closed now Sophie said the hall door had been open.

Isabella was nowhere to be found. Then the questions started. Did Isabella wake during the night? Had she gone into her mother's room? They both knew the answer to that. Isabella would definitely have gone to her grandfather if she had woken in the night. Sophie was last to bed: did she lock up properly? She mustn't have, because Isabella couldn't have turned off the house alarm. They checked the alarm and found that it wasn't faulty. And even if the alarm wasn't on, she couldn't reach the hall-door lock herself. They pulled on clothes and went searching the garden's two levels, and between the shrubbery. She might have sleepwalked – she could have fallen anywhere! But they knew in their hearts Isabella couldn't have opened the door herself. But how did she get out? Why didn't they hear something? Why didn't the house alarm go off? Oh God, why why why?

Myles made the call to the police. In a voice barely able to say what happened he told as much as he could. Sophie sat in utter disbelief, unable to take it in, her face white as a sheet.

When Eileen arrived for her day's work after her break for the wedding, she was met with a family crumbling before her eyes.

Chapter 24

When the police arrived there was another very disturbing element introduced into the situation: the possibility that the child had been taken. Myles found that prospect totally shocking. The thought of their Izzy being held by a stranger or strangers was too dreadful to contemplate.

The search began immediately. They had no way of knowing how many hours it was since Isabella had left the house, how many hours behind they already were. Door to door enquiries were begun, neighbours were questioned closely. Did they see anything, hear anything during the night? Had they noticed any strange activity in the area recently, or any strangers about the area? They were clearly distressed but they were equally unable to shed any light on the disappearance.

The area was very hilly, a small child could be easily concealed anywhere. More worrying was the sea at the back of the house. Beyond the garden there was rough rocky ground where gorse bushes grew in abundance and the land sloped down to the sea where it ended in a rocky drop into the water. At low tide a small area of rock was exposed, but low or high tide it was an extremely dangerous place, and the fear was beginning to take hold that Isabella might have wandered in that direction.

Myles didn't think so. Isabella never bothered going anywhere near the end of the garden, and even if she had there was a sturdy boundary fence and it was backed by thorny bushes on the rocky ground behind it. She couldn't have made it through there. A small child in her pyjamas? No way.

A picture of her pink pyjamas flashed through his mind. She had picked them out of the drawer herself after her bath last night, one of the ones with Dora on them. They were her favourites – she had two.

A search of the neighbourhood was begun. Volunteers armed with stout sticks searched the surrounding hilly areas. The Howth Life Boat was called in to search the rocky shoreline behind the house. An inflatable RIB was used to get as close as possible to the rocks and Navy divers were deployed to search the sea.

Sophie had to be sedated. Her severe distress caused Myles great concern about her and he called the doctor. He was very worried by her silence and the snow-white pallor of her face. But she couldn't stay still, not for a second. She paced the rooms incessantly, continually checking room after room and then, without uttering a sound, she would start all over again till Myles felt he would explode. The doctor offered Myles something too, but he couldn't be "out of it", he said, while his granddaughter was missing. They might need to talk to him, ask questions, anything.

He had phoned Bradley and Maeve earlier. The police sergeant had warned him it could be on the news. If this was reported in the media he did not want them to hear it on a news bulletin. Myles didn't want the media around. He didn't want news hounds snooping around, using his Izzy for their headlines or to earn kudos for their work.

Bradley came over immediately and was no sooner there than he was questioned by the police for any light he might be able to shed on the situation. He didn't see how he could have anything to say that could help, but he did mention the repairs that had just been finished on the roof, and the fact that there had been strangers about the house for most of the past week seeing to them.

They took another look with fresh eyes about Isabella's bedroom and they double-checked the room she was sleeping in since the storm, but still they came up with nothing that they might have missed before.

The name of the company doing the repair work was noted by the sergeant but he didn't really expect to find anything of any help there. Kidnappers in his view didn't use construction repair companies to source their targets. But he didn't say that to Myles. The less said the better all round.

Eileen stayed out of the way as much as she could while trying to provide some sustenance when needed. She kept fresh tea and coffee going and continually made sandwiches, none of which was consumed by either Myles or Sophie. The police came to the kitchen to question her – procedure, they said. But what help could she be to them, she asked. She'd just had two days off. They already knew she was never in the house overnight. Myles had confirmed this, but they were questioning everyone possible, no matter how much or how slight their connection to the house was. Apart from arriving this morning to utter chaos and disaster, Eileen clearly knew nothing of Isabella's disappearance and she was obviously extremely upset by the child's disappearance.

In the late afternoon Maeve arrived, having driven up from Kerry. Myles was very glad to see her and they hugged tightly, Maeve crying quietly and trying to put a brave face on it for her father's sake. She greeted Sophie with a warm hug also but Sophie's response was indifferent and silent. Maeve was shocked to see the gaunt face and the tormented look in her sister's eyes. She was already quite tired herself with her long flight home yesterday, and the five-hour drive up from Dingle today, but she tried her best to be some support to her sister. But Sophie appeared to be unreachable and shut off from them.

The police spoke with Myles about the possibility of kidnap and ransom. An incredulous Myles dismissed the idea immediately. He didn't have that kind of money for a start, he explained. He was retired and didn't live a lavish lifestyle. Surely if it was kidnap for ransom they would have chosen someone who was obviously wealthy.

His helplessness was driving him crazy. He was closest to Izzy, he figured, he should have *some* idea where she was, some knowledge of what happened to her.

By the end of the day they were no closer to knowing what happened to Izzy, or even how she managed to get out of the house, and indeed whether she was taken or not. There was nothing to indicate a kidnap. There was no break-in, no evidence of it, no sign of a struggle. But still they couldn't rule out the possibility. A tap was placed on the phone in the event that any demand came through, and the sergeant went through the procedure with Myles.

Eileen put a meal on the table before she left, but it was hardly touched.

Darkness had fallen and visibility on land and sea was almost down to zero for the purposes of searching, and the search was called off for the night.

Bradley stayed. There was no way he was going to leave his father and sister to face this alone. While Sophie made no comment one way or the other, Myles was glad of his company.

Shortly before midnight Sophie took a couple of the tablets the doctor prescribed for her and went to bed. Myles persuaded Maeve to get some sleep upstairs, and Maeve was very glad of it. She made her way to her old room but, tired as she was, it took her some time to fall asleep. Last night Isabella had slept in that bed and it was unbearably poignant that Maeve was now there instead of her.

Myles and Bradley sat downstairs most of the night, sometimes talking, sometimes not, sometimes pacing because tension and stress and worry wouldn't allow them to sit still.

"How did Sophie react this morning, Dad?" Bradley asked. "She's unnaturally quiet. I've never known her to be like this."

"I'm terribly worried about her," Myles confided. "I think she may be blaming herself because we can't establish whether she put the alarm on or not. She swears she did, but why didn't it go off when the door was opened? It has been checked and it's not faulty . . ."

His voice trailed away hopelessly. There were so many contradictions which they couldn't find answers for.

Myles' face had become so haggard and drawn that Bradley pleaded with him to go to his bed. Myles stayed where he was but eventually exhaustion took over and he slept on the chair where he sat. Bradley too slept for a while in the chair across from his father but he was woken suddenly by an agonised cry.

"Christ! How couldn't we have noticed that!"

Myles leapt from his chair and rushed upstairs, followed by Bradley who didn't know whether to dare hope or not. His father pushed in the bedroom door and switched on the light and stopped dead. He visibly sagged against the frame.

Maeve woke in alarm at the sudden intrusion.

"What is it?" she demanded anxiously.

"Oh Christ Almighty!" The words were wrenched from her father. There on the end of the bed, now partially covered by the disturbed bedclothes, was Isabella's teddy bear. Immediately they knew what he was thinking. Myles' worst fears leapt to life.

"She didn't let herself out. She would never have willingly gone anywhere without Ted!"

Chapter 25

The following morning at first light the police resumed their search on land and sea. No one sat on the terrace now. The patio doors were closed and the curtains were kept drawn. No one wanted to see the divers' boats out on the water; it was an unbearable sight. Overnight the emphasis had changed drastically. It was now shifted a million miles further into a chasm of blackness that stretched into infinity. A child who wandered in the night was a very different matter to a child who had been taken, and yesterday the family had preferred to think Isabella had somehow managed to let herself out of the house, even though she had never wandered in the night before. The furthest she went was to her grandfather's or her mother's bed, and back again.

Everyone in the household agreed she would not have left Ted behind willingly. Now it was a completely changed situation. Other factors had to be taken into account, factors both inside and outside the house. These were factors the police would have already been considering but they were not saying very much this morning. Still, without anything being said, the darkest of motives whirled ceaselessly in everyone's head. The atmosphere in the house today had a morbid tinge to it. Yesterday they were going to find Isabella, no doubt cold and hungry, maybe God forbid even injured, as a result of being out in the elements at night in just her pyjamas, but find her they would. It was only a matter of time.

But now? Now no one was sure of anything and the awful thoughts that were going through their heads made the whole situation all the more unbearable. Who were these people? Had they been watching the family? Had Isabella been targeted? Why her?

Myles tried hard to hold it together. His mind threw up dreadful pictures and thoughts and try as he might he found it increasingly hard to believe they would get Izzy back safely. The situation grew harder and harder to bear with every hour that passed.

It was impossible to offer any sort of sympathy to Sophie. She had locked herself mentally into a prison of torture.

Lying on her bed now, she saw it was all her fault. She saw it in their eyes, in the way they looked at her, in the way they gave knowing looks to each other. They didn't believe she had put the alarm on, and now she doubted herself. Myles had been tired out after his journey home and he had retired early. He said he was asleep almost as soon as his head hit the pillow. But she was late going to bed that night. She had fallen asleep in front of the television and so it was late when she locked up, and she could have sworn she put the alarm on. She *did* swear she put the alarm on, she insisted many times, but what she didn't mention was the worry at the back of her mind, brought back now to haunt her, the words her daughter had whispered: "Mummy . . . there's a man in my room!"

Isabella's frightened whisper haunted all of Sophie's waking hours. She had treated it as a dream, and dismissed it. Was it a dream? Was it coincidence or did Isabella really see someone? The possibility chilled her to the bone. If there was a man in her room Sophie had done nothing to protect her daughter. She didn't even check it out, she simply sent the child right back there. There was no sign of anyone or anything amiss when they went into the bedroom. But then Sophie had not got up immediately, and if there was anyone there they had plenty of time to escape. How come they didn't hear any noise or a door or anyone move about? No. It had to be a dream. But when they returned and took her daughter no one heard anything either! And doors were opened then; they left the front door open. No one came and went through walls. The chilling feeling that Isabella had not been dreaming sat like a stone in the pit of her stomach, and she, her mother, had put her back in that room alone. How could she tell the others? How could she admit to the police that this probably wasn't the first time there had been someone in the house? What sort of a mother would they think she was? Why didn't she tell them yesterday when they were asking their questions? Guilt was why she didn't say it, and she couldn't admit it to them now, she could only torture herself with it. What would her father say? And to make matters worse Maeve had to be here too, witnessing the mess she'd made of everything.

She got up from her bed and looked for something to ease the reality of it all, but thought better of drinking. Those canny police would cop it a mile off. She went down to the kitchen where Eileen straight away offered her a cup of strong coffee.

"I need something stronger than coffee," she said pointedly, in a low voice.

Eileen threw her a look, poured the coffee and placed it in front of her, and then went into the other room to see if there was anything she could get for any of the others.

Myles had a vague thought that Eileen was being extraordinarily considerate; he had never seen her be so keenly helpful before. Funny how trauma and terrible times bring out the best in someone, he thought. A little while later he came into the kitchen and inadvertently interrupted one of those little confabs between Sophie and Eileen. Something charged the air, a fleeting moment when communication was suspended, but he couldn't decipher it.

Eileen recovered herself first. "I was just suggesting a little lie-down might be a good idea."

"Of course," he answered, but he wasn't convinced.

Sophie went into the other room where Maeve and Bradley were talking. Bradley looked as bad as her father, hollow-eyed and unshaven. It irritated Sophie to see Maeve look as good as ever – well, she would, wouldn't she? Didn't she just have a good night's sleep in Isabella's bed?

Everyone was waiting for the phone to ring. Ransom, it had to be for a ransom. What other reason could anyone possibly have for taking Isabella? Their minds shied away from the other reasons. They didn't turn the television on. None of them had any wish to hear their unfolding tragedy coming at them from another source.

All of the workers who had been doing the house repairs were being tracked down and questioned.

Detective Sheehan was assigned to the case and he kept the family informed on everything that transpired. That information didn't amount to much, for any lead they thought they had turned out to be nothing, and all the while the family was waiting for the phone to ring, waiting for the one phone call they didn't want to get.

When it was time for the three o'clock news Eileen turned on the small telly in the kitchen. She didn't feel comfortable asking outright how the search and investigation were going. But she very much wanted to know if they were any closer to finding Isabella.

When Andy Fox arrived to work he got the shock of his life to hear of Isabella's disappearance. He didn't bother much at home with the telly he had in his small house; he preferred his gardening books and propagating hybrids and experimenting with his own ideas. The police stopped him from entering the house until Myles saw him; then they allowed him in. He was subjected to rigorous questioning which upset him quite a bit but it was routine and the same for everyone. He eventually got out to the garden, but the urge to work had all but left him. He took the spade from the shed and absentmindedly turned over the soil beneath the shrubs. His mind was full of Isabella following him around the garden, bringing her teddy with her, asking questions, and telling him what went on in her world. His thoughts tried hard to recall the last few days and the things she would have said to him. Sometimes she sounded as if she was confiding precious secrets in him, and in all honesty sometimes his mind wandered while she chatted away. Now and again he would make a non-committal response and she would be encouraged to chat on. In all her childish chatter could there be anything that would give them any clue as to what had happened to her, he wondered? It was like a dream to him that something had seemed very important to her lately, but what? Like a dream. That was it, her dream, she was telling him about her dream, but what was she saying it was about?

In the house all attempts at normality had finally shuddered to a halt, and the silence and tension that filled its place became too much to bear. Myles got to his feet and went through the dining room to the terrace and stood scanning the waters below, willing them to tell him something. Off to the side he saw Andy was methodically working and he was drawn over to him, as if being with someone absorbed in his work would distract him briefly.

Andy merely nodded his acknowledgement when Myles arrived beside him.

"What are we to do, Andy?"

The comment didn't require an answer; it wasn't really a question, it was more a verbalisation of pain, man to man. The words were heavy, laden with anguish and alarmingly lacking in hope. Andy adjusted his cap and cast a quick glance at Myles Nugent's face. The harrowed look he saw there made up his mind for him. He might get himself into trouble for what he was about to say but in all conscience he just had to say it. He cleared his throat nervously and fixed the cap again.

Myles sensed something coming.

"What, Andy, what is it?"

"Maybe nothin', Mr Nugent, maybe nothin', I was just tryin to rack me brain here and I remembered the little one telling me about a dream she had the night after the storm."

He hesitated about going on – the idea was so far-fetched he began to feel silly now that he'd started.

"Go on, Andy, please, anything is better than nothing."

Nodding his head at that, Andy continued. "She was saying there had been a man in her room."

Myles reacted like he had just been struck. "And?"

"Well, she hopped out of bed and ran to her mother . . ." He just knew his recollections would cause trouble.

"For God's sake, Andy, what?"

"Well, it seems her mother told her she was dreaming and put her back into her bed. I figured she was dreaming too, and maybe she was, maybe it's just a coincidence. But what strikes me is that it stayed with her so strongly that she told me the next day."

Myles placed a firm hand on Andy's shoulder in a gesture of thanks as he moved away.

Andy was alarmed. "I don't mean to cause trouble!" he called but the sign Myles made with his hand as he moved towards the house told Andy he had nothing to worry about.

Chapter 26

"Where's Sophie?"

Myles strode into the room so purposefully that Maeve and Bradley were instantly alarmed.

Maeve found her voice first. "In her room I think, she went up a few minutes ago."

Maeve and Bradley cast each other a concerned glance. Their father's demeanour as he hurried up the stairs was charged with purpose and their worry increased. Something must have happened. The muffled sounds of the voices upstairs reached them in the silence their father had left behind, but the voices soon rose in pitch and Sophie's shouting brought them hurrying up after Myles.

"For God's sake," Bradley said, reaching the bedroom first, "what is going on? Have we not enough to deal with without shouting like this!"

The sight of his sister's face stopped his words. Ashen, her lips drained of colour, Sophie looked like she was at the very point of snapping. Myles looked like he wanted give her a good shake, or knock some sense into her.

"*It was a dream! A dream!*" Sophie wailed. "How was I to know this would happen?"

"You didn't check it out, did you?" Myles shouted. "You just put her back into her bed! She could have been taken *then*, and you just put her back into her bed!"

"Stop it! Stop it! She was dreaming, she was *dreaming*!"

The incident was told to Detective Sheehan as soon as he arrived, and he questioned Sophie again till she almost screamed. This 'dream' put a very different light on the situation. If Isabella really had seen a man in her room, then the fact that she leapt from the bed so fast and woke her mother might well have foiled that attempt. The fact that Sophie didn't check about the house would have given the intruder plenty of time to escape. But the question remained as to why they would target Isabella – why her?

Maeve began to be seriously worried about Sophie. She seemed to her to be very ill-equipped to deal with this amount of pressure. Maeve watched her closely and it was clear to her that her sister was on the verge of cracking up. She said as much to Bradley, and figured from his reply that he was of the same opinion.

But Sophie wasn't nearly as ready to fall to bits as they thought. She came into the sitting room just as Detective Sheehan was about to leave.

"Why don't you ask my father about that woman he has been seeing?" she demanded. "I knew from the start she was only seeing him for what she could get out of him!"

"Sophie!" Myles exploded. "That is completely out of line!"

But Sophie wasn't going to be silenced.

"I don't think so, Father," she retorted icily. "I sensed something about her the moment I set eyes on her. If you ask me, the detective should have questions to ask of her!"

The onlookers were dumbfounded, Myles most of all. But Detective Sheehan turned to him.

"Mr Nugent? Is there something we should know?"

Myles stared back at him stupidly. Sophie had lost the plot. What on earth was she thinking of?

"Of course not," Myles retorted. "Anyway I haven't seen Betty since before I went to Maeve's."

"You think this woman could have something to do with this?" Detective Sheehan asked.

"She doted on Isabella, and Izzy was very fond of her too!"

"But do you think she could have had something to do with your granddaughter's disappearance?"

The questions were persistent and probing and there was no option but to answer them. The way they were worded made Betty look guilty as hell. Myles answered the questions in disbelief and shock. He had not seen this coming. Was it a set-up from the start? The detective believed it could well have been. Those people took great care in how the first contact was established, he said. Con artists, he called them and Myles wouldn't be the first one to fall for their line. Myles thought of the accidental meeting on Inish Mór – was it really accidental? Was Betty sitting there on the rocks waiting for prey? Was he the prey? God, surely not! He thought they actually had something there, he thought it was real.

"I need a drink," he said.

"We're almost done here," Detective Sheehan said. "You know this woman's address?"

Myles reluctantly gave the address and the detective stood up, saying, "We'll look into this and get back to you. It would be best if you don't make contact with her till we can rule things in or out."

His quizzical look at Myles sought his agreement. Myles barely nodded. There was nothing else he could do. He sat, elbows resting on his knees, his head down, while Bradley showed the detective out. Then he felt a hand on his shoulder and Maeve handed him a brandy. Sophie left the room and went upstairs.

Myles swallowed the brandy in one gulp. The implications of Sophie's accusations weighed him down, and he'd thought he was already at his lowest ebb. If it turned out that there was any truth in them, then this tragedy was his fault. He had brought it all on them, he and his loneliness, and his gullibility in believing that he could be attractive to a pretty, lively female like Betty.

"Don't contact her," Sheehan had said, and he had been thinking of doing just that. It had been his intention when he got back from the States to just call into the shop. He remembered when he saw her that last time how she had said he was not to phone, and she was insistent.

Isabella's voice suddenly shot through his head: "Betty forgot to say bye to me, Grandy."

Oh Christ! Was it that cut and dried that she could walk away without even a backward glance? Was her part in this atrocity done, so she was done with them?

Eileen told Maeve she wouldn't be able to make it in tomorrow and then she went home. Maeve figured the stress in the house was becoming a bit too much for the daily. Perhaps she needed a break. If only they could all take a similar break.

Later Maeve and Bradley were talking quietly in the kitchen.

"Go in to him, Brad, he needs man-to-man talk," Maeve pleaded. "He must be devastated over this. I know he was quite keen on her. I know that's why he came down to the cottage when she ended it."

But Myles didn't want to talk. He had talked enough in reluctantly answering the probing questions and he felt quite naked and exposed as it was. His wounds had been laid bare and salt was rubbed deep into them. His instinct was to crawl away somewhere and pray that this all came out right in the end, because if his stupid ego was the cause of anything happening to his beloved Izzy he did not want to live to see it.

Detective Sheehan was more worried than he could say as he drove back to the station. There was no indication yet of what had happened to little Izzy, as her grandfather liked to call her. That bothered him quite a bit. This case wasn't looking like it was going to fit into any usual format. He had dealt with kidnappings before and whatever the reasons for them, sooner or later they fell into similar patterns. This time there was simply nothing to go on, at least not yet. Nugent wasn't wealthy – comfortable perhaps, but certainly didn't have the kind of money to have to worry about kidnappings or the like. On the face of it there was no obvious reason he could see why this would happen to this particular family.

He could see how much the grandfather doted on the child, how distracted by her disappearance he was. The mother was an odd one though, he thought. She didn't quite fit the profile of the distraught mother. At times she looked like she was about to disintegrate completely, and at others she seemed cold, indifferent almost. He had the distinct feeling that there was something going on between the mother and her father, and perhaps that was why Sophie had come out with those accusations, but everything had to be checked out. Experience told him that leads often came from the most unlikely source, and nothing could be taken for granted or left unchecked.

But something else had long since formed in the back of his head that he didn't like one bit, something he did not voice to the family, certainly not yet. He was beginning to wonder if there would be any ransom demand at all. The kidnappers had Isabella.

Perhaps that was all they wanted.

Chapter 27

The pitch black of the country night had begun to give way to a faint sliver of grey in the eastern sky. It had been a rainy night, which had suited very well, and things should have gone as planned. Had that happened the small navy van would have been miles away from here by now and, because the night's work was only half done and the driver had yet to reach his destination, he was in a foul mood.

The way he was hard on the brakes and the gears was an indication of the anger he felt at the way the night had gone and his passenger was well aware of this, but even he knew that this was no time to allow an argument to get started over something that couldn't be helped now. Otherwise the driver was careful how he drove; the last thing they wanted now was an accident or anything that would draw attention to them.

Now, on the last leg of the night's activities, with tiredness making them both irritable, they sat in silence as the van twisted and turned down the narrow country roads. The driver had dipped his lights rather than risk them being seen by any early-rising farmer, and was sharply on the lookout.

The turn-off was on a curve and you could easily miss it unless you knew it was there and were looking out for it. Overgrown hedging made it harder to spot and the driver slowed down as he turned into a lane barely the width of a car, the sides of the van being scraped by overhanging branches.

The one-storey cottage he approached was not visible through the overgrowth; only when he stopped the van and got out could he be sure he was in the right place. The two-roomed structure before him had been disused for years now and showed all the signs of it. Built over a hundred years ago, it was low-lying and ivy-covered, making it all the more invisible from even a short distance away.

But on closer inspection there were signs of recent activity. If you looked through the hanging ivy, you could see that a new lock had been put on the door and weeds on what would once have been a natural path were trodden flat.

Without a word, the driver took out a key and opened the door. The stench of dampness filled his nostrils, there was mildew on the walls and the old paint was raised in bubbles and was flaking off. But none of that was a problem. He wasn't here to enjoy the country life.

He went back to the van and took some cardboard boxes from the back of it, careful how he walked in the still dark night. He took them into the first room of the cottage, placed them on a bare wooden table and went back for more.

He left his passenger to look after his bit and to take his cargo into the house and leave it securely locked in the other room, neither of them saying a word. There was one small window in that room, high up in the wall and much too filthy to be able to see out through, particularly as tall brambles obscured it from the outside. An old cast-iron bed and a broken chair stood disintegrating with dampness in the room.

The men used a torch inside the cottage; electricity had never been connected to it, and it wouldn't have been a clever move to switch it on even if it had.

The boxes were opened and the contents divided into smaller packaging, both men working silently and swiftly. It was too risky to leave the van outside for any length of time, even in this obscure location; the beginning of the day was gaining strength and they knew that in the country farmers were up and about at the crack of dawn.

Some of the divided packages were put back into the van, and the driver nodded to his passenger. The job was almost done, his part of it was at least, and he was keen to get away from here as quickly as he could. He was leaving his passenger and his cargo behind, but he didn't want to know anything more about that; the less he knew the better for himself, and what would happen from here on in he didn't want to know either.

He took out the van keys and would have left without saying a word but the passenger, obviously uneasy at being left there, blocked him.

"Make sure they sort out what to do about this bloody quickly," he said, jerking his head towards the back room. "I'm not going to be left here like this for long – tell them that I didn't bargain to be landed with this."

This was more than either of them bargained for when they set out to do their night's work. It wasn't on the agenda but they had been landed with the situation and neither of them was one bit happy with having to deal with the outcome. The driver knew he should use his head and just go, but he was too livid at being caught up in it. That asshole who got them into this situation definitely had it coming. He'd find out who he was.

"I just do my bit," he snapped. "If you think I'm going to tell *them* what to do, you have another think coming. The sooner I get out of here the better. No doubt something will have to be done about this but it's not up to me to make the decision. Not my call, got it?"

The other man could suddenly see himself getting all the flack for the situation and his temper caused him to be careless. "You're in this as much as I am!" he shouted. "You drove us here – you know how to get here. Don't think just because you can drive away now that you're in the clear! You can't drive out of a situation like this!"

The driver's hand went up. "For Christ's sake, keep your bloody voice down! Do you want to wake the whole neighbourhood? Why don't you just go outside the door and shout your fuckin' head off?"

The other man made a huge effort to calm himself. The driver was right; the last thing they wanted was to draw attention to themselves, but he didn't relish the prospect of being here without any idea of how long it would be.

"We shoulda been warned, it shoulda been known

and we shoulda been told. It shoulda been postponed." he grumbled.

"Well, that's a whole lot of 'shoulda been's' but it wasn't, and now it's getting too bright out and I'm outa here," was the driver's reply.

He left without another word. He drove back out of the overgrown lane and onto the curve of the narrow road. His lights were off now and he was careful how he drove, careful not to grate the gears or rev too much, keeping the engine quiet as he could despite his hurry to be gone.

Then he just about made out the form of a black-and-white dog running by the edge of the road. He swung and missed it and drove on, his mind on the bad feeling he had in his gut about this night's turn of events. It wasn't what he'd signed up for; nothing like this had ever happened before. They'd got the job done – that much was always a relief because there were always repercussions if anything went wrong. But, nevertheless, there would be ructions among the 'higher-ups' when it came out the way this night had gone, and there would certainly be a price to pay. This was exactly the kind of thing that would hit the headlines, and there would be no hiding place for any of them.

Across the fields about half a mile away, Tim Ruddy and his wife were sitting in their kitchen finishing breakfast.

"What's up with the dog?" May wondered idly. "I think he was out chasing early this morning."

Tim emptied his cup and reached for his jacket. He had work to do outside, and May always started chatting like this after breakfast. Why couldn't the woman learn to wait till his day's work was done and then she could chat away all she liked? Not that he'd always be listening, but at least she wouldn't be talking to the walls.

"Foxes, probably," he answered as he turned. "There's young ones about – saw one of them on the road last evening just before dark. No doubt some of them will be hit by cars before long." He wouldn't worry too much if they were – foxes were on the increase, bloody pests.

May nodded absently as he went out. Best get the breakfast things away.

Chapter 28

The atmosphere in the bakery shop was very subdued. The usual banter and chat gave way to sombre faces and serious frowns. The news of the kidnapping was the all-consuming topic that occupied their minds and silenced the best attempts at comfort and solace. The picture of Izzy that was shown on the news was nothing to the live bubbly child they had all seen in the shop with her grandfather. It was as if they had all lost something; the kidnapping was personal to each of them and they felt the loss and the concern deeply.

They were also concerned about Betty. She had been torn between whether or not she should phone Myles. She knew he was just back from the States; it was reported that his granddaughter was taken the night he arrived back.

Betty thought of the last day they had been together. They were down on the beach when Izzy innocently let her bomb drop. That was the end of it. There was no way she could see him again, knowing the trouble her presence was causing at home for him. Maybe she did him a favour cutting it off then. Saved him the bother. He had said he would phone but she wouldn't have it. What was the point? Anyway, he didn't phone; he headed off for a break instead.

But his granddaughter was missing and she felt it only right that she should at least phone to offer her support and sympathise with him. She had picked up the phone earlier and dialled his number. Isabella's mother answered.

Betty became hesitant, not knowing what to say to her, or how it would be received.

"It's Betty Morris," she began but the torrent of abuse that gushed down the line at her stopped her dead. Upset and confused she hung up, sorry she had made the call in the first place.

It wasn't long after that her doorbell rang. The two men on her doorstep introduced themselves as detectives and asked if she would answer a few questions. She was quite taken aback but realised very quickly that naturally they would be checking out anyone who would have come in contact with Isabella in the recent past. She stood aside and invited them in, willing to help in any way she could, but even so she began to get a very uneasy feeling in her gut.

This was no ordinary questioning. Some of their questions were not as direct as she expected, and some had an almost accusatory tone to them. Nor did they seem to accept her answers. What had been the purpose of her phone call to the Nugent house earlier, they asked? That appeared to concern them a great deal. Why would she be calling if there was nothing any more between herself and Mr Nugent? Could they not understand that she just wanted to express her concern, that he might be comforted a little to know that she was anxious about his granddaughter? No, she wouldn't be phoning again, her call had obviously upset his daughter, and she regretted that, so she wouldn't call back. Though she told them about Mrs Harcourt's outburst, she didn't say that she had felt a good deal of venom coming down the line from her. That had been a shock. She understood that Sophie was under extreme stress and made allowances for it, but it still came as a huge jolt to hear it verbalised.

With every response she gave they came back with another angle, another question, and always there was that element of doubt in their voices. They said it was routine but their approach had a very doubting element to it. Anxiety made her less forthcoming, more hesitant, and she saw the look that passed between them from time to time. They left after what seemed like ages, but they might need to question her again, they said.

Trish brought her out of her reverie.

"I really can't believe they actually suspected you had anything to do with the child's disappearance! My God, what sort of a person do they think you are? I mean, how could he think that of you?"

No one had an answer for her. Was it Myles who had sent the police? It would of course have been him who gave them her address, but she wondered with a fair amount of doubt if it was he who had mentioned her name in the first place. And she figured she would get no marks for guessing just who else it could have been.

Silence fell in the shop while Trish and Fran

assimilated the implications, both of them in shock that anyone could suspect the quiet innocuous Betty of anything, much less kidnapping! Customers were served in subdued silence, the assistants' thoughts being far from the cream doughnuts and the sesame-seed loaves.

Hearing it said straight out like that was very brutal and Betty cringed from looking for answers to Trish's questions. She had reacted the same way when the detectives were in her house, when they put bald undiluted questions to her. And she wasn't dealing with it very well since.

"Him or his family, what's the difference?" Trish was saying. "It's all the same – someone must have mentioned you, must have thrown suspicion on you, or those cops wouldn't have been at your door."

"All I can think of is Isabella. Someone has her – she must be terrified out of her wits – I'm afraid to think what they could be –"

"Stop," Fran said commandingly, "don't go there, Betty! It'll drive you mad. But was there anything you might have noticed that might help? Anyone hanging around even?"

Betty couldn't help thinking that the girls, in their concern for the unfortunate Izzy, were beginning to sound just like the detective. She sighed and shook her head hopelessly. She had been wracking her brain since she heard the news for some way of helping, for something, some tiny thing that might provide a clue.

But inside her there was the tiniest pinhead of what she figured had to be anger, and it wouldn't go away. Trish was right. Someone had thrown suspicion on her, and what did it matter who it was, the end result was the same. Was that how little they thought of her? She felt the anger grow, but she kept it hidden from the girls. She didn't want them to know how stupid she felt, because it was something of a shock to think that Myles held such a low opinion of her. She was sorry now that she had ever talked about him in the first place.

Fran was looking on the optimistic side of things. "Well, at least you still have all those nice clothes you bought, and that is something positive. You're not going to just let them rot in your wardrobe, are you? Your stars did say things would be looking up, and now you have the right clothes for *any* occasion, so that's something, isn't it?"

Trish never let a chance go. She was quick to jump on the bandwagon. "I'd be prepared to bet Betty meets someone else, and soon. Any takers?"

Betty couldn't help smiling at that. She'd be lost without the pair of them, that's for sure. But neither could she help wondering what outcome exactly Myles Nugent had been expecting when he sent those detectives to her door.

Chapter 29

Detective Jim Sheehan slid his car into the station car park and switched off the engine. He sat behind the wheel, staring into the middle distance, his thoughts a circling mass that amounted to nothing.

Two days now. Two whole days and nothing, not the slightest inkling. Nothing on the phone, except for that call from the Morris woman. She'd said she was phoning to offer sympathy to Mr Nugent, but with the daughter exploding at her like that they didn't get the chance to hear exactly what she would have said. He found the verbal assault by Mrs Harcourt unusual to say the least. In kidnap cases it was more likely that the mother would be reluctant to answer the phone in case of making a mistake, for fear of making matters worse, and he knew only too well that matters could always be made worse.

His fist came down hard on the steering wheel in frustration. Something *had* to be staring him in the face. It couldn't be that there was *no* clue, none at all, it just couldn't be. He had to be missing *something*. A child just doesn't vanish without there being something to point the way. So why couldn't he see it?

He had thought he was onto something when they mentioned the Morris woman. The way the daughter spoke of her painted a very damning picture. Kidnap was one way of extorting money if it worked, and Betty Morris was a woman who had to work hard for every penny she made. When they mentioned her at first, he thought she might have had the notion that a lump sum from kidnapping would be handy. But after interviewing her he was no further ahead than before. She seemed to be genuinely upset that the child was missing.

He sat in his car going over and over every aspect of the case in his head. It was all he could think about since he first got the call. The only fractious point in the Nugent family he could pinpoint was the opposition the mother seemed to have to her father's relationship with the Morris woman. He could see why the mother would seek to put blame on her, but that could be construed as normal family behaviour in his book – there was nothing in it that would give rise to kidnap. The Nugents were very low on the scale of dysfunctional families, not like some he had come across. The mother would be considered the odd one out there. Her reaction and attitude were confusing to say the least, and he had seen the whole range of emotions and reactions in a huge variety of situations. He wondered if she was 'on' something, and though it was not immediately obvious, he wouldn't have considered her reactions typical.

At first she insisted she had slept the night through, and only realised her daughter was missing in the morning when she went to call her for school. Then she remembered she had got up during the night and gone to the kitchen.

And what did she go to the kitchen for?

"Paracetamol," she said. She had woken with a headache.

Wasn't her sleep disturbed after that? Wouldn't she have heard any intruder?

No, she said, paracetamol always made her sleep quite heavily if she took two, and she had taken two. When asked, she said she had no idea at all what time it was when she went to the kitchen; she hadn't looked at the clock. And she hadn't noticed anything amiss then. She'd likely be right about that. She could never have passed the hall door without seeing it open, if it had been. So they couldn't even pinpoint the time the child was taken. All they knew was that it was before daybreak.

Myles Nugent was the only other person in the house that night. He had just flown home from New York the previous day after a busy trip with his elder daughter and he said he never heard a thing. Tired after his journey, he slept like a log till his daughter woke him in a state of panic.

The daily help Eileen Hyland and the gardener Andy Fox were never in the house overnight, and Sheehan had questioned both of them inside out. The gardener was a quiet man, given only to his garden: he said it was his only interest. Sheehan immediately believed him about that; the man was the essence of someone in tune with the earth. He had a loyalty to the Nugents which was admirable but Sheehan needed all the help he could get, and when he put it to Fox that anything he could tell him might well be helping Isabella, the man opened up. Sheehan was surprised at the depth of his observations, the amount of information he absorbed while he appeared to focus only on the job at hand. A lot of it though was gleaned from his reading between the lines when Isabella followed him about the garden chatting away. The one thing that stood out was the 'dream' she had the night after the storm. Sheehan knew it was Andy who had mentioned this. Odd that Sophie didn't. Unfortunately most of what Andy had to say had no bearing on the case, but by his comments Sheehan was able to get a better picture of the Nugent family and much of it bore out the thoughts and opinions he had already formed himself. The one surprise was the enmity between Andy and Eileen. The gardener said he had no tangible reason for it; it was, according to him, "just a thing in his gut". Apparently Andy was one of those rare men who listened to their instincts when it came to other people.

When he spoke to Eileen, Sheehan came to the conclusion that there was definitely no love lost between her and the gardener, but there again he detected no solid reason for it. He supposed it would have been a very unique household if there wasn't some aggravation somewhere in it. Eileen herself was a quiet one too. There was really nothing she had to say that could be of any help to him.

The fact that no ransom note or phone call had been received so far put the black feeling back into his gut, and it was stronger, and more insistent. If there was no breakthrough in the next twenty-four hours he was going to have to mention to the family that ransom might not have been the kidnapper's goal. This was not news you liked to bring to a family but it was likely they were already thinking along the same lines themselves. Families had gut feelings too, and despite their trauma they often thought very logically, but this family was hoping against hope and depending on him to save them from their fears.

Hope had no part to play for him. Facts were what he dealt with, facts, specifics, and proof, when he could find them. In this case he had nothing. He couldn't remember another case where he had absolutely so little to go on. He hated having to face the family, trying to hold their hopes up when he had no hope to give. They were not stupid people. They knew, but they allowed him to go through the motions, because the alternative was unthinkable.

He got out of the car and slammed the door. Something had to give soon. He felt the fate of young Isabella Harcourt rested entirely on his shoulders, and right now those shoulders were not up to the task. These cases were the most emotionally demanding: a helpless young child at the mercy of thugs, low-lifes and God knows what else. He was a long time in the force, many years at detective level and he knew from old that emotions did no one any favours if they were allowed seep into a case. But this was a difficult one. In this case it was almost impossible to keep his emotions out. If he only had something to go on it would give him some kind of leverage, a starting point, a fact to work from that would absorb him completely and hopefully dim the mental picture of the helpless situation of the four-year-old. He went into the station, bright fluorescent lights hurting his eyes.

A heated discussion was going on between Casey and Burke, two members of the drugs squad, and judging from the tone of the brief conversation he overheard as he passed by, Sheehan figured they were not making much progress with the case they were working on either. When they saw him they fell silent, their discussion momentarily suspended. A case involving such a young child never failed to catch the attention of everyone at the station and they all wanted to see a speedy successful conclusion. Search teams were still out looking, but they were merely going through the motions at this point and by their experience they all knew that. As Sheehan walked through the office they looked in vain for that air about him which would tell them he'd had a breakthrough and that he was finally onto something. Wearily he threw a glance over at the desk.

"Any calls?" they heard him ask.

"Nothing," came the apologetic reply.

They watched the droop of his shoulders as he passed into the inner office and sank into his chair. If this child was to be found safe and well and returned to her family he needed a miracle to help him do it.

But Sheehan didn't believe in miracles.

Chapter 30

Maeve's presence was the steadying force in the house. She kept herself busy doing whatever she could find to do, whether it needed doing or not. She felt it would serve no purpose if she was to fall to pieces along with her father and Sophie. They needed her to be strong. Some things never changed.

In Maeve's estimation Sophie was out of it most of the time. She swung between ranting and raging at everyone to being surprisingly detached from it all. So much so that Maeve was sure she was on something. What surprised Maeve was that Sophie managed to appear to be the distraught mother whenever Detective Sheehan was in the house. But this wasn't the time to tackle her about anything. Any more tension or stress and she was sure they would all absolutely crack up. Maybe she even *needed* the 'something' to get her through each hellish day.

Myles wasn't functioning very well at all. The distracted look never left his eyes, and the lines in his face became deeper and deeper with each passing hour. Without realising it, he turned to Maeve for solace and comfort, then sat in Bradley's company for a while, and then went back to Maeve again, but he was too distracted to concentrate on even the briefest conversation for very long.

This terrible situation was his fault entirely, he felt. He had gone down to Kerry to lick his own wounds, and then had taken off for New York with Maeve because it seemed like a good way of dealing with his situation at the time. He knew Isabella would have come to him in the night if she'd had a problem, and he would not have dismissed her 'dream' so lightly. She would have needed reassurance and he would have provided it. He would have listened more closely. Perhaps this might not have happened if he had been there.

But he wasn't there when needed, he had let her down. And now she was . . . she was . . . oh, Christ Almighty, please send her back safely to them – he would take better care of her. Really he would.

Bradley was there as much as he could be, and when he had to be away from the house he was on the mobile every chance he got. The way they all jumped when someone's mobile rang was torture to see, but it was nothing to the suspended breathing and apprehension they felt when the land line rang. It was never the call they wanted, never the call they dreaded.

Bradley slept there at night, something which Maeve was very glad of. If anything happened to her father or Sophie, at least she had Bradley there too.

Maeve was thinking about the search which was still ongoing. It was spread further afield now, but the divers were still down on the bay all the hours of daylight, searching each rocky cove and outcrop with the changing of each tide. She was aware all of this would come to an end before much longer. And still there was nothing, absolutely nothing. That was so dreadfully unbearable to deal with, the nothingness of it. Even the detective's bearing when he called emphasised it. Maeve could see how it was eating the man up, and how he dreaded facing them with not a shred of progress to report. She knew the search would have to end sometime, and then what? People had gone missing before and never were heard of again. That thought was too hard to contemplate and, when it crossed her mind each time, she got up to do something because sitting still only strengthened the horrific thoughts. She couldn't just sit and wait – that was negative energy – so she kept busy.

She was getting on Eileen's nerves. Eileen wasn't used to anyone else paying any attention to the state of the house. As long as everything ticked over smoothly, no one interfered with her work. She could set her own schedule as to what she would do on any particular day, as long as it all got done. Maeve did things Eileen had already done, and it irritated her. She watched tight-lipped as Maeve went about the house busying herself, oblivious to the annoyance she was causing. Maeve also decided what should be cooked. Now more than ever they needed nourishing food, she said, so she ordered it from the supermarket, and Eileen didn't know what to do with the half of it. It wasn't as if they were actually eating much. Except for Bradley who never refused food, appetites were out the window and food simply didn't come into the equation. Eileen wished Maeve would just go back to Kerry and do whatever she did and wait there.

But the others looked to Maeve. In their estimation she was keeping the whole thing together. It was she who always picked up the phone, answered the door, and then had to face them and watch the anticipation die in them when there was no news. And she was finding it all just too hard.

At the back of Maeve's mind was her cottage, her refuge, her little piece of heavenly solitude that was vital for her wellbeing. She didn't miss Dublin in the slightest. She had her painting; it was her work, her passion, and she could surround herself with like-minded people whenever she felt the need. But she had left Dingle in quite a hurry when she got her father's phone call, and now she was wondering if she had left the house securely locked up behind her. It was the studio that worried her; she couldn't remember everything she had done after she got the call. She decided to have someone check it out.

She was thinking too about her commission. She felt very guilty for thinking about it with Isabella missing and their world black with worry and anguish, but she couldn't help it. She acknowledged she needed it for herself, for her own sanity and she needed to be making a start on it.

Sophie drifted about the house, sometimes in a cocoon of silence, sometimes obviously ready to erupt, but mostly with nothing to say. What was there to say to anyone? What could any of them do? From time to time she exploded with stress and frustration and pain. And guilt.

She should have listened. She should have paid more attention to her daughter. She should have put her needs first. She should have done a lot of things. But how was she supposed to know what was coming?

How could she cope with a damaged roof, a collapsed ceiling, a sodden bedroom all on her own? What did she know about ridge tiles and roof trusses and the water-retention limits of plaster? Where was she supposed to begin? Granted, Bradley came and dealt with it on her behalf, but it was a worry, a weight on her shoulders, a complete distraction.

They were all questioned at length by the police. Like as if they were the criminals. The way questions were worded it was difficult not to feel you might be found guilty of something if you actually answered. The impression they gave was that they expected to find the culprit right there within the house. What was she supposed to say? How could she answer when her guilt would only pour out of her mouth? There was no rule book, no acknowledged format, and no guidelines as to how any individual mother would behave in the face of such a trauma. What did they expect of her? What could they know of how she felt? How did they expect her to behave in the face of her daughter being taken?

Now the family were all together again in the house, moving about like ghosts, jumping when the phone rang, trying to behave as though everything was normal. Well, a lot of it was. Bradley was back in his old role of acting like he was the man of the house, expecting his views to be treated as gospel, and whizzing in and out as if his work was the most important thing of all. Myles consulted him on everything, thereby conferring on him an equal status that Sophie saw as unfair and exclusive, and Bradley took it all in his stride.

Maeve had fallen back into her old role as if no time at all had elapsed since her departure to Kerry. She basically took over, taking it for granted that she was the only one coping in any way normally, and simply could not be done without. Sophie saw how easily her father fell into his usual habit of little confabs with his elder daughter, little knots of discussions that excluded her, and the old resentment surfaced again. There was no point in Sophie trying to include herself in these little huddles, it just didn't work. But it wasn't about Maeve, was it? None of this was about Maeve, so why the hell didn't she just go back to Kerry and back to playing with her paints and canvases?

When Sophie thought they all seemed to be otherwise occupied she went to find Eileen.

Chapter 31

For the second night in a row Myles did not go to his bed. He went into the dining room and pulled back the curtains, letting the moonlight creep silently into the room. The terrace outside looked a deserted place, not only because it was night and there were no people or police around, but because Isabella had not been out there for two days now. The feeling of her presence was fading. Perhaps, he figured, that was because he was so stressed, so strung out and worried and feelings were finding it difficult to survive in him.

He opened the doors and stepped out onto the flagstones. Where was she? Did she know they were doing everything they could to find her? No, he checked that thought, they weren't. How could they be when they had yet to find a single lead that helped? He looked out onto the water. He had no dread of looking out at it now because he no longer feared the possibility that she had fallen in. They would not find her there. Something in him was convinced of that.

He had watched Detective Sheehan closely and he felt there was some other element to this. He was convinced Sheehan believed there was, but he wasn't saying. But Myles believed the man was worried. An experienced professional he might be but Myles still saw the beginnings of a deep concern in him. Right now it didn't matter what Sheehan thought because, whatever it was, Myles wasn't ready to hear it. All he knew was that his Izzy was still missing and there were no leads, no clues, therefore knowing what was going on in Sheehan's head could be nothing but more worry right now.

The night breeze stirred the long fronds of the palm trees and he was reminded of Izzy playing on the steps with her dolls while Ted watched from his perch in the fork of the tree. Drawing a heavy sigh he looked across the illuminated bay. All around it, like a magnificent necklace, the night lights of the city twinkled brightly but all he could think was that there was someone out there among those bright lights who knew where Izzy was.

Two days. It was two days, and they had aged him a hundred years. They had aged them all. His thoughts settled a while on Maeve's excitement about her commission. She had literally buzzed in New York, and on the way home. She was bursting with enthusiasm to get started on her paintings. Ideas, she had said, were dancing about in her head, keen to leap into life and spread themselves in colours vibrant and rich across her canvases. Perhaps it was time for his family to go about their business. Tomorrow he would suggest to her that she ought to be giving thought to getting back to hers; she had her work to consider too and other people relying on her.

He leaned on the balustrade. A ferry was crossing the bay. Illuminated by a blaze of lights it moved away from the River Liffey, the reflection of its lights on the dark sea making it look almost twice its height. It glided soundlessly eastwards till it vanished from view beyond the Baily Lighthouse. It was like Isabella, he thought, out of sight but he still knew it was there. The breeze was cool and he was only in his shirtsleeves. Isabella only had her pyjamas. Was she warm where she was? Were they taking care of her?

A furious anger welled up in him suddenly. His hands gripped the cold granite of the balustrade as if they could break it. The strength in them now was nothing to the strength they would have if he could find those who had taken her.

The curtains stirred behind him and Bradley was at his side, two cups of steaming coffee in his hands. He took one with a nod of thanks. He waited for Bradley to suggest he go to bed, that they both go to their beds, but Bradley was silent. They looked into the distance as if they could find where Izzy was if they looked hard enough.

A sound behind them disrupted their thoughts. Wrapped in her dressing gown Maeve joined them.

"Couldn't sleep."

Bradley went to get her a coffee.

"Sophie okay, do you know?" Myles asked as they sat down.

"I looked in on her before I came down. She seemed to be sleeping."

Sophie was only managing to get sleep if she had taken something that literally knocked her out.

They sat in silence for a while. No one wanted to be the first to say anything negative but positive conversation had all but dried up days ago.

Myles stirred from his melancholy state.

"She really flew off the handle when Betty rang," he said. "I know the stress she is under, but I wish she hadn't done it. Now she's saying she didn't give Betty the chance to issue a ransom demand."

"I know," Maeve said. "I tried to tell her it makes no sense – Betty gave her name after all."

"I don't believe Betty had anything to do with it," said Myles, "but I suppose Sophie will see trouble everywhere."

"I can't begin to imagine how she must be feeling," Maeve replied, "and God knows how we all want Isabella back safely, but I do think Sophie is anything but rational now. And I think she is on more than the doctor's prescription too. Bradley thinks so as well. I know it's not what you want to hear right now, but I'm very worried about the effect of it all put together."

Her father made a dejected movement with his shoulders, and Maeve knew that he'd already had the same thought.

"What can we do about it?" he asked. "Right now is hardly the time to tackle her or indeed advise her, even if she would listen to anyone."

"There's nothing much anyone can do if she doesn't want to listen." Bradley arrived back with Maeve's coffee, coming in on his father's comment.

They fell silent again.

"I was thinking about your commission, Maeve," said Myles eventually. "You should be thinking of getting down to it."

Maeve looked deep into her cup at the remains of her coffee and sighed. The euphoria she had felt a few days ago had almost disappeared. The weight on her heart would only drag at her hand and her work would be heavy and lifeless. She knew that. She knew she needed to be free and light to work, to do her best work. It was why she had gone to live in Kerry in the first place. The distance afforded her a degree of freedom, freedom from immediate responsibilities and obligations, and it gave her the lightness in her heart that enabled her to create. How could she ever say that to any of her family?

The constant tension between herself and Sophie while she had lived at home was an unvarying drain on her energy, a weight on her shoulders. It was difficult to interpret her younger sister, and the next argument no matter how small was never very far away. Yet since she left so much had happened. Sophie married and moved out. Maeve used to wonder if things between her mother and father were better now that there was only the two of them at home. Bradley had already left. Getting caught between his two bickering sisters was not a situation he cared to stay in. The occasions when all of them came together at the same time were few and far between, apart from Sophie's wedding, and Isabella's birth and christening. For a while after her father retired Maeve thought him to be in very good form when she spoke to him on the phone, but she heard his optimism gradually diminish.

Maeve thought of moving home when her mother died so soon after his retirement. Her father was alone in the house then, apart from Eileen coming and going, but when she suggested it Myles wouldn't hear of it. Did he detect the change in her, see the freedom she felt? She often wondered because his encouragement to her to keep on at her painting was the deciding factor which made her stay. Now he was suggesting it was perhaps time she got back to it. She knew he was thinking of her, but how could she go now?

"I'll think about it, but not tomorrow – Eileen won't be here. But please God another day will bring good news."

Upstairs Sophie stood at the landing window looking out at the three figures close together beneath her. Her clenched hands wanted to lash out, anger and stress and resentment oozing out of her every pore. When her fist hit the window frame she didn't even notice that she had cut herself on the window latch.

Chapter 32

Quigley McGurk dug his hands deep into his pockets and bent his head into the oncoming wind. One of these days his poetry would be recognised and he would begin to live on more than his current modest income. Perhaps then he would get himself some form of transport, something he wouldn't be ashamed to offer Maeve Nugent a lift in. There were many things he didn't have that would make his life easier, and it didn't bother him, but he wasn't being too materialistic, he thought, to seek some transport deserving of Maeve.

The road into Dingle was long and deserted right now but he didn't mind that. His head was full of activity, throwing up ideas and phrases and words to beat the band, and once his mind was occupied like this Quigley had no need whatsoever of the presence of another human being. Words were his friends, his salvation, and without them there would be no light in his life.

He had spent the day so far writing furiously, getting

key words, ideas and brief phrases down on paper while they were so alive, while they were so eager to make themselves available to him. It began with a single word somewhere mid-morning. It was always just a single word that did it. It only needed to be a simple word to get him going again. But it had to be the right one. And this morning the right one had come. It just popped into his head after he had taken a phone call, and the log jam was broken. Inside, his head was like spring in abundance, and thankfully the branch was in full leaf again.

The passage of time meant nothing to Quigley on days like this. Absorbed in his work, he often went long hours without a break or even a sustaining cup of coffee. Pat Keegan would never interrupt inspiration while it flowed – it was an understood thing between himself and Quigley – he simply left him to it and busied himself with his pottery.

When Quigley finally raised his head it was to note the stiffness of his shoulders and neck. He stretched and rubbed the back of his neck, and smiled with pleasure at his day's work. He knew whom he had to thank for breaking the log jam.

Walking along the roadway now, he lifted his head to see he was almost in the town and not a minute too soon. The wind had strengthened and carried rain. By the time he reached McCaffrey's pub it had begun to come down steadily.

Inside the pub it was quite busy, and there was a delicious aroma of food. A couple of pints and something to eat would go down well, he thought, listening to the rumblings of his stomach; there was just about enough in his pocket to fund that. He threw a quick glance around.

He was the first: none of the arty types were in yet. It was usual if they had the price of a pint that they would congregate in McCaffrey's for a while at the end of the day, so he placed his jacket at the usual table and made his way to a vacant spot at the bar and placed his order and then waited for his first pint to take it back to the table with him.

His thoughts were happily reviewing his day's work, and when someone inched in, making space for themselves beside him, Quigley automatically moved sideways. Conor de Lacy hooked his blackthorn walking stick over the carved edge of the bar counter and looked around.

"You're early," he remarked to Quigley. "Nowhere better to hang around now that herself is up in Dublin?"

The flippant remark irritated Quigley. Typical of the supercilious attitude of the man, he thought.

News of Maeve's missing niece affected the close community in Dingle. But it was from a concerned point of view, not something to use to dig at someone else, as The Puff was doing. It was the talking point of the town, and rightly so. Like the rest of the country the locals were watching every news bulletin to see the little one brought home safely.

He ignored the remark.

"No news yet," Tom the barman joined in as he placed Quigley's pint in front of him, "Nothing on the news."

Quigley looked into the thick creamy head on his pint and took a long deep mouthful, deliberately ignoring The Puff.

Tom rested his elbow on the counter while he waited for Conor's pint to settle, since there was no other customer demanding his immediate attention.

"No way of knowing how long Maeve will be away, I suppose," he said. "They must be in a terrible state, the family – can't imagine what they must be going through. I was thinking of her cottage just today though, and the studio. She left in quite a hurry – somebody should be keeping an eye on it."

Conor pulled himself up straight. This was where he could make an impression, show the closeness that had developed between himself and Maeve. What better time than when The Rake was standing right beside him. How better to put him in his place, give him the impression that he was definitely in the way?

He opened his mouth to speak but the barman had moved away to top up the pint.

"I'll drop in on the cottage in the morning," Conor said when the pint was placed in front of him, his voice laden with assertiveness, "I'll keep an eye till she gets back – it's the least I can do for her under the circumstances."

Quigley was counting out the coins from his pocket, aware that Conor had a smirk on his face as he watched.

"Hope you don't mind the change, Tom?"

Tom scooped the coins into his hand. "It's all money, Quigley," he replied in a genial manner. "Better small change than nothin' at all, eh?"

A silence crashed between the three men as the hint shot home. Conor shifted uneasily, not knowing where to look, and Quigley was overcome by a sudden urge to cough.

"As I was saying," Conor went on in an attempt to divert attention away from his rapidly lengthening slate, "I'll call in tomorrow –"

"No need."

Conor turned to Quigley, throwing him a look that definitely told him in no uncertain terms to keep out of this. "I beg your pardon?"

Quigley licked the froth from his upper lip and looked The Puff directly in the eye. That necessitated looking down on him, because of Quigley's superior height.

"I said no need. It's being looked after."

Conor looked rightly miffed, but he wasn't giving up.

"And how would you know?" he asked, his tone implying that Quigley would surely be the last person to know anything about it at all.

"I've just been up there. It's all okay – no problems."

It was too much for The Puff.

"You *trespassed*?" Conor made it sound like a crime.

Tom was enjoying this. He had never seen Quigley McGurk quite so sure of himself before. Watching him stand up to de Lacy like this was a real treat, all the more so because of the incredulous expression and the rising colour on de Lacy's smooth fleshy face.

Conor had become aware of other customers watching. Perhaps they couldn't hear exactly what was going on – Quigley was very quiet-spoken – but it surely was obvious that The Rake was having his moment.

Quigley took his time and sipped his pint, unfazed by the veiled accusation or the other customers, a feeling which was new to him, and he savoured it well.

"Maeve asked me to look in on it, keep an eye out so to speak," he said calmly.

"Hah." Conor had him there: he knew McGurk was in Tralee when Maeve left in a hurry for Dublin. He drew in a long breath and prepared to let The Rake and all and sundry know that he knew him for the liar he was.

But Quigley spoke first.

"She phoned the house this morning. I checked the cottage on my way here, the studio too – everything's hunky dory," he announced and turned away with his pint, a smug smile spreading across his thin features at leaving The Puff without a retort for once. He went over to his table to join the others who had come in, leaving de Lacy looking very much put out and deflated despite the fact that he was still holding his breath.

The barman turned his face away and suddenly had to hurry the other end of the bar – as if he thought he heard a customer summon him.

Chapter 33

Somewhere that seemed very far away a car door closed hard and there were voices, a dog barking. The voices were fuzzy and distant. Isabella could tell they were angry but it was too hard to hear the words, to hear the voices clearly. The sounds were all mixed together, and altogether it was very frightening and muzzy to the sleepy Isabella.

When the shape was angry he threatened all sorts of things, from "a good swipe" to letting the dog in, and he was angry most of the time.

The voices came nearer, a door creaked, then they were in the other room but the anger was still there. It looked like it might be daytime outside because there was no strip of light coming from under the door.

If it was daytime Isabella knew she should be up and out of bed. She knew she should be dressed too but all she had was her pj's and they weren't very clean now. They got wet sometimes when she used the broken pot and they smelled, and the bed was smelly too, and it was all tossed and nobody straightened it out.

She lay on the bed trying to close her ears to the sounds of the voices in the other room. They were angry, very angry, and it made her very afraid of them. She hoped they wouldn't come in if she kept very quiet, so she didn't dare make a sound, and she covered her ears because if she didn't hear them perhaps she could pretend they weren't really there.

But somebody came and pulled back the bolt on her door.

"What in the name of – shut that fucking door, you asshole!" a voice suddenly roared. A loud bang made her jump, like someone had thumped a table, and two of the voices fell silent, and a low threatening hiss reached Isabella's ears.

Then without the door being opened the bolt was slid closed again. A minute later the other door creaked and closed and the voices were outside again, fading away into the distance.

Chapter 34

It was about a quarter to two in the morning, and so far it was a quiet night in the police station. Over a coffee break the discussion was about the Harcourt case and the depressing lack of progress. This kind of thing hit them hard, ate away at confidence, and had a bad effect on morale.

Gardaí Swan and Harris were discussing the effect it was having on Detective Sheehan which was plain for all to see. The man was hollow-eyed and pale; yesterday he even arrived in to work unshaven, something they had never seen before. They could only guess at the horrendous effect the ordeal must be having on the child's family. This was the third night, or the fourth if you counted the night she was taken. There were those attached to the station who had no illusions about getting little Isabella Harcourt home safely. To them it wasn't going to happen. There were sickos out there who had no compunction about anything they did to man, woman, or it seemed,

204

child. Swan finished his coffee and reached lazily for the phone, one of the few calls that evening.

"Hello –"

He didn't get time to say another word. The male voice on the other end spoke quickly and hung up.

"What?" Harris demanded when he saw the disconcerted look on his partner's face.

"I'm not sure I heard right, I thought he said 'the Bull Island Bridge'."

"What about it?" Harris asked.

"That's all he said, and hung up. That's it."

"Ring Sheehan," Harris said immediately. "It could be the girl."

"And it could be a hoax. You get weirdos who think hoaxes are great gas," Swan pointed out, for he wasn't so sure what it was. He didn't want to be the one who woke Detective Jim Sheehan for maybe nothing at all, some drunken asshole having a laugh. He wished he'd had even another second or two on the line before the caller hung up.

Jim Sheehan reached out a fumbling hand for the phone. He had been still awake at midnight going over and over things in his mind for about the millionth time and had only managed to fall asleep a minute ago. That was how it felt now as he reached out a hand and felt about for the handset and put it to his ear.

"Hmm, yeah?" he answered and listened to the caller prevaricating on the other end.

"Get to the point, Swan. It's two in the bloody morning!"

Suddenly the time of night or his lack of sleep was of no importance any more.

"Where? When?" he demanded as he threw back the covers and grabbed his trousers. His wife reached out a bare arm to pull the duvet back over herself. She was well used to calls in the night. Then she remembered the case that troubled him so much and she too was wide awake.

"The girl, Jim?"

"Could be."

His face had that set look she saw so often when he felt a breakthrough might be imminent. These were the times when she worried most – they could be the most dangerous. He was already shoving his arm into his jacket and grabbing his car keys. She wondered if he would phone the Nugent house, but then she realised he wouldn't, not until he had something to tell them. This could turn out to be nothing.

"Take care, Jim."

He threw her a quick nod, his face closed and grim.

"I'll be back."

Those were the three little words Jim Sheehan's wife preferred to hear at any time. She knew from old that movement in a stagnant case, if that's what this was, could well go terribly wrong. She'd told herself long ago that she had learned to live with the worry and the danger, but at times like this she knew for sure that she had not.

Something along those lines was going through her husband's head too as he drove his car towards Clontarf and the Bull Island Bridge, but he kept them firmly in the background. He needed a clear head now. His gut told him this was it. They were going to get the child back. What troubled him was, if they were giving her back of their own accord, what state would she be in? Why did they find no need to hold onto her any more? There could only be two reasons for that. Either they had achieved their objective or, or he couldn't put words to what the 'or' was. He felt it couldn't possibly be good; kidnappers didn't just hand back an unharmed captive for no reason.

His car raced along the Clontarf Road, his siren on the roof flashing but silent. There was very little traffic, a taxi here and there, not much more.

Ahead of him as he approached the traffic lights at the turn for the bridge he could see a police car already there, its lights flashing also.

Harris was waiting for his arrival. A second police car pulled up simultaneously.

"What have we got?" Sheehan asked, looking around for another car.

"Far side of the bridge, sir – light-coloured BMW. Been there since we arrived, no sign of anyone about."

The outline of the abandoned car could just about be seen glinting in the changing glow of the traffic lights on the far side of the bridge, the car itself barely visible, just a dark outline against the light of the moon.

Sheehan indicated to one of the Gardaí from the other car to accompany him and together they set off across the wooden bridge. Keeping low as they neared the far side they cautiously approached the car from the rear. There was no sign of anyone being in the car, no sign of life. Sheehan took a torch from his pocket and shone it into the interior. The keys were not in the ignition and the front seats were empty, and the back seat had just a blanket thrown across it. He tried the back door. It opened.

A child's feet, bare and white in the torchlight.

Sheehan reached out a hand to lift the blanket – it actually shook a little; he was afraid of what he fully expected to find beneath the coarse covering.

He leaned in and taking a corner he gently pulled back the blanket.

Isabella Harcourt.

Her image was indelibly scorched into his brain from the photos her family had given him for the search. She did not move; his lifting the blanket did not disturb her. His heart knew a sudden lurch and at the same time the grip of fear. There were no injuries that he could see. He placed his fingers on the side of her neck in search of a pulse, half-expecting to feel nothing but it was there, steady and strong, and he offered up a silent prayer to wherever he figured silent prayers of gratitude go. His touch disturbed her but it didn't waken her.

One thought struck him. Drugged.

The ambulance made its way across the creaking timbers of the bridge. Forensics were on their way and when they arrived a cordon was put up around the abandoned car and a portable tent was erected over it. A run on the number plate showed the owner of the car lived in Castleknock and had not yet reported it stolen. Sheehan thought it likely it had been stolen probably a few hours ago at the most, specifically for this job, the owner probably unaware of the theft and still asleep in his bed.

Isabella murmured in her sleep as the ambulance men removed her gently from the car.

Half an hour earlier two cars had travelled along the Clontarf Road in the quiet of the night, keeping a reasonable distance between them. Just beyond Kincora Road at the traffic lights by the wooden bridge they had turned right and driven onto the Bull Island. There was nothing unusual in this. Cars drove onto the Bull Island at all times of the day and night, but those who drove there under the cover of night were often seeking the anonymity of darkness for their illicit goings-on. No one ever saw anything on the Bull Island at night: they simply hadn't been there.

The BMW had been in front and, once it left the bridge and drove onto the sandy grassy surface of the island, it had turned and parked. Turning off the engine and throwing the keys on the ground as he got out of the car, the driver had quietly closed the door. He'd got into the second car which had pulled up alongside and the second driver immediately had driven back across the bridge and turned the car towards Dublin city.

Five minutes later the phone had rung in the police station and Swan lazily lifted the receiver.

Chapter 35

Myles woke as if a sixth sense had alerted him. Wide awake now he sat up in his bed and picked up the phone on his bedside locker. Why didn't it ring? Why hadn't it rung by now? He stared at the apparatus in his hand which rendered him helpless by its malevolent silence, a silence which held the safety of his Izzy in its power. Why hadn't it been used to communicate the kidnappers' demand? Why else they had taken Izzy? Anger and helplessness fought within him, the futility of having a phone that wouldn't ring making him want to fling it at the far wall. How much more of this could they take?

Sophie was on the verge of a breakdown. He'd had to bandage her hand earlier, because she never even noticed the blood after she pounded the window frame and cut herself on the window catch. She was out cold now in her room. He'd insisted she take a sleeping pill to help her get some sleep, but even that worried him because she was taking too many drugs, both prescribed and (if

Maeve and Bradley were right, and he very much suspected they were) whatever else she was taking, but up to now the stated dosage of the sleeping pills wasn't working. Myles was very worried about the mixture of stuff she was taking.

He put the phone down and swung his legs out of the bed. Looking out of his window the night was dark, too many clouds obscured the moon, the waters of the bay were choppy and quarrelsome, and morning seemed a million years away.

Was Izzy asleep? Or like him was she thinking of how it would be when she came home, when she saw her family again, when she ran into their arms? Would she feel safe then? That worried him a great deal. How could he or indeed any of her family ever assure her that she would never be taken again? She should have been safe in her own house with family around her who loved her. But she was taken from under their noses while they slept. How could he ever tell her it wouldn't happen again? He'd had the alarm company in and changed the complete unit despite the fact that they had found no malfunction in the one they had. It wasn't even an old alarm, it was only a few years old, but Myles felt he could never depend on it again for security and it had to go. The fact that the alarm might not have been activated the night Izzy was taken made no difference – he had to get rid of it. He supposed that was only one of the weird and pointless things they would find bothered them in the aftermath of the kidnapping. The fact that total strangers had been in the house while they slept was bound to have a very disturbing effect.

In the days since she was taken, the re-decoration of

Isabella's bedroom had been completed. Myles didn't want the decorators in the house at this time but Maeve pointed out that if – no, *when* Isabella came home, it might help her to settle back in more quickly if her room was ready. That made obvious sense and after clearing it with Detective Sheehan the workmen were asked, in consideration for the family, to keep only to the area to be decorated in order not to place any more stress on them, and the work was done.

As he stood at the window, Myles asked himself what had been the point when there was no Izzy to sleep in it. He was vaguely aware that his spirits were sinking very low, that he was losing hope.

The muffled sound of the phone buried in the folds of the bedclothes was like something he heard in his head because he wanted to hear it so much. When he realised it was real and actually ringing there was a frantic search to locate it and with a shaking hand he placed it to his ear.

"Mr Nugent?"

He answered with a guarded "Yes", not immediately recognising the voice of Detective Sheehan, such was his anxiety.

"Detective Sheehan here. Mr Nugent, great news. We have your granddaughter, sir."

An uncontrollable shaking suddenly affected Myles' hand and he had to grip the phone with both hands to hold it to his ear.

"H-how?"

"She doesn't appear to be harmed but we are taking her to Temple Street Hospital to have her checked out. The ambulance is taking her there now. I'm about to follow."

The sound that came from Myles cut the detective short and Sheehan knew that he was struggling with his emotions.

"I had to let you know immediately. A car will be at your house shortly to take you to the hospital."

There was no need to mention the fact that Isabella had been drugged, or the filthy dishevelled state she was in.

"Thank you, detective. Thank you, God."

Myles looked at the phone in his hand. Had he really heard that? Suddenly he was running out onto the landing.

"Sophie! Maeve! Bradley! They've found her! They've got Izzy! The police have her!"

There was scrambling from all rooms except Sophie's. He went in.

"Sophie, wake up! They've got Izzy – they have her. She's safe!"

Sophie was finding it hard to shake herself from a drug-induced sleep.

Maeve was on the landing hugging Myles and Bradley all at once, tears spilling between them.

Then there was the rush to get to the hospital.

Maeve and her father left first in Maeve's car while Bradley and Sophie, who was moving like she was made of wood, held on for the police car. They were there in a very short time – at this hour the streets were almost devoid of traffic.

Detective Sheehan met Myles and Maeve at the door and guided them to the ward where Isabella was being checked out. Myles was relieved at the fact that they had placed Izzy in a room on her own. When he entered the room she was clearly drowsy but her arms immediately went out to him.

Her hair was matted from not being washed or combed – clearly she hadn't been washed since she was taken – and there was a smell of urine from her. He was shocked at the state she was in, and livid that 'they' should treat her like this, but all he could think was they had her back. They had their Izzy back.

He lifted her from the bed and cuddled her in his arms and rocked her back and forth, and she immediately fell back asleep, gripping a handful of his shirt, her head resting against his chest. He looked up questioningly at the doctor.

"They obviously gave her something to make her sleep while she was being handed back. They may have given her something at other times too. We have taken blood samples – the results will tell us what it was – and we want to check her out a bit more, but we don't think she is physically harmed otherwise. If it was to make her sleep the night through then she should be fine when the effect wears off. In a case like this an antidote wouldn't be advisable – best to let it wear off itself. She should be fine tomorrow."

Myles and Maeve were sitting one each side of the bed while Isabella slept when Bradley and Sophie arrived soon after. Sophie looked like a walking wreck, having cried with relief all the way there in the car. She immediately tried to wake her daughter but Isabella hardly responded.

But Isabella was safe now, she saw that Grandy and Maeve and Mummy were here and the people here were nice, and the place was warm and the dark was gone, and the shape and the dog were gone and it was too hard to keep her eyes open.

Sophie surprised them all by reaching over her sleeping daughter and putting Ted beside her in the bed.

Chapter 36

The return of Isabella was on all the front pages of the newspapers, accompanied by the photo her family had given to the police to help locate her. Every news bulletin on the radio and every news programme on the television had the same news item as its headline. But for every minute piece of information the media broadcast, there was a huge question mark and it emphasised the fact that there was no corresponding piece of information that could in any way be construed as evidence.

Detective Sheehan called to the house to talk to Isabella once she was released from the hospital. Myles told her that this was the policeman who had found her and brought her home, his reason being it might predispose Isabella to feeling this man was a friend and hopefully talk to him.

It was almost true. Sheehan was the one who approached the car and found her covered by the blanket on the back seat. Myles would have preferred he had found her sooner and in the place she had been held. Perhaps then they might have something to go on.

They sat in the sitting room, Sophie, Myles, Isabella and Detective Sheehan. Isabella sat on her grandfather's lap in the circle of his arms, leaning into his chest. She looked warily across at the detective who was smiling benignly, hoping to win her trust. She didn't want to talk to him, but she knew Grandy wanted her to, and Mummy wanted her to, but she didn't want to remember the bad place.

It might make it all real again.

She didn't have many answers she could give them. Sometimes she shook her head in answer, or nodded when asked if they gave her food, or if she had a bed.

They asked her if she could remember anyone. How many were there? Who could she remember? Was it a man? Did she remember what they looked like? She was afraid to answer that; she didn't want to think about the shape, or the dog, and she wasn't sure where they were now, or if they would come back and get her again. All she could say was that he was "big and angry".

The frustration felt by Detective Sheehan was beginning to bubble to the top. He made a superhuman effort to keep it hidden. The answers were in her head, he knew that she knew them, God love her, and he also knew that in her world she did not yet feel safe enough from 'them' to be able to bring the answers to the surface and actually speak them.

Even so he pressed her a little further, backed by Myles encouraging her, but the recalling of her ordeal was too much for Isabella and she turned her head into Grandy's chest, her lower lip clearly beginning to tremble. The adults threw each other a concerned look above her head, and shook their heads in defeat. It was time to leave it. To push her now might do harm and probably no good.

For Bradley and Maeve it was time to leave, time to allow normality to come back to the house.

When Maeve was ready for the long drive back to Dingle she hugged Isabella tightly.

"Can I come to your house soon, Auntie Maeve?" Isabella asked, the urgency in her voice striking at their hearts.

"Of course you can, sweetheart. We will see when Mummy or Grandy can bring you down, and then you can come for a while, okay?"

"Can I come now?"

Grandy explained why she couldn't go now, but it didn't make sense to Isabella. Maeve left and Izzy became quiet again.

Chapter 37

Maeve took it easy on the drive back to her cottage. The last week had been unbelievably exhausting, and although a part of her didn't want to leave till she was very sure that they all would be okay, another part badly needed to be gone home to the peace and tranquillity of her little piece of Kerry, and the creativity of being immersed in her studio. Back in Howth, the general consensus was that the sooner the situation in the house got back to normal the better for all concerned.

The new roads and by-passes made most of the drive down easy enough, but when she reached Limerick city there was a slow-tractor protest in operation by farmers and the tailbacks and hold-ups were horrendous. Delayed by over an hour simply trying to get through Limerick, it being the main route to Kerry, there were also the inevitable bottlenecks on the far side of the city, between there and Tralee, where the narrower roads slowed evening traffic to a crawl.

At hold-ups like this her mind shot back to Howth and the anguish they had lived with during those dreadful few days. Her father looked like an old man on those days and nights when he hardly slept, or ate, and she worried very much about what this stress would do to him too. The change in him and Sophie since Isabella was returned was a very welcome sight.

But that was the odd bit – Isabella being returned just like that, apparently willingly, by the kidnappers without any demands since no one had found where she was being kept and therefore no one could have rescued her. She was simply returned.

What on God's earth was the purpose of it at all? What reason could there possibly be that the family were put through that hell in the first place? Maeve knew that question was really troubling her father, and that the overriding feeling in the house after the sweep of blessed relief was one of vulnerability. They were none the wiser how the intruder or intruders had entered that night, or how they had taken Isabella without anyone hearing anything. They had expected Forensics to be able to determine these things, and while theories had been put forward, nothing conclusive emerged. Myles had changed the alarm system, and had all doors and window locks checked. How could they settle and feel safe in their home again if they never found out where their weak point was, he had asked.

Sophie was just glad her daughter was back safe and sound. She decided she was putting the whole dreadful episode of the past few days behind her. Now they could get on with their lives again, and she had gone back to the shop. Myles had encouraged it and was surprised at how quickly she settled back into it, and Maeve thought it was exactly what she needed, to be immersed in something that took her mind off the week's events, at least while she was working.

Maeve drummed her fingers on the steering wheel, mentally willing the traffic to move, and at the same time hoping Sophie would get her act together now and stay off whatever she was taking. Her boutique was thriving. Apart from the fact that recent events brought the curious in, Maeve acknowledged that Sophie had an innate sense of style so her success there wasn't surprising, and she had so much going for her. But Sophie always had so much going for her, only unfortunately it appeared she was the last one to be able to see it.

Sitting in the dwindling light in almost stationary traffic on the outskirts of Tralee town Maeve still had over an hour's drive to go, and she wished now she had left Dublin earlier. She was tired and weary, the whole journey so far had been tedious, especially as it had rained often, and she doubted she even had anything to eat in the house when she got there. She had considered stopping for a coffee or tea in Tralee but that would only add another half hour onto her journey time, so she kept going.

It was quite dark when she finally pulled up in front of her cottage. Even without a light to be seen anywhere about it, the cottage looked welcoming because it was home, and that was where she so badly needed to be.

She opened the door and stepped into the living room-cum-kitchen, to a heart-warming surprise. A fire glowed in the hearth, the kettle was filled waiting to be plugged in, and some brown scones and butter were laid out on a plate alongside a mug. A sheet of paper lay beside the mug. She picked it up and read the handwritten words on it. There was no signature but the verse was thoughtfully written to restore her wounded spirit after the traumatic event in her family this past week and to warmly welcome her back.

Touched by the warmth of the words, her eyes filled up and she shook her head slowly at the thoughtfulness of the writer.

"Quigley McGurk," she whispered with an appreciative smile, "you are so full of surprises."

Chapter 38

How much she was affected by her experience was impossible to gauge. They could see straight away that the bubbly child was very subdued, and at times a large frown creased her brow, but now and again the old Izzy surfaced and she laughed lightly as she would have done before. But those moments didn't last.

Both Myles and Sophie watched her closely for indications of trauma, as they had been advised by the doctors in the hospital. Children, they were told, did not always show outward signs of distress after something so traumatic, but that was not any measure of how affected they might be.

Myles and Sophie were not so sure exactly what they were watching out for, or indeed that they would recognise it if they saw it. For the first few days they kept Isabella home from playschool, and she played with her toys and dolls as she had done before. Myles listened carefully to her play while seeming to do other things about the house. He knew from listening to her earnest conversations with the bear in the past that she told Ted everything. That bear knew all her secrets, and it was the one way he was sure he would hear what had happened to her while she was missing.

Detective Sheehan too had suggested they listen carefully to her chatting because somewhere among it all there might be a snippet of information, an unconscious recollection that would start the ball rolling for them.

He told the Nugents that the case would stay open and the search for evidence and the kidnappers would go on, but Myles wanted more than that. He wanted to know the reason why this had happened to them in the first place. He figured his reason for that was so that he could guard his family against it ever happening again. How could he protect them if he had no idea what he was to guard them against?

Ted was left in the dark as to what had happened to Izzy while she was gone. She did not tell him the ins and outs as she would have done previously. He was included in her play as usual, but Myles noticed it wasn't as exuberant as before, and she didn't mention anything that would remind her of that time to Ted.

Myles also noted that she was much less given to running about the house than she used to. When he sat on the terrace, she played by the steps or followed Andy about the garden chatting away – about what Andy didn't know half the time. But he didn't discourage her. Andy was of the strong belief that being out in the garden and watching and helping Mother Nature do her work would be every bit as therapeutic for a child as it would be for an adult. He was quite happy to have her follow him about. He told her in simple terms about what he was doing in the garden as he did it, and why he did it, because if he left that bit out she was sure to ask.

"Why do you have to dig the ground like that, Andy? Do the flowers like the rain, Andy? Will the wigglies get wet, Andy?"

Andy would answer in his slow methodical way, giving her simple answers she could understand. Myles thought he had never heard Andy talk so much before. It wasn't that he actually heard the answers but he knew from watching the body language of the two of them that Izzy was intent on listening. Sometimes Andy would point to something that Izzy would bend down to and examine at very close quarters, and Myles couldn't help but smile at the way they were absorbed in what they were doing.

He was grateful to the gardener for his patience and understanding, and made a mental note to have a word with him before he left for the day in case there was anything Isabella might have said.

On the days when Andy wasn't there, Isabella focussed her attention on her grandy. Myles had no problem with that, because he in turn was loath to let her out of his sight. When she was put to bed at night, getting her to sleep was not as simple as it had been, but that was only to be expected. Sometimes he would read a story till she fell asleep, and both he and Sophie looked in on her often. She was back in her own room, in her new bed, the decoration all finished, and Myles noted that she avoided going into Maeve's old room, and didn't like the door to be left open so that she could see in. She didn't spend time in the kitchen either as she would have done before, preferring instead to be with or near either Sophie or himself.

Sophie was surprised to be favoured with attention from her daughter these days when she arrived home from the boutique. It was obvious that Isabella was not avoiding her mother as much as she had done in the past.

But they had been told to expect some changes in Isabella's behaviour, at least on a temporary basis, and they were grateful to note so far that there was nothing they were unable to cope with.

Isabella going back to playschool was without problems, much to Sophie and Myles' relief. That was the area they expected real problems to arise. It was only when Grandy wasn't there to pick her up one day that a problem actually manifested itself. Eileen met her at the play school door as she had done frequently in the past when either Myles or Sophie, knowing they would be unable to be there, would ask her to collect Isabella. Only this time it was different.

Very different.

Isabella was dismayed when she realised Grandy was not collecting her as she'd expected. Eileen held out her hand but Isabella wouldn't take it, and she cried for Grandy, rooted to the spot and refusing to move, her sobs becoming more and more distressing and, apart from phoning Sophie or Myles, Eileen was at a total loss as how to get Izzy home. It was only a five or six-minute walk up the hill to their house but it may as well have been a million miles.

"It's so embarrassing – anyone would think Eileen was trying to abduct her," was the thoughtless remark

Ruairi's mother happened to make to someone. It was tactless and stupid of her under the circumstances, and the look Eileen gave her in return could have sliced the ground from under her. But she quickly made amends by offering to drive them home, if Isabella would get into her car.

Eileen put aside her annoyance and accepted the offer of help.

"How about I drive you both home, Isabella, would you like that?" Ruairi's mother bent down and asked kindly as Ruairi stood slightly behind her, pulling faces at Izzy.

Isabella's crying stopped and she thought about the offer for a minute. Then, ignoring Ruairi, she nodded gravely.

Ruairi immediately declared, "I'm having this side," and he climbed into the car and slid across the back seat to sit behind his mother. If he expected to raise an argument from Izzy he got none and that puzzled him. She got into the back seat and sat very quietly behind Eileen.

Try as he might Ruairi couldn't rile her at all.

Myles came home shortly after they arrived and was upset to find a very subdued Izzy. She was silent when he asked her what was the matter, and that worried him. When he asked Eileen if anything had happened that day she told him what transpired at the school, but it was her opinion that it was probably a bit soon yet after the "thingy", that the child needed more time to get over what had happened and she had obviously had more settling to do.

He mentally acknowledged that made sense but he didn't actually discuss it with Eileen. He just nodded and turned away thoughtfully. He decided not to bring it up with Isabella. It might well be better to let the whole thing die down, and give the little one all the time she needed.

But it was another thing to worry him, and she said nothing that gave him any inkling as to what had distressed her so much. As far as he could observe she didn't tell Ted about that either.

He began to feel perhaps she couldn't really articulate what exactly had happened during those dreadful days. With a heavy heart he asked himself how could she? When adults could have major problems trying to deal with events in their lives, how could a four-year-old be expected to make head or tail of what had happened to her?

But what was she keeping to herself? Did she actually remember much, or was she burying it because it was so terrible?

There was no doubt in his mind that something was frightening her still. He knew his Izzy well. He had spent hours and hours just enjoying watching her antics, her reactions to things. He knew when she was happy, surprised, angry, delighted, and now . . . fearful. He was aware how her eyes followed their every move, both his and her mother's, and how she was never more than a few steps away from either of them.

Chapter 39

Betty Morris set her alarm for morning, slid down under her cosy duvet and gave a long sigh of contentment. Spending the afternoon with Myles and Isabella was the last thing she'd expected to be doing that day.

When she went into work this morning it was just another workday, and there was nothing special to distinguish it from any other. The monotony of her life had begun to weigh heavily on her again, and she had been well aware that she was going to have to do something about it, find something that gave her focus. Work nowadays was not enough; she had been doing this job for so long now she could do it with her eyes closed, just like Trish and Fran. But they had their families to go home to, to interest them and keep them busy. Olive and Buddy having their own homes and going about their lives left a lot of unfilled space in hers. She had all that time for herself. Meeting Myles had opened her eyes to a much more interesting life out there and even if he was no longer around, she now had an interest in having something positive to throw herself into. She just had to find out what that was.

The news that 'the Harcourt child' was returned home safe and well was one of the news headlines towards the end of last week. Betty remembered a huge wave of relief sweeping over her when she heard it on the one o'clock news bulletin. She had been having her lunch and the news on the television above the cash desk in the restaurant caught her attention. It caught a lot of diners' attention, and there was a collective murmur of relief and delight when it was read out. A photo of Isabella accompanied the item, and Betty immediately choked up. She couldn't cry here, she just couldn't, she'd feel like a twit. Then she found herself wondering if her tears weren't for the loss of Myles as well as the relief about Izzy. But what else could she have done? In the face of such strong opposition from his daughter, she just had to bow out. As it turned out, she'd been right. She fully suspected that Sophie had a lot to do with the fact that the police had come to her door. Granted, they would have been checking out everything and everybody, and rightly so, but the abuse she'd received from Sophie down the line was like a kick in the gut.

It was weeks since she had seen Myles, that day on Dollymount beach. It had started out so differently, so like a parallel life that it was hard now to imagine that it had actually been a part of hers. Quick as a bolt of lightning it had all gone wrong. The innocent chatter of a small child had put an end to . . . what? They hadn't really had the chance to find out what, but if how they were together was any indication, Betty figured it could have really been something. Or was she just codding herself? Neither of them had said anything, given any indication of how they felt. Perhaps it was just as well; if she *had* said anything she knew she would feel like a real eejit, seeing as how things turned out.

That had been her state of mind as life had reverted to what now felt like drudgery.

So seeing him today in the shop was shock to the system, a shock that sent a shiver of excitement racing through her, a shock that shook her resolve and had her grinning like a Cheshire cat.

It was just after three o'clock when she saw him standing there among the customers waiting for her to notice him. He was holding Isabella's hand and the two of them were simply grinning at her. At the same time she saw the quick silent glance from Fran serving beside her, a glance charged with interest and suspense the minute she saw him too. Fran was almost holding her breath, waiting to see what would happen next. Within the next two seconds the decision was made.

Trish handed a customer her change and said, "Why don't you take your break now, Betty? It's as good a time as any – we're not busy."

Betty was too flustered to trust herself to answer, but Trish wasn't done yet.

"There won't be another rush today. So if you took the rest of the afternoon off, who'd mind?"

They went into Bewley's and sat under the huge stained-glass window. Betty was embarrassed when the waitress asked what "her daughter" would have. Myles tactfully ignored her embarrassment and ordered for the three of them. Isabella had fruit juice. Myles buttered her scone.

"I had to call in to the shop. I owe you a huge apology –" he began.

"No, you don't, it was only proper that they called, you know . . . no stone unturned and all that."

He looked at her in surprise. She was being very magnanimous but he realised he should have known that she'd be like that. He was grateful, and was about to speak, but she went on, surprising him with her insight.

"I suspect it wasn't your doing, but supposing we just leave it there, eh? Your coffee will be cold."

Her smile was infectious and he was relieved to see that there was no animosity towards him. Isabella pushed her curls back from her forehead and slurped her juice through the long straw.

"Ted went in the washing machine," she informed Betty, "when my bed got all wet." Betty looked across at Myles for an explanation and took her cue from the very slight dipping of his eyebrows. They waited to see what Isabella would say next. She skipped to the present as though the intervening experience hadn't happened.

"I have a new bed now. Ted likes it." Her head nodded in affirmation and she pushed back the curls again.

They strolled back up towards St Stephen's Green, Isabella's favourite place in town, and Betty wondered what exactly they were doing now. Perhaps she shouldn't presume anything more than the apology and just thank him for the coffee and go back to the shop.

He seemed to sense her dilemma, and as if to deflect a negative decision he asked, "Do you think we could do dinner later on? I mean, if you're free of course . . . we could discuss things then."

There was so much to be said. For Betty the matter of Sophie's opposition was still there, still likely to cause problems for Myles, and subsequently for her, if she continued to see him, and she could see no way around that. She watched Isabella calling to the ducks in the pond, watched her pleasure when some of them came her way, and watched her delight dwindle as her enthusiasm sent them paddling away to a safer distance.

I could send *him* away to a safer distance, she thought, I could go home now and neither of us would have the hurt that will come if Sophie gets her way.

But some inner instinct was alert to her cautious reaction.

And you can go home and take your chances every time you get into the bath, it said. The thought shocked her. She thought she had buried that notion a while back. And then she remembered she had only put it on hold. It hadn't gone away, and if she didn't grab life and live it to the fullest that thought might never go away. So what if it didn't work out? Nothing ventured, nothing gained and all that stuff, and didn't someone say it was better to have loved and lost than . . . well, wasn't it?

A shrill scream suddenly jolted her back from her thoughts. She whirled in time to see Isabella freeze in fright as a friendly dog stopped beside her, wagging its tail. Isabella was sobbing hysterically, and Myles immediately whipped her into his arms to soothe her. The dog was on a leash held by its owner who was simply passing by, and was now pouring out abject apologies to them.

Isabella had immediately had a flashback to that other dog that sniffed under the door, smelling her out.

233

She'd heard his sniffing again and the shout of the man who shooed it outside. Then she remembered how the door opened, and he glared in at her.

Myles tried to reassure Isabella that the Labrador was friendly but she was too upset, and clearly there was nothing for it but to take her home. Her crying stopped but her ebullient mood was gone.

Myles postponed the dinner with Betty till the following evening. They met at the Aqua restaurant on Howth pier and immediately discussed the incident in the Green the previous day. Myles said he had never seen Izzy have an adverse reaction to any animal before. In fact, he had been pretty sure she quite liked dogs. He had tried to encourage her to talk about why the dog had frightened her so much, but she turned her head away and not a word passed her lips. It had been in the back of his mind that maybe a puppy might help her recover. But definitely not now.

He also told Betty all about Maeve's commission and the trip to New York. He didn't say why he was in Kerry in the first place: that might be a bit too much information for the moment. Better to take it easy and see how it went. It was a relief to have someone he could talk to about the effects of the kidnapping on Izzy. He was too close to her; difficult to know if he was gauging her right.

He had noticed the huge gap in the 'Ted in the washing machine' story. All that had happened between Ted getting wet and Isabella being in her new bed was completely left out.

The hours flew in. He didn't want it to end, not without making another arrangement to meet. Then he could go home happy.

Myles drove her home and Betty invited him in for coffee, but she didn't ask him to stay. She wasn't *that* sure of herself. It was decades since she'd spent the night with anyone, literally.

Martin's antics with the 'child' in their bed and his immediate departure had seriously shaken her confidence, and it wasn't something she had addressed in the years since. She had wondered from time to time how it would be if she were to meet someone, but straight away she'd tell herself the likelihood of that happening was slim to none. Money, the stuff you need to fund your nights out, the stuff you need to buy clothes to go out *in* to begin with, was always in very short supply. At least money to spend on herself was. Martin's sudden departure had seen to that. After he left she had no idea where he had gone, apart from the assumption that he was in London. But what was a certainty was the fact that nothing was coming in that week or any week to buy food, or pay the rent, to heat the house, or any of the seemingly million and one other things that money was needed for. Her earning capacity was never very good. How many times over the years had she told herself that she should have finished college?

And it went on endlessly like that for years while Buddy and Olive grew up, while she educated them, kept a roof over their heads. What she would do or wear on a date were luxury thoughts she simply hadn't had the means for. It was something she'd never really thought about. And she had begun more or less to think that those times were gone for her. It was all about the younger generation, the nightclubs, the first-time buyers, crèche facilities and the like, wasn't it?

Well now, apparently not.

Betty turned on her side and pulled the duvet closer around her. She had worn some of those nice clothes she bought and then never expected to get the use of. She had felt good, and comfortable in her skin. She had looked well, and she knew it.

She believed meeting Myles Nugent was sheer fate. She hadn't figured on that, and for now she was happy to be meeting him again.

So what if there was a little fly in the ointment?

Chapter 40

Maeve was finally settling down to working in her studio. She had intended to get much more work done by now, but people had been calling throughout the last couple of days, wanting to share their relief and delight that her niece was home safe and well. They meant well and she appreciated their prayers and good wishes, but she figured she had spent too much time away from her work having tea and cake with them in her small kitchen.

Today she had some respite and worked hard clearing all the space she could of the last of other smaller canvases, finishing the wrapping of them, ready for dispatching to their respective new owners. Whenever she could and if distance would allow, she would deliver them in person. There was nothing she liked better than to see the expression on a client's face as they unwrapped one of her works. She liked to be involved in the hanging of them, and then to stand back and view them in their new home.

Clients welcomed this, she found. After all, who would know better what light would display a work to its best advantage than the artist? That amused her because it was now their property and they could hang it wherever they liked, but it was sometimes like severing a part of her, and it became almost a parting ritual at times.

The trauma back in Dublin had left its mark though. She realised the pictures and ideas forming in her head were already constructed of darker colours, a move away from the vivid splashes of colour she had been using in many of her canvases. That wasn't a problem. Artists went through many phases in their artistic lives, and most likely this was just one of them. It was interesting to see how life affected her subject matter. She could never be sure that a painting would end up being what she had set out to make it. If it took on its own life she was well pleased, for if creativity and spontaneity didn't play a hand in her works she felt she had not done her best.

She had discussed the works she intended to do for the New Yorkers with them in detail. Their comments and preferences and the lighting and location had decided what colour and shades she would use, so her change to darker hues for other works was a natural deviation she was free to explore.

She had been on the phone home each day since she came back to Kerry, enquiring how everyone was doing. Myles assured her all was well as could be and she was not to worry. Maeve felt she detected something in his voice, but she knew he was unlikely to burden her willingly. Isabella wanted to know when she could come down as Maeve had promised, and Maeve was troubled by that. Was there an excessive element of pleading in her voice when she asked to come down? Maeve was upset by it and wondered if it had to do with the fact that Isabella might be afraid in her home. That wouldn't be any surprise – wasn't she taken from there? Was it the fact that Maeve was removed from the scene that enabled her to see things more clearly? She decided to mention it to her father when they spoke again. Reading between the lines, Sophie was back to being her difficult self again, her mood swings more obvious now that there was no other upset to distract Myles. But she was going into the boutique daily, happy that sales had shot up since the kidnapping.

How like Sophie.

The huge canvases Maeve had ordered for the walls of the New York hotel had arrived and were propped against one wall, waiting to be christened with masterstrokes which she intended to deliver from the steps of a ladder, the canvases were so high. They were not so wide. Being a triptych they would be hung in a series of three in the massive foyer with a narrow space between them, each one a complete work in itself.

She could see them in her mind's eye hanging on that huge wall, a brilliant focal point of the foyer, and how well they would look, and her name and the date of completion, faint but definitely scrawled in the bottom right-hand corner.

She was about to begin the preparation of the first canvas when she heard a shout outside the studio door.

"Hello! Maeve, you there?"

That was Conor de Lacy's voice for sure. She thought he'd said he'd be in Tralee till tomorrow.

"Come in, it's open," she called.

He pushed the door and strode in, a broad smile on his face, a strong sense of purpose about him. He was surprised to find her at the top of a stepladder, loaded brush in hand.

"I'm disturbing you," he said as if it had only now occurred to him that his presence might.

But that didn't deter him from rambling about and taking in his surroundings. He looked about the studio with an air of surprise. Maeve had often talked about her painting – she frequently mentioned aspects of it, which wasn't surprising because it was obviously her passion – and he had listened politely if slightly amused by her dedication to it, but looking about now it struck him forcibly that apart from it being her passion, this was also a serious business, it had all the makings of it. All the talk he had heard in the local about the great future ahead for Maeve Nugent had to be more than conjecture. This was a future in the making and no doubt about it. Just as well then that he had the invitation he came in with.

From the ladder Maeve watched him taking it all in. She could see that he was taken by surprise, and wondered what was going through his head as he studied his surroundings, for he looked as if he had just stepped into a parallel world. She began to descend the ladder.

"Can I get you . . .?"

"No, no, no, don't come down," he insisted. "I just popped in to ask if you would like to go sailing on Saturday? Some friends of mine will be in Dingle the day after tomorrow and we wondered if you would like to join us for a short cruise down the coast, maybe out around the Blasket, eh? Weather permitting, of course, lunch on board."

If he expected her to be impressed he was a bit disappointed. She hesitated too long for his liking.

Rather than let his invitation fall flat, he hurried on, "They'd love to meet you, they're art lovers themselves – they could be quite interested in a commission."

When he left a few minutes later he had to acknowledge that it hadn't gone swimmingly well, but she had agreed to come. Saturday would go better, he decided. It would be a great day, and it would be the beginning, the real beginning. He swung his blackthorn stick as he walked, feeling better the more he thought about it. After all, why wouldn't anyone want to spend a day on a yacht cruising with him?

He wasn't much of a seafarer himself, not by a long shot. He had lived by the sea all his life, apart from a few years he had spent gallivanting about London when he was in his twenties, but he had never developed a *grá* to go splashing about on the ocean, nor indeed *in* it. His ancestors were not seagoing people, even for leisure, despite the fact that their land was practically surrounded by the ocean.

They were the *landed* gentry, and Conor always kept that in mind; the fact that it was in another time, another era, was irrelevant. Land was his preference, land that should have come to him if his forebears hadn't sold off most of it to cover their debts, leaving him to inherit hardly enough to provide him with sufficient space to stretch his legs on. But he had plans to reverse that situation in the future. After all, the future of the de Lacy line rested with him, he being the only son.

The fact that he had no gainful employment at present would never be a deterrent to the likes of Conor de Lacy. That bother was something for another day.

However, to impress Maeve Nugent he could surely tolerate a few hours afloat on Saturday. He could tolerate more than that. Conor de Lacy had a way of inveigling himself in where he wanted to be. The fact that he practically had to invite himself on board for Saturday didn't bother Conor since to him it was really neither here nor there.

Chapter 41

Betty was glad to be home. Town was crazy, and she hadn't had even a cup of coffee since lunchtime. She left her bags in the hall and went into the kitchen. Shopping was becoming an enjoyable experience since she had developed an eye and decided what styles suited her best. She didn't always feel the need to buy, but she liked to keep up with what was in the shops at the moment.

A ring on the doorbell brought her back out into the hall, stepping around her bags, as she saw an unfamiliar shape through the opaque glass. Her first thought was that whatever it was she wasn't buying, and she didn't need the windows cleaned, and she opened the door with the appropriate response already on her lips.

"Hello, Betty."

Absolute surprise stunned her. For a few moments she was speechless, then her heart sank and decades of hurt flooded back. She had thought she was no longer vulnerable to that. The years peeled away in the blink of an eye and she was back there again standing at the bedroom door, silent with shock and watching it all again as if in slow motion. Shock silenced her again now and she stood holding the door with one hand while her caller stepped towards her and into the hall.

Martin Morris was still very recognisable despite the thinning hair and the extra weight.

"What do you want? What are you doing here?" Her voice shook as she followed him down the hall, almost forgetting to close the hall door in her shock – she gave it a push as she went.

He smiled and went into the kitchen.

"Still the same little house, eh? You never extended," he said as he looked around.

"What was I supposed to extend *with*?" she suddenly demanded, full of anger at him for showing up like this after decades, when all the hard work was done.

"Just commenting," he said. "You've kept it well."

"I don't need your comments. And I don't need you. You're not welcome."

He gave no indication that he had heard her. She tried to steel herself to make it seem as though she wasn't bothered by his presence, but this was weird. She felt like her world was suddenly caught in a time warp, like she had been thrown back into a never-ending nightmare.

"I know this is a surprise, and unexpected," he said.

This was unbelievable. How could he think he could just show up after all this time and behave as though nothing had happened? As though the last twenty-something years hadn't happened. *He knew it was a surprise?* Try bombshell, *atomic* bombshell!

As she stood looking at him, he sat down at the table.

The kettle boiled and her head was immediately turning towards it like it was the only normal thing in the room. Something sent her moving towards it. Do something normal, her head was telling her, and when you turn round he will be gone. He wasn't.

"I wouldn't mind a quick cup, if you're making one," he said, "but I'm can't stay long. I have a taxi outside. He'll wait a few minutes."

Utter disbelief was making her behave like a zombie. She poured two teas, but she didn't sit to the table, and she didn't touch hers.

The turmoil inside her sorted itself into some kind of order. She was aware of wanting to kick off her shoes, but that would give the wrong signal, too much like falling back into old ways, so she put up with the way her feet hurt and blamed him for it. She couldn't help noticing the suit he wore. It was no off-the-rails purchase. And his tie had to be silk. She figured that because Myles had one that was silk which Sophie had given him at some point; then she reproached herself for thinking of Myles and this familiar stranger in the one thought. Martin used to have nice hair, she found herself thinking, it used to curl at the back of his neck when he needed a haircut, and sometimes she had cut it herself with her good scissors, the one she'd kept for dressmaking jobs and the like, because he'd let it get very untidy otherwise. Now she was looking down at a bald spot on the top of his head.

"Won't you at least sit down for a minute?" he asked her.

It struck her as odd, being invited to sit in her own kitchen. She realised she was shaking slightly and with the shock she needed the tea. She put two large spoonfuls of sugar into her cup and stirred. She didn't usually take sugar, but the sweet tea might help. She sat at the other end of the table. But the realisation that hit her next would require more than a cup of tea to sustain her.

With certainty she knew that he wouldn't be here at all if all was well with 'her' over in London, or wherever he had spent the last twenty-something years. Good God, that must be it. A slithery feeling began to creep up the back of her neck. Did he think he was coming back to live *here*? Was that what he was angling towards? Did he think that would be okay with her? She didn't want to ask any questions that might make it seem as though she was interested, and she certainly didn't want to hear what plans he had taking root in his selfish head. She didn't want this to be happening. But there was nothing for it but to face it. The sooner they got it straightened out the better. The longer he stayed sitting there could give him the wrong impression.

"Perhaps I should have let you know I was coming," he remarked calmly. "Then you wouldn't have got such a drop."

Consideration? Was he becoming considerate in his old age? No.

"Jacinta and I have split up."

Why on earth was she not surprised? What other reason could there be to bring him all the way from England to her door?

"I thought I'd come and see you, but I didn't know whether you'd be in or not. You look very well – the years have been good to you, I see."

She didn't answer. She would have choked on a response to his last comment. He talked as if she'd had a grand time of it, as if life here couldn't possibly have been any problem. After all, look at her now. How well she looked. How could it possibly have been hard for her?

She wanted to hit him. She wanted to pick up something and fling it at him. She couldn't say the same for him. He was dressed well enough, but in himself he didn't look all that well. The thinning hair and the weight weren't the only things that aged him. There was a look about him that wasn't a healthy one: he was too pasty-faced and he looked tired, and weary. He must be what, fifty-five, fifty-six now? But he looked more. And Betty knew that Jacinta was ten years younger than her. So she was still only fortyish. Maybe Martin had begun to be too old for her. Maybe all sorts of things, she really didn't care.

He looked around the room, seemingly familiarising himself with it again. He fitted into it alarmingly easily, as though he could just hang his jacket in the hall and he would be home.

"I'm sorry to hear you've split," she said, not knowing what else to say, and not wanting to say anything that might give him the impression that there was any hope here for him. She wanted that clear and unambiguous, and she found herself wondering what had happened with them over there after all this time. But that was the last thing she would have asked, and neither did she really want to know.

So they'd split. That was too much information as far as she was concerned, upsetting information. It took her back to when she'd struggled with the situation he had left her in, and how he had been there for those children and not for hers; she remembered only too well how it had felt. She didn't want to be brought back there again; she had spent a long time and a lot of heartache trying to put it behind her.

"How's Buddy and Olive?"

She had to get him out of here. He was behaving as though he'd only been away for the weekend.

"Grown!"

He couldn't miss the coldness in her voice, her reluctance to actually engage in conversation. She wasn't about to tell him that Olive and Buddy had moved out, wasn't about to let him think there was plenty of space for him to move in. She didn't ask where he was staying, or how long, but she thought it was time he was getting back there. It suddenly struck her that he might have decided to leave London and move back to Dublin, and hoped his presence here now didn't mean that he had already moved back.

She stood up, her mouth feeling suddenly dry at what she was about to say. But he stood also, stopping her words.

"I can't stay now, but I'll call again soon." He turned towards the hall.

Panic gripped her.

"I don't want you calling again soon, or any other time!" she blurted out.

His hand was on the door-latch, and he turned at her words as though what she had just said was nothing more than a load of incomprehensible babble, and stated:

"We're still married, aren't we?"

Chapter 42

Myles carried Izzy shoulder high into her bedroom. She was wrapped in a huge bath towel that went round and round her and pinned her arms to her sides.

"A sack of potatoes," he was singing, "who wants a sack of potatoes?" as he hoisted her higher and she squealed in delight and kicked her feet up and down. It was great to hear her laugh like that again. He leaned forward and dropped her on the bed, and went and took a pair of her favourite Dora pyjamas from the drawer. She had unscrambled herself from the folds of the towel and draped it around her shoulders when he turned back to her.

"Do the 'sack of potatoes' again Grandy, please!" she pleaded, jumping up and down on her bed.

"Pyjamas first," he said, holding out the bottoms.

The jumping stopped and suddenly she sat down on the covers. He threw a quick cautious glance at her face. The laughter had stopped too; she was half-turned away and she had closed down on him again.

"Izzy?"

"Not them," was all she said.

"But these are your favourites, pet."

"No."

He knew immediately there was no way that she was going to put them on. He had become familiar with this reaction since she had been returned to them. It would happen so fast that he could only assume that something had triggered a bad memory.

"What's the matter with these, Izzy?" he asked gently.

She closed her arms about herself as if for protection and didn't answer, and wouldn't look at them.

But he thought he already knew. He studied her carefully while appearing to fold up the bath towel. Then he put it aside and said, "We'll take that pair and put them away. Do you not want to wear them again?"

He got the answer he fully expected. She answered his question with a slight shake of her head, but she said nothing. He took the offending pyjamas and put them out of her sight and sat on the bed and folded the towel about her. Then he took her onto his lap, and hugged her.

"Would you like to tell me about it?" he asked softly.

She snuggled into him, her light-brown curls feeling damp under his chin. But she just shook her head and was quiet, and when he saw there would be no talk he thought it best to distract her. He took a pair of pyjamas with elephants on them, and saw there was no objection to them.

She had been wearing Dora pyjamas the night she was taken. That pair had been taken by forensics for examination.

This incident confirmed his suspicions. He was sure now that some things were triggering memories in her head. Her reactions were beginning to show a pattern, unpredictable though it was, and he felt he was recognising it.

Like the incident in St Stephen's Green with the dog.

But how do you translate snippets of impressions into something that could be seen as a fact when you have no hard evidence? What exactly could he tell Detective Sheehan when he called, that could possibly be any use to him? It was frustrating, upsetting, and sometimes even difficult to deal with.

Sophie had gone out. She'd said something about a dinner and probably being late back, but he made a mental note to discuss it with her as soon as he could, so that they both could be watchful in the hope that between them they might be able to decipher the signals Izzy was giving them.

Myles tucked her into her bed, with Ted beside her, and sat with her till she slept.

Chapter 43

It was late the following day before Myles got to talk with Sophie. She hadn't come home the previous evening. He assumed the following morning that she'd stayed with friends when he saw a text on his mobile asking if he wouldn't mind getting Isabella to school and she would see him later.

Myles didn't mind. He was usually up and about anyway when they were getting ready for their day, and Izzy mostly came to him for whatever she needed help with, as long as it wasn't anything to do with her hair. That was Sophie's department.

Sophie had a lot to do every morning. She never faced the outside world without her full face on and, despite all the tips and practice she'd had while modelling, she still preferred not to rush it. She always watched her appearance critically, constantly on the lookout for the beginnings of the faintest line that might appear, and took painstaking care of her complexion. So far, she believed, it was paying off.

She was home a little earlier that day, and was pleased if still a bit surprised when her daughter greeted her pleasantly.

"I was the best in class today," Isabella told her mother, "and Ruairi had to stand out because he spoiled my drawing."

They had heard much about Ruairi's behaviour before. Isabella frequently had stories to tell about the goings-on in her class, and all the 'bold' things everybody else got up to. She chatted away non-stop sometimes, which made the times when she became quiet much more noticeable and worrying.

When he got the chance Myles told Sophie of the pyjama incident, and that he had got rid of the pair in the drawer. Myles discussed the pattern he figured was emerging, about how he thought Isabella was having flashbacks, triggered by things that somehow related to the time she was missing. So far he hadn't heard anything that could be considered useful and wondered if Sophie had.

A sound behind him made him turn as Eileen coughed and said, "Excuse me. I'm off now, Mr Nugent. The oven will go off in twenty minutes."

Myles got a disconcerted feeling and wondered if she had been standing there for long, and wondered too if Sophie had known she was there. Then he realised that he had his back to the door and because he was standing he could well have blocked Sophie's view of it.

But the unsettled feeling persisted.

He felt there was something in Eileen's demeanour that was more than just being caught eavesdropping, if that was what she was doing. He understood that she might well be concerned as to how Izzy was doing, but asking straight out would be preferable to listening at doors.

He didn't talk to her about 'family things', even one as public as this had been, but he would have certainly answered her had she asked. It crossed his mind then that Sophie might have told her things, and if so she really didn't need to be listening in.

Later, after dinner, he sat to watch the television for a while but found his thoughts were wandering.

Something wasn't right, but he couldn't put a name on what was sitting so badly with him. It occurred to him too that Sophie didn't have very much to say when he was telling her about the pyjama incident. Maybe he was expecting too much of her. As long as all seemed okay, Sophie didn't bother herself greatly. Isabella was home now and she'd be fine – that was the way that her mother looked at things. It always had been.

As soon as he finished talking Sophie was on her mobile phone, making arrangements by the sound of it. She didn't usually say where she was going when she was going out, or who she was going with. He wouldn't have expected her to, but it was only common courtesy when you lived in your father's house and expected him to take care of your child while you were gone, he figured. He sighed, and wished Sophie took more interest in things other than Sophie.

He went to answer a knock on the hall door and was pleased to see Detective Sheehan there. Myles showed him into the sitting room and indicated a seat. The policeman sat clasping his hands between his knees and waited for Sophie to come from the kitchen, where dinner was about ready to be taken up.

When she arrived and sat down, Myles sat opposite Sheehan and asked, "News?"

The detective was pleased to be coming here with something to say, as against all the times he faced these people with nothing to report. His report now wasn't much but since they'd had nothing up to this point it was a welcome break. Where it would or wouldn't lead was something else.

"An abandoned van was found about fifty miles outside Dublin, driven into a ditch and left partially covered by overhanging branches. The local guards checked it out and found it had false plates, and most likely was stolen. They immediately called us."

"*Driven* into a ditch?"

"They examined the scene carefully and it had all the hallmarks of being deliberate," the detective replied.

"What has it got to do with anything?" Sophie asked, surprising them both.

Before this Sophie had allowed her father to lead the way when it came to asking the questions, or seeking information.

"Forensics has gone over it with a fine-tooth comb, so to speak, Mrs Harcourt, and they came up with a hair. We have checked it out and it is one of your daughter's. We believe she was wrapped in a blanket and transported in the back of the van. I have been waiting for the forensic report to come back before I could bring you this news."

They were silent while the pictures of Izzy in the van cut deep impressions into their minds. They wondered how she was put there, who put her there. This was putting meat on what was up to now only their own imaginings, but they knew that if the case was resolved they might well have much more unsettling images to deal with, and they wouldn't be only imaginings, they would be factual.

"Any other evidence?" a clearly troubled Myles asked.

The detective shook his head. "Not yet. We don't know where the van had been – we are making enquiries as to whether anyone saw it – but at least this is a start, and I want to emphasise that the file will be kept open till we have the person or persons responsible."

Myles wondered about that. He was well aware that the police had files that were years old and still not resolved.

Chapter 44

Sophie was dressing with particular care and the effect was stunning. Isabella was downstairs with her grandfather and Sophie knew he would put her to bed while she was out. He had been out himself last night so he would hardly be going out again tonight. She hadn't asked, she just assumed.

She knew he was still seeing that leech but she had learned to keep quiet on the matter. The usual malleability of her father had dissipated a good deal since he had met the leech.

Since she had thrown suspicion on Betty while Isabella was missing, her father was less inclined to be sympathetic towards her. She had lost a lot of his support then but it had been worth it to think of the police arriving at the leech's door and questioning her. Sophie hoped they had given her the third degree.

Torturous interrogation would have been better.

She wanted to prevent Myles from taking her daughter

into that woman's company, she figured she was a bad influence, but she knew her father often saw the leech during the day, and on her days off, and he always took Isabella with him. To stop him doing that would be to shoot herself in the foot, for then who would look after her daughter and collect her from school while she worked?

It certainly would not be Ruairi's mother – she'd had it too with the way their children always seemed to bounce off each other the wrong way. Sophie had sensed it when she'd asked her to pick up Isabella when she was collecting her son. Sophie was fed up hearing about how badly Ruairi behaved in playschool; she was no longer sure he was a good influence.

Eileen appeared to be out of the running as well. Since her trauma, Isabella didn't seem so keen on her either. She never stayed in the kitchen any more when Eileen was there – instead she would go out to Andy in the garden and follow him around for a while. And right now Sophie certainly didn't want to be without her father to look after Isabella while she was out at night.

The shop was going particularly well. Being in the news as they were lately had a positive side to it as well, as it turned out. The publicity brought customers in, people who would not have known her boutique before, but people with the wherewithal to pay her prices. So that was good, and it enabled her to look further afield for designers, and bigger-named designers at that.

But tonight was not for concentrating on work, or Isabella or her father, or even the leech.

Tonight was for herself and Gary and she tingled in anticipation as to how it would end. She viewed herself in the full-length mirror, turning and looking over her shoulder at the deep scoop of the neckline of her dress and how the silky fabric sat smoothly over her hips like a glove. Her heels were the highest she dared wear, making her legs look endless, and smooth and tanned in very sheer stockings. As she picked up her bag, her eye caught the photograph of Peter on her dressing table. For a split second she looked at it, then shrugged slightly and left the room.

Myles was struck by how well she looked when she came into the room downstairs.

"Date?" he asked. He knew it was a rhetorical question – obviously it was a date.

"Do you mind looking after Isabella for me?" she asked sweetly, checking the time.

"Of course not . . ." he began but she was already heading for the door.

A taxi had pulled up outside.

"Mummy, kiss, Mummy!" Isabella ran towards her, and Sophie bent and air-kissed her daughter, not wanting to spoil her lipstick.

"I may be late," she said, then she was gone.

Myles sighed to himself and didn't expect to see her again till the next evening. She wasn't telling him anything about this new man in her life. He was happy about it, thinking it was good for her to be out and about again. She was far too young to do otherwise, and he figured she would say something when she was good and ready. What pleased him most was the change in her. Her dark argumentative mood-swings seemed to be a thing of the past, well, the recent past at least, and he fervently hoped it would continue so.

Yes, life was good these days, thought Sophie. Apart from the fact that business was booming, she put it down to the man who was sitting opposite her now, a man who was tall enough for her to wear her highest heels, good-looking enough to keep her eye from straying, and successful enough to be able to afford her. He focussed on her intently and exclusively, a trait that ensured that he passed with flying colours in her book. His hand reached across the table and covered hers. It was a firm hand that sent a tremor of excitement through her, leaving her in no doubt that they were of the same mind.

It was early the following morning when she woke. The light streamed through the east-facing windows of the bedroom and she stirred lazily and turned to Gary, still sleeping beside her. Last night had been wonderful. It was so long since she had known such release, such utter pleasure. A feeling of relaxed wellbeing filled every fibre of her body, and the urge to be so close to him again began to grow rapidly. Her fingers tangled themselves in his hair and pulled his mouth down to hers. When his arms tightened around her demandingly she felt such a surge of pleasure that a little cry of joy escaped her lips.

When he emerged from the shower, briskly towelling his hair dry and seeing Sophie still stretched out languidly on the bed he asked, "What does one do around here for breakfast? I'm ravenous."

"Coffee," she answered lazily. "That's about it, I'm afraid."

She stirred herself to get him a cup of black coffee while he dressed.

Gary was first to leave for work – he had to contend with the chock-a-block morning traffic – and after he had left she got up and showered, then selected something from the wardrobe to wear to work.

On their way to the apartment last night she wondered if she was doing the right thing. No one but Peter had ever slept in that bed, made love to her in that apartment. It was akin to a sacred place, a place where life had been good, where she had been secure, loved, happy. She was surprised at herself for suggesting it.

But the angst and torment over Peter since he died did not surface and come to the fore as she had feared. When she entered the apartment with Gary following behind, the rooms were strangely neutral, benign, and she turned to him with a new light in her eyes, and this morning she felt she had finally put Peter to rest.

Now she couldn't dilly-dally about any longer no matter how much she felt like it. She'd have preferred to hang about and savour the afterglow of their lovemaking but she just had enough time for a quick coffee after she had dressed and put on her make-up – it was good that she had left some of her clothes here.

It was a lovely morning. The tide across in the bay was full in and the sun glinted on it from a clear blue sky, making it sparkle like a million diamonds. That was how she felt . . . like a million diamonds.

Pulling the door of her apartment shut behind her, she went down the stairs to open the shop.

Chapter 45

Maeve looked into her wardrobe and sighed. She didn't exactly have much in the way of sailing gear, or anything that could pass for it. Sailing was never even on her horizon. She enjoyed boats and the luxury yachts that came into the harbour as much as anyone else but she was happy to enjoy them from the solidness of terra firma. The impressions their sleek lines and tall masts imparted to her artist's eye could turn up sometimes in her abstract works, along with a riot of colour and ripples and reflections, but there her love affair with the sea ended.

So why was she looking in her wardrobe now for something to deck herself out in, so that she would at least blend in a little to a nautical background? She was still wondering about that. But Conor had been so animated about this mini-cruise, and she had been caught off guard. He had taken her hesitation as acceptance. And that was that.

There was a lot she didn't know about Conor de Lacy, now that she came to think of it. She supposed this trip would probably disclose another side to him.

She did have a pair of flat white canvas shoes somewhere, if they didn't have multiple splashes of paint on them, and she had a pair of lightweight trousers that would suit and a T-shirt, and she took out a sweater to put round her shoulders. Dingle harbour was often very calm, but she was well aware that once beyond its protective boundaries it could be a very different situation. She tied her hair back in a ponytail and figured this was as much like a 'sailoress' as she was going to get.

Conor arrived in his car to drive them to the harbour. He knocked on the door of her cottage and pushed it in.

"Maeve! You look stunning. Onassis would have nothing on us, now would he, eh?"

If he were alive it would be no contest, she found herself thinking. She struggled to hide her amusement. Conor was wearing a navy and white horizontally striped crew-neck sweater which made him look five times wider, and a navy baseball cap. Baseball caps and Conor definitely did not go together. It looked like a pimple on top of his head, but by the way he carried himself it was obvious he didn't think so.

"Looks like being a good day for it," she smiled as she seated herself in the car, a black Alfa Romeo GT. She looked at the leather upholstery and the wood trim and figured this car had to be at least thirty years old or more. Probably Conor's father's car, when he was alive.

Why was she being so unkind to him in her thoughts, she asked herself? She had to be careful how she phrased her next comment.

"Lovely leather. I see you are into vintage cars as well as sailing, Conor."

He adjusted the cap. "Man of many interests, that's me. This is part of my inheritance." He tapped the steering wheel. "Couldn't bring myself to let the old girl go."

When they arrived at the dock she followed him to a long sleek cruiser, where he stood briefly at the bottom of the gangplank, lifted his cap and greeted the people on deck. She smiled up also and had a heart-stopping moment when it looked as if they were unsure who exactly he was. But the moment passed so quickly that she thought she must have imagined it, or else it was the blinding bright sunshine making it difficult to see.

She was greeted warmly and introduced to the others on board. There were three other couples, one of about her own age, and the others older. The women were well-tanned and made-up and dripping with gold jewellery. They didn't look like sea water ever got anywhere near them. They didn't look how she had imagined friends of Conor's would look either.

"So you're the artist," one of the men said, putting a champagne flute into her hand. She smiled at him and took the glass. Champagne in the morning? A bit rich for her.

"So how come a looker like you has hooked up with de Lacy?" the man was asking.

She didn't know she *had* "hooked up with de Lacy", but she was relieved to see that they obviously knew Conor more than was at first apparent, even if the "de Lacy" had something of a derogatory tone to it.

"I've known Conor a while, but we're not 'hooked up' or anything."

He gave her a knowing wink, having first looked around to check he was not being observed. "I'm very glad to hear it – can't have these younger fellows snapping up all the best-looking women."

While he had been commandeering her attention, they had cast off and she saw they were moving slowly out beyond the mouth of the harbour. She moved away from him, saying she must mingle with the others as well.

Her glass was almost empty, and she realised she had been swallowing without thinking because her mind was taken up with the thought that she was going to have to keep her distance from this insistent fellow guest.

Conor was sitting on the sun deck and called her up, but the higher she went the more unsteady she felt. She smiled to camouflage her uneasiness and gripped the handrail tighter. The tide was turning ahead of a westerly breeze, and the vessel rose and sank into the dips and hollows of the sea, as they made their way west towards the Blasket Sound.

The waters were even more choppy as they approached the open Atlantic Ocean and Maeve was finding it increasingly difficult to ignore the disturbance in her stomach. It was her admirer who brought attention to the white pallor of her face.

"Maybe you should go downstairs and lie down?" he suggested.

Not very likely, Maeve thought, and anyway, down by the throbbing of the engines was the last place she wanted to be. Conor was looking at her as though she was spoiling his great plan, but he did show concern for her.

"Perhaps you need the air up here? Cabins can be so stuffy if you're not feeling well."

He went and fetched her some water, but there was no getting rid of her seasickness. By the time they rounded the head south of Dunquin she had begun to be sick.

"Conor, I have to get off this boat," she whispered, her voice so weak that he had to lean close to hear her.

But her hosts could see that for themselves and guided the yacht north and headed for the little pier at Dunquin.

She didn't want Conor to leave the boat with her. She preferred to be on her own, and figured if she could get a taxi or a lift back to Dingle she would be fine.

She insisted he stay, while their hosts insisted she couldn't go alone. She wondered vaguely if they were keen to be rid of him. It took her no time at all to find her land legs again once she was on terra firma, but there she was again, being unkind to him once more now that she was back on solid ground.

But at least he was able to locate them a lift back to Dingle, while she sat in a small café fortifying herself with a cup of tea and homemade cake. It had been a strange morning. The atmosphere with the others on board was odd, distant somehow, despite Conor's genial manner. Apart from a brief moment when they asked her what she painted, they didn't appear to have much interest in the subject.

Conversation in the car on the drive back to Dingle was minimal. The driver did his best to be amiable, curiosity about life aboard a yacht and the lifestyle of 'yachties' made him chat away with many questions.

Conor did his best to respond but his thoughts were elsewhere. It had gone all wrong and he was dead annoyed. Those on board didn't play their part. Granted it was a part they didn't know they had, but he had been certain that once they were all on board and a glass or two was downed then it all would go brilliantly well, they would have a great day, and the thrill of cruising out around the seaward side of the Blasket Islands would be the highlight of the day. He was aware they were cool with him, but they were fine with Maeve, even though he could see they didn't really 'click'. Truth be told, they had no interest in art, but he'd had to tell Maeve something.

And he hadn't banked on her not having sea legs, and being sick like that. Now she was very quiet, her head back against the headrest and her eyes closed. His efforts to impress his way into her life had gone all wrong and he felt further back than where he had begun.

He answered the driver as pleasantly as he could, smiling and seeming relaxed while expertly concealing his anger and his frustration at having his plans thwarted, but he was very mad about it, and it had to be someone's fault.

Chapter 46

Quigley knew it was time to leave his friends behind in McCaffrey's and head home. He had work to do. Time of day or night made no difference to him when he was possessed of the urge to create and there was nowhere better he liked to be than sitting with pen and paper, or in front of his laptop, whichever was to hand. He had spent a few hours working this morning – that was Quigley's way – he just worked when the juices were flowing and for as long as they flowed, and would go back to it whenever it called. Quigley always figured his poetry 'called' and when it did he answered.

Anyway he was out of cash, and that meant it was more than time for him to leave, so he finished off his drink and figured it wouldn't be too much longer before the rest of the crowd left also. But they were not going his way, so it was pointless hanging on for a lift.

If Pat Keegan had been there he would have offered to leave with him, but they all knew that he liked to walk and think, so when he bid them goodnight and set off it was just the norm.

He walked up Green Street and turned left into Goat Street. There was no one around and the air was balmy with light breezes, a pleasant night for a walk. His long legs were glad of the exercise in the cool night air after the heat of the pub, and in no time at all he was striding along Upper Main Street, lost in creative thought. He paid no heed to the traffic that passed him by. There wasn't much anyway, just the occasional car. It would be unusual to meet a fellow walker for hardly anyone walked into or out of town any more, not at this time of night. His house was just outside the town and for him this was only a stroll, a walk he could do in his sleep and would take no more than six or seven minutes.

He was deep in thought and at first wasn't aware of the fact that there was a car behind him. He moved over onto the grass verge to let it pass even though he wasn't obstructing it and the rest of the road was empty, but the car didn't overtake him. Curious now, he turned and looked back just in time to see the car veer left towards him. For a split second of disbelief he watched as it came directly at him, then he leapt out of its way. His feet slipped on the damp dewy grass and he came down heavily on his left side. The searing pain that shot through his arm took the breath from his body, and the weight of his fall caused him to slide down the other side of the verge, where it sloped into a ditch. He heard the car speed away. He lost consciousness then with the pain, and was very cold when he came to. Pain shot in waves through him and he was beginning to find it difficult to know where it was coming from. Trying to shake the urge to slip into a sleep, he reached with his free hand for his mobile phone. He'd had it in his breast pocket when walking along the road and he patted the pocket now with his free hand. Panic gripped him when he touched the flat empty area of his pocket. He tried his other pockets, knowing even as he did so that his phone wasn't there and that it had fallen out as he fell. It had to be somewhere close, and he felt around the slope as much as he could, hoping his hand would land on it in the dark, but he didn't feel the phone and couldn't see in the dark. If it had fallen into the water at the bottom of the ditch he knew it was finished.

With difficulty he turned onto his back and attempted to sit up. The ditch couldn't be that deep – he should be able to see the road, get help, but he found that he was held fast. He had crashed through the bushes that grew from the ditch and his hair was entangled with brambles that held him securely.

With his free hand he tried to disentangle his long hair from the dense brambles, but they had sharp thorns and he realised his hand was badly scratched and bleeding and that his efforts were only making matters worse. Pain caused him to slip in and out of consciousness, and he had no idea of how long he was lying there, but he figured he was there a while because of the way he was tiring.

In his more conscious moments he tried to consider the situation he was in, and he had the lucidity to realise it was anything but good. Shouts for help went unanswered and he began to see that getting out of here might take a while. It was already late and the number of people passing along the road at this hour was zilch; certainly none would be walking, and drivers would not see him where he was.

Water from the bottom of the ditch was seeping through his clothes. His shoes were filled with it; his feet were freezing and his trousers were already very wet. Somewhere in his pain-riddled mind it occurred to him that if he was facing the other way he might be able to see what he was doing to free his hair, but an attempt to turn his body so that he was on his knees instead of his back failed when he slithered in the wet ditch and came down again on his arm.

The ringing of his phone forced its way through his pain and he stirred, trying to figure out where the sound was in relation to him. It was close; in the silence of the night it sounded so shrill, and so close. Possibly up by the side of the road, but he couldn't see it, and he couldn't reach it.

It stopped.

He sank back against the ditch, back into the pain-filled blackness. At some point he regained consciousness and made a super-determined effort to help himself. Repeatedly he dug his toes into the side of the slope till he could gain some kind of grip – he needed to be sure he had enough of a foothold to take his weight. Then he painfully forced himself inch by inch upwards on the slope. Held by his hair, his body was rotating on the slope like the hands on a clock going backwards. His feet were now on the grass verge, his head held firmly by the brambles halfway down the ditch. But the effort was too much. He was dragging his injured arm and pain threatened to swallow him every second, and finally the blackness closed in on him again.

Chapter 47

Maeve walked down the long corridor in Kerry General Hospital in Tralee town and looked into the ward she had been told Quigley was in. She was met by half a dozen male faces turned expectantly towards her. But she didn't see Quigley. Assuming they must have moved him elsewhere, she turned to try the next room.

"Maeve," she heard and looked back. A patient in a bed by the window lifted a hand and gave her a little wave. She looked at the fellow and figured he was mistaking her for one of his visitors. It was a coincidence that he had called her name. She turned again to go, but when he called her again more insistently the familiar voice stopped her and she looked hard at him. He was so badly cut about the face that it would be hard for anyone to recognise him. Her heart gave a lurch with shock. Good God, was that Quigley?

She came across to his bed, her eyes wide in horror at the multiple lacerations she saw. They were many and most of them small, but some looked sore and slightly infected.

"Quigley, my God, what happened to you? They said you had a broken arm!"

Then she noticed the plaster cast encasing his left arm.

And then she noticed the haircut.

"Your hair! What happened to your hair?" she gasped when she realised it wasn't tied at the back of his neck. His thick long dark hair was reduced to a shorter cut, completely changing his appearance.

He gave a rueful little laugh. The glossy curtain he'd used to hide behind for so many years was indeed gone. She sat beside the bed and leaned forward, taking hold of his right hand, then noticing how it too was covered in small lacerations.

"Quigley, what in God's name happened to you?"

It was nice, her holding his hand, and he couldn't help thinking what it had taken to achieve that. It even felt worth it.

"Accident on the way home from McCaffrey's," he said, enjoying the concern in her eyes, "and no, it wasn't the drink, I only had two. Some eejit in a car couldn't drive straight. I jumped onto the verge so he would miss me, then I slipped on the wet grass and fell through the brambles into the ditch. Broke my arm."

She couldn't get over the change the haircut made. She could have sworn she would know Quigley McGurk anywhere – he was unmistakeable with that thick long hair which was sometimes tied back, more often worn loose. The face she looked at now was a face she expected to be more familiar with, and she realised just how much it had been hidden. His hair now framed a good strong-featured face rather than hiding it.

"My hair was so tangled in the thorns it had to be cut to free me," he told her.

"Pat said you were in the ditch all night," she said. "He phoned me this morning."

"Don't remember much of it," he replied, "but what I do remember seemed like forever. And the bloody mobile fell out of my pocket as I fell and I could hear the damn thing ring, but I couldn't reach it. It was so frustrating."

"And your arm?"

"Broken, two places, I'll be like this for weeks. Thank God it wasn't my right one. I'd be *rightly* banjaxed then, wouldn't I?"

At least he had a sense of humour about it. She couldn't get over how much he was talking. Shock and trauma might do that, she thought, but it was nice, and she hoped he didn't revert to his usual silence when he recovered.

"How did you get rescued then?"

"Someone cycling to work, they said. I had managed to twist my body upside-down and my feet were visible from the road. I don't know who, but the police should know. I'll find out later so I can thank them."

"And the car – did you see who was driving it? He could have killed you!"

Ah yes, the car, the way it had tailed him for a while. He realised now that it had actually been tailing him, even briefly – at least it had slowed down behind him when there was absolutely no need. The road was empty, the driver had the whole place in which to overtake. But he was playing games, dangerous games that could have had a worse outcome. And was it a game or did he really mean to mow him down? Quigley had no way of knowing. Nor had he any way of knowing if he had said anything about the incident before he regained full consciousness. He could have talked under the anaesthetic. People did, he knew that.

"It was dark," he said, "it happened so fast . . ."

"You should tell the police, Quigley, you can't just let them think you were drunk. Look what he did to you."

He was nodding when he realised that this was one of those times when he would have used his long locks to hide behind and maybe even to prevent having to give an answer. Of course he had recognised the car; he hadn't seen it on the road often, but he had recognised it, and what he was going to do about it he had yet to decide.

"I'll be here for a few days, they tell me – by then I might remember it all more clearly."

She didn't press him. If he wouldn't report it there was nothing she could do. But she was curious because she felt he was reluctant rather than needing time to remember. "Tell me how your work is coming on," he said, changing the subject.

She told him about the huge canvases she had begun work on, and her ideas for the subject itself, and described the hotel in New York and where they would hang, and how she envisaged them looking there. She insisted he come to the studio and see them for himself as soon as he was able.

For some reason she made no mention of the disastrous morning she'd had on board that yacht with Conor. Something stopped her. But she noticed he was getting sleepy. The effects of the anaesthetic hadn't completely worn off, and he looked like he was about to just drop off. And she had the drive back to Dingle to do. She released his hand and stood up to go, and he stirred.

"I'll come in again, if you think you could stand another visit," she smiled, and then she bent down and kissed a spot between scratches on his cheek. He lay back on his pillows, his eyes already closing, a little smile stretching a cut lip.

Yes, it was definitely worth it.

Chapter 48

The atmosphere in Betty's small kitchen was tense, and she wasn't sure whether or not she had done the right thing. They sat around the table, laid with a dinner set which was the remains of what had been a wedding present – the tureens were long gone – and tried to come to terms with what she had just told them.

Olive she wasn't too worried about – she felt she could correctly gauge her reaction, or close to it, but Buddy was harder to read. He always had been. He was the man of the family from the time he was not much more than a baby himself, and he had grown up with very little to say when it came to anything that involved the emotions or any matters along those lines. He kept his own counsel, and left the women to do the talking. Not necessarily to do the sorting, because some things couldn't be sorted – he knew that, having learned it at a very young age – but to do the talking, and ultimately they all just carried on.

There was much that had no answer, no resolution, you just got on with it. You could be angry or hurt, or even guilt-ridden over something you had no hand, act or part in, but you still just had to get on with it. 'What ifs' were pointless, a waste of time and energy, and only served to prevent you from giving the present your best. But it didn't stop you wondering, from time to time. And this was one of those times.

"Buddy, you're not saying very much," Betty remarked quietly, thinking how silly it was to be stating the obvious.

He put his knife and fork down. "Do we know what he wants?" The question gave away none of what he was thinking. He had no recollection of his father. A photograph which was on the sitting-room wall when he was a child was the only memory he had. A picture that was taken in the back garden on a sunny day, when he held a small hand up to shade his eyes from the sun, standing beside a man seated on a kitchen chair with a toddler on his lap. His father, seated and holding his sister. Thanks to that photograph, Buddy always imagined that the days with his father were sunny, but he came to realise they couldn't have been, or he would have stayed. All that remained was the photograph. A photograph taken at a time before the man himself had time to make a lasting impression on him. His absence was what had made that impression.

All through Buddy's life he had been aware of that absence. How much difference would his father's presence have made? What effect would it have had on his children if he had been there for them, how different would they have been as people? How different would it have been to have had a normal family, what did he miss as a result and why did it still bother him so much?

"What worries me," Olive was saying, "is why he said he'll be back? We don't even know him. He's a stranger."

"But he is our father." Buddy's voice was flat, devoid of the slightest hint of his feelings.

Betty was becoming more concerned as to how her grown son would handle this situation.

"He was never a father to us, not after he left, not for a minute," said Olive. "And how much could we have known him anyway? We were only babies, for God's sake!"

Betty looked across at her daughter. She seemed to have her feelings sorted already, but she hadn't stood here in this kitchen and looked at her father sitting there as if he had never left. As if the intervening years were of no consequence. As if they were all waiting for him to return so they could pick up where they had left off. Betty began to see where Buddy's silence was leading him.

"What do *you* want, Mam?" Olive asked. "You're his wife – sorry, I don't mean that to sound bad, I'm sure it cuts, but that seemed to be the one thing he hooked onto while he was here."

Betty pushed her vegetables about her plate. None of them was eating much despite the hours she had spent working it, but then she had known this would probably kill their appetites stone dead.

What she wanted was to be free of the responsibility of it all. She was afraid it might depend on her reaction whether or not their father played an inclusive role in their lives. It shouldn't be that way, but she was afraid it might. And she could end up being blamed if he was excluded. That was human nature for you. What she didn't know was what *they* wanted. They had yet to meet him. They could very well want him in their lives. And that would put him up to a certain point back in hers. And she couldn't tell right now how she would cope with that.

She had decided to wait till they were both here to tell them their father was back in Dublin and had called on her, and said he would call again, but she wasn't convinced she was going about it the best way.

They had arrived in such high spirits earlier on. She had given them no inkling what this was about and it struck her forcibly as she spoke that they were expecting something completely different. She watched the excited expectation vanish from their faces as her words sank in.

She knew, and figured they did too, that no matter which way they went this was certainly going to have an effect on their lives, a different consequence on top of how they had been affected so far, and she knew they would be affected by how she felt also. Perhaps loyalty to her would cause them to make a wrong decision for themselves. She feared that. No matter which way she went, it would have consequences for them, and there was nothing she could do about that.

"Did he ask about us?" Buddy wanted to know.

"He asked how you both were," she replied, the short answer she had given him coming back sharply to mind.

"And what about Myles?" Buddy asked suddenly, "does he know about this?"

She shook her head. "This is not really about Myles," she said gently. "For me this is about what you as my children want, and how it can be balanced with what I as your mother, want."

Silence followed while they thought about what she had said. But what would be the best outcome for everybody, and was it possible to find it?

"So why did they split?" Olive wanted to know. "Has he run out again?"

"I didn't ask."

Betty was struck by her daughter's bitterness. This visit was bringing out facets of her children's character she hadn't seen before, and it upset her to see how they hurt.

"There's something else we haven't mentioned," Betty said.

They looked at her warily. Didn't they have enough going on at the moment? Neither of them asked, they just sat and waited to be told, almost feeling it would be worse if they invited it on themselves.

"There are his children in England. He has two, if you remember, two girls." It was hard to get the words out, even after all this time.

Neither Olive nor Buddy spoke.

"They'd be your stepsisters."

There was no noticeable reaction, and it was impossible to gauge their feelings. She let the fact sink in.

"Why would they want to know us?" Olive asked. "If he has left them to come back here, I don't imagine they would exactly be delighted to know us."

Betty felt she had a point. Buddy simply nodded but stayed quiet.

"I was just mentioning it because no matter how anyone feels about all of this they are still relations, family.

And none of this is their doing either, no more than it is any of your doing."

"They wanting to know us, or vice versa, is probably something that will take some time to come about," Buddy surprised them by saying. "I think this is all too raw for anyone to make a move along those lines. You don't know how anyone will feel with time. Then their children might come looking for their Irish relations."

"Let sleeping dogs lie?" Olive asked.

Buddy just shrugged, but his thoughts had a diffusing effect on the situation. He was probably right, there was perhaps no big rush to make decisions now, but Betty knew the situation wasn't going to go away.

No matter what else, Martin was still their father, and she could well understand the draw he would be to them. Decades had passed since he left, but the tie was still there. Olive's bitterness was proof of it, and Betty realised the truth in the saying '*Blood is thicker than water*'.

Chapter 49

Sophie sat at her dressing table, putting the finishing touches to her make-up. The conversation she'd just had with her father had annoyed her. She had known it would arise, more likely sooner rather than later, because she was out so much these nights. Isabella wouldn't stay with anyone when a baby-sitter was needed; she would only settle if her grandy or Sophie minded her. Sophie had seen it would become a problem.

The problem, as Myles saw it, was that Sophie didn't ask in advance if he was going to be there. She just assumed he would be, and made her arrangements as she wanted. They needed to discuss it and come to some arrangement between them.

It crossed Sophie's mind that if her new romance was messing up his arrangements with the leech, well, so much the better. He should get sense and find someone more appropriate, as she had. But she was happy, and she supposed she shouldn't be too hard on him. It would fizzle out. Of course it would.

Gary knew Sophie had a daughter, but he hadn't met Isabella yet. That was okay, because he had told her that he had two girls, and she hadn't met them either. She didn't like to think about that. She didn't want to think of having to share him with anyone, not yet anyway. She put the idea out of her head that he'd been married. It didn't suit her to think that he had loved someone else, loved her enough to actually marry her. She was well aware that practically everyone had a past these days, it was par for the course, but when they were together there was definitely only the two of them. Each time they met she relaxed into his company with complete ease, savouring every minute, and was very aware that he felt the same. He took her so completely out of herself that she felt she was capable of anything with him beside her.

She would introduce Gary to her father of course, and he would then introduce her to his daughters, but not yet – they were still greedy about sharing their time now. They were planning a break away together soon, and Gary thought perhaps after that would be time enough.

She sprayed herself with perfume and surveyed her reflection in the mirror, happy at what she saw. Gary couldn't resist her, his eyes told her that every time they met, and she wallowed in the admiration. When he wasn't with her he was on the phone, impatient for their next date, and they always stayed over in her apartment afterwards. It was a perfect arrangement, and she did not want it disturbed.

So her father saying they needed to check with each other as to when he would be available to baby-sit Isabella was a pain. Gary wasn't as available with his time as she was – he had to make arrangements to see his daughters, so Sophie preferred to fall in with him.

When she came downstairs Isabella and Myles were sitting on the sofa, Isabella in her pyjamas ready for bed and curled up against him.

"Can we talk about this when I get home?" she asked, hoping she could defer it again till another time.

"You'll be back later?" He sounded surprised.

No, of course she wouldn't be back later, she would see him tomorrow evening, but she didn't say that. She gave Isabella her kiss and went out to her taxi.

All thoughts of responsibilities or home life vanished at the sight of Gary Marchant waiting for her at the bar. His broad physique quickened her pulse as he stood to greet her. It always did. His kiss lingered, his smile was subtle and intense as he helped her off with her jacket.

"You look stunning as ever," he said and the rich quality of his deep voice sent pleasure coursing through her. They moved into the restaurant later and continued deep in conversation, engrossed in each other, oblivious of all around them.

In her apartment later they lay in each other's arms, their desires finally satisfied for now.

Myles put the phone down. A frown furrowed his brow. Something was troubling Betty, he could feel it down the line, but she insisted everything was fine. It was in her voice: it had lost its usual lightness, its tendency to make a joke, its readiness to laugh. It wasn't like her to hold back from him, but he was very sure she was doing that now. Perhaps it was family stuff. Her son or daughter's problems maybe, and he understood she would be very reluctant to discuss that, if that was it. It was how he would be with Sophie's problems: he would tend to keep them to himself.

But Sophie was a changed woman lately since she had met this new man. He was happy for her, and he hoped it would all work out. This guy seemed to be good for her. There were none of the pendulum moods, or the covert drinking, or the preoccupation she'd suffered since Peter was killed.

Maeve and Bradley were both convinced that she had been using something, particularly at the time of the kidnapping, but that was gone now. Sophie was on a permanent high and, unlikely though it was, he fervently hoped it stayed that way. He didn't expect her home tonight. When she had a date it was usually an overnight, so he knew she wouldn't be in later. He put Sophie out of his mind as Betty's subdued form came back into his head.

It wasn't like her to be down.

He turned out the downstairs lights and went upstairs and into the bathroom. Just as he turned on the tap a shrill scream cut the night silence. Isabella's cries rang out from her room and sent him running towards her. He knew she was dreaming. It wasn't the first time she had woken with a bad dream since she was missing, but they seemed to be getting worse. He pushed wide the door to see her sitting bolt upright in her bed, terrified and sobbing. He turned on her Mickey Mouse bedside light and grabbed her in his arms and tried to soothe her but in her dream and terror she struggled against him.

"Izzy! Isabella, it's okay, it's okay, pet."

The sobbing subsided, but seeing that big shape at the dark doorway again telling her he would get the dog if she didn't stay quiet was still very real, so real that she was afraid to turn around, he could still be there if she looked. And she had heard the dog barking. She knew he was only outside.

Grandy soothed her, telling her it was all gone now, she was safe, he would mind her. But you didn't know when that big shape would come again.

Myles stayed with her till she slept, and watched as her little chest rose and fell with large silent sobs in her sleep.

He had to do something. He didn't feel she was getting any better. As time passed things were coming out, things he was sure were connected to her experience, and the nightmares were the worst. No matter how gently he tried to coax her, she refused to talk about what frightened her, or what the dreams were about. The shake of her head was barely perceptible, and no words passed her lips.

Chapter 50

The following evening Myles decided to call around to see Betty. Her voice on the phone last night was laden with something that had bothered him all day, and he felt he might be of some help if he was to call on her for a visit. Perhaps she would prefer that to talking on the phone.

When he had made sure Isabella was fast asleep he took up his car keys, and reminded Sophie to keep a listen out for her, just in case.

He was glad to be out of the house. Trying to discuss things with his daughter when she was pulling the other way was futile. Sophie was not taking kindly to having to arrange in advance with him for her dates. Her father was treating her like a child, she complained, and she wasn't pleased. She was less pleased when he told her of Isabella's nightmare last night.

"I thought she was doing fine these days," she had said, as if he was trying to manufacture problems simply to annoy her.

"She's anything but," he'd replied. "Haven't you noticed how she hangs about so close to you or me when we are home? Don't you see the difference in how she follows you around? She never used to do that. She used to be so absorbed with the games she'd imagine with Ted and her toys that she didn't pay any attention to where you or I were. You may not have noticed, but that has all changed now and clearly she is still troubled."

She ignored the remark that insinuated Isabella had previously preferred to keep clear of her mother. "That's only natural after what happened," she sniffed. "Give it time, it will wear off."

Why on earth did he keep looking for problems, she wondered? He was being overprotective, and just what were they actually supposed to do when Isabella flatly refused to speak of it?

"I'd like to think it will," Myles said, "but at the moment it's getting worse rather than better. That dream she had last night – she woke absolutely terrified – you haven't seen it, you've been out . . ."

She turned a defensive look on him, cutting his sentence short.

"I know it's pure coincidence," he agreed quickly, "but that's just how it happens to be. If you saw how afraid she is . . ."

He left the sentence unfinished and Sophie's flicker of a glance saw the worried look in his eyes. Her father wasn't given to exaggerating, that much she knew was true.

"What do you suppose we should do?"

Myles had to confess he didn't know, but they agreed they were going to have to come up with something. Someone somewhere must be able to help.

Now he switched his concentration back to which turn was Betty's. He indicated and turned his car left into her narrow road, turning his thoughts away from home issues. He was glad he had come. Betty always lightened his heart.

Her road was lined with parked cars. Front gardens here were built with only a small gate for pedestrian access. These houses and narrow roads were built when not many people had cars, were doing well if they had one bicycle in the family, and so the roads were never expected to have to cope with two or more cars in almost every family. Betty's home was up ahead on the left-hand side and there was already one of the neighbour's car parked in the space outside it and the nearest available space was on the other side a few houses down.

Myles backed into it, taking care not to block anyone else's gate and switched off his engine. He reached over and picked up his jacket and then he saw the man at Betty's door. He didn't look like he was canvassing for anything; he carried no bag or clipboard. He was slightly heavy-set, and well dressed from what Myles could see from the car.

The door opened and, after what appeared to be a brief greeting, he stepped inside. Myles didn't actually see Betty, but he decided to hold on. He wouldn't go to the door till the caller was gone. He didn't want to interrupt; he assumed the man would only be there a short while. He didn't mind waiting.

Forty minutes later he was still waiting and had begun to feel conspicuous sitting there in the car. People didn't know him around here, and he had become very uneasy with the situation. He turned on the engine, ready to move off, and gave one final glance at the door.

Still closed.

He put on his indicator and pulled away from the kerb with a deep uneasy feeling in his stomach. When he put that together with how Betty sounded on the phone last night, he didn't like what was rummaging around in the back of his head. What was she not telling him?

He pushed those thoughts away, and reminded himself how good they had been together since he came home from the New York trip. Search as he might, there was no indication there that he could find which would tell him that there could be someone else.

He didn't believe Betty was like that. She was straight with him. That was what he liked so much about her from the start, the honest way they interacted with each other. She couldn't have been like that if she wasn't up-front with him.

He drove out of her estate without thinking where he was going, as if he was on automatic pilot. The light-heartedness was gone, the upbeat feeling that he could be some help to her by turning up here this evening had dissipated in a wash of doubts, and he was annoyed at himself for taking so much for granted.

Sophie's words were among the first to push their way to the front of his consciousness.

"You'll never know where you are with someone like her. Her sort are users, believe you me, and you clearly can't see your hand in front of your face with her around!"

How he had silenced her then. He wouldn't listen, she said. She was right about that: he refused to listen to her biased conjecture. But Sophie had also been vociferous to the police when she put them onto Betty about the kidnapping and she had been so adamant then too. And she had been proved so wrong in that instance. So why were her damning words so loud in his head now?

He knew the answer to that as certainly as he knew his own name. He loved Betty Morris. And he couldn't bear not to have her return his feelings. And he couldn't bear to think of someone else visiting her either.

But some other man was.

Chapter 51

It was a fine bright morning and Maeve had been working away for hours now. Her commission was coming along nicely, if slower than she'd planned, but then they were the biggest canvases she had worked on so far, so it was bound to be different. She came back into her kitchen and put the kettle on. Her mind was ranging over things that had happened in the past number of days.

There was Quigley's accident for a start, if it was an accident. He hadn't reported it to the police, and she wondered at that, but he was out of the hospital, and that was good.

According to himself, the shake-up had triggered great inspiration for him, so maybe it wasn't all bad; good had to come out of it somehow, he said.

And his comments in turn had given her an idea, if Quigley would go along with it. Before that there was that disastrous cruise with Conor and his friends. She hadn't seen him since. Neither had she come across any of them in the town as she thought she might. She thought he might have called in just to see how she was, but perhaps she had embarrassed him too much in front of his friends at having brought such a landlubber on board, and at having to leave the boat at Dunquin.

She decided after having a quick lunch that she would call in to Pat Keegan's house to see Quigley on her way into Dingle. She had to go anyway – she was out of titanium white.

"Think of the Devil," she said as she looked out the window.

Conor de Lacy was coming up her path.

"It's open," she called as he approached.

He stepped into the room and greeted her warmly. He gripped her shoulders and kissed her cheek, and looked around the room as was his way, as though he was claiming possession of all he surveyed. His sudden kiss surprised her. Conor was proving to be full of surprises when he liked. She hoped he wasn't here with another daft sailing idea, or the like.

"You look great, Maeve. I'm glad to see you recovered well."

"I'm fine, Conor." She had been since her feet touched solid ground again, as he well knew.

He noticed her jacket. "Have I called at a bad time? Are you coming or going?"

"Just going, I need paint." She put her purse into her shoulder bag. "What do you make of what happened to Quigley?"

The accident last weekend was still a talking point. If it had been the accident on its own it still would have caused a lot of talk. Quigley McGurk was not known for falling home drunk, so it had to have been a pure accident. But the hair business and the way it had trapped him and magnified his ordeal had caught the imagination of everyone. And then Quigley being transformed as he was with both the cast on his arm and the haircut, especially the haircut, had those who knew him very animated about him. He was coming in for a great ribbing over the haircut, but the surprising thing was he was taking it all in his stride.

People were asking Pat Keegan who his 'new' lodger was, and Quigley was having his leg pulled unmercifully about how bad the poetry business must be if he had to resort to selling his hair to make a few bob.

Conor took his time answering, and Maeve got the impression, just for a second, that he was searching for an appropriate response.

"Terrible thing, terrible thing," Conor said, "and his hair gone too, terrible."

She picked up her bag. There was no hanging about today with cups of tea or the like. Her paintings had been started and she had things to do.

"Actually I think it quite suits him," she offered. "Makes such a difference, don't you think?"

No, he damn well didn't think, and he hadn't expected that reaction either. But it got worse.

"I think he should have cut it off ages ago. It has made such a change to his appearance and to his personality too."

She was sounding far too animated for Conor's liking. Already The Rake was ruining his day. So what if he was a rake with a new haircut? That was one thing, no big deal; he was aware that women weren't superficial enough to be that impressed with new haircuts for their own sake, but The Rake with a new appearance *and* a new personality to match was just too much! It was a situation that Maeve Nugent seemed to find appealing so it was just utterly sickening altogether.

"I had better let you get on with your day, Maeve." Conor turned and opened the cottage door. He had to think this one through.

Maeve saw his car outside on the road, facing towards Dingle. If he was going in she could leave her own car, as finding parking in the town could be tricky, and getting a lift or a taxi back would be no problem.

"You headed into the town?" she asked offhandedly, rather hoping he was. "Could you drop me at Pat Keegan's, by any chance?"

Pat Keegan's! He knew well it wasn't Pat she was going to see. As if he was actually going to drive her to see that dammed phoenix, and then drive away and leave them together. Not bloody likely.

Anyway he had no wish to be in the vicinity of Quigley McGurk, even if it was only to the gate. He hadn't been into the hospital to see him. That was the last place he'd have wanted to go. Of course he had heard what happened, who hadn't? Stupid man, imagine not being able to walk home without ending up in a ditch. There was talk about as to how it happened, of course there was, and as far as he could gather The Rake's account so far didn't throw any light on who the driver was that night. That was good.

When Conor heard the talk his response was a vague, 'Could've been anyone.'

"Ah, no. Just came from the town," he answered Maeve now, a little too quickly. "Thought I'd drop in as

I was passing, have to get on back to the house, expecting someone, you know."

His smile was thin, but determined. Still, she thought it odd that his car was facing the wrong way, if he was heading home.

He bade her farewell, and she had to wait before she could take her own car out while he turned his long old-fashioned car, with no power steering, on the narrow country road outside her cottage.

When she reached Pat's house he told her that Quigley was ensconced in his room working, and had been for the last couple of hours, or thereabouts. He offered her coffee while he shouted upstairs for Quigley.

"Usually I wouldn't interrupt him, nor he me when work grabs us, but I'm sure he'll be glad to see you," Pat said quite matter of factly as he poured the coffee.

When Quigley appeared Pat declared he would "leave them to it and get a bit done himself", and took himself and his mug of coffee across to his studio.

"How's the arm?" Maeve asked when Quigley came into the kitchen. He looked a lot better than the last time she had seen him. Most of the cuts to his face and hands were nicely healed up, just a little of the redness of the longest ones still visible.

He lifted the cast away from his body slightly and said for the umpteenth time, "I'm glad it's not my right one, I wouldn't even have been able to shave, but I'm managing, thanks. I'm glad you called in."

"Something I can do for you?" was her first thought.

"It's just nice to see you." He qualified his spontaneous comment with, "Well, I haven't been out by your cottage since I got out of the hospital."

Oh. She didn't know what she had expected him to come out with, but that wasn't quite it.

"How is the work going?" he asked as he checked a movement of his head. He had yet to lose the habit of flicking his head with a quick jerk to toss his hair back.

"Well," she began hesitantly, "that's what I called in for as well. I wanted to put a proposal to you about that."

He looked at her curiously and intently, and immediately she was aware of the direct eye contact. The old Quigley would have died rather than do that.

"I was thinking about when my work is finished and hanging in New York. I've been feeling I'd like something to go along with it. It's just that I feel it should have something that will complement and harmonise with it."

He was clearly not following her drift. Her work needed no accompaniment, or anything to embellish it in any way, and he wondered where she could possibly be going with this.

"Maeve, what are you talking about? Your work doesn't need anything else. It's a complete statement in itself. Are you having a confidence crisis or something now that the work is actually underway?"

She smiled at the concern for her artistic confidence. Quigley was admonishing her, and she wondered if he realised the extent of the change in himself.

"I was thinking about *your* work," she said emphatically. "I was thinking that you could write some verse to accompany my paintings. Something that would blend and unify the two art forms, and yet they would each be complete in themselves. What do you think?"

He was speechless. He daren't look Maeve Nugent in

the eye, and allow an honest view of his feelings, but the prospect of his work hanging in New York, as part of a whole, or as works in their own right was enough to stunt his new-found confidence with her.

She grinned at his flabbergasted reaction. "Good idea, yeah?"

Yeah, it certainly was, but he couldn't jump on her bandwagon, it wouldn't be right. It sounded like she had it all worked out, but she didn't have to do this for him.

"I know what you're thinking," she told him assuredly. "Why should I do that, you are asking, and why all sorts of things, but the fact is I'd really like something it, I really feel it would *work*. The idea excites me and the two works would be individual. We would each be responsible for our own works, yet they would be a pair, and I really do think they would complement each other. If you agree I will run it by my clients, and see what they think. Work by a poet from where their ancestors came from will appeal to them, I'm sure of it, and I really do want you to agree." Her hand landed lightly on his good arm. "Please, Quigley, I really would like it."

How could he refuse when she put it like that? His poetry hanging alongside her works in New York! His insides were turning to jelly, and he could see how sincere she was about it, and that she wanted it because she really believed it would work, it would be different. The thing was he thought it a terrific idea himself. It would be a new departure, poetry and art conceived as one, yet individual creations born with an intangible link.

"Well . . . see what they say, and if they go for it . . ."

"Yes!"

He laughed aloud at her reaction. Maeve Nugent like

298

a child whose wish had come true. But so was he. If this worked out, oh, if this worked out . . . well, they would just have to wait and see.

"Just one thing though," he said.

"What's that?"

"I'm a poet, but not from here."

He thought of how fast this year was going, and was reminded that in a few months it would be back to the lecture hall and his students. It was another world altogether there and he loved it, but this year out was precious too, and if he could make his mark, some kind of mark with his poetry it would have been worth it. There was another mark he'd very much like to make too.

Maeve laughed. "That's okay. I'm an artist, but not from here either."

Quigley felt a wave of good portent, followed quickly by a wicked feeling of perverse pleasure that surged through his bones that this was a million miles away from what the driver of that car had in mind last weekend when he ran him off the road.

He wanted to see it in his eyes first, let him know he had recognised him. Face him, man to man, and let him worry about it.

Chapter 52

Bradley called in when he knew that Isabella would be home from playschool, and his father would most likely be there too. Since the 'incident' he had taken to coming in more regularly, and he knew his father was pleased about that. Previously he had been all wrapped up in his job at the 'heli-hire' as he liked to call it, but the 'incident' had changed a lot of things, a lot of attitudes in the family. That was good, he decided, and now, as he came through the dining room, he saw Isabella out on the terrace with her small pink watering can which Andy had put some water and plant food into, and she was very busy feeding 'her' flowers. Andy had planted up some pots, with her help, and it was now up to her to 'make' them grow.

The pots were Andy's idea. He cleared it with Myles, saying he thought she needed something to absorb her, something that held its own therapeutic element, if not remedy. It wasn't in Andy's nature to put in his tuppence-worth uninvited; his idea was in response to a comment that Myles himself had made when worry made him talk man to man with the wise and prudent old Andy. So Andy told Isabella that he was so busy in the garden that he needed some help. He said he had so many flowers that he had to put some on the terrace in pots but he had too many to be able to look after them all. They would need watering now and then and he wondered if she could do it.

Izzy didn't need any persuading to look after the plants. She swelled with importance when she told Myles that she was 'working' in the garden with Andy. And she surprised them both by saying that she should have a wigglie in her pots so her plants would be best.

It was the good side of Izzy on good days, and when she was happy she was like her old self again, and there was no indication of the terror she felt from time to time.

But the dreams still came, and the 'shape' still threatened her with the dog, and the terror of being locked in that dark smelly room on her own still came to her in the night. They didn't know this for she still wouldn't talk, but they had to deal as best they could with the effect it had on her.

Looking at her now, intently busy with her watering can, pushing her curls out of her face, and the water sloshing as much on the granite surface as into the pots. it was almost impossible to believe she was anything but a happy four-year-old.

When she caught sight of her Uncle Bradley she called him to see her plants growing, and told him about how the wigglies lived in the pots making her flowers grow.

Bradley was hugely impressed, and she was hugely satisfied with his reaction.

Myles came out to join them, saying Eileen would bring some coffee. When she brought out the tray and placed it on the table, Isabella ran down the steps to Andy, to discuss her plants, they assumed. Then she came back and finished watering them.

"What is it, Dad?" Bradley asked, seeing the frown that had appeared on his father's face.

Myles had got a sense of something being wrong just then but he couldn't grasp it sufficiently to analyse it. He was unable to identify the essence of the feeling that had suddenly made its presence felt in his gut, and he simply shook his head in response to Bradley.

"I haven't seen Sophie in a while," Bradley went on as his father remained silent. "How is she doing? Is she coping at all after everything that happened?"

Myles brightened. His daughter was a different woman these days, and he was glad of it. He didn't see that much of her himself. Since they had talked of sharing the minding of Isabella, Sophie arranged her nights out in agreement with her father, nights out which always included the following day too.

He didn't mind that. The change in Sophie was worth it. Her form was good, if a little impatient, but then Sophie always had to have what she wanted right now, even as a child, and he was sure too that she had stopped taking whatever substance it was that she had come to rely on, or at least it seemed her dependence on it was reduced. And that was a huge relief.

"She's fine. Actually, I don't see that much of her. She has a new man in her life now, he takes up a good bit of her time these days, but I have to say I'm glad about that."

Bradley thought about it. It was over a year now since Peter had died, and his sister was a young and beautiful woman, so that was very welcome news.

"I passed her apartment recently, saw her car outside," he said. "I wondered if she had moved back there."

Obviously not yet, even if she was there that particular night, but Bradley was thinking ahead – if she moved in with this new guy, it probably wouldn't be to the same apartment she had shared with her husband and daughter. So maybe there was a possibility that he might have a shot at buying it yet.

"Have you met him, this new guy?" he asked Myles.

His father smiled. "She's keeping him very close to her chest so to speak. She doesn't make a habit of saying very much about him at all, apart from the fact that he lives in Meath and is in insurance. No, I haven't had the pleasure."

"Insurance? Meath?"

Bradley's tone caused Myles to ask, "Do you know him?"

"Probably not – it's just that we have a client from Meath who hires out a chopper from time to time to take clients to various functions here and there. Insurance too, probably coincidence though. Guy named Marchant, Gary Marchant."

Myles looked surprised. "That's what she calls him. Gary. So you do know him."

It was Bradley's turn to frown. Marchant was not a common name. There couldn't be two Gary Marchants from Meath in insurance, surely? A silence fell over him as he thought how best to answer his father's question. The Gary Marchant he knew was in about his late thirties, a high flier in more ways than one, big in insurance, and married.

"So what is it, Bradley?" Myles looked at him closely.

"Well, I could be wrong, but to the best of my knowledge the Gary Marchant I know is married, if it's the same guy."

The news didn't shock his father as he thought it would.

"Does he know the connection between Sophie and you?" Myles wondered.

"No, that's not likely. Even if he happened to remember my name, Sophie is a Harcourt. I don't see how he'd ever connect her and me unless he was told."

"Of course, but she does know he's married, because she told me he is separated. Isn't that so often the situation these days?"

Bradley had to agree that was true. He had often dated someone who had a 'past' as they would say, and children or an ex-husband would be referred to. It was not so often that he met someone who didn't have a 'past'. Being without a past as such himself, he was beginning to feel like the odd one out on the social scene. Statistics showed thousands of new relationships were formed, making new families where stepchildren and stepparents made up a high percentage of the new family units.

He wondered if Sophie knew all the facts about her new man – after all, she had only known him a short while – and if this fellow really was separated, or if she knew otherwise and simply wasn't saying. Bradley was a man of the world, and he knew a lot of what went on out there.

He also suspected that Sophie was not beyond going after what she wanted. But if this Gary Marchant was messing her around then he would look on it differently. After all, this was his sister, his own sibling, and that made it different, particularly when this self-professed separated man hired a chopper and showed up at the airfield on regular occasions to fly with his wife and children to County Clare for "little breaks" in Dromoland Castle.

Chapter 53

Myles was beginning to feel that things were building up to an almighty explosion at home, and he was glad to be getting a break from it tonight. He sincerely hoped Bradley was wrong about Sophie's new man still being married, and as well as that she wasn't keeping to her part of the arrangement about the baby-sitting. They argued about that, and he found himself wondering how Isabella would take to the idea of Bradley minding her, at least the odd time, if of course Bradley was willing.

And there was poor Isabella and her situation. She was becoming reluctant to go to her bed at night-time because of the dreams. She began to find all sorts of reasons to stay up later, and many nights she fell asleep on the sofa beside him, and then he would carry her to her bed and hope she wouldn't waken in the process.

So an evening with Betty would have been just what he needed to restore his spirits, his sense of humour, and his faith in mankind in general. But tonight it wasn't working.

Myles put his family issues out of his mind and concentrated on the petite woman across the table from him. The effect she always had on him was to put his worries out of his mind, and her light heartedness never failed to affect him, making his world lighter too. At least that was the way it had been till he saw another man go into her house and stay longer than he'd have liked.

He waited now for her to mention it, make some reference to it, but she didn't. But tonight she seemed to have something on her mind, something she declined to talk to him about. The atmosphere between them had become strained, and he didn't know how to fix it.

If he asked her straight out whether there was someone else, he could risk offending her greatly, but if he didn't the question would continue to torment him. Either way he was beginning to feel he couldn't win. This was sliding out of his grasp and there seemed to be nothing he could do about it but sit and watch it go. Eventually, after attempts at trying to lighten the mood which promptly fell flat, he figured if he was the one to initiate the topic and ask the questions then the confirmation might not whack him so badly when it came.

"More wine?" he asked even though her glass was still half-full and she seemed to have forgotten it was there.

She shook her head absently, and then said, "Sorry, my mind was elsewhere."

He took the bull by the horns. He had to know.

"Betty, is there something up?"

She looked across at him strangely. "Like what?"

He placed his elbows on the table and rested his

chin on his hands. It was now or never. "Well, I'm not sure . . ."

He almost gave up then, lost his nerve. If he didn't say anything it just might all go away. But to think like that was stupid; he knew it wouldn't go anywhere except deeper into his troubled thoughts.

"I called around to your house the other evening."

"You did? When?"

"After we had been talking on the phone. I thought you sounded a bit down, and I figured I'd call and see if I could cheer you up."

"Oh, right." Her eyes came up to meet his with a genuine question. "Why didn't you knock?"

He hadn't expected that response, but then he wasn't exactly sure what response he expected to get. But, now that he had brought up the issue, he was suddenly concerned about what her reaction would be when he told her that he had waited outside. Spying, she might think. It sounded to him like he was spying, how else could she take it? He was trying to formulate an answer that wouldn't prompt an inflammatory response.

"Why didn't you knock if you came around, Myles?" She seemed genuinely puzzled.

She watched as his search for an answer marched all over his face, and then her head went slowly up and down as she remembered what night that was. It was her turn to search for a way to respond. He saw her quandary and his heart sank, and suddenly he did not want to hear the answer.

"You saw him, didn't you? That's why you didn't knock," she said flatly, not looking at him.

He felt anger. She was admitting she had someone

307

there and she wouldn't even look him in the eye while she said it.

She sighed heavily. This was getting harder and harder all the time, and more complicated. She hadn't wanted to mention it. It had nothing to do with them, Myles and her, and she didn't want it to impinge on their relationship. But she realised then that, whether she liked it or not, it already had. She looked directly across at him. His expression showed her how the sight of another man at her door had troubled Myles.

"I'd have expected you would trust me better than that," she said, and then *he* was rightly stuck for an answer.

What was he supposed to think? This was ridiculous, they were sounding like a couple of teenagers having a tiff. But then he realised there was no different set of rules for the heart a second time around.

But she apologised immediately.

"I'm sorry, Myles, that was uncalled for – under the circumstances that was uncalled for."

He waited for her to continue.

"You've always known I'm married, right?"

"Yes," he agreed, a sudden feeling of dread creeping over him. He wasn't going to like this, and it must be the last thing he had expected her to say.

"I haven't seen him since he left, or heard from him in all that time since then, and suddenly he shows up at my door recently. When you saw him – that was the second time he's called."

She was finding it difficult to talk about it, but now that it was begun she found she wanted to go on despite the difficulty.

"Maybe you don't want to know this," she suggested.

His hand reached out and covered hers, his looking enormous over her small neat one.

"Betty, you're not yourself at all tonight, anyone could see that, and something is weighing down on you. I don't know what or how much you want to tell me, if anything, and I don't even know if I ought to or want to hear it, but you have to talk to someone about it."

He didn't know whether he wanted her to go on or not. He was the blow-in in her life, and he was suddenly aware of how very precarious his position had become in the last few minutes. The last thing he had expected was that the man he had seen at her door would be her husband. Husbands meant history and children and connections going way back and much deeper than any he had, and he felt that put him on a very tenuous footing. In a battle for her feelings he could be seen as a Johnny-come-lately.

When he thought about it, it looked at the time like the man felt he had every right to be there – there was that assurance about him that he would be invited inside. Myles had known that from his bearing.

But he could understand the dilemma she was in. The one shred of consolation he could see now was that she had not sought to have her husband back, but back he was, and causing havoc by the sound of it.

"Why is he back? What does he want after all this time? And more to the point, what do *you* feel about it?"

She didn't answer immediately. Any response she might give now could well be interpreted in a number of ways other than the way she meant it. She knew that, and she didn't want Myles to get the wrong impression.

"He says they have split, but what concerns me most

is how it will affect Olive and Buddy," she said thoughtfully. "They have really never known him, they were too young to remember him, but he is still their father and I can well understand how this would throw them into a flap."

She thought of the very differing reactions of her children, but she was aware too that those reactions could change. They were thrown as much as she was, if not more, and given time to think their opinions might be different.

"Part of them feels they don't need him, they have done fine so far without him, and that's true, but the other part of them probably always wished they had a father like everyone else. Before this they never had to make any kind of decision about him – there was one situation and that was that he was gone, simple as that – but now they do. Now they have to decide whether to accept or reject this stranger who has come back and thrown such upheaval into their lives. And it leaves me in much the same boat. If I reject him they might feel they have to as well, out of loyalty to me, and I don't want them to be influenced by that – but it could be very hard for them to leave that out of the equation."

Their dinners were going cold, unnoticed by them both. Betty fiddled absentmindedly with her fork, her concentration on the predicament she saw herself and her little family were in.

Questions were circling in Myles's head, questions about what that deserter was doing back, about whether or not it was a permanent return, and what was he expecting of the family he deserted, if anything. He wondered what sort of man would have the temerity to show up like that after a lifetime of desertion, and he worried too that such a man would have the audacity to elbow him out of the picture very quickly.

As much as he dreaded to hear the answer, he had to ask the question.

"What do *you* want Betty, for yourself? You have to decide that. If he is to come back into your lives, you have to decide how much you want him in your life. Is he to be on the periphery, or more than that? You need to work that out for yourself. Don't get me wrong here. I'm simply saying this time round you should go by what *you* want. You owe yourself that much at least."

He had no right to try to influence her, much as he would have liked to. But Olive and Buddy were grown adults. What was done to them in the past was unchangeable, and he hoped they were mature enough to realise that their mother did not have to 'make it up to them' now.

The waiter came and their plates were taken away, and there was no dessert ordered. Coffees were brought, and left to go as cold as the dinner was.

Myles ordered a taxi and there was more silence than talk on the way home.

"I understand what you are saying, Myles," Betty whispered, as the taxi turned into her road, "but I am so afraid of how it will go. I can sense a need in them to know him, and that's not surprising – he is their father after all – and I am so afraid of being accused of 'depriving' them the second time around, however illogical it might sound. I know they are grown adults, but even so there's no knowing what way they will see things . . ."

He sat in the dark of the taxi and all he knew was

that he did not want to share her. For him it was all or nothing, but the choice was not his, she had to choose. She had made no attempt to answer his question as to what it was she wanted, and it seemed to him that what she wanted most was to keep her children happy at all costs, at least as happy as she thought they had been, but she did not seem to see that it was not in her power to guarantee that outcome, no matter what decision she made.

They were both aware that something impenetrable had fallen between them, each on their own side of the divide. Myles felt it was for Betty to make her choice and to make it with her own happiness to the fore, and Betty was of the opinion that Olive and Buddy's happiness depended on the choices she made. She was torn between what she wanted and what she thought was best for her family, but what Myles saw was a reluctance to send this errant deserter packing, whatever the reason.

He didn't feel it appropriate to make a move to get out of the taxi when they arrived at her house, and she didn't invite him in. He waited in the car to see her safely inside while she opened her hall door, but she didn't look back, and with a feeling of helplessness he indicated to the driver to drive on.

Chapter 54

When he arrived home his spirits were at rock bottom.
He reproached himself for not having told her how he
felt. It might have made some difference to her decision.
But he felt he wasn't in the equation, he wasn't part of
her family, they didn't have a history or offspring who
were now thrown into turmoil as to how to handle this
crux.

He was surprised to find Sophie still up. Usually, on
her nights in, she saw to it that she got her beauty sleep,
but tonight the lights were still on and he heard the
sound of the television in the sitting room.

When he pushed open the door he knew immediately
Izzy had had another dream. She was asleep curled up
beside her mother on the sofa, her curls hiding her tear-
stained face, and Myles knew instantly without Sophie
saying a word how the evening had gone. He cast an
inquiring look at Sophie, who looked back with a new
understanding in her eyes. Till now some part of her had

wondered if her daughter just wanted the company, the attention, or if it had become a habit that got her attention. She hadn't believed how much these dreams were upsetting Isabella till she saw it herself.

"That bad, huh?"

"Yes, she wouldn't go back asleep for me. I couldn't seem to comfort her other than to bring her downstairs and let her fall asleep here."

"I'll take her back up," Myles said. "Then we have to talk about this."

He lifted the sleeping Izzy from the sofa and carried her up to her bed. When he had covered her up, he waited a while to see that she was well asleep before leaving the room.

Sophie was in the kitchen making coffee.

"None for me, thanks," Myles said, coming into the room. "It will keep me awake."

He would have liked to think he could go straight asleep and sleep peacefully, but there was too much on his mind for that.

"What are we going to do about Isabella?" Sophie asked, concern showing noticeably on her face. "She needs help with this. Perhaps we should have a child psychiatrist look at her. What do you think?"

Myles thought about that. If they went that road it could be a long-drawn-out one, one that might very well be hard on the child, and could leave her with residual effects from having to see a psychiatrist at such a young age. It would certainly trouble him that they needed such help for her so young. From what he knew of these things there was rarely any quick fix for patients.

"Dad?"

"I have to say I'm uneasy at the idea of a psychiatrist, Sophie. I can't help but feel that if only she would talk about it, it would help. But I know she obviously isn't able to do that here. And –"

"Here? What do you mean by 'here'? She can't talk 'here'? Why not?"

He pulled a chair out from the table and sat down.

"You know, Sophie, I'm sure it's the fact that she was taken from this house that is causing these dreams. I mean, think about it, we don't know why it happened, or why we got her back like we did, but we do feel we can keep her safe now. But in her young mind she should have been safe before, and she wasn't. Is it any wonder she has nightmares? How do we know she doesn't live in fear of being taken again?"

Verbalising it like that made Myles feel like a monster, and it gave Sophie some insight into the depth of horror her daughter could well be living with. If Myles was right they had done nothing at all to allay Izzy's fears. They expected her to continue in the same situation that had resulted in her being kidnapped, and were doing nothing about it. How could she be expected to get over it like that?

"So what do we do? Move?" Sophie was thinking that was a drastic solution to have to take but it looked like there might be no other way.

Myles was a bit more practical. "What if we took her away from here for a while? Would that be of any help, I wonder?"

"Away? To where, for how long? I have the shop to run, you have to remember."

Going away didn't sound like a good idea to Sophie.

315

How would she see Gary? It was too soon yet to be going 'away' indefinitely anywhere, for any reason, and expect him still to be there for her when she got back. The thought annoyed her. She wanted to feel more secure with him than that.

"I was thinking, Sophie, what if I took Isabella down to Kerry for a while – stay with Maeve – what would you think of that? I think the break would do her good. I think it might help – at least she should feel safe there. Perhaps we should try something like that before we go the other route. We could see what Maeve says."

Normally the suggestion to bring her sister into the picture would have annoyed the hell out of Sophie. But, as Myles' suggestion settled in her head, Sophie liked it. It could be a solution to a number of things, at least temporarily, and it just might help Isabella, if her father's line of thinking was right. At least it was worth a try. And think of the freedom she would have to herself. It never crossed her mind to ask her father how long he was thinking of staying.

"Would Maeve have enough room?" was the question she came out with.

Chapter 55

Quigley was quite happy with himself since his accident. Things in his life had changed so much as a result, he was almost glad to have his arm in plaster. Certainly it was no hardship when he compared it to the way things had been. It almost felt like the real him had finally succeeded in getting out of the hard shell that had formed around his exuberance for life and which had been stifling it for years now, much to his mortification on countless occasions.

He could breathe freely now. He could enjoy a good laugh. He even felt taller than before and that was good, because he walked with his back straight now – the stoop was gone, and he held his head up. He could look the world in the eye and smile. And the world smiled back. That was the best bit.

Well, the second best bit.

The first was when Maeve Nugent had called to the house after he had come home from the hospital.

317

Imagine her wanting him to write verse to accompany her works for New York! He thought it a great idea, from an artistic viewpoint of course, and the work he created for this commission was going to be of his finest. Her request had nothing at all to do with his accident; he knew that now though he'd thought it did in the first instance. Maeve Nugent wanted his work because of her high regard for it.

That was definitely the best bit.

The instance in which he inadvertently bumped into Conor de Lacy in McCaffrey's pub recently came in a very good third. Quigley had been sitting on a barstool waiting for his pint. The place had filled up and people were standing beside and behind him along the length of the bar, waiting to be served also. When his order arrived he took the first sip and paid Tom, then made to return to Pat and the others at their table.

People made way for him, mostly because of his arm and also because he was vacating a precious bar seat, with friendly comments and a bit of ribbing about only being able to "take one at a time" as he held his pint with his good hand.

But Conor had just arrived in and made his usual beeline for the bar, expecting to occupy his usual spot. Seeing Quigley in his way he stood his ground, assuming and fully expecting The Rake would move first.

They eyed each other eyeball to eyeball, Conor conscious for the first time that he was physically being looked down on. The Rake didn't blink an eye, and he found it unsettling. But Quigley's low comment when it came was worse.

"Not jumping aside this time," he said, his voice

steady and firm. He watched the expression change in The Puff's face, the slight narrowing of the eyes and the instant hard set of the jaw-line that gave him away and spoke volumes.

Conor had no choice but to move aside. Quigley took his time in moving away towards the table, compelling The Puff to wait, very briefly, but it was a wait. Quigley was employing psychological tactics. And it was alien to Conor de Lacy to be in the underdog position. He turned towards the bar again, his face a mask of fury before he could calm his temper enough to disguise it. When he ordered his drink he was once again his usual charming self.

No one else had paid much attention, or seen any significance in the stand-off, but the barman had seen the exchange from his vantage point behind the bar. And, as he watched, Tom was aware that he was looking at more than a mere battle of wills between the two as to who would move aside for the other first.

Now what in hell's name was that all about? he wondered.

Quigley joined the others at the table again, outwardly joining in the *craic*, but he had seen in Conor de Lacy's eyes the fear that he, Quigley, might very well yet spill the beans on him.

It was what Quigley had been waiting to see, what he had known he would see. It would keep The Puff in his place. Better still, it would tell him clearly he really ought not to mess with Quigley McGurk, or the Gardaí might happen to find out what really occurred that night in the dark along by the ditches on Upper Main Street.

Tom put the pint in front of Conor. Conor lifted it

and took his first sip before giving Tom the usual sign, but Tom had had enough of that. He couldn't spend a nod or a wink, no matter how many of them he collected, even if they had the de Lacy name on them. He had gathered a whole heap of them by now, and had placed then religiously and quietly on de Lacy's slate. That was where they stayed ad infinitum, and feck all use they were to him.

He placed an elbow on the counter and leaned across to Conor.

"What was all that about?" he said in a low voice with a tilt of his head towards where he and Quigley had had their very subtle showdown. "What's with you and McGurk?"

Conor swallowed a big mouthful all in one go, and coughed pointedly, deliberately gaining himself time to think. What the hell was gone wrong with this place tonight? It suddenly felt like the very fabric of the walls was out to get him: first McGurk, now the barman.

"Don't know what you mean," he replied nonchalantly. "I stood aside for an injured man –"

"Didn't look like that from where I'm standing," Tom was being relentless, "injury or no. If I didn't know you better, I'd swear it looked like he had something on you . . ." He allowed a mischievous grin to spread over his face, taking the menace out of his implied accusation, but the meaning struck home, and the brief flash of a lightning reaction he saw in the irritated face across the ancient wooden counter from him added flesh to the bones of his budding suspicion. He thought it might be interesting to put the same question to Quigley when he got the chance. He had seen sparks fly between these two before, but now Quigley definitely appeared to have the upper hand, and the self-belief to back it up, while de Lacy seemed more like someone who'd had the rug pulled out from under him.

Tom smiled inwardly at de Lacy's discomfort. He thought it was time to call a halt to the 'facility' as well while he was at it. He kept his voice low, and followed the annoying grin with a very definitive wink.

"I think the slate's had it too."

Chapter 56

Isabella was pulling her pink travelling case out from her wardrobe, in her excitement pulling a number of other things she didn't need out too. She struggled to get the case onto her bed. She had to make a start. Mummy wasn't home yet to help, so she decided she ought to get going on her packing. They were travelling tomorrow and she had to be ready. If she was all ready to go they wouldn't be able to change their minds about the trip.

But what to put into the case? Any other time they went anywhere it was always Mummy who put her things in, Mummy always knew what would be needed, and all the right things always ended up in her case. So she began to empty things from her chest of drawers, but they wouldn't all fit into the case and they didn't look all smooth like they would if Mummy did it for her. So she took some things out and they fell on the floor. Her case was suddenly too small.

And there was no room for Ted. She had to have room for Ted.

The sound of the hall door closing brought her out onto the landing.

"Mummy?"

Isabella ran down the stairs, keen to enlist her mother's help with the packing.

Sophie needed to kick off her shoes and put her feet up for a little while. The shop had been very busy all day, and just like when she was modelling she still was not used to the discomfort of being in high-fashion shoes for hours on end. Feet that wore killer heels could not expect to actually have room for toes as well, but Sophie being Sophie would not be caught dead in anything else.

Isabella ran into the room, almost breathless with excitement.

"I'm nearly all packed, Mummy, come and see what I've done!"

Isabella caught her mother by the hand, but Sophie wasn't going anywhere till after dinner.

"Calm down, Isabella, I'll come and help after we've eaten."

"Can we stay a lot of days? Did Auntie Maeve say we could?"

Myles came into the room. He and Sophie gave each other a loaded look. It silently acknowledged that neither of them had seen Isabella this animated in quite some time.

"Are you packed too, Grandy?" The child was becoming anxious.

Myles sat on the sofa and, as was her habit, Izzy automatically came and perched herself on his lap, as he knew she would.

"Listen to me, pet," he said quietly while he wrapped his arms around her. "We have plenty of time to get packed, or to finish packing. The train doesn't leave till lunchtime tomorrow, so there is no need to worry. We'll be there in plenty of time. And Auntie Maeve will be in Tralee to meet us and take us to her cottage. And we'll have a lovely little holiday. And after dinner I will wash up and then Mummy will help you with your packing, okay?"

The dimples deepened, the curls bounced with the vigorous nodding of her head. Everything would be okay. Mummy and Grandy would see to it, Grandy had said so.

Sophie was looking forward to having time totally for herself. It had not been mentioned how long a stay her father and Isabella were going for. Maeve did not have much in the way of accommodation. The cottage was small, only two bedrooms and they were small, and she was doing her New York work as well. So Sophie figured that two extra people being around for more than a few days could turn out to be a bit of a nuisance.

She would like them to be gone at least a week. The freedom she would have! Perhaps she and Gary could have that break now that they had been talking about. They could spend as much time together as they wanted, all day in bed if they liked, and no having to bother about having Isabella minded, or having to go home, or anything else. Having unlimited access to that body of his was her idea of heaven.

Bliss.

And another advantage was that this time in Kerry would take her father away from the leech for a while, but now that she came to think of it he hadn't been out in the evenings this week so far. That got her hopes up.

This was definitely the best time in her life in a long time. It was in a positive helpful frame of mind that she went to her daughter's room after dinner and sorted out what Isabella would need for her little holiday in Dingle.

Myles packed his bag without all the ceremony it took to get Izzy's ready. His thoughts were very mixed. He couldn't help feeling that he was doing the right thing, taking Izzy away from the house. It was so obvious that the child couldn't wait to be gone. Already the change in her was noticeable.

She simply had to talk to Maeve about it when Grandy phoned to see if they could come down. "Grandy said he will bring me to see Fungi while you are working, Auntie Maeve. And I can bring Ted too, can't I? He doesn't need a bed – he sleeps with me."

That night getting Izzy to bed was no problem. The sooner morning came the sooner they would be going. She had better get to sleep then, so morning could come.

Myles didn't get to sleep as easily. Izzy's behaviour convinced him that the source of her trouble was definitely the house, and if it continued after they came home . . . well, he didn't want to consider what they would have to do then. But for now he was very positive about the trip, and he looked forward to more benefits for Izzy in the next few days.

He would have liked to have been more positive about the situation with Betty too. She was very tied up in this thing that had landed itself upon her lately, and he knew she felt obligated to Olive and Buddy. Was it an unexplainable guilt thing because they were reared without the father they should have had, or did she still have some feelings for that sorry excuse of a husband of hers? Why else would she allow herself to be swallowed back into a relationship with him? She hadn't ruled it out when he asked. She hadn't actually given an answer to that question. There were many questions he wanted to ask, but most of what he asked she left unanswered. Myles was sure that he would have had a clear picture of what he would do if he were in the same situation. The one thing they did agree on was that she had to sort this out, and clearly the sooner the better.

She didn't say much when he'd phoned her to let her know he was taking Izzy to Maeve's for a while. That was a good idea, she said. She hoped Izzy would benefit from it, she said. What she didn't say was that she would miss him, or ask when he might be back.

Chapter 57

"I've put you in the front room, Dad, and I'll take the back with Isabella," Maeve informed her father.

He took the two bags out of the car boot to carry them into the house, but Isabella grabbed her bag and was all business trying to carry it up the garden path. Having slept for over an hour and a half on the train, she was still full of beans.

"I can take it in, Grandy," she insisted, but after struggling about halfway up the garden with it she allowed him to take over. She went ahead with Maeve into the cottage and ran up the stairs to see the rooms and was delighted when she saw she was sharing *her* room with Maeve. Maeve had managed to find bedcovers with a fairy princess on the coverlet for her, and Izzy thought sleeping on this low fold-up bed was going to be fun. Myles carried the cases up and put Isabella's at the end of her bed.

"I don't know what your mother has in that case,

Izzy," he said to the child, "but she must think we are never going home."

A peculiar look flashed across Isabella's features, and her smile faded quickly. As she ran downstairs to see what Maeve was doing, he realised he had said utterly the wrong thing. He could see now that Izzy did that sometimes – run away from you when you inadvertently said or did something that reminded her of things she would rather not remember – and he realised she had been doing it for some time, always on the pretext of something else catching her attention elsewhere. He wondered how many other signs he had missed, how many other ways she could have been trying to communicate with them about what had happened to her.

Maeve was at the cooker putting the finishing touches to the dinner when he came down.

"I hope you don't mind your room being lilac and cream, Dad," she joked.

He half-smiled. There was a worried look in his eyes, but she didn't ask why. Isabella was within earshot at the table arranging the cutlery.

"I hope we're not putting you out too much, Maeve." He had noticed the fold-up bed opposite the single bed in the back room, with just space for a small bedside locker between them.

"Not in the slightest," she answered. "I got a loan of the fold-up for Isabella, so we will be right beside each other so we can whisper bed-time stories – isn't that right, Isabella?"

"And Ted can listen as well," Isabella piped up. "He likes stories too."

But there was no storytelling that night. Despite her

nap on the train Isabella was asleep very quickly once Maeve had hugged her goodnight and Grandy had tucked her in.

When Myles came back into the kitchen Maeve had poured them two whiskeys. He took his gratefully and settled himself opposite her at the fireplace.

"I think you're doing the right thing bringing Izzy down for a while, Dad."

He was glad to hear she was thinking along the same lines. So much was up in the air as to how they could help Izzy, but judging by Izzy today it was already working.

"We'll do our best not to be in your way, Maeve. I know you have your commission to do. I'll see to it that Izzy won't be in your way, I'll keep her busy and –"

"Dad," she interrupted him, "it's great to have both of you here. It will be no problem at all. Just relax and be at home, for Heaven's sake. I'm so glad you're here. I'm going to enjoy it too. And tomorrow I want you to come and see how I'm getting on with the works. You're the only person who has seen where they're going to hang, so I want your considered opinion about them."

He laughed at the idea that he could have an opinion on her work that she'd value, considered or otherwise, but he was pleased that she wanted it in the first place. He looked at the hearth brightly lit with many candles which made a blaze of flame. It was too warm for a fire, but Maeve didn't like sitting by a dead hearth, and he swirled his glass as he looked into the golden liquid.

His talk went back to Izzy.

"The change in her when her mother and I told her we were coming for a little break was incredible – it was like getting a flash of the old Izzy again. I'm more convinced than ever that being in that house is the problem."

"But it's her home."

"Not really hers. I mean, yes, it is her home, but only until Sophie decides whether or not they move out. Sophie is seeing someone nowadays, so it looks like she is finally moving on with her life."

Maeve was very interested in that.

"Sophie has a new man?"

"Oh, you didn't know?"

Maeve laughed. "Sophie doesn't make a point of getting on to me to let me know what is going on in her life. It's not something we do."

Myles figured that. Pity, he would have much preferred that his daughters were close. But much as he loved them both he had to admit they were like chalk and cheese, and they probably got on better because there was distance between them.

But Maeve was interested. "So, tell me all about this 'new man'? Is he deserving of my beautiful sister, do you think?"

"I hope so."

Myles watched the flame on a candle flicker in a draft.

Maeve could read her father well. "Come on, Dad, you can tell me. I can see you have reservations. What's wrong with him? Two left feet? Sticky-out ears?"

He was amused at the way she chose to prise the facts out of him. Her approach was so different to the way Sophie would have gone about the same thing. He found himself thinking that some fool of a man was searching in the wrong place for his elder daughter, and it was time he got his act together, and got himself on the right track.

"Worse," he said. "Sticky-out ears can be fixed relatively easily. Bradley thinks this guy is married."

"Oh." She absorbed that information with a nod of her head. "How does Bradley know him?"

"Apparently he has told Sophie he is separated, but it's likely he could be the same guy who hires choppers from Bradley's firm occasionally."

"I hope for her sake he's not mucking her about," she mused. "She's had enough to deal with over the past year, God knows."

"That's what worries me, and she does seem very keen on him. I haven't seen her so upbeat in a long time. Since before Peter was killed actually. You thought she was on drugs or something when you were there last and you were most likely right – Bradley thought so too – but I don't see much evidence of that kind of thing nowadays, I'm glad to say. So I hope all goes the way she wants, please God."

They sat and chatted a long time by the candlelight. There was a peace in this cottage that would seep through your bones very quickly and soothe the tired spirit. Upstairs in the back room Isabella slept soundly, lulled into the secure place where she used to sleep before her kidnapping.

When Maeve finally crept into the room she was afraid she might waken her, but there was no chance of that. Izzy was away in a happy dreamland judging by the angelic look on her face. Maeve leaned over and picked Ted off the floor and tucked him back under the covers.

Chapter 58

Breakfast the next morning was a very leisurely affair. Maeve moved about the kitchen making toast and frying rashers and eggs. There was no dash for anyone to be anywhere, except for Isabella – she wanted to see Fungi. She was assured she would see Fungi, all in good time.

"Any plans for today, Dad?"

"Relax, enjoy, and more of the same," he answered.

He was in better spirits this morning. Watching Isabella did that for him. This break was for her, but there was no rule that said he couldn't enjoy it too.

Later in the morning he and Izzy went across the yard to the studio. Izzy knew Auntie Maeve did paintings, but that little bit of information in no way prepared her for the surprise she got when she stepped inside the door. Grandy had said she must not touch things, or run around inside because the paintings Maeve was working on were for people who were going to buy them, so they had to be very careful.

With a huge sense of awe Izzy stood looking up at Maeve on the ladder. The picture she was working on was *very* big. Izzy had not thought pictures could be that big, and she stood almost rooted to the spot. Everywhere there were paints and brushes and canvases and bottles of varnish and all manner of artists' things that Izzy found fascinating.

"Well, what do you think?" Maeve addressed her father.

Myles looked over the work approvingly and remarked, "You certainly have got the dimensions right, and I love the mix of colours. That will look stunning in the foyer, and you're right to make it larger than life. It will be very impressive."

She came down the ladder and stood back beside him to evaluate it herself again.

"I have asked Quigley McGurk to write some poetry to accompany it. The clients think it a great concept – I was on to them to see how they would like the idea. The verse will be carved into a limestone plaque using Celtic symbols but with a modern twist to them and will hang alongside the paintings. I'm dying to see them all in situ."

Myles nodded his approval. "It will be a very impressive installation, I'm sure. Who's doing the sculpture?"

"Pat Keegan, the sculptor whose house Quigley shares. We're keeping the work in the community – but Pat was the best anyway so why go elsewhere?"

Izzy was taking it all in. She would love to have a go at what Maeve was doing, but she knew they wouldn't let her get up on the ladder like that. But she could do it on the table. That might be okay. But Grandy decided they would go for a walk and let Auntie Maeve get on with her work.

They went out by the back of the cottage and turned into a field that led them towards the mountain that could be seen rising up at the back of the house. Grandy told her all about the trees and the plants on the way and he pointed out the holes in the ground where the rabbits lived, and told her the names of the wild flowers growing in the field and she picked a colourful bunch for Maeve.

The view across the bay was stunning, and Myles could well understand what it was about the area that Maeve loved. From where they rested they could see the back of the cottage and the studio, and to the left in the distance was the sheltered harbour of Dingle, about which the town spread itself comfortably on the small flat plain on the southern side of the peninsula that stretched from the foot of the mountains to the shore.

While her grandy sat, Izzy went into raptures about each different flower she pounced upon to pick and add to her little posy for Auntie Maeve.

It was then that Myles noticed that Ted wasn't with them.

When they got back to the house the back door was open and Myles could smell coffee. But when they went inside it wasn't Maeve who was making it. A tall dark-haired man with his arm in a sling was at the countertop making a good fist of managing to complete the job with only one hand fully useable. Maeve was nowhere to be seen. Myles was taken aback at the sight of the stranger in his daughter's kitchen, but the man greeted him with a broad smile and reached out his good hand.

"Mr Nugent, good to see you again. Maeve said you were down."

Myles looked hard at this unknown friendly person, and then recognised him.

"Quigley, my God! I didn't know you, how are you?"

The change was amazing, he hardly looked like the same person at all, but then his face was hardly visible before; the hair was what used to be Quigley.

"This must be Isabella." Quigley reached out his good hand and ruffled her curls.

She stood looking up at him in silence, her eyes wide with curiosity and surprise.

"Izzy, this is Quigley, Auntie Maeve's friend."

Isabella nodded but said nothing.

"Let me do that for you." Myles took over the making of the coffee and added an extra cup for himself. "Maeve know you're here?" He immediately checked himself. "Sorry, didn't mean it to sound like that . . ."

But Quigley just laughed. "Called in to see how the commission is going."

He always referred to it as "the commission". Not the first of many, but to date the most prestigious of many, and he insisted on giving it its proper title. Quigley had never needed a reason for calling to see Maeve before and now because her father was there it sounded like he needed one. It felt odd.

Myles talked about the New York trip and about how Maeve was such a big hit with her clients and their friends.

"I thought they were never going to let her come home to do her work," he joked. "There was one particular son who kept insisting we stay one more night so that they could show us 'just one more of the sights' as he would say."

That was met with silence.

"What happened to the arm?" Myles asked.

"Accident on the way home from McCaffrey's one

night," Quigley responded. "Fell into a ditch, couple of breaks, another few weeks to go yet in the plaster."

Myles was nodding as if he had understood the implications of falling into a ditch after being in the pub. Quigley saw that he had the wrong end of the stick altogether.

"Hadn't the money to be that bad," he defended himself with a grin. "Car came up behind me, and I slipped."

Something in his voice made Myles shoot him a curious glance.

Quigley decided he hadn't seen it, but he knew instantly that he had given too much away already.

"I'll give Maeve a shout for her coffee," he said and veered the conversation away from the subject.

"I will!" Isabella suddenly sprang into life.

She had been watching Quigley in silence since coming into the cottage, so much so that they had forgotten she was there. Now she ran out, bouquet still in hand, and crossed to the studio where she crept in quietly because they had stressed upon her how careful she must be in the studio.

"Auntie Maeve, Whigley says your coffee is ready," she announced, "and these are for you." She held the posy forward.

Maeve put down her brush and wiped her hands with a cloth, exclaiming how lovely the flowers were. She found a jam-jar and filled it with water and placed the flowers in it, saying she would keep it in her studio so that she could see it all day while she worked.

Izzy was pleased, and delighted with the big hug Maeve gave her. "Can I do some painting too?" she wanted to know.

Maeve promised she would get her a canvas to work on for herself, and they went across to the kitchen, where she handed round some muffins on a plate and poured Isabella a glass of milk.

The adults were busy talking when Isabella, sitting at the table between them, began to cry. It was a stunted cry that she tried to hold in but it was too much for her. The adults were stunned into silence. It became a very distressed cry and Myles immediately recognised the tone of it.

"Izzy, what is it?"

She just sat staring into her milk, a pathetic little figure in tears. Myles was distraught. He had been so sure she would be safe from her demons here. But it was too late, her nightmare had intruded on her safe haven and Izzy was back in the dark place, the 'shape' was standing over her in the dark of the room, his big fists clenched and ready to swoop down on her if she didn't drink her milk. It had a horrible taste and she couldn't swallow it, but the shape said he would let the dog in if she didn't get it down. He wanted her to drink it quickly, he was in a hurry. Another man who was very annoyed was shouting at him from the other room that she never saw into – the door was half-closed but there was a small light coming from there, she could see it under the door when the door was closed – and he was getting very angry and shouting back at the other person. She was so terrified she couldn't stop shaking and she shook so much that she was spilling the horrible milk on her pj's and on the smelly bed, and the man was cursing loudly and leaning into her face, and she didn't want to see his red eyes glaring at her. She screamed in panic when he grabbed her, not realising it was Myles taking her into his arms.

"Izzy, Izzy, sweetheart, it's okay now, it's okay, pet." He rocked her back and forth in his need to comfort her.

Maeve and Quigley were shocked into immobility.

Then Myles noticed the milk.

He indicated to them to take it away. Gradually Isabella calmed down but the sobs took a while to subside. Myles was muttering soothingly to her, reassuring her that Maeve didn't know that she didn't like milk any more. Appalled at what she had inadvertently triggered, Maeve's hand covered her mouth in shock and she looked agonisingly at Quigley who gripped her free hand in support. The gesture was so full of understanding that Maeve gripped his hand back and held on. The incident had shaken them all, but Izzy eventually came back to herself.

"I'm so very sorry, Isabella. I'll get juice in the shops for you, would that be better?" Maeve asked tentatively.

The head of curls nodded slowly, wordlessly, and Isabella accepted a warm hug.

She asked if she could do some painting now and Maeve found her a small canvas and some acrylic paints from the studio, and Isabella settled herself down to paint at the kitchen table, a serious expression troubling her young features. To see her apparently lost in her own imagination again it was hard to believe that only a few minutes ago she had been in the grip of blind terror.

Later, when he got the chance, Myles explained that forensics had taken the pyjamas Isabella wore during her kidnapping for examination. They had found traces of Izzy's own urine, and milk, and they identified a drug that would have made her sleep dissolved in the milk.

Chapter 59

Olive sat and admired Buddy's kitchen. Perched on a high stool at the kitchen bar she milked her coffee and dropped two sugars into the porcelain mug. He had made great improvements since moving in. She was surprised at the contemporary style of his furnishings, and the matching neutral shades with splashes of strong colour here and there made it look very elegant indeed.

"The house looks great, Buddy, but I never would have thought you would be the modernist. Would've had you figured for the classical type."

He was surprised at that. He never would have gone for the classical look; he was a man of the moment, and he had to have the 'look' to go with his new lifestyle, his new freedom. You'd think she would have known that. Funny how you think you know someone you have grown up with, lived all your life in the same house with, and their tastes turn out to be completely different than you thought, and you doubt if you knew them at all.

"Why would you have thought that?" he wondered aloud.

She stirred her coffee endlessly, he remembered the habit, and he remembered how it used to annoy him. Some things remained the same no matter what.

"You never liked change at home," Olive replied. "Mam used to have a problem when it came to replacing any of your stuff, so I'd have thought you'd have preferred the tried and true, simple as that."

"Different when you have your own place, when you get out there and make your own choices."

She agreed he was right there. What you do when you move into your adult life might not exactly be what you had previously decided on. Often long-held ideas get thrown out when a new situation arrives. There was always more than one way forward. She wished she could see more than one way forward now. Worry had her blinkered.

"So what are we going to do about this situation, then? I'm really worried about Mam."

Buddy wasn't as worried about his mother as Olive seemed to be. He reasoned that she would cope since she'd had the wherewithal to make it this far in her life. She was a woman with hidden depths, depths she'd had to go to find the resilience to get the three of them through a tough life. But he was well aware that she felt she was in a real dilemma now, and he hoped she would make the right decision for herself.

But what decision would he and Olive make?

"What do you make of him coming back?" he asked.

Olive was less vociferous now. When pushed for an answer she always hedged. She had great go in her when it was her own idea she was working on, but put her in a tight spot and it was a different matter.

"Maybe he missed home . . . us . . ."

"Oh, for God's sake, that's rubbish, and you know it. Here hasn't been home for him for decades. He left it very easily so maybe it wasn't home even then. He left *us*, remember? And he was our only means of support. We were babies, for God's sake! What kind of a man leaves his own babies?"

"Plenty," she said flatly.

That didn't make it feel any better for Buddy. All he ever wanted was to have a daddy like all the other lads, someone to go to matches with, someone to look up to, or simply the luxury of not being the only male in the house and always feeling it was up to him to put everything to rights. He always felt the odd one out, and he never knew the ropes. He had no role model. He just fumbled through his life. His daddy did that to him.

"I know Mam feels she owes it to us to –"

"That's nonsense! Mam owes us nothing. She spent her life working for us, thanks to that bastard! If anyone owes anything it's we who owe her, big time."

"Perhaps you should tell her that then – she'd appreciate it I'm sure."

"You should get your priorities right, Olive. You want it every way, you want everything to be hunky dory, but there're other people involved here. You're not considering that. You probably have a romantic idea of your long-lost daddy coming home. Wake up, girl."

That wasn't exactly true. She only wanted what she should have had. She didn't remember her father at home, she had been too young. It would have been nice to have a dad like all the other girls. They were their daddies' girls. "My daddy said this and my daddy said that" were words she would carry with her all her life, and their daddies were bringing them here and bringing them there, it never ended. Doted on, they were, and they could twist their dads around their fingers, she knew that from listening to them. But she didn't know what all of that would feel like. She didn't know what a lot of things would feel like, and it was too late for all of that now, but if Martin stayed here there was a chance that she might like having a father, albeit belatedly. Buddy probably had a point in what he said, but she couldn't help it, he *was* her dad.

"There's not just him, there's his family in England. We have siblings. Wouldn't you like to know what they are like? Aren't you even interested in that side of it?"

A sister was a lure to her. But Buddy didn't feel the same. Olive found it hard to believe he had no interest at all in them.

"They're *his*." It was a derogatory tone he used.

"So are we."

He said nothing to that. He did not feel as cut and dried as he sounded, and that annoyed him. He should be able to sort this in his head and be done with it. He had sorted it all out years ago, and decided then he was done with it. But was he? Why wouldn't it go away as he wanted? Simple, because the bastard was his father, and that was the nub of it. Buddy was still a relatively young man. Did he want to go through the rest of his life wondering if he had made the right decision?

"So what do we say to Mam?" Olive wondered. "I've a feeling she's waiting to see which way we bounce. But I do know one thing – she's not herself since Dad showed up. I could say she was happy before, but I couldn't say that for sure now. The decision we make could bring him back into her life, and I don't think she wants that. But she doesn't want to make a choice that would keep him out of ours if we want him around, and I worry that we can't have her choosing something against her will because she doesn't want to be the one who deprives us of this chance to get to know our father."

She sighed heavily. It was complicated. There were long-term effects now no matter which choice any of them made.

Buddy wondered just how well they could possibly get to know him – the man was unreliable and untrustworthy – and his response was adamant.

"Mam won't do that. That would be stupid, give her some credit. We are grown adults, we have to make our own choices, not look to Mam for answers."

Olive sighed. Apparently relationships didn't get any easier when you were older, despite what you might think.

"I know that, but I suspect she would feel responsible in some way – isn't that mothers for you?"

Buddy hadn't given that angle any thought; it wasn't in his male psyche. He dwelt on the reality of the situation, the practical side that you could actually *do* something about.

"Doesn't she have Myles Nugent? What about him? Doesn't how she feels about him have some bearing on all of this?"

"He's in Kerry with his daughter and granddaughter, but he did see Dad going into Mam's, and so it's sort of all up in the air at the moment. How long will he wait, do you think? A husband comes out of the woodwork and is seen going back into his wife's house. Myles might think he doesn't have much chance or much to hold on to."

There was nothing Buddy could do about that – what was Olive telling him that for? It wasn't as if he could actually fix it. People had to make their own choices.

"Look, Olive, you do whatever you think right for you. And I'll do whatever is right for me. I just hope it doesn't cost Mam what looks like a decent man. I think *he* has a bloody thick neck coming back after all this time as if nothing had happened, and stirring all this up now."

Olive sighed heavily. Despite the things she said, she didn't have it sorted any more than he did.

Buddy was angry with his father. He was angry with her and everybody and everything. But it was nothing to the anger he felt for himself. He'd had this all sorted for years. And now he had let that spineless deserter succeed in throwing a spanner well and truly in the works.

Chapter 60

Martin Morris washed his hands at the small bathroom sink, and did a quick mental reflection on what he thought of as 'the state of play'. It wasn't going too badly. He didn't expect to be welcomed back with open arms, he had to be realistic, but he was here in Betty's house, and it was early days yet. Quietly he opened the bathroom cabinet and had a quick look inside. There was the usual stuff he would expect to see in a woman's bathroom – some painkillers, some jars of various creams, a spare emery board, a small scissors, and a razor, but it was a small pink lady's razor. There was nothing there that would suggest to him that a man might use this bathroom on a regular basis – no spare blades, no razor, no male shower gels or toiletries. That was good.

He took a quick look into the bedroom before coming back downstairs. Nothing he saw was cause for concern. That was good too.

At the kitchen table Betty wished that she was a smoker. Now would definitely be the time when she would go back on them, if she had been trying to give them up. Yeah, silly thought, but she would. She was aware that he was too long upstairs, but she didn't feel she could say anything about it. Any reference, no matter how remote to bathroom functions was absolutely taboo in these circumstances. Nonetheless she wished he'd come down. Come down and find her filling the room with cigarette smoke.

When he did come back into the room, something about his bearing caused a thought to flit across her mind, too fleeting to grasp its meaning. But the way he settled himself into his seat bothered her.

Compared to his home in England, Martin found this house claustrophobic. He had done well when he left with Jacinta. He was full of great ideas then about all he would provide for her, the life they would have. He had worked hard, no one could take that away from him, and he had done what he promised, he had provided well. Jacinta had worked too; after each baby she had gone back to work. There was nothing they had wanted. When they moved to a bigger house in a better area and then stocked the garage with a better car for both of them, he allowed himself a good measure of pride in all they had achieved.

So where did it all go wrong, he could almost hear Betty wondering. She didn't ask and that was a bit off-putting. She wasn't asking anything, which made it a bit harder to assess what his chances might amount to in the future – the near future, he hoped. But if she had asked he knew exactly what he would have told her.

They wanted different things from life, Jacinta and him. Their interests were miles apart and Jacinta liked the pub scene, and holidays with her friends. As the children grew they had less and less in common, but their lives were good and neither of them wanted to do anything about it. It was the easy option, but it was a dangerous option. Dangerous for a marriage, that is. Well, a relationship then – he hadn't committed bigamy, he reminded himself, he wasn't that much of a louser. He didn't like to dwell on what Betty thought of him one way or the other. He didn't want to think of how low he might have to go to find his starting point again with her.

But the cosy indifference he and Jacinta existed in invariably led to trouble, third-person trouble, affair trouble, and more than one. She got away with it relatively easily in the beginning. Trust is still there; you believe what you are told at first, that's what you choose to do. He believed her, he'd believed Jacinta, he would say. She was a people-person, always was, and people like that have the advantage. He hadn't been living with her for a good while now, he had moved out some time ago, and he hadn't seen his daughter or his son in months. They had moved away from home, both of them, to other cities. They were getting on with their own lives now. He didn't want anyone to know that he didn't have much contact with them, because they might well say he deserved it, and he supposed they were right. But he had his children here too, and perhaps there was a slight chance that they might want to see him. Yes, it was expecting a lot, but he hoped against hope. He had to give it a shot, he'd say.

But there was a lot he wouldn't say.

347

He wouldn't say that the account he gave should be reversed. He wouldn't mention all the affairs he'd had, or the fact that Jacinta believed his stories for longer than he thought she would. He wouldn't say that she didn't deserve to be treated as he had treated Betty. Betty didn't deserve it either, but he wouldn't say that, not now, not yet – that would be for later when she needed to hear his remorse.

Nor would he say that neither Jacinta nor his children wanted to see him again. Or that she had finally thrown him out only a couple of weeks ago. If his children had been in other cities he might have tried them, but they preferred to be with their mother.

Yes, this house was very small, and it probably would take him some time to get his feet 'back under the table' so to speak. He fully expected that. But he had money, Jacinta had the house and her job, she'd be okay. But their bank account was in his name only, and when you had money there were things you could do.

But first things first.

"Did you tell Olive and Buddy I'd called?"

It was distasteful hearing their names in his mouth; he came out with it as if it was the norm. But Betty could not do otherwise than say yes, she had.

"Do you think they will see me?"

"I don't know. You have to realise this is very distressing all round. They had you relegated to the past, they hardly remember you. You have to remember they were very young."

She wished she could tell him no, they didn't want to see him, but he was their father and she didn't have the right to say anything decisive on their behalf.

"I'd like to be in their lives, Betty. I know it won't be easy for anyone, but I'd like to try."

He was finding it hard to read her. She wasn't saying much and that didn't help. He couldn't ask directly how she felt about him being around. That would give her the opportunity of rejecting him outright, and she might then feel she couldn't go back on her word, even if she wanted to. And she *could* change her mind; women were known to do that, weren't they?

He figured it would be best to play it by ear, take his time, and allow it to build slowly. It would be better than being on his own, and he would have a good woman in his life again, much preferable to having to go to all the trouble of finding one; at his age he didn't want all that bother. It was a tough world out there, too much competition from younger studs, younger slimmer guys who had the energy he lacked. And the hair he was losing. Anyway, better the woman you know and all that.

"I'll tell them," Betty stood up purposefully.

It told him clearly that his visit was over. For now, he thought, over for now.

She rummaged in her handbag.

"If it's okay with you, Betty, I'd like to call again."

She drew a piece of paper from her bag and held it out to him. As she did she realised what had struck her when he had come down from the bathroom. He actually thought this was going his way. It showed in his bearing, in the old but familiar look that told her he was sure of himself, sure of his chances.

"I don't want you calling again," she said very deliberately, looking him straight in the eye for almost the first time since he had arrived. "I have a man in my life now, and I love him. There's no place for you."

Despite the outright bluntness what struck him was the complete lack of any malice in either her eyes or her voice. Her tone had that quite level structure to it that a voice carries when the truth is being spoken: he knew it and it threw him completely. He hadn't seen this coming. He had misread the situation very badly.

He looked warily at the paper in her hand as if it had the capacity to bite him.

"What's this?"

She was glad that she had decided on how to deal with this if he called again as he said he would. Glad that she'd had time to discuss it with Olive and Buddy. She was happy that they were all in agreement that this was probably the best way to deal with the situation for all of them. It committed no one to anything, and it gave them time to proceed, if they wanted to, at their own pace.

"Their phone numbers. If you really want to meet them, and they agree to see you, then arrange to do it elsewhere."

Chapter 61

A satisfied smile graced Sophie's face as she padded silently, her feet deep in the thick pile of the carpet, to the window. She drew back the bedroom curtains quietly, not wishing to hasten the end of their time together, and soaked in the glorious morning sunshine. There wasn't a sound in the house, and it was a welcome silence, like an invisible cloak of stillness that bound the lovers in a cocoon of their own making.

But behind her Gary was already stirring in her bed and reached out an arm for her. It gave her such a full sense of pleasure when he stayed over, slept in her bed, woke to her alone. And this time he had stayed two nights in succession. It was the most positive sign, she thought. There was a tangible sense of timelessness in the house with no one else to rise and disturb this delicious blissful scene.

There was no Isabella to get ready for playschool, and there would be no Eileen with the radio going a bit on the loud side in the kitchen.

Myles invariably came into the kitchen in the mornings and turned it down with his usual "You don't mind, Eileen, do you?"

She never did apparently, at least she never said, so why she bothered to have it loud in the first place never crossed Sophie's mind till now. But now there was only a tranquillity that she allowed to seep into her bones.

Myles and Isabella were in Kerry, and she had given Eileen two days off, in a decision to create a romantic idyll. She had planned for her and Gary to be together as much as possible while she had the house to herself.

There was her apartment, of course, but most of her things were here, and the house was far better stocked than the apartment ever was. It pleased her that it was all the same to Gary where he made love to her; his desire for her was unbridled wherever they were. He lifted his head off the pillow and looked around for her.

"What are you doing over there?"

He pulled the covers back invitingly. Sophie laughed and moved like a wisp and was back in beside him, and yet again her body was urgently moving in unison with his, their craving for each other never satisfied for long.

She was first to shower and then went downstairs. She wanted to have breakfast ready when he came down. She smiled at herself, at the idea of her doing the housey thing – it wasn't her scene but it really wasn't so bad.

"I have to see the girls this evening," he mentioned as he milked his coffee. "I mentioned it last night," he looked up to see she remembered "and I have a couple of business arrangements for later in the week."

Her spirits fell.

She had been hoping he would change his plans and

stay. He liked to keep in regular touch with his daughters, she knew that, because they were still so young, but it didn't help her to feel any better about it. She resented the time he gave them, particularly when she had other plans as to how they could spend her free time.

She said nothing.

"I did mention it, Sophie." He looked across at her, waiting for her acknowledgement. "I need to see them as much as they need to see me. You have a daughter too – I'm sure you know how it is."

What could she say? She should be commending him for taking fatherhood so seriously – so many wouldn't bother as much as he, but right now she just wished he was one of them.

"I understand," she replied, smiling through her annoyance. "Of course I know how it is."

He looked at his watch. He did that a lot, and it went against the mood she was trying to create. He got up from the table, came to her and planted a lingering kiss on her lips.

"I'll miss you, Sophie, I always do. You're something else, y'know that?"

Another lingering kiss.

"We'll have to try and arrange that weekend you were talking about, soon as I see a gap," he said as he picked up his jacket and patted the pocket for his car keys.

"I'll ring you," were his three parting words.

Not the three little words she wanted to hear. Not yet, but three vital little words nonetheless.

"Do."

Perfect, the time they had just spent together had been perfect. It was difficult with his work trying to get times that suited them both. His work was demanding, clients at his level expected a lot, and his daughters obviously were precious, so if she was being a realist she supposed they didn't do too badly finding time for themselves, all things considered. But Sophie didn't like to be a realist. That often meant making allowances, and it went very much against the grain for Sophie to have to make allowances.

Chapter 62

It was a bright afternoon. The rain of the early morning was well and truly gone, leaving clear skies over the peninsula as far as the eye could see. Isabella was settling well into her break at Maeve's house. The incident with the milk appeared to be forgotten, and she was sleeping peacefully at night. Maeve said the clean fresh Atlantic air coming in off the sea took some getting used to and probably was knocking her out.

Myles admitted it was knocking him out too, and that wasn't a bad thing. He didn't care for lying awake in Maeve's lilac and cream bedroom being tortured by thoughts of Betty and her husband.

Apart from the fact that she had told him she was technically still married, she had never made much reference to her spouse, at least not in his own right, only in relation to them all as a family. Thoughts of him alone didn't seem to exist. She was a free agent, she thought like a free agent, behaved like a free agent and that was why he found it so threatening to see how the man could be 'back' with any expectation of having a future with her. What troubled Myles was how she obviously had some culpability or undealt-with emotions around the whole thing. That left her vulnerable, and that in turn meant anything could happen.

"And then he jumped really high and his mouth tipped off my hand," Isabella's excited breathless voice broke in on his thoughts. "He has *hundreds* of teeth and he splashed water all over us, he was so *big*, he was *that* size!" She stretched her arms wide to show Maeve how huge Fungi was, her eyes still wide with the amazement of it all. "Grandy said we can go again, can't we, Grandy?"

She kept jumping up and down with a splashing sound, emulating Fungi breaking the water and rising up into the air.

After the rain stopped, Myles had kept his promise to Izzy to take her to see Fungi. Down at the harbour, when they boarded the boat which would take them out into the bay, the excitement was palpable on board. All eyes were peeled in all directions while every wave that broke caused a ripple of excitement. Cameras and video recorders and even mobile phones were at the ready to catch pictures of the famous dolphin doing what he was famous for. But for quite a while there was nothing to see but the sea, the waves, and the shadows of the broken cloud on the water as the sun made an appearance then vanished behind a cloud again. A shout rang out and all eyes turned to the one direction as a splash was seen not too far from the boat.

Then stillness and silence as everybody watched for the first sighting. Then suddenly the magnificent mammal broke the surface quite close and performed a series of plunges while great excitement broke out on board. Myles held onto Izzy as she leaned as far as she was allowed over the side.

"Could I come next time, do you think?" Maeve asked. Isabella enjoying Fungi she just had to see.

"He could touch your hand," Izzy told Maeve, fully expecting her to be filled with awe if such a thing did happen to her.

The following day was showery and it was after lunchtime before the sun made an appearance, and Isabella contented herself for a while by doing drawings with a canvas and the acrylic paints that Maeve had given her. She decided to do her version of what Maeve was doing on the big canvases in her studio. While she was busy at the table, Myles settled himself down to do some reading. Throwing a watchful eye towards Izzy, he was happy that she was absorbed in her painting.

Some time later Quigley came upon this peaceful scene when he knocked to say hello.

"Come in, Quigley, good to see you, how's the arm doing?" Myles was glad of the company.

Isabella looked up at Quigley and nodded when he asked if she was well. The men sat chatting a while and Isabella sat and quietly threw a curious glance now and then at Quigley and his arm in the plaster cast. It was an interesting thing: she had never seen anyone who had broken their arm before. It was when Myles went across to the studio to call Maeve that Isabella addressed Quigley.

"Does your arm hurt, Whigley?"

"Not now," he answered, amused at her pronunciation of his name, "and it will be better soon."

Some friends had scribbled comments on the plaster and he invited her to put something on it too. She drew a figure of a man with a small head on a big body in blue acrylic paint, and acknowledged Quigley's remarks on it with just a little nod. She remembered him telling Myles about his accident when he was in the cottage the other day.

"How did you fall in the ditch?" she asked, dipping her pencil-thin brush into the little jar of paint. The question surprised him, but then he was surprised that she seemed interested in the first place.

"I slipped on the wet grass in the dark."

She considered that information for a second or two, and a frown came on her brow as she put paint-brush to canvas again and continued with her picture.

"Did you mind in the dark, Whigley?" she asked, still very intent on her painting.

He was unsure of how he should answer. The question seemed loaded, more by the tone of her voice than the words, but because he was a bit stumped as to how best to answer he decided to stick to the facts, and water it down a little for her.

"Well, nobody could see me to help get me out till it got bright."

The moment the words had passed his lips he thought it was the absolutely wrong thing to have said to a four-year-old, particularly this four-year-old. But she looked at him with renewed interest. He was a big man, a grown-up, and nobody had come to help him in the dark either. She could empathise with that, and it surprised her that such things could happen to a grown-up. But the way he put it didn't seem to bother her in the slightest; in fact she was actually commiserating with him.

"I didn't like the dark either," she confided, still not lifting her head.

It was a bit of a shock when he realised she had used the past tense. He saw the frown was still on her little face, but her mouth was set firmly and she appeared to be very absorbed in what she was doing. From Maeve he knew what was known of her captivity, and that wasn't much, but it was enough for Quigley to realise the significance of what Isabella was referring to.

"No?" he prompted quietly, not wanting to interrupt her train of thought or hinder her response by distracting her with other questions.

"It was smelly and dark, and there was a big dog . . ."

The door opened just then and Myles and Maeve came in. Catching the atmosphere in the room and the end of the interrupted sentence, Myles threw a questioning glance at Quigley. A flicker of a look passed back from Quigley and was enough to convey silence and no one spoke, waiting for her to continue. But the moment was gone and she gave her attention to her painting.

"I'm doing Fungi in my picture," she told them, and the matter was closed.

"That is the first time she has uttered a single word about it," Myles remarked.

They had been lucky to get a seat. All around them McCaffrey's was buzzing, the place crowded with locals and holidaymakers alike, and a *seisúin* was going full swing down the far end of the bar. Myles was feeling very hopeful that more might follow now that Izzy had broken her silence, that something she would say would give them a clue as to who took her and why.

"What made her come out with it, d'you think?"

"She was asking about my arm," Quigley replied. "She was curious about the plaster and seemed interested as to whether it still hurt or not, and when I said I had slipped in the dark it seemed to trigger something in her and she just came out with it. I didn't know how to react really when I realised she was talking about that."

Myles was thinking if Isabella was going to say anything else it probably was more likely to happen here rather than back in Dublin, and he hoped they would have time enough here for that.

"You know what they say about an ill wind, Quigley? Looks like your accident has acted as the catalyst that encouraged her."

He was convinced the house itself at home was a problem for her.

Quigley was thinking of the telling expression on her face as she talked, and thought how awful it must have been for her, especially being such a young child, and he just nodded to Myles' comment.

He put his pint to his lips and caught sight of Isabella's drawing on his plaster cast again. It struck an odd chord with him this time. It didn't look quite so harmless now. Then he noticed the eyes, the paint-brush dots he hadn't seen earlier, and they were not smiley eyes, and the childish blue paint figure with its small head and too big body had somehow lost its innocuous appearance.

Chapter 63

Eileen went about the house clearing up, picking up after her two days off, the annoyance showing clearly in the mutterings she made to herself as she went. You would think that 'madam' could at least have used the dishwasher or the washing machine during that time, if indeed she even knew how. How like Sophie to use her father and daughter's absence for her own ends. By the look of the house she must have had a great time of it indeed.

Not that Eileen was particularly house-proud; it was just that it was her job and it irritated her to have a double dose to catch up with like this.

She was in the middle of everything when she heard the doorbell. Bloody sales people, there was no end to them lately knocking on doors about the area, everything from catalogues to 'wash your windows'. She went to the door after the second ring, fully expecting to put the run on whoever it was outside, and was taken aback to see Detective Sheehan there.

"There're not here," she said shortly.

He ignored her comment. "May I come in?"

She stood back and let him in, wondering why he would want to come in after she had told him there was no one home.

"Are they away?"

She told him 'they' were in Kerry for a break, and Mrs Harcourt was at work. He nodded as though satisfied.

"Probably do that little child a world of good, to get away from here, wouldn't you say?" he mused, looking at her inquiringly.

The direct gaze unsettled her a little. Why should he ask her? What would she know?

"Do you know when they'll be back?" he asked as his gaze wandered about and came back to rest on her again.

"They didn't say, they don't tell me these things. Mrs Harcourt might know."

She wished he would just go. She didn't want to be standing here in the hall talking to him. There was something else, she could feel it, but he just stood there pursing his thin lips, as if making a decision and taking his time about it.

"Do you think," he gestured with his head towards the stairs, "that I might have a quick look in the room the child was sleeping in when she was taken?"

Her mouth opened wordlessly for a split second before she gathered herself together.

"Well, there's no one here. As I said they are away, and it's not up to –"

"I will let Mr Nugent know I have been here, and I don't think the family would mind me taking a minute or two, do you?" he said, cutting short her hesitation, or was it objection? He couldn't decide, but he moved towards the stairs nonetheless, assuring her there was no need for her to accompany him, he wouldn't be long. He was aware that his presence was causing her some unease; she hadn't managed to hide that.

Eileen moved towards the kitchen, a bit perturbed by his presence. There hadn't been an occasion before where he had called to find there was no one home but her. Since the return of Isabella he had called once or twice, as much to see how the little one was as anything, because from what she could make out the Gardaí didn't have much more to go on than before. Sheehan was hardly going to tell her any progress they might have made – he would keep that to tell the family himself – so why was he upstairs now? What was he doing? She fiddled about in the kitchen, waiting for him to come down to show him out, but he seemed to be an awfully long time up there. She kept her ears peeled but she heard nothing, at least nothing that would indicate what he was up to. She heard him walk along the landing and back to the room again, and he came down the stairs to the hall door and went up again. There was more walking about. Then silence. She strained her ears but could hear nothing. She was worried, this wasn't right, and she couldn't figure out what he was up to. When he came downstairs again, he had a thoughtful frown on his face. She came out to the hall to meet him.

"You have been working here since when, Mrs Hyland? Since after Mrs Nugent died, is that right?"

She wasn't expecting him to question her. They had done that already, in detail. She felt reluctant to answer.

She thought he was taking a bit of a liberty. But she couldn't see any problem in answering, apart from the fact that she just didn't think he should be asking.

"That's right."

"And you are here every day, is it?"

"Most days."

"And you leave at what time?"

He looked as if he was mentally writing this down, and she watched his face closely for any indication of where this was going, but he didn't have years in the force as a detective for nothing and his poker face told her nothing.

"As soon as Isabella is home and there is someone else here, I can go."

He nodded thoughtfully as if mentally trying to fit a jigsaw together.

"And you do. Go, I mean."

It was more of a statement, and she didn't feel the need to give him an answer. She moved purposefully towards the door, an indication that she thought he should be leaving, but he stood his ground and made a put-put-putting sound with his mouth. He looked all over the hall from the alarm box on the wall to the door-latch and up the stairs again.

"One minute," he said and turned and ran up the stairs again. She heard him walk the length of the landing from the door that led onto the fire escape back to the bedroom door. She felt her unease grow. After a few seconds he came down again.

"So in the course of your day's work you could often be here for some hours on your own, Mrs Hyland, would that be right?"

Her hesitation was slight, but he picked up on it just the same.

"Yes."

He moved to the hall door and opened it himself. Bidding her goodbye, he went out and pulled it shut behind him.

He walked the few steps to his parked car and sat in and buckled his safety belt. He put his key in the ignition and turned the engine on but he went nowhere immediately. He sat wondering if his hunch had any chance of paying off.

Eileen pulled herself together and went to look out the sitting-room window. She was disconcerted to see him still sitting there.

Back in the station Detective Sheehan sat at his desk. He flicked a pen around between his fingers, each time tapping the end of it on the desk before doing it again and again. Something was staring him in the face. He'd had that feeling in his gut right from the start, but he had yet to nail it down.

He thought his visit to the house today would help. It had added to his conviction that he already had some of the answers. He had some of the pieces of the jigsaw. He was just looking at them the wrong way round. He couldn't move on the theory that suggested itself to him as to how it could have been done, and possibly why, but if he was right it was a very logical theory. The trick was to find something that would substantiate it. Mrs Hyland's unease today added to the certainty growing within his gut.

Finally, with his brain twisted enough for the moment by concentration, he got up to leave. Perhaps it would do him good to get home reasonably early for once. Maybe that was what he needed, a few hours without thinking about it. Perhaps a few hours vegetating in front of the telly for a change might rejuvenate his grey cells.

Pulling on his coat, he checked his pockets for his mobile phone and made a call home saying he was leaving now and he would be home in about half an hour.

At least that was what he hoped if the traffic wasn't as bad as it had been earlier. A crash near the East Wall entrance to the Port Tunnel earlier on that afternoon had a tailback of traffic backed up as far as the Alfie Byrne Road and onto the Clontarf Road beyond the station, a tailback that had lasted a few hours.

The station was in the process of shift handover, but Casey and Burke were still at Casey's desk looking over papers and discussing their current case. Burke was perched on the edge of the desk.

"It's not enough to bring her in," he was insisting, "and if we don't make it stick and she walks, then we've blown it, and I don't think it's worth the risk."

Casey stretched his arms over his head, scratched his balding patch and rubbed his hand down the back of his stiff neck. Sometimes the frustration of his work could be so exhausting.

"Christ, we have to get her on something!"

Sheehan heard the familiar weariness in Casey's voice as he passed the desk.

"We've been so close before. If I have to spend another day on that bloody Hyland woman I'll fuckin' lose it, I swear to God I will!"

Sheehan stopped dead in his tracks. Maybe he was going to be home later than he thought after all.

Chapter 64

Isabella was tired. They had gone for a long walk today over the fields towards where the mountain began to rise behind the cottage, and now she was in her pyjamas curled up on the sofa beside Myles. Maeve was finished in the studio for the day, happy with the way her work was going, and now she cleared away the dinner things while Isabella told Ted about how their day had gone while on their walk. Ted wasn't getting as much of a look in these days as he was used to. Perhaps Isabella had moved into another phase of her life, maybe as a result of what had happened to her. Some of her innocence was gone; she had learned something of life the hard way, and prematurely. But for now she was happy to chat away to him. She no longer believed he actually listened, but it was a habit more than anything now.

Myles' mobile phone rang. He automatically moved Izzy and stood up when he looked at the name of the caller.

"Hello, Betty."

He hadn't really expected her to call, and now that she had he was half-afraid of what he was about to hear.

"How are you?"

He left the cottage and went outside for privacy. It was a very calm evening but he felt anything but calm inside. She said she was fine. Her voice was quiet, subdued, and it gave nothing away. If anything he thought she seemed a bit nervous.

"I was wondering how Isabella is – if the change of scenery is helping any?"

"Actually she broke her silence yesterday. She seems to have developed an affinity with one of Maeve's friends here who has a broken arm, and she was actually telling him something of what happened."

There was a long pause.

"Was it any help?"

His mind kept winding forward to what he was expecting her to get around to. He didn't want the conversation to get there.

"Not really. She was interrupted and she stopped talking then. She may get back to it."

"I hope so."

He couldn't put it off any longer. Now that she was on the phone he had to ask the question.

"And you, Betty, is everything okay with you?"

He felt she had been waiting for him to ask, and that wasn't fair. He shouldn't have to help the axe-man do his job.

"Yes, fine."

There was a long pause, as if she was deliberating as to how she would say something. Just say it, he wanted to tell her. She didn't have to find a delicate way, it wouldn't be any better clad in niceties, and it would just be wounding to try to sweeten the blow.

"I only have a minute, Myles. Olive will be here any minute to pick me up. We're going to dinner in Buddy's, but I am happy about the fact that after all this time I finally got to give Martin his walking papers. Well, I'm so glad Isabella has broken her silence. Will you say hello to her for me?"

He had no proper response ready, at least not a suitable response. It wasn't what he had been expecting, or had been preparing himself for. Over the phone he heard her doorbell ring and knew she was walking to answer it. He heard her greet her daughter. He found his voice finally.

"I'll tell her . . . thank you."

"Olive's here, Myles, I have to go."

She was gone. He couldn't believe that he had let her go like that. What would she think of him? Dumbstruck and silent when he should have taken the ball on the hop.

He came back into the cottage, his mind still reeling with surprise.

Maeve took one look at his face and found it impossible to know if her father was frowning with bad news or was deep in thought, so she asked hopefully, "Any news?"

Chapter 65

Quigley had taken quite a liking to Isabella. She was exactly the way he would like his daughter to be, if he had one. Her constant unstoppable exuberance was a tonic. Despite her down times, and there were some noticeable ones, she continued to bounce back again. He so enjoyed her chattering company. And so he took to going to Maeve's cottage to see her. She allowed him into her confidence on little things, but so far she hadn't said anything further about her kidnapping. He flattered himself that she had taken a shine to him too, in her own little way.

He felt Myles was glad of his company too. With Maeve working a lot across in the studio Quigley thought Myles was at a little bit of a loose end. So they joined forces and kept each other company.

This was something that pleased Maeve. Lately she thought she could detect her father's spirits had lifted. He didn't actually say, but she thought that mystery phone call had something to do with it. Still, she wouldn't have spent so much time with her work if it hadn't been for Quigley's presence. It was interesting having him around so much lately. Since his accident he was another person, as she kept telling him. She claimed that whoever tried to run him off the road had really done him a favour. He had objected at that.

"I never said someone tried to *run* me off the road," he'd protested.

"No, you never said it like that, that's true."

Maeve Nugent was too cute altogether.

When the weather allowed, the trio took the occasional trip together. Myles, Quigley and Izzy. Quigley showed them the sights of the Dingle Peninsula. Sometimes while Maeve worked they took long walks and sometimes they were glad of the use of Maeve's car.

On one particularly nice day they drove into Camp, and after a pleasant walk around the little village they then drove west to Stradbally where they had lunch in a lovely small restaurant where home cooking and local recipes comprised the entire menu. A visit to an arts and crafts shop followed and Isabella wanted to bring a pressie back for Maeve. She chose a small ceramic bowl with mauve flowers because it was nearly the same colour as Maeve's bedroom, and she could put her jewellery in it. After a post-lunch walk, they set off again for home. Continuing west they left the very scenic Brandon Bay behind them and the road began to climb into the mountains and towards the south-west. With Myles at the wheel, this road took them over the Connor Pass. The famous pass was a series of hairpin bends with no room for two cars to pass in some places and once committed to it there was no going back. Here and there Myles had to pull over onto loose shale against the side of the sheer rock mountainside so an oncoming car could go by.

"I'm very glad we're on our way back," he declared. "There is no way I would drive over this pass again today."

Adding interest and danger to the sometimes hair-raising journey, sheep were free to ramble over these mountains and often presented themselves on the roadway, to the delight of some passengers and possibly the annoyance of drivers. Isabella loved them and rolled down her window to lean out towards them, but they scampered away, much to her disappointment.

While Myles watched the road like a hawk, Quigley explained about the big red stain on the backs of the sheep, because Izzy had asked if they were bleeding.

Back at the cottage she took out the paints Maeve had given her and decided to "do" some drawings of sheep. Quigley invited her to draw one for him on his plaster cast. She thought that a great idea and she began to draw but she had forgotten about her earlier drawing on the cast and, when she saw the blue paint figure she had done before, Quigley was suddenly aware of a frown and a slight intake of breath.

"Do it on this side," he encouraged her, indicating a clear area away from the blue paint.

"This side is better," Isabella agreed. "I don't want my nice sheep beside *him*."

"The blue man is not nice?" Quigley asked innocently as she was intent on the drawing. He didn't think he was really going to get an answer because there was a long pause. He waited, watching her draw. The tip of Isabella's tongue was sticking out between her lips as she concentrated hard on the animal's spindly legs. She had decided to do the legs in black, like the real sheep.

Then he saw the slight shake of her head and the frown was back again.

"Oh right, why not though?"

At the back of his mind he was wondering where Myles was. She gave the wobbly animal a dab of a red mark on its back. It didn't look remotely like the real thing, but Isabella seemed very pleased with her effort.

"'Cos he was *there*," she confided finally.

It was barely audible, as if she feared her utterance might somehow conjure him up. The memory of him surfaced large in her mind now and the very thought of him terrified her. She remembered feeling the only place she was safe was on the bed, because if she stayed there the shape didn't threaten her. Sometimes he would open the door suddenly and glare in at her, just to make sure she hadn't escaped.

And sometimes he came in with something for her to eat but she wasn't hungry. She was always cold, and sleepy, but not hungry. The shape didn't care whether she ate or not; he took away what she wouldn't eat and gave it to the dog. But he made her drink the milk.

A memory flashed into her head of trying to look under the wooden slatted door once, but she heard the snuffling of the dog on the other side of it as he put his nose to the bottom of the gap, smelling her.

Sometimes in the dingy room, her fingers trailed along the cold flaky emulsion. She remembered picking quietly at the blistered paint, the flakes falling to the floor, and how they stuck to her bare feet. If the shape noticed he said nothing, as long as she was quiet.

Quigley said nothing, just pushed back her curls from her forehead with his free hand.

"Eileen was there too."

373

She whispered this as if she was divulging a great secret. Silence followed these words, and he realised immediately there was huge significance in her utterance.

He had no idea who this Eileen was, but Isabella either hadn't thought of that, or didn't realise it. He decided that didn't matter for the moment. He played along.

"You *saw* her too?" he asked quietly while he made a show of watching the drawing closely, hoping to draw her out a little more while pretending he was more interested in her painting than what she was saying.

She shook her head again.

"I didn't *see* her: *he* locked me in the smelly room. I heard them fighting in the other room."

Quigley assumed the *he* referred to the blue-painted figure. His heart was racing; it seemed like she was telling him evidence the police had so far been unable to unearth, despite their best efforts. If what she was saying was true, then maybe, just maybe this was a real breakthrough, something the police should know.

"Do you think that leg is a teeny-weeny bit too short?" he wondered, pointing at the sheep's leg and peering closely at the drawing.

Isabella looked at it consideringly.

"Did you hear what they were fighting about?" Quigley asked.

"No, just the voices in the other room. I'll make it a bit longer, will I?"

She decided there and then she didn't like dogs. Sheep, she liked them, but not dogs.

She dabbed with the paint again, engrossed in lengthening the fourth limb and then looked sideways at him, a questioning look on her face.

"That better, Whigley?"

Chapter 66

In the house in Howth Sophie put the handset back on its base. Myles had just phoned saying they would most likely be home in a couple of days or thereabouts. Sophie wasn't exactly pleased. She had expected they would be gone longer. Or rather she had *hoped* they would be gone longer. Myles had said Isabella was doing very well, the change of scenery had obviously been good for her, but he didn't want to put Maeve out any longer than they had to.

There was a lot Myles had not said. He did not mention what Izzy had told Quigley yesterday evening. He still had to sort his feelings on that. If he was honest, guilt was foremost among them. *Something* should have been obvious to him. If what Isabella said was true and he had been taking proper care of his little family, he should have noticed something amiss.

Nor did he mention his long phone conversation with Detective Sheehan earlier on. From what he could garner from that conversation, something had happened in Dublin that resulted in Sheehan not being so surprised when he phoned him with what Izzy had said. The man would not say – he just said there had been "developments" and Myles knew he neither would nor could elaborate at this juncture. On Sheehan's advice they ought not to return home just for the moment. He would let them know when the "coast was clear" as he put it, and please note that "nothing was to be said to Mrs Harcourt on the matter".

Myles reacted to that request with an understandable indignation, but Sheehan insisted it was for the best, as an informed Sophie might inadvertently show it in her manner or behaviour, and he assured Myles that Mrs Harcourt would actively be helping the investigation by her lack of knowledge on the matter, for the moment. Put like that Myles had to agree with him. But he knew she wouldn't like it.

What Sophie didn't like now was the consideration for Maeve. Maeve had to get her work done. Maeve had a commission. Maeve had customers who were waiting for their order, and she needed to be getting on with her work. Maeve this, Maeve that! So what!

Sophie had customers too. She had people waiting for their orders as well. She had been running a successful business longer than Maeve. Where was *her* praise? Where was the pride in what she had achieved? It was all about Maeve, Maeve, and still bloody Maeve! How could he stand to tear himself away from his darling first-born, the bloody artist?

Myles had said she was spending a fair bit of time with them, so they would likely stay a couple more days at most then they would be home. Sophie drew a deep breath. She had to calm herself. Gary would be here to collect her in a few minutes, and she mustn't be flustered, or annoyed. He mustn't see anything but a calm, sexy, stunning Sophie, ready to shower every attention on him.

She marvelled at herself these days. Peter still came to mind regularly, but his memory was much more benign and didn't torment her as before. She figured that was the result of how strongly she and Gary felt about each other. There was no room for negative feelings from the past. Peter would understand. Peter had always been good at understanding her.

Peter would have died for her.

She squashed that thought immediately. How had that managed to creep in when she was so happy now? She lost her patience with a necklace she was trying to fasten at the back of her neck. She flung it away from her.

The doorbell rang. He was here, and she wasn't ready! She was making her way downstairs when the door opened.

"Bradley! Oh, I thought –"

What was *he* doing here now?

Bradley looked up and saw her on the stairs, and he withdrew his key from the lock and closed the door behind him.

"Hi, Sophie, how are you?" He noted how eye-catching she looked. Obviously she was expecting someone other than him. Had she thought he was Marchant?

"I'm just going out, any minute now," she said briskly.

"Don't let me hold you up. I had a meeting in the golf club and I just dropped in for a quick hello. Any news from the deep south?"

She was surprised at him having to ask; she figured she was always the last to know anything.

"Dad was on earlier. He says they may be home in a couple of days."

"That's good." He looked towards the kitchen and noted the silence there. "Has Eileen gone home already?" He'd hoped for something to eat, preferably handed to him, and hot.

"Eileen's never here this late."

She seemed agitated. Was his presence bothering her? He decided he wouldn't stay. He could get a takeaway on the way home and was sorry now that he hadn't eaten in the club when the meeting was over. They had a fine restaurant there. A quick coffee then and he would leave her to it.

Sophie vanished upstairs as he made his way to the kitchen and came down with a necklace in her hands.

"Would you mind, Bradley?"

She held it out to him, and as he fastened the clasp the doorbell rang again.

There was a sharp intake of breath as she hurried out to answer the door.

A male voice greeted her and the door closed; a short silence followed. Bradley was just about to milk his coffee but something drew him out into the hall, coffee mug in hand.

The two men looked at each other, surprise registering on both faces. Bradley's grip on the handle of the mug tightened. Sophie looked from one to the other, sensing an undercurrent of something running between them. She suddenly was struck with how this could look to Gary, and she hurriedly made introductions.

"This is Gary Marchant," she said to Bradley. "Gary, my brother Bradley."

If she expected smiles and handshakes that certainly wasn't what she got. Bradley's face hardened, the surprise instantly replaced by a dark look, but it was Gary who remained surprised. Surprised and aghast. Sophie was flummoxed by the tension between them, and was anxious to clear the air. But what could she say that would clear up this awkward situation and make everything alright?

"I hoped it wasn't him," Bradley said to her, ignoring Marchant. "Dad told me you had a new man in your life, name of Marchant, and I hoped it wasn't him."

Even before she knew what he was talking about she sensed something awfully wrong but, Sophie being Sophie, she refused to believe her instincts when it didn't suit her

"You know each other? Gary?" She looked to him for clarification. There was no immediate response, and she sensed him emotionally backing away from her. That was one feeling she was prepared to believe, and alarm took hold of her.

"Gary?"

Gary Marchant instantly knew it was over, but surprise held him speechless.

Bradley helped him out there.

"Your boyfriend has a wife, Sophie . . ."

"I know that," she snapped, cutting him short. "Why are you doing this, Bradley? They are separated. Tell him, Gary," she flung a hand wildly in Bradley's direction, "tell him!"

The look on his face spoke volumes, but Gary said nothing.

Bradley cut in. "Separated? I don't think so. They spend a fair bit of time together as a family for a couple who are separated. Like last week, flew down to

Dromoland with the family. Again. It must be a regular home from home by now – regulars at the airfield they are – isn't that right, *Mr* Marchant?"

They both heard her intake of breath. She wished with all her heart Gary would say something, tell her what her brother said was all wrong, convince her otherwise, anything so that this wasn't happening, but the disbelief in her eyes was slowly being replaced by hatred.

"You said you had business appointments!" she accused him. "You said you couldn't see me because of that, and because your children were so young –" Her voice broke off as the extent to which she had been deceived suddenly slammed home with gut-wrenching force.

"Sophie . . ." he began but it was as if the sound of his voice had broken a spell and Sophie utterly snapped.

"Get out! You slimy bastard, get out before I take your bloody *life*!" she screeched. She grabbed the coffee mug from Bradley, the hot liquid spilling over his hand, and flung the mug at Gary. It missed and smashed against the wall, but the action galvanised him into movement. For a split second he struggled with the latch on the door, then he managed to wrench it open, and was gone.

Silence crashed down on Sophie and Bradley as the door was slammed, leaving them both stunned and speechless. The burn on Bradley's hand throbbed, but all he could think was the cheat got a quick exit, far better than he deserved.

"Come inside, Sophie, I'll pour us a drink."

She was still standing staring at the closed door, incredulity immobilising her. This was not happening! This could *not* be happening to her. Two minutes ago Gary had called to take her out. They were going to dinner. They would be oblivious to the rest of the world, they would be lost in their overpowering love and they were coming back here and he would rock the foundations of her being with his lovemaking . . .

But now he was gone, *gone*, and it was Bradley's fault!

"Sophie . . ." Bradley forgot the burn on his hand, the eerie stillness of his sister concerning him more.

"You had to go and ruin it, didn't you?" Her voice was like the rumble of a rock-fall before it crashed with devastating effect. "You with your righteous little life and your moral uppity attitude! Why don't you join the real world and stop judging others? Why did you have to come here tonight anyway?"

He was alarmed at how she was reacting, and ignored her remarks. Yes, she was in shock, but he sensed something else, a degree of hysteria, panic.

He attempted to draw her out of the hall and into the sitting room where he intended to get her a shot of brandy, and perhaps stay till he was sure she was going to be okay. But her manner and bearing surprised him. She shook him off vigorously, as if his touch seared her skin, and she strode into the kitchen.

"You can go, too," she said through clenched teeth. "Who needs either of you!"

"I'll stay a little while," he offered.

"You will not! You've done enough damage for one night!"

He didn't expect thanks or anything like it. He had done what he thought she would have wanted, and did it out of concern for her, but despite the obvious shock he still found her reaction unbelievable. But even if he had said nothing tonight, Marchant's own reaction had said it all. He was taken so unawares that he stood there facing his nemesis and Sophie could simply have read it all there on his face. Then the miserable cheat had just crept out, leaving devastation behind him.

"Sophie, I'm sorry –"

"Sorry? Ha! What would *you* know about sorry? You couldn't wait to spill the beans on him! What kind of a sicko *are* you?"

He certainly did not want to leave her alone just then. He felt he at least ought to make sure she was going to be okay before he left. He made allowances and did his best to ignore the remarks she flung at him. Her voice was rising once again into a screech. There was a wild look in her eyes, they darted everywhere. She was searching for something on which to pin her pain, something formidable that could take this unbearable hurt and anger without disintegrating, something very unlike her.

Bradley's concern was mocking her; *he* had done this, and he had done it knowing he was unable to fix it.

"Get the hell out!" she roared at him. "Or do you want to enjoy watching what you have done? Get some perverse pleasure out of it, will you? Happy now, are you? Why don't you go and get yourself someone to keep you busy, stop you interfering in other people's lives?"

Her insinuations struck deep, and he could ignore them no longer. With a heavy heart he went to the door and let himself out, the throbbing coffee-burn on his hand forgotten. But the situation he left his sister in caused him great concern. She shouldn't be on her own right now.

Chapter 67

The following morning Eileen arrived to find a disintegrating dishevelled Sophie. She did not say or ask anything: whatever had her in this state was no concern of hers, and she preferred not to know. Sophie should have been in the shop by now, but by the look of her she was fit to go nowhere. Maybe if Eileen helped out she would decide to go to the shop, albeit a bit late.

Eileen made herself a coffee before she set about her work. It was grand with the rest of the family down in Kerry. Not that they were hard to work for. On the contrary they generally left things up to her, allowed her to set her own work pattern, and sometimes even her hours. Mr Nugent was fine like that, easygoing, laid-back, trusting . . . and unobservant. That was the best bit, and it suited her down to the ground.

The whole debacle with the child missing was a bit tough though. For a while there, recently, she had thought the game was up, but it had all turned out well, and no one was any the wiser.

She took the credit herself for the safe return of Isabella. Intervening like that was the best she could do. She had to: she couldn't leave the little one in that situation. It had been a risk, and Eileen was not one for unnecessary risk-taking, and she might not have done anything at all about it if she had been able to sleep at night.

The rest of them blamed her for the situation. They said she should have known about the change of bedroom. She was supposed to cop things like that. It was of course the easy way out for them, blaming her and taking the heat off themselves. But they should never have taken the child; that was the stupidest thing ever. Every one of them acknowledged that in one way or another. Kidnapping was a major offence, it carried a maximum life sentence, and it was certain to bring the full force of the law down on them. But they still blamed her.

They had been lucky. The child was home, unhurt, and there wasn't much else the Gardaí knew about it, at least so it said in the papers, and on the news. No leads. Those reporters were sharp; very often they knew stuff the cops didn't – you'd see it all the time on the telly when the 'undercover camera' blotted out faces because it was stuff the cops either couldn't make stick, or didn't know.

But it was all right now. The heat was off, and things had gone very quiet, died down. But she didn't want anything to do with the business any more. She knew the Nugent family would be extra-vigilant now. And it would leave her too exposed if anything went wrong again.

She poured herself another coffee. There were sounds from upstairs of Sophie moving about. Maybe she would go to work and Eileen wouldn't be bothered by her. That would be handy. The doorbell rang. Bother. The postman was early today. She rambled out and opened the door.

"Mrs Eileen Hyland . . ."

The colour drained from her face. The very bearing of Detective Sheehan and the Gardaí on the doorstep signalled trouble. She was so surprised that she barely acknowledged that she had heard.

"You are under arrest for the kidnapping of Isabella Nugent."

The clipped officious tone chilled her to the bone. But she was made of that element that got her back up at the very idea of being confronted by the cops and she quickly backed off.

"Who do you think you're accusing of kidnapping? I had nothing to do with that! Get your dammed hands off me!"

They were too used to the tactics she employed, struggles or evasive movements were a waste of energy and the handcuffs were on before she knew it.

Sophie appeared at the top of the stairs. They were taking Eileen! They couldn't do that! She needed her!

"Detective Sheehan! What is going on here?" She pulled her dressing gown tighter around her, and she started down the stairs. She ignored the other two Gardaí.

"Mrs Harcourt, I have just informed your housekeeper that she is under arrest for the kidnapping of your daughter."

Sophie laughed. It was a high-pitched snort of disbelief, and it made the men look at her twice. Sheehan was not about to hang around. He was here for a specific purpose, but he easily recognised the state of Sophie and offered his concerned opinion.

"My advice would be not to bother about this one, Mrs Harcourt. You just get yourself sorted."

His meaning was obvious but she was fractious enough to feel affronted. While she stood at the hall door, they frogmarched a highly protesting Eileen out the door and into the waiting patrol car. Sophie watched with incredulity as a hand bent Eileen's head down to prevent her banging it against the doorframe, and the last sighting she had of her was a scowling Eileen hemmed in the back seat between two burly policemen.

Chapter 68

Myles came into the studio. Maeve knew by him that a decision had been made. She put down her brush and wiped her hands on a cloth.

"What is it, Dad?"

"I've just been talking to Detective Sheehan."

She waited for him to continue. Since Isabella had spoken out, things had moved fast in Dublin by the sound of it. The family were having a hard time of it trying to come to terms with what had been going on under their noses. Myles in particular was quite broken up about it. All the facts weren't out yet, but hopefully the questioning of Eileen would reveal more, and give answers to the questions that were tormenting him.

"I should have known, Maeve," he said for the umpteenth time. "How could I not have noticed something? What sort of a father and grandfather have I been?"

His voice was laden with guilt and grief at the thought of what had befallen his family in their own house, where they should have been safe. It was understandable he would feel like this, but it was hardly possible for any of them to know the criminal mind, Maeve said, or to gauge how daring and devious they would be where their activities were concerned. She told him this many times, but it made very little impression on him.

"Don't torment yourself like this, Dad. You did the right thing bringing Isabella here. If you hadn't seen the need to get her away from the house for a while, the truth might not have come to light. It's thanks to your insight that it did."

He smiled a weak smile. He could always trust his elder daughter to bolster him up when it was needed.

"Anyway, I think we'll leave tomorrow. Sheehan has done his business and the coast is clear, you might say. You've been great having us here, but we need to be getting on home."

"Does Isabella know yet?"

He shook his head in answer. From where he stood he could see his precious granddaughter over by a large sycamore tree in the garden with Quigley. She was sitting on a swing someone had hung from one of its branches years ago, before Maeve took the cottage, and Quigley was sitting on the grass nearby, supporting himself on the elbow of his good arm. They had become almost inseparable since she and Myles had arrived in Dingle; they were like two wounded spirits who found something akin to solace in each other's company. Myles marvelled at how easily Quigley was able to become part of her world, how they connected on some level that allowed them to understand each other so easily.

"She will miss him," he said as he watched, and Maeve agreed with him.

"Do you know what I keep thinking?" she asked, her gaze following his, and a little smile twinkled about her eyes.

"What do you keep thinking?"

"It sounds silly, I know, but I keep thinking that it's almost as if she has decided Quigley can replace Ted in some ways."

He looked at her in surprise and would have dismissed her words without a second thought, but then he saw it as she did, and realised how perceptive it was. He nodded his agreement as another thought occurred to him.

"Quigley will miss her too but then he will have some compensation, I think."

"How so?"

"Do I really have to say?" he grinned. "Quigley McGurk was coming over here well before Izzy and I arrived."

She did not elaborate on his comment but busied herself with her brushes again: she had walked herself into that one.

"He won't be here that much longer. His year will be up soon and he'll go back to his university and his students. I remember when he first arrived in Dingle how he talked about how much he loved his work."

Myles listened, absorbing the unspoken inference as well as the spoken words.

"And now he is passionate about his poetry," he replied.

And you, he thought.

"All I'm saying is that change happens and we shouldn't be too cut and dried about things, you know?" he said aloud.

She gave that little movement of her eyebrows which

she did when she knew exactly what her father meant, and when she wasn't going to make a reply to his comment.

"I'll order a taxi for the morning," he said.

He said no to her offer when she insisted on driving them to the station, saying he preferred to say goodbye at the cottage.

"I'll miss you both," she said, changing the conversation's direction, "you and Isabella. It's been great having you here. I hope you'll make a bit of a habit of it now."

He nodded agreeably to that without replying. She noticed how contemplative he had become as he stood looking out towards the swing for a brief moment, as if preparing himself for a difficult task. She was well aware that the last thing he wanted to do was to spoil that happy contented place that Izzy was in at the moment. The nightmares appeared to have stopped, and she was sleeping the night through without a bother.

It was pure heaven to Myles to think that her torment had eased. To watch Izzy now was to look at the old Izzy but, wonderful as it was, they could not stay here indefinitely.

He took a deep breath, went out of the studio and crossed the grass to the swing. When Izzy caught sight of him he was smiling.

"Will you push me please, Grandy?" she called.

He obliged, and delighted in her excited squeals as he urged her to hold on tight.

"Whigley, look at me!" she cried out as she sailed higher and higher.

But Quigley was watching Myles, and noticed that his face held that preoccupied look of someone with something on their mind. Presently Myles allowed the swing to slow down despite her demands for him to continue.

"We will have to get a swing for you in our garden at home," he said, searching for the best way to broach the matter of going home.

"I like this one," Izzy declared defensively, her feet finally touching the ground.

"We could have Andy fix one up for you – he would know the very best spot for it."

She said nothing to that, but the laughter had left her at the reminder of home.

"Mummy misses you, you know, because we have been longer here than we planned, so it's time for us to go home, Izzy."

"No! No, Grandy, I want to stay here!" she insisted.

He saw her anxiety. She left the swing and he noticed how she moved closer to Quigley. It cut him to the quick to see it. He had done that, by not protecting her properly.

"I want to stay here!"

"It's nice at home now, and Mummy is all on her own. Eileen is gone now. She won't be back any more."

Isabella still made no reply and he wondered if the significance of what he had just said had sunk in with her. He shared a fleeting glance with Quigley. While he remained sitting on the grass, Quigley took Isabella's hand and offered the back-up Myles needed.

"Your grandy is a very brave man, you know, Isabella. A little bird told me that he got the police to take Eileen away. She won't be going back into your house. Ever."

She threw a quizzical look at Quigley. He saw her eyes shift to the blue-painted man on his plaster cast.

"All the bad people are gone," he told her quietly, "and they can never come back either – your grandy has seen to that."

Without being able to articulate either what she thought or how she felt, Izzy knew that Quigley was her friend, and he wouldn't say that if it wasn't so.

"But your grandy will bring you down again to see us often, isn't that right, Myles?"

She gave a faint little smile in response to Grandy saying of course he would and the two men shared a look of camaraderie.

Then Isabella wrapped her arms around Quigley's neck.

"Will you come and see Fungi with me next time, Whigley?"

Quigley came to the cottage the following morning to be there to see them off. The driver placed their bags in the taxi, and Myles hugged Maeve tightly.

"Perhaps now you can get on with your masterpieces in peace," he smiled. "The world is waiting to see them!"

Isabella hugged both Maeve and Quigley and was still waving out the rear window as the taxi moved down the road and the cottage disappeared from sight.

Quigley followed Maeve back into the cottage, which suddenly felt very empty and silent. He realised she was making a big effort to hold back unshed tears. He put his good arm around her shoulders, squeezed her supportively and placed an empathetic kiss on the top of her head. Joy surged through him as she moved fully into his embrace, and she wrapped her arms around his waist and rested her forehead against his chest. When she lifted her head he had no hesitation in placing his next kiss full on her lips.

Chapter 69

When they arrived at their house in Howth it was strangely quiet. Usually there was the sound of Eileen doing whatever she was busy with, and the radio going in the kitchen. Myles didn't expect Sophie to be there either – she would be at the boutique. But there was an out-of-the-ordinary silence for their house.

Isabella entered with obvious reluctance, as if she expected Eileen to jump out at her from somewhere, and she was only happy when she had gone into her own bedroom, and all the rooms, and found that Grandy was right. Eileen *was* gone.

Myles listened to the message left on his answering machine. It was from Bradley and worried him, not so much for what he said, but for the tone of his voice.

"Dad, ring me when you get this."

Myles dialled Bradley's number. It was answered immediately.

"Dad, I'm in Beaumont hospital. Sophie is here. She'll be fine, but . . ."

"What happened?"

Bradley paused, not wanting to give his news over the phone.

"Bradley?" His father's tone said he wasn't about to wait to hear whatever it was.

"She's okay, Dad, but it seems like she overdosed . . ."

"What!"

"She'll be fine, they said. Really, but they are taking some tests . . ."

Myles didn't wait to hear any more. "I'm on my way now."

He didn't stop to see if Isabella could be minded by Ruairi's mother – he simply bundled her into a taxi and they arrived at the hospital within half an hour.

Bradley met them in the foyer. The furrows of worry showed deep in his father's face as he hurried to meet him. His whole bearing asked the wordless questions.

"She'll be okay, Dad, she's upstairs. They've just taken her to a ward."

"What brought this on, Bradley? I thought she was happy, her new man and everything . . ."

Bradley's silence caused him to look at him quizzically, and their previous conversation came back into his head.

"He was, wasn't he?"

Bradley nodded.

Myles sounded as if he had been holding his breath. "The bastard! How did she find out? *When* did she find out?"

"I was in the house the other night when he came to collect her. He and I recognised each other. She was devastated."

He didn't elaborate on the argument that ensued or that he left her alone then, even if it was at her insistence.

"I was worried about her. She wasn't answering her phone and she wasn't in the shop, so I called in to the house a couple of hours ago."

He shivered at the thought of what could have happened.

Myles felt it emanate from him and placed a grateful supportive hand on his shoulder.

"Have you seen her since?"

"Briefly. She looks dreadful, but they say she will be fine."

Sophie was sleeping naturally when they reached the ward. At his father's request, Bradley agreed to take Isabella home. Myles would stay till Sophie woke.

He spoke with the doctors while he waited and also did a lot of thinking and a lot of looking back. Back to when his daughter's problems really seemed to assert themselves. After Peter's accident Myles had expected her to be dysfunctional for a while, that would have been normal, but it also should have decreased with time under normal circumstances. So what was different about her bereavement? Why did she not adjust, and why was she haunted by it? Had it led to her dependency on drink and drugs? Maeve was right, and Bradley had seen it too, but he, her father, did not want to accept it. Perhaps it was his fault, perhaps he should have supported her more. Perhaps if he had it would not have come to this.

He sat by her bedside and waited and thought what to do.

Eventually he went to find a bathroom and returned to see her awake.

"Dad." Sophie's voice was a whisper, pain and anguish filling her eyes as she turned and saw the pain in his.

He gripped her hand. "We'll talk, Sophie, when you're up to it . . ."

But she didn't want to wait. "I didn't mean it, Dad, you have to believe me . . . I just wanted it to stop . . . I never meant *this*."

He put her hand to his lips and then patted it, relief flooding over him. He looked into her face, her eyes in dark sockets in a dull transparent skin, and found anguish and pain there, but there was also truth. He nodded in agreement and gratitude, unable to find words adequate to convey his feelings.

"I never meant this, Dad, I'm so sorry."

"Sophie, can you tell me what troubles you so? Why are you so unhappy?" he asked quietly.

The curtain was partially pulled between hers and the other bed in the room, and the other patient was snoring quietly.

Sophie looked away from her father and closed her eyes against her pain.

Don't do this, Sophie, he mentally pleaded, please talk to me, let me help.

She freed her hand and began to gather the edge of the sheet in a fidgeting, nervous motion.

He had to listen very closely to hear her.

"I can't live with it any longer, and I can't forgive myself . . . he shouldn't be gone . . . it's my fault . . ."

Myles watched her closely, seeing the anguish that went so very deep, but he didn't understand it.

"Tell me, Sophie," he urged her, "let me help."

"No one can help."

She sounded helpless, resigned. He waited.

"Peter had drugs taken when I asked him to go for

that takeaway. Recreational was how we saw it, if there is such a thing," she said bitterly. "He shouldn't have been driving, but I insisted. I was as high as he was, and he went to please me. I killed him, it was my fault, and he won't forgive me! He won't forgive me!"

Her voice broke and her body shook with the telling of it, and hard sobs were wrenched from deep within her. She inhaled a deep breath as if she hadn't had sufficient air in a long time. Myles said nothing, just waited quietly, seeing something of the hell she had been living in since the accident.

"He won't forgive me and I can't bear it but I didn't mean this!"

Her hand waved distractedly around the ward. Her eyes followed the motion in disbelief. She was shocked to find herself here, shocked to know that only for the fact that Bradley was concerned for her, even after how horrible she had been to him, she might not be here at all . . . God, it was frightening to think what had almost happened, what she almost did. She heaved as a deep shudder shook her visibly.

"I just wanted to escape it all for a while – Peter, and the trauma of the Isabella situation. And Gary didn't help. While I was with him I could block it out, but now it is as bad as ever and I can't live with it, I need something to block it out . . . and then Eileen . . . oh God, to think I thought she was my friend! She was supplying us, Peter and me, and then just me, because I can't live with what I've done."

He put his arms around her, and she sobbed as she hadn't sobbed since she was a little child. He waited for it to subside. He gave her his handkerchief. They sat a long time in silence while Sophie silently realised that she had to do something about herself.

"My God, look what I've come to, Dad. I'm no better than a junkie, and lucky to be alive."

"Sophie, listen to me, will you? You are my daughter and I love you. You mean so much to me, so much to us all and we want you to be well, you have so much to live for. Maybe you can't see it right now, but we can. Peter made his own decision, whatever the reason for it, and he chose to drive that night. It wasn't your fault. Peter never struck me as a man who did things he didn't want to do."

Her father was right in what he said. Peter never had taken telling; that had been her own ego telling her she could twist him around her little finger. Had she ever *really* been able to do that? Probably not, but if felt better to think she could.

Myles sensed the resignation in her and told her gently what he had been thinking while she slept. "Don't you think you should do something about this problem?"

She knew he was talking rehab and she had known he would bring it up. She surprised herself by her willingness to acknowledge that she needed help.

He realised that he was surprised too. He had expected resistance, denial, at least some degree of opposition. But he was not about to give her time to change her mind.

"What if we found a nice private place? Somewhere private and discreet?"

Chapter 70

Detective Sheehan rang, asking if Myles was home. He wanted to talk to him.

"I'll be in for the evening," Myles answered. "Call anytime." Myles put the phone down. "Detective Sheehan – he's calling round."

"You want me to go, Dad?" Bradley asked reluctantly. When it came to 'the Isabella matter' as he preferred to think of it, he believed his family needed all the support they could get, for however long it took.

"You stay put," Myles answered, "no need for you to go."

Isabella was sleeping peacefully in her bed. Her nightmares hadn't resurfaced, thankfully, and it was a comfort to Myles to check on her and stand a minute or two just watching how peacefully she slept. There was a time when he had wondered if he would ever see it again.

When Sheehan arrived he was all apologies. "Sorry about the time, got delayed, the story of my life, I'm afraid."

He settled himself in the armchair Myles indicated and accepted the coffee offered to him. He gazed into the blazing fire, apparently lost in thought. Myles waited.

"Great to see a real fire, you know. Not many houses I have to visit bother with them any more. Can't beat it, eh?"

He supped his coffee, obviously enjoying the home comforts. Then he put his cup down, as though he had come to a sudden decision.

"Well, to business," he said abruptly.

Myles and Bradley were all attention.

"It's an interesting story, you know, that Mrs Hyland has to tell. We thought at first she would never talk. She has family involved in this, clearly didn't like the idea of spilling their beans. But kidnapping is a major crime, carries a serious sentence, and I think in the end she was afraid that taking the rap for it would fall on her, unless she spoke up and co-operated."

He shifted his position and seemed to be considering what he had just said. They waited again.

"I have to say, it was an ingenious idea, the way they worked it. If it hadn't been for your granddaughter unconsciously recognising her voice, and indeed remembering it, we would have had great difficulty connecting Mrs Hyland to it. Or finding out why it all happened in the first place."

The truth was they probably never would have, but he wasn't about to say that. The public had to have confidence in their police force at all times. That was what he drilled into his men. Mostly it worked. To himself alone he acknowledged how indispensable 'lucky breaks' were in their type of work.

As he spoke Myles and Bradley had questions

forming, but he always looked as if he was forming the next bit of information, and they didn't want to interrupt his thinking, at least not yet.

"Drugs of course were their business, and very lucrative they are too. Especially when you can get away with it the way they did to date. We did have some help from a farming couple who live near the place where they held Isabella. They became suspicious when they noticed some activity in the derelict cottage on the land next to them. Apparently their dog found it very interesting all of a sudden, although Isabella had been returned that night. The Drugs Squad has been trying for quite a while now to figure out where they were stashing the stuff. That was one place."

He glanced up from the fire and fixed them with a look that signified outrageous neck.

"Your spare room was another. Yes, I know it's unbelievable, but that is where Mrs Hyland came in. It was her job to find a suitable place in a 'safe house' from which they could operate the distribution in small easy-to-manage amounts and obviously yours fitted the bill perfectly. Being a 'daily' was her cover."

Myles was completely shocked, so much so that questions he wanted answers to refused to form as he tried to take in the enormity of what he was hearing.

She was actually using his home, his *house* as a distribution base for their drugs business. And that, apparently, was her primary reason for being there in the first place. No wonder she wasn't very obliging. She wasn't a 'daily' by choice.

Sheehan was used to all sorts of reactions: silent shock and vociferous outrage. If he wasn't interrupted he usually just carried on.

"After she had decided that the activities of the family,

the house itself and the location would suit their purposes she was able to arrange things to suit them. She had the perfect opportunity – hours alone in the house. She even had a hiding place fixed under the floorboards in the spare room, where the packages were kept. She actually brought someone in to construct this suitable hiding place. Expertly done too, she says it was, not detectable unless you knew what you were looking for. She could remove as many packages at a time as she needed to carry in that bag of hers, quite without raising any suspicion whatever. I would like to take a look at this hiding place while I'm here, if you don't mind."

Myles found his voice. "But what of the man Isabella saw? And those who took her? What were they doing here in the night if Eileen was their distributor?"

Sheehan was coming to the most daring bit.

"Those were the guys who actually landed the drugs, and deposited them in this house. At low tide the rocky shoreline at the back of your house is exposed. A small dingy could land there unseen. It is too far below the houses to be troubled by lights, and the height of the hill would muffle the sound of the engine, and as you know it is not a difficult climb up through the bracken and undergrowth that proliferate on the slope beyond your garden."

"But my house is alarmed! I have it checked twice a year!"

Sheehan cut in. "But Mrs Hyland had a key for her own use and the alarm code, correct? She had copies made and passed them and the code on. She gave them detailed instructions as to where everything was, and the layout of the upper floor. And they came in from the back via the fire escape and the door at the top of it. The alarm can be switched off by means of a box there, right? And because it has an LED screen rather than a voice it suited then perfectly. And the nearest bedroom to that door is the spare room, yes?"

Myles nodded stupidly.

"I thought it might be a good idea at the time to have a box at that door," he said lamely. He looked dejected.

"It was, Dad," Bradley said, "but we don't know the criminal mind, do we? How could we ever think the likes of this could happen?"

Sheehan sat and waited while the incredulity of it sank in. He didn't really need to go to see the hiding place or the alarm box for himself. Mrs Hyland's fear of being charged with kidnapping had made her give explicit details under questioning, and he had no doubt that they would prove to be exact, but he had to see them from an official investigative point of view. Forensics would be over in the morning to examine the room again, take fingerprints from the recess and the surrounding area. Sheehan impressed on Myles and Bradley the importance of no one going near it till forensics had been back.

"How – how long has this been going on?" Myles demanded incredulously. "How often were these thugs in my home?"

"Not as often as you might fear, I think, Mr Nugent," Sheehan assured him. "The removal of the drugs from here was done in broad daylight, a certain amount of packages at a time, in a canvas shoulder bag Mrs Hyland always carried. When a new shipment arrived they divided it up, some of it went elsewhere, and some of it came to your house, from what Mrs Hyland says. The rest of the story will, no doubt, come from other members of the gang, her son among them. We have had him under surveillance for quite some time, a slippery eel if ever there was one."

Myles had a mental picture of Eileen and her large bag which she was never without. Now and again it had crossed his mind that she must have everything but the kitchen sink in it. God! If only he had known. If only he hadn't been quite so dammed trusting!

Bradley had been taking all this in, but realised Detective Sheehan hadn't mentioned Isabella yet.

"What about Isabella? Why take her?" he demanded.

The answer was simple, Sheehan said.

"Isabella was basically in the way that night. She wasn't expected to be in that bedroom, and Mrs Hyland was genuinely at a wedding, we checked it out, so she didn't know to warn them."

Bradley thought of the panicking of Sophie when she phoned him after she had seen the damage to the ceiling and the rest of Isabella's room by the storm, and how it was such a relief that they had the spare room for her to sleep in. Little did they know the danger they were putting her in.

"They took her because they had no plan B. An alternative would never be allowed – packages could go missing, and they couldn't leave your house still in possession of the drugs – their lives wouldn't have been worth it, and they knew it. Easier and safer for them to complete their drop and take the child and then try to make it look like she had wandered herself. That's why the hall door was left open. It was badly thought out – they were taken by surprise and they didn't know what else to do with her."

That horrendous time came back to Myles' mind and replayed itself as clearly as if it was happening only now.

"But what of the fact that Isabella claimed she saw a man in her room the night before? What about that?" he demanded.

According to Sheehan, Eileen hadn't been informed about that but she thought it was probably a new guy on that run, to familiarise him.

Myles and Bradley found the whole story very hard to credit. Sheehan said that Eileen had claimed under questioning that there was no threat to the family. The whole operation depended on its secrecy, and the family never knowing of the activity.

"What of the other gang members?" Myles wanted to know. He couldn't rest easy till they were sure they were all apprehended, and their activities put to an end. Sheehan was able to tell him they believed they had all the main players, and there was no further threat to his family.

"No further threat!" Myles exploded. "Someone has my house key, and my alarm code!"

But there was something he could do about that immediately. He would change the code this very night. The locks he could have changed tomorrow, all of them. Detective Sheehan allayed his fears. "There is no way they will be back here, or anywhere. That gang have been well and truly routed."

He asked to see the spare room again and the landing door to the fire escape. He had hoped to do that while he was here, but Myles asked him to leave it till morning.

"I don't want Isabella to waken and hear a strange voice on the landing. She is doing so well since we were in Kerry . . ."

"Of course, of course, that was thoughtless of me," Sheehan said. "Of course, I will call in the morning."

"That would be better, thank you. Isabella will be at school in the morning."

When he had left, Myles poured brandies for himself and Bradley, and they sat and discussed the entire mind-boggling episode, the daring and the extreme audacity of the gang. Eventually a feeling of lightness and relief settled on them. The ordeal was over in the main. They might well be asked to testify, Sheehan had mentioned, but that would probably be a good way off yet. Isabella would not have to be exposed to any further situations, he assured them, and Eileen's disclosures together with the evidence gathered by Burke and Casey would be enough to put most of the ringleaders away for a very long time.

"You know, I never was very keen on Eileen," Bradley remarked. "There was always something about her. Had no objection to her cooking though. And I'll tell you something else – Andy Fox never liked her either! You could tell. The way that man avoided her!"

"Ah – Andy! You know, they don't make them like Andy any more. You could trust him with your life. I'm sure he won't be sorry to see the back of her. Good Lord, when I think back to the little confabs I used to come upon between Sophie and *her*! No wonder the conversation would dry up all of a sudden. I hope she gets life. She deserves it for what she put this family through."

Bradley was thinking of Sophie. "I must say she really has been going through hell, hasn't she, thinking she was responsible for Peter's accident? That's a lot to be carrying around with you. But still, I thought she would put up fierce objections to going for treatment – you know how intractable and wilful she can be."

"You know, Bradley, it came as a huge shock to her

to wake and find herself in that hospital. She was so shocked and upset it was palpable. I think that's what did it. After that, the decision was easy for her. Thank God you called into the house when you did – she owes you her life."

Bradley laughed softly and swirled his drink. "I'd never say anything about that to her – she has more than enough to be going on with – but you can bet she won't like that notion for one minute."

Myles just smiled when he thought of the natural familial aggravation between his children. Was there ever the perfect family, he wondered? The fire had died down and he decided it was too late to put more fuel on it.

Bradley stifled a yawn.

"There's a bed upstairs for you," Myles said.

"It's beginning to beckon, I think," was the tired reply.

Myles looked in on Isabella before going to bed himself. She had just woken up and wanted to go to the bathroom. When he tucked her back into her bed, he brushed back the curls and kissed her forehead and said goodnight. She wrapped her arm around Ted and pulled him close.

"When you come home from school tomorrow we will go and see if Betty would like to come here and you and I can do dinner for her," Myles told her as he tucked the duvet in all about her.

Well, it would be a start, Myles was thinking.

"What do you say to that, Izzy?" he asked softly.

But Isabella was already fast asleep.

The End.

If you enjoyed *Broken Moon*

by Anna Kelly, why not try

Daniel's Daughter also published by Poolbeg?

Here's a sneak preview of Chapter One.

Daniel's Daughter

Anna Kelly

POOLBEG

Prologue

Angela Brennan looked in horror at the man lying on his back on her kitchen floor.

A minute earlier he had been on his feet, grappling with her. In unbridled anger he had closed his hands around her throat. Only her terror-induced struggles had at first prevented his mallet-like hands from getting a solid grip.

Then, as her struggles grew weaker, his grip tightened and became vice-like. Her world grew dark and a myriad of thoughts flashed through her mind, not least being the fact that there was no one to come to her aid. There was only Thomas, nine years old, and he was out somewhere in the fields as usual.

From the small loft window in one of the outhouses Thomas had spotted the man prowling around. Then he saw him go into the house by way of the back door. In alarm he jumped down via some stacked bales of hay and ran across the yard. He heard the scuffling inside as he reached the back porch. He burst into the kitchen and, seeing his mother's plight, picked up the first thing that came to hand – the coal shovel from the stone hearth. He began to hit the attacker on the back.

In fury Christopher Cleary rounded on Thomas, who dropped the shovel and ran like a shot to the other side of the table, where fright made his legs unsteady. Cleary made to follow, but instinctively Angela thrust out her foot and suddenly her attacker was going down. The side of his head and the corner of the table met with an awful smack, and the force twisted his body so that he landed face up. The fall knocked his cap from his head, and long greasy strands of hair lay like black snakes beside his ear.

He stared up at her. Sick with fear and unable to divert her eyes she stared back. In an instant he would be back on his feet again, and God help her then.

He didn't move. Just stared.

Thomas edged his way back around the table cautiously, silently, and looked down.

"He's dead," he said flatly.

"He's not!" Angela's eyes involuntarily transferred to Thomas in disbelief.

"He is!" Thomas insisted.

"Fuck it!" his mother swore. Then she thought again. "How the fuck would *you* know?" She eyed the prostrate form warily as she spoke, watching for the smallest sign of movement.

"I've seen dead birds in the field. And a dead dog too. They had the same kind of stillness as that."

Revulsion took hold of Angela. Her uncle's eyes still stared up at her from the floor. Just as she couldn't get her eyes away before, now she couldn't bear to look down. And neither could she move away without having to step over the body. He had landed quite close to her feet, and the prospect of coming in contact with him again, however slight, immobilised her.

Thomas held out his hand. "Gimme your hand, Ma."

She did. She closed her eyes and jumped across the body. The two of them stood back then, unconsciously holding onto each other.

"Jesus, Tomo, what are we going to do? Oh God! Oh fuck it, fuck it!"

Thomas looked up anxiously at his mother. He could feel her shaking. She was becoming increasingly agitated, her head moving continuously in an irregular manner, her fingers beginning to dig into his shoulder. Then she began to babble and what she said made no sense to him – he even heard her mention the name of Redser Reilly. He feared his ma was losing it. Suddenly his young mind knew with certainty that if anyone was going to deal with this situation it was going to have to be him.

"Come on, Ma," he urged as he encouraged her towards the door. "We'd be better off out of here."

He wanted to get out of the kitchen himself. He guided her up the three steps that led into the front hall and then into the drawing-room where he sat her down in an armchair. He tried to think what his nan would do if she were here. And suddenly he wished she was. Nancy Brennan could cope with anything. Well, almost. Thomas then thought of some brandy. He remembered hearing his nan call for brandy once when a neighbour's child was knocked down on D'Arcy Avenue. He looked for brandy now in the long sideboard opposite the marble fireplace, while keeping a watchful eye on his mother. She was mumbling a load of stuff that seemed to have no bearing on what had just happened. She was nodding to herself as if something had just fallen into place, and only now made sense.

"I knew it all along, I knew it, I knew it wasn't my fault," she was saying.

"Drink this, Ma!" He held a glass to her lips.

She kept pushing the glass away. "I know now," she was whispering, "I know now."

Thomas was getting terribly worried about her, and he didn't *really* know what to do, try as he might to make it look like he did. He needed to con himself as much as his mother. He tried with the brandy again.

"This will help, Ma. Just have a little sip," he pleaded.

She took the glass and drank, then looked at him with more awareness in her eyes.

"Are you all right, Ma?"

She nodded determinedly.

"Did he hurt you badly?"

She would have answered him but for the fact that a noise startled them both. In their fright they could not decide where it had come from, or exactly what sort of noise it was.

Both of their heads swivelled towards the door together, then in alarm they looked at each other, wide-eyed. A terrible silence prevailed while they waited for something awful to happen, their hearts almost stopped in suspense.

Angela got to her feet and felt Thomas's restraining hand on her arm.

"Don't go, Ma," he whispered, even as he moved with her.

As stealthily as a cat stalking a bird they moved into the hall and towards the kitchen. Thomas had left the door open, and from the doorway they stooped low and looked across the room under the table.

Christopher Cleary was gone!

"Oh Christ!" Angela moaned.

"He can't be gone!" Thomas couldn't believe his eyes.

"I thought you said he was dead!" Angela hissed.

"Well, I thought he was! But where *is* he?"

She feared he might still be in the house. She was too afraid to turn around. It occurred to her that she should phone someone. They needed help. What if Christy was lurking around? What if he had collapsed and died outside in the yard?

"Ma, he's the oul fella we always see on his bike," Thomas was whispering.

"Thomas," she said, trembling, "that oul fella is not just any oul fella. He's Daniel's older brother, and he's pissed off that we got this place, instead of him."

The boy's mouth fell open. He stared at her in disbelief.

"Swear to God!" she insisted, her throat sore and her voice rasping. "Patrick told me. Now, come with me, I'm going to phone him."

She immediately felt a little better. Patrick Cullen would know what to do.

Chapter 1

In D'Arcy Avenue the Brennan family was at dinner. Paddy Brennan was making full use of his audience to expound his usual theory: Angela Brennan was useless. Totally fuckin' useless. He'd been saying it for years. Any time he got half a chance. An uneasy but familiar embarrassed silence befell those around the table.

"Part-time," he was saying derisively, "what bloody use is that? Why can't you get a proper full-time job like anyone else, for Christ's sake? There's two of yis there to feed, y'know!"

As he spoke he wagged his knife in Thomas's direction. Thomas had long since learned when to keep his head down. He cast a quick glance sideways at his mother. Angela's eyes were fixed on her plate. With her fork she stabbed at her food, and it was clear she had lost her appetite.

Nancy came to her daughter's defence. "It's better than the last job," she pointed out. "There's more hours and the money is better –"

"It's no better than the countless bits of jobs she's had

since she left school!" Paddy cut in. "And as for the money? It'll probably go on hair dye or more bloody muck for her face! And what fuckin' improvement will *that* make? Tell me that! None!"

Twenty-one-year-old Finbar had heard it all before. He got to his feet.

"Where do you think *you* are going?" his father snapped.

"I have exams tomorrow," Finbar answered shortly. "I have to study."

Fergus got to his feet also. "Me too. Excuse us, Mam." He followed his twin out of the room.

Paddy fumed but said nothing. He was losing his audience, but he knew he was on thin ice when it came to the exams. Nancy wouldn't hear of anything getting in the way of them. Thomas took his chance and slid quietly from his chair. No one said a word as he followed his uncles up to the bedroom. He climbed onto his bed and picked up a comic.

"I'll be quiet," he pleaded, "you won't even know I'm here."

Finbar and Fergus gave each other an understanding look and said nothing.

In the kitchen Paddy sat facing his wife and daughter.

"It's a pity *you* hadn't the brains to pass *your* exams!" he flung at Angela. "It would've answered you better than to go whoring around –" With a cry Angela leapt to her feet and ran from the room, but her father followed her into the hall, his voice roaring after her up the stairs, "At fifteen!"

Upstairs a door slammed loudly. The whole house felt the vibration. Paddy returned to the kitchen, slamming *that* door equally loudly.

Nancy was scraping the unfinished dinners into the

bin, including her own. Her nerves were at breaking point, and she was heartsore and weary of the same argument.

"If you didn't keep on at her she might have the confidence to get something better," she said quietly.

"Oh, so now it's *my* fault, is it?"

"I didn't *say* that."

"That's what you meant. You're the one who wanted her to have that bloody young fella in the first place. He should never have been born. If I had had my way –"

"Keep it down!" she hissed. "We know what you would've done if you'd had your way!"

The voices rose as one word borrowed another.

In her room Angela clamped her hands over her ears. Then she turned on her stereo and turned the volume up. But that only further fuelled tempers downstairs, and the arguing got worse.

Suddenly she grabbed her jacket and clattered down the stairs in her high-heeled shoes and left the house, slamming the door behind her. She half-walked, half-ran down D'Arcy Avenue, desperately trying to hold back the tears, and was grateful for the fact that it was already dark. Seeing a bus approach the stop ahead, she ran forward, put her hand out and stopped it. It took her into town, where she wandered for hours, cold and miserable. On Batchelor's Walk she paused in her aimless rambling to rest by the Liffey wall. The Liffey looked like a long, black, oily streak stretching endlessly into the night. There was no wind to ripple its surface, and the reflection of the streetlights on the narrow quays seemed unable to penetrate its depths. A late frost glistened on the thick granite walls of the silently ebbing river and on the roofs and windscreens of the cars parked alongside the uneven flagstone footpath. It was a bitterly cold night. She moved on. The balustrade of O'Connell

Bridge provided little protection from the freezing cold air arising from the water. The cold of the ancient granite easily penetrated her short, lightweight skirt, and she regretted having dashed from the house with only a flimsy jacket against the night air. She wished for the warmth and comfort of her own bedroom.

She was the problem. She and Tomo.

There had been peace in their house. Then Thomas arrived. The arguing began as soon as her pregnancy was confirmed. Her father went spare altogether. Not wanting her in the house. Not wanting the baby. But her mother had put her foot down. Nancy Brennan stood firm for the first time in her life. They'd manage. Somehow they'd manage. No one asked what Angela wanted. The arguments became constant. They were always about her, or Thomas, but never included her.

In his own inadequate way Paddy Brennan was still trying to come to terms with the disaster which had foisted itself on their lives. When she became pregnant he was devastated. Though not the youngest in the family, Angela was his baby, his little girl. His angel. She adored him. Never ever did he dream that anything would or could spoil their relationship. But this unwanted bastard she carried demolished all that. He couldn't bear to think of his darling girl being mauled by some spotty, sweaty wimp, and her enjoying it. The thought repulsed him. When did she start this carry-on? She was only fifteen, for Christ's sake! How many had she been with? Oh God, he couldn't bear the sight of her swelling belly! How could she continue to pretend to be his little innocent? The hypocrisy of it! Anger surged through him like some raging torrent. Well, he was finished with her for sure. He had no daughter now, and she had done it herself.

Neither could he understand Nancy's new-found determination. That surprised him and made him angry at how she could defend her whore of a daughter the way she did. Did she not think of his position as head of the house? To him, it was ganging up on him. Usurping him. Women! You couldn't trust them. How dare they do this to him? How was he going to face his workmates when "it" couldn't be hidden any more? He could just imagine it now, the snide remarks behind his back in the job. He'd be talked about for the duration. He was determined that he wasn't going to cough up to pay for its rearing. Money was tight enough as it was. They could go out and get jobs. The pair of them. He worked all the hours he could and he wasn't going to be taken for some kind of soft touch of an eejit. In fact, it would answer her better to leave his house and get herself somewhere else out of his sight. Get rid of it. Before it became too noticeable. While they still could. But there again Nancy surprised him, railing against him, appalled at the very mention of getting rid of it and insisting their daughter be given the support she needed. Support which would cost *him*. The arguments raged on never-endingly.

Nine years now and if anything, things were worse. Thomas was more of a handful the older he got.

Angela was freezing cold now. And it was late. She was on early in the shop in the morning. She made her way to the stop and took the bus home.

Calmer now, she walked back up the avenue, noticing as she went that the light was on in the Reillys' porch. So the job was finished. It looked well. A bit over the top perhaps, a conservatory-cum-porch on the front of a terraced council house, but it was well done. Of all the neighbours on the avenue the Reillys were always the first to get something new. Nancy always declared she never knew how they did it. No one in the house ever seemed to have a proper job, but clearly there was no shortage of money. Thomas was constantly telling them the Reillys had this and the Reillys had that, despite the fact that Angela was forever telling him not to hang around with them.

She had slowed down passing the house, taking as good a look as she could in the dark.

A car came to a sudden stop beside her and a man jumped out of the back seat, pushing the door shut behind him.

She stopped in her tracks in fear. The car sped off up the road, and she found herself standing facing "Redser" Reilly.

Word had been that he was "out" again but no one had seen him. Till now.

For a split second she hesitated, then she tried to side-step. He moved so as to block her way. She tried the opposite way. He blocked her again. He was enjoying this. The grin on his face chilled her. It had to be nearly ten years since she was last so close to him, but time had not diminished his ability to strike instant fear in her. Most of that time he was back "in" again.

Aggravated assault was his favourite thing, but there were also rumours about drugs.

Everyone believed the rumours – after all, there was no smoke without fire. Redser's viciousness was legendary around the estate. No one could remember a time when he was not a problem. From a young age he was in trouble, regularly getting into fights just to prove he was the toughest. When he first pulled a knife it was in the church where he carved his initials into the wooden pew. To do this in the church had the desired effect. Only a "hard man" would dare do such a thing. But a knife slicing wood was no kick. It wasn't long before the feel of the blade in real flesh gave Reilly the high he wanted. Either he was lucky or his expertise developed quickly because he managed to cut without causing a life to be lost – because that was never his goal. He preferred to see the terror in his victims' eyes before the lightning flash of the blade followed by a thin red line forming on the skin. At first he cited any imaginary insult as a reason why he attacked someone, but he soon gave that up as a waste of energy. He was Redser Reilly. He needed no reason. He did it because he could. The gang that gathered around him thought themselves favoured to be associated with him but soon found that once Reilly selected them there was no way out. He ruled over them with absolute power and was known to be involved in one way or another with most of the local crime and gangland feuds. Spending time inside was seen as yet another feather in his cap and Reilly used these experiences to his advantage, often having planned his next "job" even before his release after the last one.

It was often Tomo who brought the stories home, relating what he had heard from the youngest member of the Reilly household. Now, the eldest of the brood stood before Angela, and the knowledge of what he was capable of greatly intimidated her. He was barely the same height as she, but he was built like a bull. Solid and broad, the result of much pumping iron.

"Well! If it isn't little Angela! Long time no see."

It sounded more like a jeer than a greeting. He manoeuvred himself so that he had her back to the garden wall. She could smell the alcohol on his breath.

He could smell her fear. She flattened herself against the wall to stay back from him.

"Yeah," he almost slobbered, "it's been a long time . . ."

His eyes swept over her, taking in the improvements the years had made to her.

He made her feel dirty.

"Let me pass." Her voice sounded small and weak.

He feigned surprise. He held his arms out to the sides. "I'm not stopping you."

She was almost afraid to move in case he grabbed her.

"Go, if you want," he said. "Or maybe you like it where you are, right?"

His face came sickeningly close. The blade-one red stubble on his shiny scalp earned him his nickname. She slid sideways. His hand was instantly on the garden wall, stopping her.

"Remember – you haven't seen me! Got that?"

She nodded wordlessly, her eyes wide with fear.

"If you talk," he growled into her face, "I'll know it was you!" He traced a stubby finger down the side of her face.

She recoiled as the touch of his hand made her skin crawl.

"It'd be a pity to spoil that lovely complexion . . ." He removed his hand with a snigger of a laugh. He loved the smell of fear. He stepped back only enough for her to move without brushing against him and she started to run up the road. There was no one else around, and the sound of her running feet echoed in the quiet of the night.

Her family had lived on D'Arcy Avenue as long as she could remember. The avenue, with its thirty houses and their small front gardens, some still fenced off with black painted railings, had not changed much over the years. Her house was the last one at the top of the road, on the corner.

There was a large open space facing it. An eyesore, where gangs congregated at night and where bonfires were lit. This was where Redser Reilly and his gang graduated. Used syringes and condoms were often found, but it was the horses which caused the most annoyance to local people. Tethered to stakes in the ground by long ropes they sometimes broke loose and wandered into gardens. Local youths owned them and rode them bareback around the fields. Thomas had his mother pestered. He wanted a horse. It was all he seemed to think about. He spent all the time he could over in the field. Sometimes Angela would look out her bedroom window and see him riding up and down, despite her having told him umpteen times to stay away. She had often opened her window and roared across at him to come in this minute. That in turn would bring a shout from her mother downstairs to give over shouting out the window like a common rossie.

Now, as she approached the garden gate she was relieved to see that the light was on in the big front bedroom window. She would not feel safe till she had closed the door behind her.

The house was quiet. For now.

Her mother would be in bed reading, as she often did, till the small hours of the morning. Most likely her father was sound asleep, snoring. Tomo was in the back bedroom he shared with Finbar and Fergus.

Quietly Angela let herself into the house and listened.

The only sound was her father's snoring. She slipped the bolt on the hall door, and went up to the small boxroom that had always been her bedroom.

As she passed her parents' door she heard, "That you, Angela?"

"Yeah."

"Night, love!"

"Night, Mam."

Exhausted, she was asleep almost as soon as her head hit the pillow.